# *Pretty Instinct*

## By S.E. Hall

Felicia~
In for me!
Out for you
XO
SHall

SE Hall

Pretty Instinct

Toski Covey of Toski Cover Photography
Sommer Stein of Perfect Pear Creative
Editor: Erin Roth, Wise Owl Editing
Formatting:  Brenda Wright

SE Hall

table of contents

"Today, we gather to mourn the death, but also celebrate the life, of Anna Christine Carmichael. She was—"

A sharp elbow jab in my gut startles me, sending a shard of pain radiating up my side. "Conner," I hiss a quiet warning from the side of my mouth while squeezing his thigh. "Sit. Still."

His big, crystal blue eyes widen in surprise, the tone I've taken sharper than usual and obviously scaring him. So badly in fact, water begins to pool in his bottom lids and I'm instantly consumed with regret. I wince, hating that I've hurt him, hating the fact we're even here, my own tears threatening. But *damn*, we have to get through this funeral with our heads held high.

*She'd want that.*

"Should I take him outside for a while?" Jarrett, sitting on my left, clutching my clammy, lifeless hand in his larger one, whispers in my ear.

*Jarrett Foster.* What would I do without his unwavering, unconditional friendship? Along with his brother, Rhett, and my own brother, Conner, I have the three most important, and now my only, reasons for living and living strong. They're more than enough and well beyond what I deserve.

I answer him with a quick shake of my head and thanking smile, then bend forward to grab last week's pamphlet and a little pencil from the box on the back of the pew.

"Here, Bub," I nudge Conner, demonstrating the appropriate pressure to exude with one's elbow. "Draw me a picture." I hand him the tools of distraction and whisper, "I'm sorry. Love you."

His slight pout, which had been lingering from my scolding, disappears, replaced seamlessly with a childlike grin, lifting my shroud of guilt.

Now if there was only something to distract me as well. I need my own miracle mini-pencil, beguiling me so I forget where I am and why I'm here. But no, I'm painfully, consciously aware of this room, the stagnant air suffocating and pungent with the smell of old money and deceit.

"I'll draw a picture of Mom, okay?" His booming question drowns out the pastor, earning judgmental glares from the gallery, the harshest of which belongs to our father. Ah, the distinguished Councilman, turning around from his seat in front of us, tightly drawn face glowering.

I lift a hand, one finger dangling down, and twirl it in a circle, silently directing the old man to turn the fuck around and then use the same hand, different finger, to "wave" at his shrewdly frowning Personal Assistant.

Yes, his glorified, whoreified secretary accompanied him to my mother's funeral, so very thoughtfully rubbing his back the entire service.

And not one adult in this overcrowded room of corrupt show ponies has the gumption to say a thing about it. Or perhaps ask why the dearly departed Anna Carmichael's, the woman you all supposedly cared enough about that you're here today, children are seated in the *second* row, *behind* the piece of ass?

I'd call them all cowards, but cowardice means not having the backbone to stand up against what you know is wrong. It's far too generous a compliment for what they actually are—empty, programmed vessels of pure evil no longer cognitive of right from wrong.

"Yeah, buddy," I pat my brother's leg and flash him a reassuring smile, "draw a picture of Mom."

When the pastor asks if anyone would like to come up and say a few words, I anxiously wait, my breath held and my muscles tightly coiled, still foolishly hoping in my naïve, sixteen-year-old heart that my father will stand.

Of course he doesn't, my dash of hope doused as promptly as it'd risen. Nor do any of the other regaled socialites in the room. Swallowing disgust, I drop Jarrett's hand and move to make a stand myself, *for my mom*, when one of my angels speaks.

"I got this," Rhett assures me, shuffling between the pew and our legs to proudly walk forward. He owns his post proudly, his posture and defiance glowing in his eyes leaving no room for doubt he's got something to say, beside the easel displaying a large picture of my mother, a beautiful snapshot taken back when she still smiled through her whole face. Her piercing blue eyes, the exact shade of Conner's, glow from here, perhaps finally seeing all.

*My sweet Rhett*...beautifully out of place in *this place*. He's too kind; an empathic soul who writes poetry and leads with his heart...naturally his parents and the fools in this high-browed town use their suspicions that he *must* be gay to tromp on his spirit daily.

He clears his throat and stares directly into my eyes, despair meeting his fury. "When God made *a lady*, Miss Anna was who he envisioned. She cared about us *faggots*," he glares at his parents, "their burnout brothers," he throws Jarrett a cocked smirk, "and loved her amazing children more than anything." His face falls solemnly for a moment as he regards Conner and me. "She had more money than anyone in this room and only wanted the things it couldn't ever buy. It couldn't buy her the love and honesty of those who should have given it freely." My father flinches subtlety in his seat as Rhett visually pins him in place. "It couldn't protect her kids from evil and it damn sure won't buy our silence any longer. You'll never be able to hurt her again, because there's no room for the likes of Suttonites where she's gone, far away from here. The lot of you miserable motherfuckers can all rot in Hell, which I imagine is a lot like this place, where you belong. So Sutton's finest, all together now: kiss her, my, and her children's asses and fuck right off!"

With both hands and middle fingers high in the air, he waves his two gun salute like a boss as he kicks over the podium and strolls down the middle aisle, banging open the doors to outside.

*By far* his best poem ever.

### Seven years later

"There any left for me?" The deep, croaky morning voice at my back doesn't startle me in the least. Not only had I heard him coming, the stealth of a Clydesdale, but my defenses are already on high alert.

Jarrett either woke up with a set of brass balls or amnesia this morning, talking to me all normal and shit, as though he's not in for an ugly round of *Liz is pissed*.

I spin haughtily to face him, eyes on fire and the pulsing in my neck probably visible. "*Surely* you're not talking to me," I hiss. "My coffee, my bus, and my," poke, "fucking," poke, "RULES!"

He rubs his bare chest, specifically the spot I just finished jabbing repeatedly as I yelled at him. "Damn, woman, what the hell's your problem?" His hand tries to sneak around me to snag the coffee pot, but I'm way ahead of him, sliding my body to the right and blocking his attempt.

"You fuck on my bus last night?" I demand, kicking his shin so he backs away from the caffeine. Not that I need to ask; a rocking *fourteen ton* tour bus is pretty unmistakable. Coupled with the hickey above his pierced left nipple and the stench of skank sex wafting off him…the glove fits, we shall not acquit.

I'm also positive that whatever bitch fell into his bed last night has no idea what she let get away. All she saw was a hot guy in a band—*all* of him, I'm sure—lots of bad-boy piercings in his brow, lip, tongue and nipples, an unbelievable body he needs to quit poking holes in, and a face that'd charm the panties off a nun. I hate that he lets them have even a single part of him without earning and appreciating the amazing person he is, but I hate even more when he does it on my bus.

"Maybe. But she left before you got up, and he wasn't even here, Mama Bear. So what's the problem?"

I raise my chin indignantly, my arms crossed over my chest. "He could have been. I could've picked him up early, or changed plans. Then what? Huh?"

"But you didn't, and now she's gone." He shrugs and flicks my earlobe playfully, same as he always does when he's trying to appease me. "So quit bitching about couldas."

I swat his hand away, still pissed *and* short my crucial dose of caffeine. "That's exactly how it starts, Jarrett! You slack on a rule, take an inch here or there, next thing you know? Poof! Anarchy!"

"You're insane." He snickers at me, scratching his boxer-clad crotch, *probably crabs*, and reaches around me *again* for java, which I let him get his hands on this time. "You raggin'?" he asks, those denim eyes of his taunting me over the rim of his mug.

No preamble, I pull back and slug him in the gut, smiling and quite satisfied as the hot, *poached* coffee splashes over onto his hand. "This may come as a shock to you, but females *are* capable of getting pissed without being 'on the rag,' which is a disgusting way to say it! Don't you ever just get mad?"

"Well sure. Your point being?" He sticks his hand in his mouth, sucking on the burn...worse thing you can do for it.

Mercifully, knowing he'll suck all day wondering why it isn't getting any better, I turn on the cold water and pull his hand under the flow. "*My point is*, how are you able to get mad, obviously not ever *raggin'*, but it's inconceivable I'm able to do the same? I may be behind on my CNN, but I've yet to hear that menstrual cycles and the ability to get angry have been scientifically linked as exclusive, you sexist pig!"

"You know it, baby." He digs his face into my neck, oinking.

I giggle and squirm because it tickles, *not* because he's irresistible or forgiven. But this is the same way all our arguments end, since we were ten and his family took up residence across the street. I'm serious—he's too adorable for his own good and we always secretly make up—but I never verbalize that he is, in fact, off the hook.

"Please don't do it again, though, Jarrett, I mean it. If I hadn't been feeling charitable, I'd have ripped her out of here by her hair." It was actually more the whole "if the bus is rockin', you might throw up at what you'll see if you go knockin'" than charity, but I won't mention that tidbit. Hands planted on my hips, I resume a deadly serious scowl for emphasis. "I won't let *anyone*, even you, disturb his harmony. He wins, and—"

"Every other motherfucker loses," he finishes for me. "I know, babe, I agree."

"I mean, seriously, how hard is it to get a hotel room or go to their house? Are *all* hoes homeless?"

"Homeless hoes—ha! Good one," I hear a mumbled echo and laughter in the distance.

"Well, since you're awake, listening," I warn the other two, obviously shrinking in their beds away from my *so-called* wrath and *clearly* scaring Jarrett into *non*-compliance, "you best be takin' notes. I won't have this conversation again."

Rhett's head pokes out of his cubby, ebony hair sticking up wildly in every direction, and flashes me a smile alight with pride and agreement. It's his usual way of supporting me without blatantly dogging his brother out, or heaven forbid, siding with the female over his "own kind."

12

The Foster brothers are always assumed twins, though they're actually a little over a year apart, Rhett the elder at 25, and they couldn't be more different. First of all, Jarrett's got a tiny selfish streak, whereas Rhett is unfailingly self*less*. Rhett's darker hair is soft and wavy, while Jarrett's is coarse and tickles your hand. They're both tall and muscular with navy blue eyes, but Jarrett's are always dancing with less than subtle motives, reflecting the sarcastic, crass thoughts in his head, while Rhett's are docile and considering, looking *into* you.

When I want to joke, laugh, and generally cut up, I go see Jarret, his jovial, carefree spirit refreshing. But when I want to "be," maybe with deep, meaningful words and insights, maybe in the solace of comforting silence, I seek out Rhett.

I love them identically, though.

With Rhett still peeking at me, I stick my tongue out at him and cross my eyes, but keep my voice stern for the rest of them. "I'm leaving to go pick up Conner. This place better reek of Lysol and lollipops when we get back." I swivel on my heel, grabbing my shit and slamming the door behind me. At the bottom of the steps, I stop to collect myself, and a lungful of fresh air.

"You good?"

My head jerks to the right where my uncle Bruce, our driver, makeshift manager, and only decent relative Conner and I have, leans against the side of the bus having a smoke. I wish he'd quit the nasty habit. My mother's only brother, he lost his wife to *cancer*, for Christ's sake…and yet he smokes like the aging, slightly overweight engine that could. Sometimes I wonder if he's tempting death, trying to speed up the wait until he can see his wife and sister again, cause a pack of non-filter Camels a day is definitely a solid plan.

"Hell no, I'm not good. Jarrett brought a whore on my bus last night. You know anything about it?"

"Nope." He throws down his cig and grounds it out with his boot. "*My* wh—uh date, took me to hers last night. I never came back by the bus after the show."

13

I love how he calls them "dates," ever protective of what he perceives to be my fragile ears. My aunt Kerri had died only eight months after my mom. Figuring my uncle had said more than his fair share of goodbyes, when I *finally* got legal rights to Conner, and more than enough of Sutton, I bought this bus and asked my uncle to come along. He'd jumped at the invite, going on three years ago, and he's been keeping us right of the center line, one mile of highway at a time, ever since.

"Nice." I roll my eyes. "Get them all to clean up, please. I don't want Bubs walking in to a pigsty. And use *bleach* on the toilet. No telling what treats, only *treated* with penicillin, Jarrett's guest left behind."

"You want me to go with you to get Conner? Rhett can run clean up."

"No," I laugh. "We gotta get moving soon. Bailing you out of jail would take too long." Uncle Bruce *loathes* my father, bumping up his cool points to astronomical levels. I walk towards my car, last time I'll be driving her for a while, and call back over my shoulder. "Seriously, get their asses up. Be scary or they won't listen."

"Aye, aye, Captain!"

"Bethy!" he yells the second I clear the door. Our mom called me Bethy, so Conner does too, *now*. But up until the day she died, it was always Liz or Lil' Sis, which now often comes out "Sister."

"Umpf," I grunt, barely managing to stay on my feet as he plows into me, full-body tackle style. It's always how he greets me, whether apart two days or two minutes, and it started to actually hurt when he got over two hundred pounds. He met that mark long ago, so you'd think I'd be used to it, but *no*. It often hurts like hell. I don't know that my petite, female stature will ever welcome an overzealous frontal attack by a twenty-seven-year-old, far from lightweight, grown man.

I'll eat my own tongue before ever complaining, though.

"You miss me, Bubs?" I ask, voice lined with the wheeze of still recollecting my breath.

"Uh huh." He grabs my hand, pulling me toward the door. "Goodbye, Dad!" he yells to no one.

"Whoa, hang on." I strain to stop him, pulling back on his hand and considerable inertia, searching around for our father. "Conner, we gotta get your stuff first. Where's Dad?" I visibly shiver, choking on the word *Dad*, repeating it merely to keep the conversation aligned for Bubs.

"I don't care." He tugs again on my arm. "Back to the bus!" Gotta love my kickass brother, always straight to the point and untactfully honest. Another thing "just that way" for so long now—I don't exactly remember if he had a filter *before*. He was cocky, an athlete, musician, popular...but I kinda remember some couth in there somewhere.

"Thank you, son." The icy baritone echoes off the vaulted ceilings, raking along my spine. It kills me when I react, my own body betraying me with instinctual, physical aversion, reminding me of the power he still, in fact, holds. "Elizabeth," he regards me curtly when fully descended from the overly grand staircase and at my side. "You're well, I assume?"

"Well, I assume you're still a prick. Am I right?"

Conner titters from behind me and I turn to give him a clever, victorious grin. *That's right bud, score one for our team.*

"Dear Elizabeth, as always, such an eloquent young lady."

"Dear Father Time," I point to his face, "tucking and sucking in vain, as always, I see. Where's Alma?" Our housekeeper/nanny since I could walk, she's one of the select few I trust in this world, and the *only* reason I let Con visit *him* in this house without me. She *better* be here; he's not allowed to be alone with Conner, *ever*, and he knows it. There may be some liberties I fought like hell and still couldn't get taken from him, but on this rule, I'd won. And if I hadn't, Conner and I'd be deep in the tropics somewhere, sunbathing, snorkeling, and hidden.

His shoulders, cloaked in a suit far too dignified for him, shake with his sneering chuckle. "She's around here somewhere. Ask your brother if you don't believe me. Or feel free to go search for her yourself." Rubbing his chin, stoic mask resumed, he waits for me to call his bluff. When I remain in place, he fires off his next jab. "How's *the band*?"

"Why do you ask empty questions? You don't care what the answer is, so why ask?" I slap a hand over my heart dramatically and puff out my bottom lip. "I hope it's not for my benefit, Daddy Dearest. Please don't ever worry your feeble mind into thinking I need filler conversation with you. In fact," I step toward him and snarl, "I'm bloated and gassy from what little we've already spoken." I rub my belly, wishing I could burp on command like Jarrett. "So get me his bag and we'll be leaving. Unless there's anything we actually *need* to talk about? Say, about Conner?" Speaking of Bubs, I glance over my shoulder, finding him talking gregariously to the large fish tank, tapping noisily on the glass. If not for Alma being the one who'd have to clean it up, I'd be rooting for him to break it.

"Nothing other than what I've been telling you. He belongs—"

"With me." I shove a shaking finger in his face. "And that's where he'll stay. I *only* let you see him because *he* asks. Never forget, old man, we hold the cards, *not* you." Even as I speak it, I know it's not true. As long as Conner wants to see him, asks for him, despite every instinct in my body, I have to let him. The visitation mandate my slimy father somehow got wormed into the agreement sees to it. I hate Con going anywhere near him and worry from the time I drop him off 'til the time I safely pick him up, but again...until Conner remembers something, finds his voice, my hands are tied.

"Why do you insist on dragging someone in his condition across the country on your meaningless bout of rebellion? The money can't be taken back, it's yours, whether he's with you or not. Let him have a *home*, a watchful eye."

I step even closer into him, rage and resentment seething in my veins, ringing in my ears. "He *was home*, not on my *watch*, when he got in this *condition*. And our mother saw to it we have that money, you pretentious fucking bastard. Don't you dare talk as though you have one ounce of generosity or concern for him in your body!"

He pulls the pansy ass handkerchief from his pocket and wipes my spit from his leathery, over-processed face. "Always a pleasure, Elizabeth. Do try not to get him killed."

"Wouldn't want to steal your M.O."

Nothing. No jolt of shock at the accusation, no flabbergasted denial, not even so much as a "what's that supposed to mean?" He simply doesn't care enough to feign plausible deniability anymore, sure he's untouchable. One in the ground, the other not talking—I'd probably be feeling pretty good about my odds too. Unless I was going up against me. Which he is. As long as I have breath in my body...*he is*.

His footsteps echo off the pristine marble floor as he turns and walks briskly away. *There's* the version of him I know best—his back to us. He won't stop and turn around, smile longingly at the daughter he's lost, beg her to forgive him and explain away her suspicions. I quit wishing for it long ago; an icy indifference has taken its place. Nor does he so much as hug his son goodbye, killing my sense of obligation to tell him we'll be gone a while this time, heading across the country as soon as we leave here.

Allowing one fleeting sigh, my eyes take a rapid sweep around my childhood home before I gather myself and reassume my armor. "Come on, Bubs, we're going. Grab your bag."

"Can we take the fishes with us?"

"You don't want those fish, Con. They're tainted. I'll get you some fish of your very own. Okay?"

"And Pez?" he coaxes me with a goofy, adorable smile. Completely unnecessary because I'll give him anything he wants, but my favorite sight all the same.

"Of course. Always Pez."

# CHAPTER *two*

When I promised Conner I'd get him some fish of his own, I wasn't lying...but I also wasn't thinking *right this second*. He however, was, pointing to every single building we've passed in the last ten minutes asking, "Is that the fish store? Is this where we're getting my fish, Bethy? Don't you need to turn right there, Sister?"

Pulling over in a random parking lot, I can't help but snicker. To hell with what the doctors say, my brother's all kinds of cunning, brilliantly wrapping me around his little finger every chance he gets.

"Where are we? This isn't the store." He slumps in his seat, shoulders hunched and a pout tugging down his mouth. "You were only kidding me about the fish, huh?"

See what he did there? Doesn't know what he's saying *my ass*.

I scoff and blow a big raspberry at him. "You know better, you clever little monkey. I'm getting directions real quick, Bubs. I don't know where the fish store is."

We'd never been allowed pets growing up; too messy, loud, undignified—pick an excuse. Therefore, I have no clue where to buy one. The Foster brothers, though...they always had some sort of creature in a cage, bowl, or box when we were young.

Dialing Jarrett, I practice the "I'm sorry oh and can you help me" speech in my head as the call connects.

He answers on the first ring, sounding panicked. "You okay?"

"Yeah, we're fine. I kinda need your help, though."

"Shoot," he pops off, no questions asked, no apology demanded first. He's kinda great that way.

"First," deep breath filled with shame, "I need you to forgive me for being an over-the-top bitch this morning. You know I love you and I don't mean to be so harsh, but I can't have—"

"You're forgiven, already were. What else ya got?"

I let free the nervous sigh I'd been holding and roll my head back and around, the ease in my shoulders glorious. Deep down, I knew he'd forgive me, but sometimes I worry that he, or Rhett, or both, will finally figure out I'm a handful, more trouble than I'm worth, and leave me. "I'm parked in front of Keene's Appliance Store right now and need to know where the nearest fish store is. And could you please clear a spot for our new pets? Conner," I turn to him, "where do you want your fish to go?"

"In my room." He nods his head up and down eagerly. "Yes, in my room, for sure."

"A spot in Con's room, please." And for five seconds it seems that easy, until inner Liz rears her complex head.

"Wait, what if they spill? I guess I can get a lid. Oh, you better pick a spot by a plug, for the bubble thingy. Not by a window, too hot or cold," I huff, "I don't know." I *don't* know anything about this whole spontaneous project, let alone trying to pull it off on a tour bus.

Conner's in the big bedroom in the back, all the rest of us in the bunks or the pull-out couch in front...and I'm suddenly regretting giving him a choice for the tank's home. Lord only knows what he'll do with the fish all secret-like back there; I'll have to keep the food, and net, and whatever else they come with in a safe place. I squeeze my eyes shut, breathing somewhat labored, panic level rising, and try to find solace in the fact he didn't ask for a dog. *Unjinx, unjinx. I did not just think that.*

"Yo, Mama Bear!" Jarrett's amusement rings in my ear. "Curb the crazy, it's fish, not a fucking alligator. It'll be fine. Go get the man some damn guppies and I'll have everything ready. There's a place called The Tank on the corner of Riker and 23rd, in the shopping center. Head there."

"Okay, you're right. Only fish. We can do fish." I breathe out all the unnecessary worry, firming my grip on the wheel. "See ya in a sec."

"That one," Conner yells, sliding his pointer finger across the tank, chasing one fish, then another, and so on. "And that one!" His feet shuffle a mile a minute, excitement uncontainable. "Sister," he turns to me, "they got a red one for Jarrett and a blue for me!"

"I see," I say, giggling at his enthusiasm. "We'll take the red and blue one," I tell the young guy helping us.

"Anddddd," Conner's voice is a full scream, "the yellow one and orange one and blue one for Rhett!"

"Two blue ones," I amend to the helper, raising a warning brow as he sighs and rolls his eyes. *Don't even go there, dude. Help my brother, service with a smile, or else. Ruin this for him and you asked for what you get.*

"Bethy," he says softly, the sadness in his voice snaring my attention, "they don't got a bright pink one for you. You gotta pick a different color."

I lean in and examine all my choices, darting around the tank so fast my eyes can barely keep up. "How about a couple of those tiny little bright green ones?"

"*Yes*," he drawls out in fascination, "great choice. What ones for Cami and Uncle Bruce?"

*Thoughtful angel, never forgetting anyone.*

"They can share with me," I assure him, patting his arm. "I think that's enough, Bubs. We don't have room for too big of a tank and you don't want them to be crowded."

He considers that, tapping his index finger on his chin, then finally happily agrees. Carrying one of the clear bags with his blue and red fish toward the front, he positively bounces the whole way. *Yep, we can do fish.* Together, we gander around as the guy tries to chase down the rest of our order with the tiny net, Conner scooping up all kinds of castles, ships and treasure chests to go in the tank.

"Remember, not too much, Bub. They need room to swim."

"Two things?" He holds up that many fingers, begging me with his sweet smile. When I agree too easily with a bob of my head, he goes in for the kill. "Three things?"

"Two." I stifle a laugh…trying desperately not to cave and tell him to grab four.

"Jarretttttt, I'm home!" Conner screeches the minute the door to the tour bus opens, his poor fish ricocheting off the sides of the bags from his exuberant shaking. I'm unsure why he always calls out for Jarrett first, the boys both equally good to him, both in our lives the exact same amount of time. I wonder if Rhett ever asks himself the same thing, or if it hurts his feelings? Knowing Rhett like I do, the answer is undoubtedly yes.

"There he is!" Jarrett smiles, standing from the bench seat to give him a hug. "We missed you, bud. You have a good time with your dad?" He glances over Conner's shoulder to me as he asks. He worries too, after living through it all right by my side.

"Ask if he saw Alma," I mouth.

"Did you see Miss Alma today, buddy?" he questions casually, my jaw clenched tight as I wait for the answer.

"Yes, she loves me. Bethy too." My brother can contain it no longer, already over any conversation not about his pets. "See my fish?" He shoves the bags in Jarrett's face. "The red one's yours. You can name it if you want."

Still behind them observing, I roll my hand, wanting Jarrett to confirm specifics. He winks, reading me like a book. "Awesome fish, dude, we'll put them in a bowl in a sec. What'd Alma make you to eat today?"

"Grilled cheese. Rhett, Bruce the Moose, I'm home!" Jarrett and I both chuckle at Conner's clear dismissal of any further banter. He says he saw her, and he's back with me now, seemingly unharmed, so I guess all's well enough for me to move on.

Jarrett leans in to conspire in his ear. "Your uncle ran to town, but Rhett's in bed, go wake him up."

Such a shit, sending Conner to do his dirty work.

Once he's bouncing down the hallway to torture *anyone* in the vicinity, Jarrett sits back down and pats the spot beside him for me to take. "How bad this time?"

I flop my head on his shoulder, letting him entwine our fingers. "Not too. Short and bitterly sweet." I tilt my head and grin mischievously up at him. "I got in a few good jabs."

"I'd expect no less."

"I didn't see Alma, though, which worries me. I just wish Conner wouldn't ask to go. I wish he'd remember why he shouldn't *want* to go."

"You sure about that? Maybe it's better that he doesn't remember. There's a lot of bad shit stuck in my head I wish I could forget, ya feel me?" He squeezes my hand and brushes a kiss at my temple.

In a way he's right, I don't want Bubs to have those visions in his head, waking him up at night, confusing him. But without his recollection, and him saying it out loud, I can't ever prove what I *know* to be true. And therefore, I can't

23

keep him from our father. It's never ending, these thoughts, the internal debates on the lesser of two evils. *It's exhausting.*

Conner played soccer and football from youth to high school; our father didn't attend a single game. He was in a garage band for almost three years; Daddy Demon never heard a single song. He didn't give a shit about Conner before *the accident*, which I'd bet my left tit was *far from* an accident, but now he's hell bent on playing house with a twenty-seven-year-old man he barely even knows? I haven't figured it out, *but I will.*

My thoughts are splintered by a nasally shriek. "Get out, you retarded freak! What the fuck is wrong with you?"

I'm on my feet and down the corridor in a flash, Jarrett hot on my heels.

"Bubs? Bubs, what happened?" I ask as calmly as I can, dropping to my knees and wrapping my arms around him. He's curled into a ball on the floor, rocking back and forth and banging clenched fists against his head. "Conner, stop," I command, trying to restrain his arms, gasping in piercing pain when I catch his accidental elbow to the jaw. *Always the damn elbow.* "Shit," I howl, shaking my head and rubbing it quickly before going back in. "Jarrett, help me! Rhett!"

They're already there, caught in the flurry of commotion, one of them now flinging me out of the way so they can stop Conner from hurting himself. This time it's my back, a sharp blow knocking the air from me as I'm tossed aside, landing against the edge of a bunk. I've gotten pretty tough over the years, so I take the moment to ignore the back and rub on my jaw some more, working out the ache.

Cami, our bassist and the one who'd set this catastrophe in motion, scrambles down and out of her top bunk, pulling a t-shirt over herself. "Liz, you can't expect us to live like this! Your pervy fucking brother was creeping on me again. I don't care what the hell's wrong with him, I have a right to privacy!"

You live on a tour bus with four men, sleep nude, and have an expectation of privacy? Anyone else think that train of thought is asinine? Not my job to show her the light, though, that epic fail is all on the fools who raised her "cry wolf when convenient" exhibitionist ass. *Helluva job.* But more importantly, I haven't the time or energy to waste on the about to be *ex*-member; I have to take care of my brother, the innocent, precious soul she name-called and scared to death.

Rising slowly to stand nose to nose with her, I concentrate on my breathing as a source of center, reminding myself the last thing Conner needs to see is violence. How badly he reacts to it, over-exaggerated even for him, is one of the biggest reasons I suspect foul play that summer I went to camp. If I dust this bitch right now, I'll make things worse for an already petrified Bubs.

It's this concern alone that saves her life. Otherwise, I'd have already mopped the floor with her and made her like it. "Cami, what's wrong with you? He didn't mean a thing by it."

"I'm sick of it! I've bit my tongue long enough. 'Nobody upset the retard' gets old," she air quotes snottily, testing everything in me not to lower those hands for her. "He's always spying on me. I almost think he's faking it just to get a peep show!"

Yes, that is exactly it, diva. He's been faking it for seven long years in hopes of one day getting a glimpse of your uneven mosquito bites. *Way to go, Cami the Case Cracker!*

I literally have to take a minute and simply stare at her for my brain to compute such venomous hatred coming out of nowhere. Cami's lived on this bus with Conner for months. I've even seen her help him with his puzzles a time or two, so the level of animosity pouring from her now is shocking and completely unexpected.

"He was looking for Rhett, you delusional, heartless bitch. He wanted to show off the new fish he got and mixed up the bunks." My voice cracks and I gulp down the threatening sob, a cumbersome bubble in the middle of my throat. "But luckily, Conner isn't doomed. He'll be fine in a few minutes, still an angel. *You*," I take a step in, crunching her toes under my own and making sure to curl my lip and bare my teeth, "however, are screwed for life. There's no hope for the kind of evil inside you and I'm only sorry I didn't see it sooner. Ugly and mean to the core is no way to go through life, Cami. I'd pick the way Conner does it over yours any day of the week. Now pack your shit, next stop is yours."

"You can't be serious! You're kicking me out of the band, whose only chance in hell is me, because I don't want some freak staring at my tits?"

"Jarrett?" I plead, flexing my fists in and out, praying for willpower I don't usually possess.

"On it." He inches himself between us. "Get your shit together, Cami, you're out. And shut the fuck up while you do it. I don't hit women, but you call him another name and I'll damn sure smack a bitch."

"You can't just dump me, I don't have a car! Unbelievable," she scoffs.

"And your tits *aren't.*" Jarrett scores one for the whole team. "But we'll take you where you need to go. *We* have some decorum."

While he stands guard over her, I move to the front of the bus where Rhett's corralled Conner. Squatting down in front of him, I pry his hands away from over his face. "Hey, look at me."

"S-sorry, Sister," he chokes out in a trembling voice.

"What are you sorry for, huh? Being amazing, kind, and good lookin'? Being a winner? Cause that's what you are!" He doesn't answer me, burying his face behind Rhett's shoulder. "What's the rule, Conner?" I jostle his leg. "Huh? Tell me the rule."

Still shaken and ashamed, he doesn't answer, so I do it for him. "You win and every other motherfucker loses, right?"

"Right," he grunts from his hiding spot, Rhett rubbing his back and smiling at me.

"Who's the winner?"

"I'm the winner." He peeks one eye out at me. *Precious.* How could anyone ever be mean to that face; those huge, innocent eyes, filled with unconditional love, and those sweet dimples?

"You're damn right you are." I hop up, grabbing his hand to raise his arm triumphantly in the air. "Ladies and gentlemen, boy and girls, Conner Matthew Carmichael is the winner!"

The boys clap and hoot while Cami rolls her eyes and continues to stuff shit in her duffle. Now Conner beams ear to ear, all again right with the world.

"I'm keeping her fish," he boasts and we all die laughing.

*Oh shit, he was holding the bags of fish!* And now he's not, surely lost in all the commotion.

Looks like we're making another stop.

"And I'm getting the top bunk back!" Jarrett chimes in, sick of sleeping on the pull-out.

*My boys, so resilient.*

# CHAPTER three

After the longest two hours of any of our lives, with suffocating amounts of tension in the air, we finally make it to the rest stop Cami designated. Lucky for her, we'd still been in our homeland of Ohio when she'd lost her shit, so she was able to call someone to meet her a small jaunt down the road. Otherwise, I *would* have offloaded her randomly. At least, I think I would have.

Throwing down his cards in the middle of our four man game of Uno, Conner's up and ready as soon as we stop and he sees a park out the window.

"You didn't say Uno," Rhett teases him as he picks up the scattered cards. "I win."

"Move," Cami barks at Conner, trying to shove past him and knocking her case into his hip as she does so.

"I'm not playing with her," I warn Jarrett in a menacingly low snarl. "Get her the fuck off my bus before you have to alibi my whereabouts at the time of the murder." I'm truly floored, no idea of the deep-rooted venom she'd hidden. And maybe she's just having a *categorically* bad day…but I won't risk her having another one on my bus.

Jarrett hurries to the door, throwing an arm around Conner's shoulders. "Let's scoot back, buddy, give Cami room to get off the bus."

"Where's Cami going?" He looks around, confused. "Cami, where are you going?"

"The fuck away from you!"

Instinctually, Jarrett has Conner moved back already, thank goodness, 'cause I'm done, up with a fist full of her hair and my arm reared back as Rhett chuckles from behind me, his arm squeezing around my waist.

"Almost over," he whispers, his lips brushing the shell of my ear. "Hold it together long enough for her to get off the bus and you never have to worry about her again. Come on." He untangles my fingers from her greasy strands and walks backwards, dragging me with him. "Come sit down with me until she's gone."

I only do so under duress. He holds me down forcefully on his lap, my head falling against his chest. As relieved as I am that the debacle's seconds from being over, it's created a whole new problem. "We have a gig in a few days and no fucking bassist. What're we gonna do?"

"I can play!" Conner raises his hand, eavesdropping from way over there.

Jarrett nudges him with a shoulder and heads to sit down by us, Cami completely unloaded now. Time for our little family to have a meeting, minus Bruce. He'll stay put in his captain's chair, steering clear of any drama.

"You play great, Con." And he did. He was talented, even wrote some songs way back when. "But we need you on tambourine, remember?" Jarrett lovingly reminds him.

Every show, Uncle Bruce watches over Conner, right off stage, shaking his tambourine like a champ. I feel awful that all he can do now is shake the noisy thing from the wings, but it's too unpredictable to let him on stage, some crowds nicer than others, venues ranging from large and rowdy to small and accommodating. We adjust accordingly.

"That is right." His brow wrinkles. *Sweetness.*

"Don't worry, we'll think of something." I stand, moving to the door, figuring Cami's long gone. "You wanna stretch your legs in the fresh air a minute, Bubs?"

A jaunt in the sun is as much to clear my mind as his. I have no idea what we'll think of, and I'd dragged them all on this misadventure, only to have it now collapsing. Although originally my idea, it's become all Rhett and Jarrett have. Even if we call it quits today, I have Conner and a fallback nest egg, but the boys were ostracized socially and financially from their shitty "family" the minute they'd stepped onboard. Well, officially, anyway; the groundwork of such was laid *long* before. They'd finally given their parents the excuse they needed to justify their douchery at tea parties and such: *"It's okay to shit on our kids because they..."*

So I can't just cancel the gig. It may be no big deal to me—this was never about being discovered or getting signed as the next "big thing" in my eyes—but I suspect it's become exactly that to Rhett and Jarrett.

I need a miracle...preferably one that has some empathy, or at least fakes it with their mouth closed, and can pluck a mean bass.

What started as stretching our legs for a minute turned into an afternoon picnic and a game of Frisbee golf. I'm heading to hole five, a par two (the trash can), cleaning up what's left of our lunch when something, or some*one* rather, catches my eye.

*Hello, miracle.*

The glint of the sun reflecting off the guitar slung across his back is what first snags my attention, but the favors he's doing that pair of Levis is what's keeping it.

Hell yes, I noticed. How could I not? I am, after all, a healthy twenty-three-year-old woman.

"You thinking what I'm thinking?" Jarrett creeps up behind me, scheming in my ear.

Positive he's not thinking *"I wish I had an hour all my own to let that guy fuck the legs off me,"* I turn my head back to him and attempt undeterred sarcasm. "If my answer to that question is ever yes, feed me lots of fish. Brain food. Not any from Conner's tank, though."

*Which reminds me…*eh, we'll wait for Bubs to mention it.

"Seriously smartass, we gonna stand here and pant 'til he notices us or we gonna go ask him?"

"Ask him *what*?" We both know I'm full of shit—I know exactly what he means. And yes, in a perfect world, this would appear to be divine intervention…guy with guitar conveniently located at same rest stop as band coincidentally in need of a guitar player, but I far from believe in a perfect world. I do, however, let my head fall back for just a moment to take in the clear, endless blue sky and wonder, filled with warmth at the thought. *Good lookin' out, Mom.*

"I can't let a stranger on the bus with Bubs. What if he's a mass murderer?" *What if he's not as pretty on the inside as he is on the outside?*

"Ah, Mama Bear, run him through all the tests. You're careful. And he might say we're crazy and tell us to fuck off. Let's ask before we worry about it."

Biding my time, I chew on the inside of my cheek and look back, confirming Conner's still tossing the Frisbee happily, Rhett watching him. "You asking or am I?" I sigh, hopefully masking the foreign tingle of anticipation working its way up my battered spine.

"He's hetero, I can tell from here. I say we send in," he flicks a finger back and forth between my boobs, "the big guns."

"Don't lick your lips!" I shove him, mouth agape. "You're like my brother. That's illegal in at least forty states, *and gross.*"

"You didn't think it was gross when—"

"Enough." I slap my hand over his mouth hastily. "I'll go, but you stay right here and watch, closely. He makes a move for a weapon, dial 911 *as* you run to rescue me."

"On it." He grins at me, full of victory, a hint of his earlier teasing still lingering in his expression.

Girding my loins, I think, *do women have loins and can they be girded or is that only a guy thing*? Summoning my courage, I move with slow, hesitant steps in the miraculous unknown's direction, reminding myself with each one that it's for the boys, the band, the overall goal of staying the hell out of Sutton. And it is, but I'm kidding myself if I don't admit I wouldn't be this anxious if I was walking up to an ugly man. Or even a kinda good-looking man. *Shallow much, Liz?* Nah, I have no control over biological response.

Almost there now, his head lifts and turns at my approach, connecting eyes as sable brown as thick molasses to my own. He was tummy-turning enough far away. Up close, he's better than photoshopped, a clear-cut case for Guinness Genetics. His lips are full, much plumper than my own, and he has a strong nose and jawline, both very masculine, the latter covered in a dark scruff. His hair is the same rich chestnut as his eyes, not too short, but definitely not too long. "Just fucked" hair (isn't that what they call it?) be damned. He's got "just fucked her and she had to hold on" locks, unruly in the most intricate fashion. The black boots at the end of long, thick legs are scuffed, faded jeans worn, *well,* and the long sleeved black thermal he's wearing? Oh, he *wears* it, or rather, every muscle in his torso holds it up flawlessly.

Bottom line—he's easy to look at.

"Are you a deranged serial killer and/or rapist?"

I like to open subtly.

"No, are you?" His timbre is deep and gravely, sending my vagina subliminal messages. Something along the lines of "yup, you want it." With a voice like that, I'm praying he isn't a chain smoker. To fuzz this perfect picture with the stench of an ever-present cloud of smoke would be one helluva slap in the face of the Almighty creator.

"No," I answer too defensively, this instant, highly unusual attraction frying my staple "too cool to care" attitude that, up until right now, I'd like to think I pull off fabulously. "You any good?" I lean and point to the instrument on his back, brows bowed in questioning antagonism.

"Define good," he deadpans, head down as he pulls the guitar off his back and puts it back in its case.

"Hendrix."

"Not left-handed." He shrugs as he straightens back up and captures my gaze.

"Page."

He laughs, treating me to one seriously enlightening sound, accompanied by the sexiest blindingly white smile. "Then no, not even close to good."

Damn, I should've gone with a mediocre guitarist! Now I've backed myself into a corner, Stranger Danger not giving me anything in the form of segue. Struggling, I shove my hands in my back pockets and rock nervously back and forth on my heels, forced to come up with another revealing yet seemingly aloof question.

"Why do you ask?" he rescues me.

"Our band." I toss my head back toward the bus. "We need a bassist. And since you're hitchhiking, I thought maybe—"

He drops down from his perch on the top edge of the bench and stands, well over six feet of sinister sex appeal stretching out before my eager eyes. "Do you *know* what a hitchhiker is?"

"What?" I shake my head to clear it and take a step back. "Yes, of course."

"You sure about that?" He eats up the steps I'd retreated, placing his body close enough to mine that I can literally *feel* the battle of push and pull between us. "'Cause where I come from, hitchhikers stand *at* the road, where you can see them. It increases their chances of actually landing a ride." His left eyebrow curves up at one end and that same eye, I swear it, twinkles at me. "Seeing as how I'm sitting at the back of a desolate rest stop, I'm either the worst hitchhiker in history," another step closer, "or you're labeling me with the wrong tag."

Some weird sensation creeps up my neck, then my face, ending with a tingle all over my scalp. Confused, I reach up to feel my cheek. *What the hell? Am I blushing?* I had no idea my body was capable of such an act.

*Am I a delicate, femininely light blusher or one of those hideous, red as a beet, blotchy kinds?* Also, and *most importantly*, what is it with this guy? I don't blush, I certainly don't notice what brand of jeans a guy wears, and...I don't usually enjoy challenging yet intriguing conversations with strangers. In the blip of time I've spent with him, I've morphed into a completely unrecognizable version of myself, one I really don't like...*and I wasn't overly thrilled with the original.* Nothing, no one, ever surprises me in a good way or brings to curious life parts of me I thought were long since dead or didn't exist at all.

Seriously, girls in high school? Complete anomalies. Gushing, blushing, obnoxious freaks of nature. I was never one of those girls and won't allow myself to become one.

"I don't play bass anyway, just dabble on that thing some." He casts a fleeting glance at his case. Close enough that his breath grazes my already heated cheeks, I can clearly see that his pupils have dilated, a sure sign he's fibbing and being modest. *He can play.*

I step back again, beginning to resent him, this may be *vagabond*, for daring to stir my damn *Kool-Aid*. Nine out of ten receptors in my brain, although I have no clue how many a human brain actually has, are screaming at me to tuck and run far, far away. My heartbeat is thumping against its own cage like I just freebased crack and I haven't turned to look for Conner in at least a full five minutes, neglectful and careless.

*Yeah, not good. Time to regroup.*

I need to come up with a solution that doesn't make my nipples wanna cut glass.

And yet...I shift my eyes right, seeing that Conner is fine, and find myself speaking again as though I didn't just have a back-out plan damn near planned. "Jarrett does. Play bass, I mean. He plays almost anything, and well." My chin juts up and out, pride in my boy not to be tamed as I give him a curt nod. "So if you can hang on guitar, he can switch to bass no problem."

He rubs his chin between thumb and forefinger and considers me, but in a classy, eyes above the neck kinda way. This time the *right* brow lifts in contemplation as he slides his tongue back and forth across that enchanting bottom lip. Women worldwide would pay top dollar for the chance to watch this guy do *anything,* algebra even; *trust me.* I'm cataloguing his habits *strictly* in case he does end up on the bus—left eyebrow up is playful and joking, right brow means serious and analyzing.

"Why don't you let me try this, since you suck at it? Cannon Blackwell, *not* a hitchhiker." He offers his right hand. "And you are?"

"Liz."

A frown line mars his forehead as he awkwardly draws back the hand I didn't shake—no way I'm actually going to risk touching him, as in, his skin, my skin. I'm becoming even more confused about the array of rabid, conflicting emotions stirring within me as the moments pass.

"Do you have a last name, *Liz?*"

Evading his question, I take a deep breath, and let 'er rip. "Here's the deal. I pegged you for a wandering musician, and we need one. You'll have to pass a background check, body search, and piss in a cup for a drug test before you step one foot on my bus. We're not a die-hard, international sensation, just a small band having fun. You split all the money from the gigs with Jarrett and Rhett, less a small cut for Bruce and Conner, and I pay for everything else. In return, you agree not to do drugs, on or off my bus, *ever.* You can do whores, not any of my business, but also, not on the bus. You *can* drink onboard, but never so much that you get sloppy in front of my brother." After a long, loud exhale, I let my shoulders drop, done with the winded, practiced speech I've given before, and take another step back.

"What's the name of the band?" *That's* what he got out of that spiel? Definitely not the usual initial response I get. Most people start asking exactly what shows up on a

SE Hall

background check, or what drugs the test picks up, things like that.

"See You Next Tuesday."

His head cocks to the side, a few brown locks falling near his eye, and he smirks. "Your band is called cu—the uh, c-word?"

"Now did you hear me say the word cunt?" I challenge, twisting my lip in jest.

"Do *you* play, Liz?"

"Why?" I ask, a hint of defiance.

"Well, you're as feisty as you are cute. Not sure I can handle a triple threat. You play too and I may be in trouble." He smiles; well, his mouth does some upturning, mind-fuckery type thing. I'm not exactly sure it'd be considered a smile.

"Sister!" blares through the peaceful afternoon air, and then again, more desperately. "Bethy! Come find me!"

I hold up one finger, silently requesting a minute, and turn, smiling at Conner running toward me, Jarrett right behind him. "Come 'ere, Bubs! I want you to meet someone."

*Tell me* he's not a genius with super powers—his timing is spot on. I'm on the fence with this guy. No kill us in our sleep vibes or so much as a flinch at my gamut of requirements, he should be an automatic yes. Yet I'm torn, all my hesitancies resting on the scary *good* vibrations he's giving me. I need to continue focusing on what's important, my ace "people reader," who's joining us now, and *not* the ass on the new guy. I find Cannon Blackwell disarming...and quite frankly, it's pissing me off.

"I thought you got lost," Conner pants, habitually throwing his body on and around me, igniting a reminder twinge in my back. "Jarrett! I FOUND HER!"

I wince, dislodging my arm from his deadlock to stick a finger in my ear, wiggling it around to stop the ringing.

36

"Right behind ya, buddy," Jarrett chuckles in a normal volume. "Good job, though."

"Bethy needs a Bubcuff," Conner states, holding up his wrist.

Jarrett grins at me sideways. "I think you may be right there, Con Man. Liz, do you need a Bubcuff?"

Ever since I was granted custody of Conner, almost a full two years of red tape after I turned eighteen, I'd made him wear what came to be known as the "Bubcuff" any time he's not right beside me. It's nothing more than a thick, brown leather wristband, but Conner thinks it's magic and sends me a signal if he gets too far from whomever I've entrusted him with.

I do what I have to do. You lose your brother, who faces certain challenges, in the middle of a carnival and then come talk to me. And in my defense, Bubs is actually the one who first suggested I was able to find him because of the bracelet. I just didn't correct him.

"I wasn't lost, Bubs. Jarrett knew where I was the whole time, but thanks for finding me. I should have told you where I was going too. Can I have a *soft* hug?" I reach my arms out, hoping he caught my specific request.

Thankfully, he did, wrapping him arms around me half as tight as normal, kissing my forehead as he pulls back. "Soft enough, Bethy?"

Eaten up with happy and the goofy grin to match, I nod my head. "Perfect. Now, there's someone I want you to meet."

When I turn Conner by the arm, Cannon's watching us with, hmmm, I don't know him well enough yet to say with what exactly. But none of my intuitive hackles go up, so it's not anything offensive, nothing I'm usually braced for when introducing someone to my brother for the first time.

"Conner, this is Cannon Blackwell. He plays—"

"He almost has my same name!" I'm interrupted with a shout.

"You're right, they do sound a lot alike, but I wasn't done, bud."

He ducks his head. "Sorry, Sister."

I tilt his chin with my finger, not specifically acknowledging the pouting as the doctors advised me, and continue on. "He plays the guitar and I was talking to him about maybe giving the band a try. Cannon," I shift my body, opening my stance to include them both, "this is my big brother, Conner. He plays the tambourine for us."

"I'm the second other boss of the band." Con steps forward, puffing out his chest.

What Cannon does next, reflexively, not only casts away any doubts that may have still been lingering in the back of my head, but also testifies largely toward my preliminary sizing up of his character. "It's nice to meet you, Conner." His hand's already extended. "What kind of music does your band play?"

I sneak a glance at Jarrett to find he's already looking at me, wearing a "told ya so" smile on his lips. *Cannon's in with him.*

"Not my sister's music. She won't let us. We play Rhett's songs, and other people's. It's called Al, At—"

I place a hand on Conner's back, helping out a little. "Think Evanescence has a baby with City & Colour. We call it Alternatwang. Jarrett and I wanna rock, but Rhett writes the songs and *should* have been born the gritty Everly Brother, so we compromise."

He nods, surprisingly not needing further explanation on our genre. "So, Conner, I'm sittin' here, minding my own business, when your sassy sister comes over and asks me to jump on a bus full of strangers. Sounds crazy to me. I'm hoping maybe you can tell me why I should join your band?"

"Where are you going?" Conner asks him.

He bounces his shoulders and looks off in the distance. "No idea," he barely wisps out.

"Do you like Pez?"

Cannon turns back to him slowly, an amused spark of interest lifting *both* brows, which I note to mean "you've pleasantly surprised me." "Sure, who doesn't like Pez?"

"I got a bunch on the bus, let's go!" Conner yells, grabbing Jarrett's and my hands, dragging us back the way we came. "Come on, Cannon Blackwell, we're heading out! Woo woo!" His train noise carries off on the breeze.

# CHAPTER four

"You may have passed the Conner test, but I wasn't kidding about the rest." I hold up a hand to stop him from climbing the steps on board. "Let me see your driver's license."

This is the part where I go back to, and stay in, sister mode. For a moment, I got lost in the smoothness of his tone and allure of his seductive, discerning eyes, but now we're back to business. You're about to cohabitate with my brother. Everything you've ever done and might be inclined to do again, anything in your bloodstream, all your secrets…they just became my business.

While he's digging out his wallet, I yell into the bus, "Uncle Bruce, will you bring me a piss cup, please?"

I take his offered license and pull out my phone, typing all his information into the background check website. *Magnificent invention.* About the time a processing swirl appears on the screen, Bruce comes clomping down the stairs and thrusts the rapid-screen kit into Cannon's chest. "Take one nap and you start picking up heathens," he grumbles.

"Go piss in that and bring it back. Bathroom's right over there." I point.

"When do I get the full body search?" He smirks.

"When you get back," Bruce rumbles at him, shifting closer to me.

40

Although I feel kinda sorry for him, I can't contain my laughter as Cannon's face pales and drops, along with his jaw. "Relax," I coo sarcastically. "If you pass the drug test, I'll let you skip the cavity check."

"You're a siren," he mutters, shaking his head.

"A what?"

"You know, a Siren. Those witchy mermaid girls who sang sailors to their deaths." He winks at me. "It's a compliment."

"I'm unfamiliar with that fable." I flush in flattered embarrassment, reveling in the spark of femininity for a moment before I'm back to business. "And I'm certainly not what you describe. I'm cautious and realistic. You don't like it," I flit my eyes about, landing on anything but him, shooting for boredom and disconnection, "say no. We'll be on our way and you'll never have to see us again. Your call, Superstar."

"Mmhmfhp," he mumbles to himself, stomping off to the bathroom. How nice it'd be if my outside *actually* matched my inside, that in my soul, I was, in fact, the hard-ass bitch I emote, the kind of girl who's impervious to the sight of his ass walking away.

I'm a fraud. And apparently, according to him, a Siren.

Confirmed wholly by the fact that I could testify with 200% certainty that Cannon Blackwell puts more weight on his right leg than left, also the side on which he carries his wallet, and his left ass cheek hitches up a smidge higher with his manly, slightly bow-legged gait.

"Dare I ask?" my uncle says, stepping away and lighting a cigarette.

"We need someone to replace Cami." I wave my hand in front of my face and sneer, sweeping away the smoke as well as any remnants of wishful longing, which I *don't* want my uncle to see. "Almost seemed like a sign, him sitting right in front of us with a Gibson on his back. By the way, I approached him, so maybe you could ease up a little?" I lift a brow, beckoning his empathy.

My phone dings and I slide it open, checking his results. 'No Criminal History.' I turn the screen toward him and grin. "Feel better?"

"Where's he from?"

Consulting the phone again, I do a rapid scan. "Looks like Indiana for the most part. No known aliases." I see a Sommerlyn Blackwell listed to the side, relation not specified. Mother, sister, daughter or wife? *We shall see.*

"Sitting on a park bench, only a bag and guitar? I don't like it." My uncle's forehead wrinkles, four lines of worry to be exact.

Of course I'd thought the same thing, coupled now with *who the hell is Sommerlyn?* But I *refuse* to google anyone. If someone was to return the favor, they'd find a contorted, misinformed butchering of all that is Carmichael. I'd much rather someone have the decency to ask me for the real story, or at least what I know of it, directly from my mouth.

Or mind their own damn business.

So other than making sure you're not "wanted," and I don't care if it's dead or alive, or on drugs, I try to do the same. My investigations are warranted for safety, not nosy philandering. And they stop when I have the few critical answers I warned you upfront I'd go seeking. Is it odd and mysterious that he was chillin' in the middle of nowhere? Of course. But my gut's usually spot-on, and it's telling me Cannon is harmless.

The crunch of the gravel gives away his return and my head darts up, almost guiltily, from my phone. "Everything come out all right?" I goad, shooting my uncle a "get lost" look over my shoulder. For some reason, I'm gonna save this guy his dignity and actually skip the body search, and Bruce would fiercely contest that.

What I assume is his weak attempt at a snarl emerges as he hands me back the cup. "I'm handing a cup of my urine to an intimidating as hell little thing I just met in hopes of being accepted onto her bus of mystery. If that's *all right*, then sure." His shoves both hands in his front pockets and sighs aloud. "I'm starting to think the lemonade vendor I hit up earlier thinks it's funny to slip LSD in people's drinks and I'm hallucinating this whole very strange day. That or I'm not actually awake right now."

"You're awake," I rip the label off the cup and scope out the results, "and apparently, not on any hallucinogens. Congrats, you passed."

"So just a strange day then. That, or you really are a witchy little thing, casting some weird spell on me." He smiles then, the curve of his lush lips cocky and spellbinding itself.

"Listen, I know this all seems *super* invasive, but Conner's safety is imperative; he's the most important job I'll ever have. And the band needs a replacement. For Rhett and Jarrett, it's become a way of life. So if I'm gonna solicit random gypsies in order to save it for them, which obviously," I usher a hand at him, "I am, then I have to be extremely careful. You'll start to feel more comfortable, I promise. And if you don't," I pause, shocked that I *want* to choose my next words correctly, "you, of course, have the option to leave any time you want. We'll drop you off anywhere you say, anytime you say it. You have my word. Besides, you got anything better to do?" The last part's a long shot; he exudes class, responsibility and every other key component of "something better to do."

He dips his head, staring at the ground while smoothing one hand back and forth over his rich sable hair. "Sadly, no."

"Why's that sad?" I hear it pop out of my mouth spontaneously.

Chuckling, he pulls his head up. "I'm a twenty-seven-year-old, recently unemployed *and* unengaged, falsely accused hitchhiker. Though," I get a wink, his glumness evaporating, "being thought a gypsy is cooler, thanks for that. Either way, this isn't exactly how I saw today ending when I woke up this morning."

"No house?" I pop a foot up, leaning back against the side of the bus, as comfortable as I've ever been...in several ways.

"Technically, the house is hers. She'll take it." I assume *she* is the other half of "recently unengaged."

"Family? Kids?"

"Small family, parents and a sister. No, no kids."

I mentally debate if I've asked too much, deciding no, and that it's probably best to keep him talking. Every shred of information I can elicit makes it easier to let him join us, plus I'm intrigued. "What happened with your job?"

"Was never really *my* job. Like a moron, I agreed to work for her dad, learning the business to one day take over, since I was set to be family. Without being told, I can assure you I lost that gig the minute she kicked me out of the car. Say," he shifts his stance with a coy grin, "what's with all the questions? Do I get to treat you to the same cross-examination?"

"No way." My head waggles back and forth furiously. "But I'm not climbing up in your life like you are mine, ergo, I get to ask the questions."

His mouth pops opens, most likely to call me out on the fact that I did walk over and climb in his life first, but I cut him off...who's got time for semantics?

"Ok, last one and I'll stop. For a while." I laugh, knowing that'll be a challenging promise to keep. "How exactly did you end up squatting in a rest stop a long way from home? What was your plan if I hadn't bulldozed in?"

"That was two questions. You owe me." He smirks. "This is where she kicked me out of the car. Didn't have time to grab my phone, so I was sitting, not squatting, waiting for her to come back. For the first two hours anyway. I think *three* hours is probably long enough to figure out she's not coming back, don't you?"

That's just sad, and I don't want to answer him honestly, but that's the only way I know how. "Yeah," I frown *for* him, not at him, "she's probably not coming back. I'm sorry." I shrug, offering a sympathetic smile.

He closes his eyes and pinches the bridge of his nose, first chuckling lightly, the miniscule shake of his shoulders the giveaway, turning soon to all-out laughing. I have no idea at what, maybe he's finally cracking…sounds like he's had a definitively shitty day. He eventually settles and stares at me, the resolve moving over his face gradually. "Liz No Last Name, her cool brother, Conner, grumpy uncle who hands out cups and already hates me, two other guys and a band named Cunt, headed wherever. That about cover it?"

"Pretty much."

"Okay." He picks up his two belongings in the world, a guitar case and duffle bag, and heads to the steps of our home on wheels. "I'm in."

"After you." I move aside and put an arm out for him to go first. "Welcome to our humble abode."

He boards, maneuvering himself and his baggage up and in, and I follow, consciously fighting the urge to admire the view.

I lost that fight. Honestly, though, it was like matching Holyfield against Thumbelina from the word ass.

I clap and rub my hands together. "Grand tour time. The boys are in the top bunks, so you'll be on bottom there," I point to the bed underneath Jarrett's, "and I'm across from you. Jarrett snores if he drinks even one beer, so we all hear it any way, but you're getting the better deal, trust me. Rhett tosses and turns above me all night. I lay in mortal fear he's gonna fall through and crush me."

"You wanna trade?" He laughs, pausing his duffle bag in mid-air, not sure now which bed to toss it on.

"No, that's okay. I'm used to it. Ok, next." I nudge past him in the narrow space. "One bathroom, here. Use any of our stuff you want until we stop to get whatever you need. Just don't use the toothpaste in the green and blue tube. That's Conner's," I turn and pin him with my eyes, "and *yes*, he'll notice."

"Got it." He nods firmly. Still nothing—no jokes, no questions, just accepting Conner at face value. I'm not sure yet of his angle, or if he even has one, or how I feel about either option. I'm always braced for defense and his lack of any type of reaction is throwing me off. "Where's everybody else?"

"Conner's room." I point to the door at the very back. "Xbox. You can join them if you want."

"Thanks, I'm good." He sits down on his new bed, guitar case between his bent legs. "Where should I put this?"

"Oh, sorry." I climb on the edge of my own mattress, too short for the good rides, and lean across the aisle, teetering on the tips of my toes to reach the top bunk storage. I open the space above Jarrett's bunk; he keeps all his stuff in Conner's closet. "Okay, hand it up to me," I twist, hanging on with one hand and holding the other out to grab his gear.

"Whoa, be careful there." He rises and grabs my hips, releasing them just as quickly, as though electrocuted by the current I damn sure felt as well. I'll decide later what the jolt to my heart rate meant, surely it was merely the discomfort of being touched. His hands move hesitantly right, then left, eyes roving over me in the same sporadic sweep. "I don't want you to fall, but I'm, uh, not sure where to put my hands." His face reddens, matching my own, I'm sure—since I'm now a blusher—and I swiftly duck my head and jump down.

"Why don't you go ahead and put your stuff up there," I suggest. "You're more than tall enough to reach." Why I didn't let him do it in the first place rather than lean all kitten-like across the way, I have no idea.

While he's busy doing that, I scoot away and grab a pop out of the fridge, taking a seat at the table. He takes the hint and soon joins me.

"So where we headed?"

*Oh shit, that's right!* We aren't moving. We should be.

I hold up one finger and lean out in the aisle. "Uncle Bruce!" I sit up straight again and smile at Cannon weakly. In fact, he probably thinks I'm nauseous or something; even I can feel my freakish attempts at facial expressions.

"What?" My uncle saunters through the bedroom door and over to me.

"We gotta get our poop in a group! Shouldn't we be mobile by now?" I raise my brows at him questioningly.

"Poop in a group? Is that like get our shit together?" He asks and Cannon chuckles.

"Yes, same. Either one, you pick, let's do it!"

"So he's coming?" He cocks his head in Cannon's direction. "Didn't want to take off 'til *you* were sure."

Well color me the absorbed asshole. They've all been packed in that room like sardines, not goofing off at all, but giving me range to make a decision. A decision we should be making together. At the very least, they probably thought I'd have enough courtesy to let them all know when I had decided for sure. "Sorry." I glance guiltily up at my uncle through my lashes. "Will you get them? Let's have a quick meeting."

I'm staring down at the table, picking nervously at my fingernails, when they all settle around me. Well, except Conner, who never *settles*, but rather bounces half onto the seat, half onto my lap.

"Guys," I start, stopping to clear the ball of shame clogging my throat, "I'm sorry I made you wait so long. We're all a part of this decision and I'm not sure what came over me." *Yes, I am.* "Forgive me?" I look up now, eyes pleading with each of theirs, one at a time. Especially Rhett's. Hell, I haven't even seen him in the last hour, but I'm assuming Jarrett filled him in seeing as how he's not attacking Cannon as though he's hijacking us.

Bruce simply gives me a warm smile, proud I'm making it right. Conner wraps me in a big hug and Jarrett laughs before speaking.

"If I was mad at you even half the times you seem to think I am, I'd never be happy." He leans over in what he thinks is whispering to Rhett, "Raggin'. They get emotional and paranoid."

Rhett, always the last to bounce back, hasn't flinched. His face tight and unrevealing, arms crossed in front of him, he fixes me with a pointed glare. If a less trusting person than myself walks this earth, it's Rhett Foster. Always assessing, forever prepared for and expecting worst case scenario, his guard never relents. It's why he's such a brilliant songwriter and drummer, he's broodingly intense and analytical to a fault.

"Call me crazy, but shouldn't we hear him play?" he asks, voice as sinister as his mood.

*Again, oh shit! Now I know they must all think I'm flying by the crotch of my jeans. Picking up a band member you've never heard play? Might be a bit much.*

As if reading my thoughts, which he so often does, Rhett mocks me with his condescending sneer. "Forgot that part, huh?"

My mouth opens and closes at least five times before Cannon's up, back, and seated again, Songbird ready to play. "What do you want to hear, Conner?"

Jarrett's laugh matches my grin; everyone else on this bus would stake their life on what Conner will say, what he always says.

"'Beautiful Boy,'" he answers, as predicted, bouncing in place as the corners of his mouth reach for his ears. "My mom always sang me 'Beautiful Boy.'"

Long before anything happened, *this* is something he remembers. I'm glad, it's a wonderful memory, but not the only one I need to know about.

"Well, let's see if I can manage half as good as your mom." Cannon winks at him, adjusts his guitar, and strums the first chord. "You gonna sing with me?"

Conner's head bobs up and down and I turn away, gathering myself. No sooner than I've squeezed back the looming tears and gotten myself collected, I'm lost now in my brother's glee and Cannon's hauntingly smooth voice and superb playing. He went and did it. He changed it up, holding me paralyzed in his gaze as he sings out the new line, "and your sister's here."

My gasp is embarrassingly audible, the first tear I've shed in front of Conner in years escaping and tracing a line down my cheek. I don't reach up to wipe it, rather embracing the release, sticking out my tongue to lick it. The taste of being beguiled mixed with my pain is salty and bittersweet.

When he's finished the song, Conner's boisterous clapping breaks the silence, drawing us all back to the present. "That was really, really good, Cannon. I say yes!" Bubs praises and casts his vote.

I snicker softly, leaning over to kiss his sweet cheek. "I vote yes too. And it was beautiful." I peer back at Cannon. "Very."

With a brisk jerk of his head and a wink, he then turns to the boys expectantly. "Anything else?"

"I'm sold." Jarrett slaps his shoulder and keeps striding past him to the back. "Con Man, come play *Halo* with me."

I catch my balance on one hand as Conner rumbles the whole bench in his excited departure.

"Guess I'll get us on the road then. Welcome to it." Bruce shakes Cannon's hand, pats my head, and walks to the front.

And then there were three.

Rhett hasn't taken his eyes off Cannon once this entire audition, nor does he now. I'm unsure who I feel worse for, Cannon, the victim of palpable scrutiny, or Rhett, the ever-tormented soul.

"Rhett," I pat the seat beside me and slide over, "come sit down, ask your questions."

If push comes to shove and Rhett is truly unhappy, Cannon goes, bottom line. But sometimes I have to help

Rhett figure out if his first reaction is what he *really* feels, or if it's merely the product of his lifelong branding.

"Come on," I coax him again, holding out my hand.

Grumbling, he takes it and eases down beside me. Our thighs touch under the table, his leg bouncing up and down feverishly, which I calm with my hand to his thigh. "Cannon, why don't you tell us a little about yourself?" I *beg* him with my eyes to pacify my admiringly anal best friend with a repeat of the testimony I'd already forced out of him.

"Okay, sure." He clears his throat, swiftly pushing back some errant coffee strands off his forehead. "My name is Cannon Blackwell. I'm from Indiana, twenty-seven, graduated from IU, Business Management." He stalls, rubbing a hand on his thigh nervously; it's obviously daunting to recite his autobiography on the spot. "Never been married, although I was engaged up until," he consults his non-existent watch, "almost five hours ago. My fiancé, Ruthie, and I were driving home from visiting her parents. We got in a fight and she dumped me on the side of the road with only my guitar and bag. Well," he laughs and waggles his head, "she actually dumped me out with nothing, then pulled over not far up the road and threw those two out, but not my phone, unfortunately. I figured out she wasn't coming back about the same time Liz found me."

Hiding any pity, I smile, tempted to reach across the table and pat his hand, which I manage to squash. And it doesn't escape my attention that the Sommerlyn on his background is now narrowed down to mom or sister, because there's never been a wife, he told me no kids, and the fiancé now has a name, Ruthie.

It dawns on me that we've reached an impasse of stony silence and I turn my head to Rhett. He's doing that steeple his fingers and tap the ends together thing he's long since mastered, his inner contemplations shining off him like a beacon. "Well, thank God," he finally says. "Here I was worried you might be shady. Pissing off your fiancé bad enough to drop you on the side of the road and never come back? Nah, nothing shady about that."

Rhett is scarily good at that—slicing you to the quick with not so much as an extra blink, no inflection whatsoever in his voice.

Cannon readjusts in his seat, sitting up a little straighter, letting the broad stretch of his chest and shoulders speak for themselves. "Liz. Approached. Me. *Then* I pissed in a cup and let her run my background with no safeguards provided by any of you in return. For all I know, you're all cracked-out criminals, yet here I am, climbing into your sanctuary and giving life and what it throws at me a chance. This is the craziest thing I've ever done in my life, and honestly," he grins and shrugs, "it feels pretty fucking good."

I swallow down my laugh and resist high-fiving him, happily shocked. Rhett just got served. Is it okay to still say "got served?" Who cares—that shit happened—and it's making me feel...hmm...please stand by while I put words to it.

"You write lyrics?" Rhett asks him.

He shakes his head. "Nah."

"You should."

# CHAPTER five

Cannon, we've all discovered, is a perfectionist. Refusing to let us adapt our set list, he was bound and determined to learn our music before the wheels on this bus hit Vegas, and he succeeded—seven songs in less than forty hours. By the time we need to head over to the venue, we've all had mere patches of sleep here and there, everyone's fingertips are numb, and my voice is crackly. But everyone hung in there, and Cannon's far more ready at this early stage than I could have possibly hoped. And it turns out he can hang on bass quite well...I knew he was downplaying his musical capabilities the minute I asked.

There's no official backstage area at Elite, a favorite stop of ours here in Vegas, but we've played it several times and not only are the owners awesome, but it's small and the crowd is usually regulars, so I'm comfortable with Uncle Bruce and Conner at the table front row center in the audience. One less thing to worry about, since Cannon's new and hell-bent on playing every song, still making me somewhat antsy despite his stellar determination and progress. He's definitely a natural, though, with an amazing ear and memory, so if anybody can pull it off, my money's on him.

"Hellllloooooo, Vegas!" I grip the mic and get their attention. "It's good to be back in Sin City with ya'll! You miss us?" The crowd whistles and hollers, several familiar faces out there. "Didn't I tell you when we left, I'd—" I cup my ear, asking them to finish.

"See You Next Tuesday!" the room yells in unison.

"That's right," I chuckle in the microphone. "And here we are! Surely it's Tuesday somewhere! Now, has anybody seen my boys? Rhett, Jarrett, get your asses out here!"

Lords of the ladies, they both strut out all casual like, every ovary in the room their captive. Thank God Conner's in the front row, his back to the pair of imposter D's bared in offering behind him. *She isn't a regular.* I would've remembered her blatant self. Jarrett eats it up, flirting right back, his shirt "accidentally" riding up as he straps on his bass. Rhett, as usual, gives a quick wave above his head and scurries behind the seclusion of the drum kit.

"Wait," I look around, then back to the crowd. "Where's my guitarist? Hmm." I point to my chin and tap. "I know I had him around here somewhere. Cannon, oh Cannon, come say hi to this kickass crowd!"

Out he walks, six feet of unmistakable chiseled perfection, poured into tight, dark jeans, a plain gray t-shirt, black cap turned backwards, and boots. The roar of the females is deafening, but I barely notice over the rushing in my own ears. He truly is eye catching, the kind of guy you notice even if he's merely checking the mail in his sweatpants. Your heart speeds up and your mouth goes dry. Your eyes wander all the way down him by themselves and you can't stop your mind from wondering what he's packin' under those clothes.

"I can't believe you talked me into this, *Siren*," he grumbles in my ear as he passes.

"All right, all right," I push down my hands to settle the crowd as much as my own libido. "So now you've met the Cannon. I gotta tell ya, it's damn insufferable being trapped on a bus with these three. I've got some aggravation to get out. Ya'll ready for that?" I glance down at Bruce, pointing and motioning to ask if Conner's earplugs are in. At his thumbs up, I lift my foot and stomp my black combat boot down hard on the stage, signaling Rhett to count it off.

We open with one of our own, "Cloaked." Rhett wrote it amid his senior year of high school, "dark" lyrics softened only by the natural rasp in my voice and emotion I can't hide as I sing it. It's a song about all of us, hidden, "cloaked" under the guise of loving, well put together families. At the second chorus, the words that bled from Rhett's heart onto the page, "the real me you never choose to see hates the real you," evoke all they're meant to in me. I shove both hands in my hair and tug my way through the lyrics.

Cannon's short solo is up and I look at Jarrett, his face etched with the concern he's trying to temper. We'd practiced it no short of twenty times, but...my head swivels high-speed, face alight and foot stomping out the beat on its own. *He nailed it.*

Cannon's quite humble, ducking his head, not a clue how good he is. Beyond relieved, amped up and feeling alive, I watch him, waiting for him to look up from his fret. And when he does, high on emotion and before I know what I'm doing, *I wink at him.*

My face must wear the disbelief that suddenly hits me because his chuckle blends in with the closing chords. The roar of applause gives me a reprieve long enough to shake off that whole out of body experience and square my chin.

"For our next song, we're gonna switch it up a little. I'm betting you've never seen this before." I pause while Jarrett and Cannon cross the stage and trade instruments. I don't care who you are, but especially if you're a musician, *it's fucking hot.* "Secret's out—my boys are *multi-talented.*" I fan my face to toy with the crowd. *Uh huh.* When they're ready and the cat calls have quieted, I turn and look at Rhett. "Let's give 'em their 'Walking Papers.'"

Never breaking eye contact with me, he taps it out, then bangs his drumheads like he wants to shred them. We wrote this song together, on the roof right outside my bedroom window. It took us eight nights to get it perfect,

54

seven if you discount the thunderstorm delay. It's actually an upbeat song, written about the good kind of walking papers...when you're finally free to go your own way. But tonight, Rhett's not feeling the same vibe that went in to writing it, nor the playful tempo. No, his face and rueful eyes hold a storm.

That's exactly how things are, always have been, with Rhett. Periods of smooth sailing, just long enough to fall into a welcomed sense of ease, and next thing you know, he's back to sullen anger, always brimming right below the surface. Even when he's in a good place, you're always but a thunderstorm delay away from meltdown. I stay focused on him, my back to our audience, trying to convey love and comfort through my voice, my gaze, and the sway of my body as I sing *to* him. When the song ends and he's still stewing, I spin around to rejoin the show and energy of the audience. One song of Rhett's intense, cutting glare is plenty, and the non-verbal solace I'm sending isn't getting through. He's somewhere wicked and it will take more than a smile across stage to bring him back.

I don't turn around again for the rest of the show, refusing to be dragged down into something I can't fix right now. The next four songs sound great. Jarrett's energy is always high and contagious; Cannon's nailing every single note. He even "got jiggy with it" for one of our faster numbers and sang into my mic during "Sideswiped," our signature ballad. I'm giddy with how well it's gone, giggling as I again address the audience. "As always, we wanna thank Elite and all of you," I throw an air kiss on both hands out to them, "for having us. To say goodnight, I'm gonna sing one more. A phenomenal songwriter said it all for me and I'm hoping he doesn't mind if I borrow it, 'cause I do so a lot."

Bruce nudges Conner's shoulder, his head popping up from his drawing as he yanks out the earplugs. "My song, Bethy?" he screams.

"Your song, Bubs, love you."

Lights dimmed, I close the show the way I always do when he's there, with only my voice and Jarrett's acoustic accompaniment, but for the first time, and what I'm sure will be every time from now on, I switch and use Cannon's new "sister" line when I sing "Beautiful Boy" to my brother.

While the guys had gotten ready to go out on the town, in the city of sin after all, I'd laid down and watched a movie with Conner. He'd fallen asleep before Optimus Prime even started stomping flowers, and I'm hoping there's some hot water left for me to finally get a shower. I creep out of the bedroom and down the hall quietly, more than a little surprised to see Cannon sitting at the table, wet hair, jeans only.

Guys may be oblivious to, well, almost everything, but you can't tell me they don't know what the shirtless, barefoot thing does to a woman.

They know. Sneaky bastards.

Bare-chested Cannon won't soon be forgotten, my brain working overtime to take in, preserve, and memorize each chiseled nuance of his magnificent torso. Not overly muscular, but more than toned and defined, he should never hide behind pesky shirts. There's a very light dusting of dark hair between clearly outlined pecs, leading a line down to… *Oh, happy, happy trail.*

Anyway, I should probably speak out loud now.

"Didn't feel like going out?" *They better have invited him.*

He bounces his shoulders and barely shakes his head, rolling a beer bottle on the table between his hands. "Not really my thing. I'm more of a homebody. Conner asleep?"

I chuckle. "Yeah, he didn't last long. I'd have sacked out with him but I'm long overdue for a shower."

He stands and casually strides toward me and for a moment I can't breathe, every muscle in my body tightening and my skin tingling like I'm being poked with tiny needles.

56

He reaches around me to throw away his empty bottle, excusing himself, yet I don't budge an inch.

"Hold still," he croons, reaching up to my face and gathering….and eyelash. "Thumb or forefinger?"

"Huh?"

Pinching the two digits together, he explains. "Pick if your eyelash if gonna to be stuck to my thumb or forefinger. If you're right, you close your eyes, make a wish and blow it away," he smiles tenderly, having just introduced me to the most enthralling game I've ever played.

"Thumb," I scarcely get out.

He opens his squeeze and sure enough, there's my runaway eyelash attached to the pad of his thumb. He leans in, warm, fresh breath fanning my face. "Close your eyes and make a wish, then blow. But don't tell me your wish."

I do as he's instructed, the spell broken and my eyes popping open when he chuckles. "Only one wish Lizzie. That was like a whole list."

"Oh," I mumble apologetically and dip my head.

"Hey now, no biggie. In fact, you seem tense," he says in a low, docile voice, dangerously close to my ear. "I bet you're exhausted, always doing for everybody else. You go take that nice, long, hot shower."

If Jarrett could see me right now, he'd be laughing his ass off and I'd never hear the end of it. My tongue's swollen in my mouth, unable to form words, and I fear greatly that when I finally move, my trembling knees will buckle.

I'm starting to remember why I've never dated. Bossy, bitchy, motherly, or invisible, I have all those down pat. Whatever the hell *this* is, not so much. If I *do* open my mouth, I can pretty much guarantee that whatever I'll say will come out stuttered and he'll add bumbling idiot to his list of Liz-isms.

"Go on." He smiles, giving me a small nudge at my back. "And I hope your wish comes true," he winks. "You hungry? I could fix ya something while you're in there."

Like my head's too big for my body, I awkwardly bobble it no and stumble to the row of drawers in the wall, digging for something to wear to bed. Deciding on a t-shirt and shorts, I *attempt* to nimbly slip into the bathroom and shut the door. If nimble is now defined as gawky, clumsy, and with the grace of a blind, three-legged elephant…I *may* have pulled it off. Alone at last, no one's scrutiny or questions upon me, I slide the door closed, collapsing into a puddle on the floor.

*What have I done?* I've knowingly invited a walking, talking panty shredder onto my bus! How am I supposed to run a band, a family, take care of Conner, all while trying not to spontaneously combust?

I'd ask a girlfriend for advice, except I don't have any of those. I have the boys. Okay, what would they do? I run every conversation we'd ever had on such matters through my memory bank and come up with one thing. Jarrett would "knock one out."

*Ingenious*—I'll relieve my frustration and festering attraction any time I take a shower. Then I'll be able to act somewhat normal in his presence and eliminate that bitchy voice in my head constantly screaming, "What the fuck is wrong with you?!" Yes, excellent idea. I'm well versed in hand-to-self combat; I got this. With a plan, I climb in the shower and get to work. My white blonde hair washed, all 5'3" of my body takes another three minutes, and then I'm ready to let my fingers do the walking.

Closing my eyes, I let my head fall forward, bracing one hand on the wall. With the warm water easing its way down my back, I relax more with each deep breath and begin to picture Cannon Blackwell in my mind. Tall, lean and sophisticatedly handsome, country club to my punk, male to my female. Teasingly, my hand slowly creeps its way down my quivering stomach, one finger hinting at what it wants. I bite down on my lip, keeping my gasps and moans as quiet as possible, that single digit now two, rubbing a circle with the perfect speed and pressure.

Is this how a man does it? Gently, knowing exactly what you like and need? Or do stronger, larger hands, with delicious callouses on their musical fingertips make it feel even better? Not *a* man, *that* man, the perfectionist, plays me like a melody dying to escape into sound, consuming my mind's eye as I diddle my way to orgasm.

Breathless and disoriented, I sit down under the warm spray and pull my knees to my chest. Of course I feel *better*, but still somewhat lacking, shallow, as though I only skimmed the surface of a bubbling heat inside me. When I'd had sex before, it'd been more about healing, sharing pain with another person whom I could trust, hugs and light kisses turning into something else. What I feel right now is completely different, a wholly physical pull toward a man I find unrealistically attractive. I yearn to taste his lips, learn the speed of his tongue, the punishing brunt of his force. What would he smell like when he sweats against me? What illicit words would he grunt in my ear as we writhe against each other?

Lost again in my fantastical thoughts, the chilled water on my back startles me from a lust-filled fog and second round of pleasuring myself. I've never gone off twice, frustration and carpal tunnel always kicking in long before second fruition, but indeed it just happened, my hand again finding my center on its own, while I was dreaming awake.

Using the wall to help me stand, I step out, right under a vent. The cold air blowing down on my naked, wet, and highly sensitized skin motivates me to hurry through drying off and getting dressed. When I've brushed my teeth and run a brush through my hair, I take a deep, collective breath and open the bathroom door.

"Feel better?"

Dammit if I don't twitch, startled. This guy is erasing everything I thought I knew about myself, rattling "nothing rattles Liz" into an embarrassing fawn. And the truth is, I knew it the minute I saw him, but welcomed it anyway. I confess, I wanna feel. *Sue me.*

"Much," I finally answer him, climbing under the covers of my bed directly across from him. He's lying on his side, looking at me, undoing all the good of the "relaxation technique" I'd performed on myself. In five seconds, I'm once again strung tight as a fiddle. "Well, um, good night," I mutter, rolling to face away from him.

"I had a great time tonight," he says softly. "Thanks for the chance."

"Oh, you're welcome, thank you for helping us out. And don't worry about Rhett, he'll come around."

*Maybe.*

"Speaking of that, can we talk some?"

I turn back over to face him, despite my better judgment, grateful for the low, protective lighting. "Of course. What's up?"

"I've told you guys an awful lot about myself. And I know you nixed any personal questions, which is fine, but if I'm gonna be on the bus, maybe you could enlighten some on the dynamics?"

"Like?" I ask, puzzled.

"Conner's your brother and Bruce is your uncle, got that part. But how do Rhett and Jarrett come in to play? 'Cause I gotta tell ya, they had to drag Rhett out with them tonight. He actually threatened to dismember me on his way out. I think he might standing outside with his ear to the bus right now, waiting for an excuse to kill me."

I wouldn't be surprised, no more than I was at the fact he'd left us here alone in the first place. But Rhett knows if I need help and call out for Conner, my brother would have Cannon's ass in seconds, no pause for conscience or repercussions, and snap his neck like a twig. And I suspect he needed some space to come to terms with the fact that he too has realized Cannon's harmless. Rhett *roots* for bad—it's easier to immediately dismiss someone than give them a chance. He just sees that as their "chance" to hurt you. With that mood of his on stage tonight, I'm glad he went out. This bus feels claustrophobic enough already.

"Rhett's a little overprotective, but his heart is in the right place. He loves me and Conner, that's all. We've been through a lot together, so he's leery of new people."

He shifts, elbow propped up, cheek in his hand. "You guys all grew up together, or—"

"Yep."

"Enough already, no need to elaborate." He chuckles.

"I won't."

"All right, I can take a hint. So, where are we playing next?"

"I know we're here another night, and then, I honestly have no idea. We'll have to ask Bruce." I yawn, settling deeper into my pillow. I close my eyes and try to even out my breathing, our close proximity, the dim lights, and the hushed, nighttime voices making it infinitely more difficult than normal. But I can feel the weight of his stare on me; he hasn't moved, more questions dying to claw their way out of his mouth. I've asked a lot of him and his blind faith, so I decide to throw him a bone and lift my sleepy lids. "What?"

"Why do you do all this?" He twirls a finger around in the air. "The band, the traveling. Why do you do it?"

"Just because I don't know all our stops doesn't mean I don't like it."

"I think that's exactly what it means. You're on top of every little thing with Conner, Rhett's shift in mood, things you *truly* care about."

I roll my eyes in the near darkness, fending off his way too keen observations. "You're wrong. I love the band."

"That, I know. It's abundantly clear you love each one of them. But do you love *being* in the band?"

I hate this, the receiving end of examination. Like cooking a bug on the summer sidewalk, my skin burns, throat itches, and I feel unguarded, without my armor. *When are the guys getting back?* He's already managed to creep into my secret thoughts, now he's trying to unarm me out loud as well.

61

"Too much, I'm sorry. Forget I said anything." His voice gentles as he rolls to his back. "Goodnight, you witchy little thing."

"Night," I mutter, as unsettled and far from sleep as I could possibly get.

# CHAPTER six

The enticing aroma of bacon and muffled, persistent laughs from Conner wake me the next morning. Stretching, I pivot and crane my neck to peek out the bunk, praying Conner's not doing the cooking.

"Bethy, where are my fish?" He'd been ready, obviously waiting for the moment my head emerged, finally having noticed the absence of his pets, which I was hoping he'd forgotten for good.

"We'll get some more, Bubs, I promise," I croak out in an unattractive morning voice. "And good morning to you too."

He bounds over, grabbing my hand to drag me from the warmth of my bed. "Cannon and I are making breakfast!"

Hurriedly checking my wardrobe for any possible malfunctions, I run frantic fingers through my hair and subtly dig the gunk from my eyes. "I smell that. Whatcha guys making?"

"Cannon, what are we making?" he asks, causing me to snicker.

Cannon turns to us, grin in place, from his post at the small range. Where I'm sure I look like Helga the Undead, Cannon looks better than any breakfast, his hair damp, making it appear almost black, barefoot and wearing only jeans...*again*. He owns shirts, I know he does, I've seen him actually wear them, so what the hell is with the constant bare chest?

"What *are* we making, Conner? You know."

My spine stiffens, hands instantly balling into fists. What's his game, teasing Bubs? I open my mouth to ask him exactly that when Conner snaps his fingers. "Breakfast sandwiches!"

Cannon winks. "There ya have it!"

My head flicks back and forth between the two of them, jaw slack and brain melting circuits trying to comprehend what just happened.

"Anybody awake?" Bruce calls from outside, followed by a bang on the door. He refuses to sleep on the bus, always getting a hotel room. Handy, since we're maxed out on beds.

Cannon lets him in, then heads straight back to the sizzling pan. "Morning, Bruce, you're just in time for breakfast."

"None for me, thanks," he pats his belly, "I had the buffet at the hotel." He catches my eyes and his own narrow. "What's the matter with you, girl? You look like you've seen a ghost."

"Huh? Oh, nothing," I dismiss it. "I'm gonna go freshen up. Boys, get up if you want food!" I call, reaching up to rouse them both as I walk past their beds to the bathroom. I have no idea what time they got in, but I know they're never too tired to miss out on food.

Shut in the bathroom, I dare a glance in the mirror. Precisely as I feared—Morning from the Crypt. I wonder if my uncle was referring to all this pageantry or if my face bore shock at Cannon and Conner's interaction? And what the hell was with that guy? Swaggering in all sexy-like, whispered questions across pillows, cooking, challenging Conner productively, kindly? Too big for his own britches, that's what Cannon is. You manage your way through one set and never wear a fucking shirt and all of a sudden you're omnipotent?

By the time I've brushed my teeth, dug the rats out of my hair, and washed my face, I'm still no closer to contentment. It's strange. I'm not sure if I'm impressed, repressed, or just plain jealous. I'd like to think no one deals with Conner better than me, and yet…I've become complacent because it's easier to answer his questions than force him to think on things himself. It makes me feel selfish because the shortcut saves time for me; I'm ashamed of myself and a little resentful that it took Cannon mere hours to put me in check.

Well, a shit sister or not, I can't hang out in the 2 x 2 bathroom all day, so I lift my head, fortify the practiced mask I usually wear, and head back out to the people I love most in the whole world and one newcomer who intrigues me more so than anything, ever.

True to their species…they're having a food fight.

I should probably be mad, the thought of clean-up exhausting me already, but it's impossible. Conner is downright squealing, Jarrett is ducking under the table, bumping his head, and Rhett—*Rhett is laughing*!

I watch in silence, my heart bursting at the seams, for what feels like minutes. Cannon's the first to notice me. His eyes enlarge guiltily as they connect with mine. "Busted," he mumbles out the side of his mouth. "Cease fire, I repeat, cease fire."

The other four culprits come out from under tables, attempt to wipe their faces, and slowly turn to find me, all wearing smug grins of culpability.

"Jarrett started it!" Conner points, folding first.

"Damn, Con," he pinches him on the arm, "way to rat me out. She hadn't even asked yet!"

A blob of ketchup drips off Rhett's chin, pieces of egg fall from Conner's hair, and my uncle is licking jelly off his hand.

*This is why I do it, Mr. Soul-Searching Questions.*

At the thought, I steal a peek at Cannon, the foreigner who is rapidly finding his way into the rhythm of the band, our family, amazingly aware and filling gaps I, for one, hadn't realized existed. An unnamable twinkle in his focused gaze back at me says he knows exactly what just flashed through my mind.

It's profound, a little eerie, and probably more my own wishful thinking than actual, but I swear I feel the ease of a "connection" creep up my body in a comforting heat.

With everyone pitching in, we're able to get the bus back to pre-explosion condition in no time, leaving the rest of the afternoon wide open.

"We could practice some more," Cannon offers buoyantly, his fingers twitching. I think it's legit how enthusiastic he is to master his role in the band, seemingly dedicated already, but Rhett...not so much.

"Not today," Rhett grumbles on his way back to bed, wiping the last bits of ketchup from his face. "I'm sleeping. It's the exact same song list anyway. I think all of you should go explore the city and leave me in peace and quiet."

"That is a *great* idea!" Conner takes off running to the back, getting his shoes, I'm sure.

"Well, I guess that settles that." I get up, throwing a scowl in Rhett's direction. "Looks like we're going out, guys. Gimme ten to get ready."

"Ready!" Conner appears, proudly holding up his wrist, armed with the Bubcuff.

"I need a second to get ready, Bubs, k?"

"I have a better idea," my uncle cuts in. "I'll take Conner with me, see if we can't find some new fish somewhere. The rest of you go have some fun."

"I am so down with that plan." Jarrett grins, rubbing his hands together. "Lead me to the tables!"

Groaning, I roll my eyes, not at all interested in gambling the afternoon away, and a tad apprehensive about Conner out and about in Vegas without me. "That's okay, Uncle Bruce. I can take Conner to a show or something," I offer casually as I pull out something to wear.

"I'm going to get fish with Uncle Bruce, Bethy. Okay, bye!" Conner calls out, already pushing our dear uncle out the door.

*Alrighty then, no show.*

I dart after them, yelling out the door. "I'll have my phone on me! Stay right with him, Conner! Call me if you need anything!"

My uncle waves back with his hand like "yeah, yeah" and I watch them hail a cab, sending up a silent prayer that everything goes well *and* they find a fish store.

"They'll be fine, Mama Bear." Jarrett tugs on my shoulder. "Come on, let's live a little!"

I'm not sure I know how to do that, and I'm positive I don't want to be initiated Jarrett-style. "Cannon, anything you feel like doing?" I ask, crossing my fingers that he has something other than gambling and showgirls on his mind. "Do you need to get stuff? Maybe a phone?"

He glances between Jarrett and me, indecision riddling his face. I can smell the gears grinding. He can't decide whether to say yes to my idea and spoil Jarrett's fun, stomping all over "Pledge of the Penises," or not.

"Why don't we head out and play it by ear?" he suggests. *Ah, very nicely done, Switzerland.*

Fine by me. I have no idea if he has a toothbrush or if his family has issued an APB, but I tried. My deed here is done. If he's not worried about it, neither am I. Except for the toothbrush part, which actually does concern me because the thought of him having busted ass breath inhibits my fantasies of him giving me mouth to mouth.

"Don't you, uh, need a toothbrush? Deodorant?" I shuffle back to my pile of clothes, acting to head into the bathroom to change, but really barely moving, ears perked up waiting for the answer.

"Had both in my bag, thankfully."

*My dreams are safe. And sanitary.*

"Okay then." I shrug and retreat to change.

"Good thing, yo," I hear Jarrett say through the door, "I can't have my wingman funking up the place!"

"You're all funking up the place! Get the hell out!" Rhett barks. He's a pitiful drinker, always has been, completely unable to man a hangover.

We all scurry around like frightened mice, trying not to make a peep, escaping the bus as fast as possible. And not even a half hour later, I find myself staring blankly, bored, at a life sucking slot machine.

How do people sit for hours at these things? Slot machines have to be the most mind-numbing, monotonous hunks of junk ever invented. It's probably more exciting if you take bigger risks than milking a twenty in a penny machine, but I've had all the excitement one girl can stand.

"Easy there, daredevil." Cannon's silky whisper fanning my ear gives new meaning to excitement. "You're gonna set off all the bells and whistles if you're not careful. Sixteen cents a push, damn."

"I'm holding my own." I turn my head ever so slightly back to him. He was telling the truth earlier—he definitely has hygiene products with him—he's mere inches from me and all I smell is fresh man.

"*That*, I'd bet on every time." He winks, leaning over me and pushing the max bet button before I can stop him.

"Hey!" I look from the row of half-naked ladies to him then back again. "You lucky thing, you won! I'm up eleven dollars now. Woo hoo, make it rain!" I holler, ready for the waterfall of pennies...to *not* rain down in the tray! "Of course I get the broken one! What the hell?"

"Pay no attention to the slip of paper coming out," his smart ass chuckles behind me, pointing to the anticlimactic dispensing of my fortune.

"Oh, yay!" I grab the slip in my hot little hands. "Let's go cash out. I'll split it with ya. And where's Jarrett?" I glance around. "I'm over this place."

Cannon rubs a hand over his mouth, trying to hide the smirk his dancing eyes share freely. "Um, he'll meet us back at the bus later. He found alternate entertainment."

"The waitress or the dealer?" Each girl was young, cute, and salivating over both the guys when I'd left them at the blackjack tables earlier.

"Actually, a last minute entry. Gal who took the seat beside him. I'd make a joke about third base, but that'd be too easy." He laughs, ushering me to the cashier counter with his hand at my elbow.

I flinch at his touch and pull away from it. There are four people, only, allowed to put their hands on me, and he's not one of them. He may do a lot more than graze my elbow in my dreams, but he's far from earned even that inadvertent, small gesture in real life.

"I don't get it. Third base?" I ask, breaking the palpable uneasiness.

"The seat at the end of the blackjack table is nicknamed third base. If that person doesn't know what they're doing, the whole table's screwed. So I thought…third base was her seat, third base is probably where Jarrett's at with her right now?" He lifts the left, playful brow. "Never mind, bad joke."

"No, I get it now, good one," I placate him with a small smile. "Okay," I hand my ticket to the cashier then angle my body to his, "where to now?"

One hand goes to rub the back of his neck and his eyes shift down to the hideous casino carpet. "W-well," he stammers.

I *should* make him stew in his own pot of bro-code, but he won me eleven dollars, so I'm feeling generous. "You want to go to the store now, don't you?"

His head pops up, timid smile gracing full lips. "If you don't mind?"

"If I minded, I wouldn't have suggested it. *In front of Jarrett.*" I smirk at him condescendingly. "Chickenshit."

"I know." He puts up both hands in surrender. "I'm a pussy, but I'm a pussy who'd like my own razor, and unless we're stopping at a laundromat soon, some skivvies and socks as well."

"Thank you." I take my cash and shove it in my pocket. "You'll have to enlighten me. What the hell's a skivvy?"

He holds the door open as we enter daylight, the sun and fresh air invigorating after my stint in casino hell. Those places have dim lighting and no clocks for a reason. The masterminds want you to forget you're wasting away your day and life savings inside their clutches. *And* they eliminated the only fun part, the money pouring out before your very eyes? I wonder if Wayne Newton knows about this!

I wonder why I know who Wayne Newton is...

"There's one!" He grabs my hand, my short legs barely able to keep up with his hustle to the empty taxi, his hurried grip so taut that I can't pull away when I try.

"One what? A skivvy?" I ask, looking around, for what I still don't know.

"No," he snorts, "a cab, come on."

*I am coming on, bossy! You're dragging me to on.*

"Where to?" the driver asks us.

"If you happen to know what a skivvy is," I gleam at Cannon from the corner of my eye, "someplace to buy one, please."

"Smartass." He bumps my knee with his own; again, I notice, but don't flinch outright this time. "Target, Walmart, whatever's closest."

70

"Tell me already! What the hell is it?"

"Skivvies?" He stares at me questioningly. "You know, it's another word for underwear."

"No," my head shakes, "no, it's not."

Bent over, he laughs like nobody's listening, deep, sexy and with his whole body. If there was an instrument that made such a glorious sound, I'd learn to play it immediately. "Oh, Lizzie, I wish I could take credit for such a great word." He wipes his eyes, shoulders still jostling with residual laughter. "How have you never heard it?"

"Because my people speak English?" I question with a clever grin, hoping dearly that it overshadows what I'm really feeling inside right now. Either I'm delirious from endorphins and all the damn touching, or he just called me *Lizzie*.

With all the variations of my name available—Liz or Mama Bear from the boys, Bethy via Conner or my mom, even my father and his *Elizabeth*—never has it been Lizzie.

It's charming and feminine and...*what only Cannon Blackwell calls me.*

Yep, definitely the endorphins.

"What is it about this cab that makes you want to stay in it? The sexy driver? The alluring scent of ass and feet?"

"Huh?" I flinch, his hot breath tickling my ear. "What?"

"We're here. Or as *your people* might say, time to get out."

# CHAPTER *seven*

The first cart had one loner kamikaze wheel, doing its own thing, spinning against the grain of the other three.

Number two had clearly been run through some gum or gunk recently, the front right wheel sticking and stopping short every few seconds.

Cart three bore a suspicious looking glob of green-yellowish *something* on the handle. (It was clearly a booger, but I think Cannon would have lost it had I actually confirmed it out loud, having tried to stifle a gagging noise when he saw it.)

If *anyone* else, except Conner, of course, but *anyone* else went back for a different cart this many times, I would go "Ran out of Paxil ON the day I got my period while finding out I was allergic to chocolate" on their ass—totally lending credence to Jarrett's theory. But when Cannon, who we've already established is a perfectionist, does it, I can't even feign annoyance; something about the way he does OCD is as fascinating as it is comical.

The female clerks on lanes 1-3, all watching in amusement and appreciation, are more than obviously thinking the same thing if the twirling of their hair and high-pitched giggles are any testament.

*Finally*, he finds one he likes, his "yes" joined by an air fist, and gets a good push going. While rolling, he hops on the lower bar, *riding* the cart down the aisle as I speed up my steps to catch him. "You want a ride? I'll push ya," he offers, which I immediately decline, starting to aimlessly toss stuff in the basket.

I make it over one aisle before he goes coasting by me, all smiles.

"You sure you don't want a ride?" his voice trails behind him.

I snicker to myself and ignore him, searching for a men's vitamin Conner might actually take, ones that don't "taste like shoes, Bethy." My women's version has no taste, but trying telling Bubs that.

"I am *so* sorry." Cannon's panicked apology grabs my attention from the label I'm reading. I slap a hand over my mouth to contain snorting laughter, the scene before me, since I can clearly tell no one's actually hurt, instantly hilarious. "Are you sure you're okay? I really am very sorry," he pleads, hands shaking as he checks over the old lady he apparently almost ran over with his cart surfing.

"Watch where you're going!" She shakes a bony finger at him. "And *push* the cart! This isn't an amusement park, young man!" Tsking him and shaking her head, which is covered in curlers and plastic, she turns and hobbles away, turning her scathing glare back twice to make absolutely sure he caught her disdain.

I'm biting down on my lip so hard it's throbbing, still stifling laughter, when Cannon turns to me. "Did she look okay to you? I don't think I hurt her, she said she was fine. You heard her say that, didn't you? Sh-she walked right out in front of me." He gulps, pushing back his hair and blowing out a long, deep breath.

"Cannon," I say sternly, pulling him from panic to my eyes. "She was fine, relax. Now," my face cracks, the grin not to be caged any longer, "bring the cart to me, with both your feet on the floor, and then step away slowly."

Head dropped, his boots scuff the floor as he begrudgingly drags the cart over to me like a scolded puppy. "I told you the poor old woman you almost killed was fine. I can only assume you're still pouting because you can't *ride* the cart anymore?" I tease him.

Slowly looking up, one side of his mouth curling, he winks. "Kinda."

"You're terrible." I chuckle, dragging the wheeled weapon away from the scene of the crime. "Come on, Andretti. And please try not to accost any more senior citizens."

We wander up and down several more aisles, both grabbing useless crap we don't need, talking and laughing the whole time. Shopping with Cannon is…fun, effortless…light; I think probably anything would be. He's not easy to talk to, the famous cliché, because talking to someone new, gauging and censoring every single word I say to them, is *never* "easy." Rather, he's engaging, and interesting, and funny; it's as comfortable as it will probably ever get for me.

And maybe I don't get all his jokes right away, but he gets mine! He has a natural, charismatic way of making you feel like the funniest person in the world…and I'm basking in it. My dry wit isn't for everyone, almost no one, in fact, but he's confirmed what I've suspected all along…I'm funny as fuck.

"Why are you buying three kinds of toothpaste? You're fancy, huh?"

"I told you, Conner's very particular that no one uses his. And I'm not about to share with the boys. They never put the cap back on, so the end gets all mucked up."

"Why don't they buy their own?"

"They just don't. I'm here, and I don't mind." I turn and lean over the edge of the cart, letting an armful of toothpastes, razors and men's shampoo fall, Cannon's eyes on me critical and discerning.

"You don't take a cut from the show payments, it's your bus, *and* you buy everyone's stuff. What gives?"

"I don't take what I don't need and I like helping my friends. Simple." It's more of an answer than I usually give. I've also already given him my back, heading to the hair products. "Which one do you think?" I ask when he makes it to me, holding up a box of magenta in my left hand and black-purple in my right.

Cannon's eyes pop out in bewilderment. "Um, neither. What color's your hair naturally?" He glances up to my obviously bleached hair.

"Ugh, ugly boring brown. No, thank you." I shake the boxes, reminding him again to choose.

"Brown like your eyes?" It comes out more a breath than actual words.

"Yes, now—"

"Except when you wear a light top, white or pink. Then they look more hazel, with a pretty green cast to them."

Rhett was right—*he's lyrical.*

We face off, unmoving, my hands still holding up the boxes, his searing gaze never veering from mine. *I'm Lizzie, and he's thoroughly considered my eyes.* A slight heat tinges my cheeks and I curtly duck my head and try not to fidget. He then shifts from around the other side of the cart between us and stands closely, studying the shelf behind me.

"I'd go with this one." He steps back, talking up to me now. "Warm Chestnut Brown. Not that you don't look great now, but I'll bet it's spectacular when you just do you. If you're making a change anyway, why not change back to the real Lizzie?"

There it is again, that word. *Lizzie.*

"Yeah, ok." I shrug, putting my choices back, grabbing the box from his hand and tossing it in the cart. "It's been a while since I've done au natural. What the hell."

"Perfect choice." He winks at me, leaning against the cart that he's now pushing very responsibly. "We get everything then?"

"Did you want to get a phone? Somebody might be worried about you."

"No need. The only person that might be worried is my sister, Sommerlyn. And I don't know her number to call anyway. I always just pulled up her name in my cell."

*The mystery of Sommerlyn solved—sister.*

"What about Gertrude?" I ask innocently.

"Who?"

"Gertrude, Esther, the fiancé?"

"*Ex*-fiancé. Ruthie."

I toss an unconcerned hand at him. "Whatever, I was close, all old lady names."

"Gertrude," he mumbles with a grin, shaking his head. "I doubt it, and couldn't care less either way. But now that you brought it up, I don't want Sommer to worry. Maybe I could use your laptop to sign in to my email and send her one? My parents too I guess, while I'm at it."

"Sure." I nod. "Good idea. I guess we're done then." Our cart overfloweth, impulse buys completing covering all the things we'd *actually* come for, including a six-pack of black boxer briefs and a bag of who gives a shit what the socks look like.

"I saw fish tanks on the far wall back there. We should check if they found Conner any new fish. If not, we can hook him up."

So thoughtful, but has he missed the ten times I've already texted my uncle? Not only do I know they found a pet store, but also every move they've made all day.

"No, they found some," my voice dips, heavy with appreciation, "but thanks for thinking of Conner. You're good with him."

"I'm good with him, he's good with me. We're friends. Why?" He stops unloading onto the conveyer belt to meet my gaze. "Were you afraid he wouldn't like me? That any of them wouldn't?"

*They're friends?* Part of me wants so badly to believe he genuinely sees Conner that way, *so* badly, in fact, that I'm battling back tears right now. But the other part of me, the

76

girl who's jumped on the backs of grown men and beat on their heads as hard as I could for being insensitive, loud-mouthed assholes, is skeptical. And worse yet, what if he's a fake, saying these things slick off his tongue like a shyster needing a place to crash, just telling me what I want to hear?

That would be the worst kind of cruelty; deceitfully laid false-hope. At least a dickhead rocks it out loud, removing all doubt and not wasting my time, or Conner's. Or the flip side of being cruel, condescending sympathy, isn't brutal *or* deceitful either, just annoying.

No, a wolf in sheep's mind-fucking clothing would be the worst. And would hurt Conner the worst, pissing me off the greatest.

"Conner likes everyone, Jarrett too. Least of my worries," I finally respond, trying to scoot in front of him without actual contact when he tries to pay the cashier. "I've got it. You're maybe $30 of the ridiculous amount of shit we bought."

"And you're in for an $8 box of brown. I can pitch in. I'd like to."

Dina, according to her nametag, is outright laughing at us, a couple of goons making a spectacle, stubbornly shoving our credit cards and hands over the top of one another's at her.

"I. Am. Paying," I grind out in a low, definitive command. "Now step away from Dina's register, you're scaring her. Much like the grandma earlier," I mumble the last part under my breath.

"Oh, I'm not scared," Dina beams and pops her gum. "You two are hilarious. Most excitement I've had in my line all day."

"Well, Dina, will you be scared when I tackle him to the ground and start sawing on his throat with the edge of my Black Card?" I smile back sweetly.

"Don't worry, Dina, she's all talk," Cannon assures her. "But I'll go ahead and *let* her pay." He backs up, crossing his arms and grinning devilishly. "No arguments at the pharmacy though, young lady. I *am* paying for your crazy pills."

Ooh, so Cannon likes to play, does he? We'll see about that when I've got the mic tonight.

Four score and eight years later, we've lugged all the bags from taxi to bus. The counters, table, and floor are covered in white, plastic-contained crap we don't need, nor have the space to haul. Good thing all these men eat like they have tapeworms.

I can hear Conner and Bruce's voices coming from the back, one directing happily, the other complying while grumbling. Jarrett's still at the ballpark—third base, I get it now—and Rhett's lying in bed, watching us work with a scornful sneer on his face.

I try to ignore the sinister, happy-sucking vibes he's putting off, chanting over and over in my head that I love Rhett and wholly accept him as is, the same charity he affords me. Cannon's stacking leftover drinks in the corner, the tiny fridge bursting full halfway through the load, whistling "In My Life," *my* favorite Beatles song. I'm secretly watching him, strangely enchanted at his ironic song choice, when Rhett fires off the first shot.

"Hey, Jiminy Cricket, you pay for your own shit?"

*That* joke I got; the "give a little whistle" cartoon, but it's only a joke if it's funny. Rhett's not kidding around, he's being mean and purposely antagonistic. I was hoping to get all this put away before alerting Conner's curious self to our presence, but it doesn't look like that's gonna happen. No doubt once I call Rhett out, he'll call back, loudly, and Conner will hear. Gotta be done though.

"Actually," I seethe, hands braced on hips and body now facing him ready to square off, "he tried to pay for your shit too, Sunshine," I sneer, since we've obviously entered the name-calling portion of the festivities.

"What shit of mine would that be? I didn't ask for anything." Rhett starts to exit his bed at the same time I feel the heat of Cannon moving close against my back.

"It's fine, Cannon," I mumble where only he can hear me, then speak the rest louder for Rhett's benefit. "Why don't you give us a minute?" I can more than handle Rhett; I'm far from scared of him. What I *am* afraid of is the alarming amount of testosterone suddenly clogging the atmosphere.

"Nah, I think I'll stay," he says from behind me. "He was talking to me, after all."

"And now I'm talking to her," Rhett growls, having joined us and standing practically on top of me, speaking to Cannon over my head. "Butt the fuck out, new guy."

I place my hand on Rhett's chest, his heart pounding against it. "Rhett, stop, you're hungover and grumpy. Have you eaten? How 'bout I make you—"

"I'm not hungover or hungry," he cuts me off, his voice as raw and as laced with threatening explosion as I've ever heard it, especially directed at me.

"Then what's wrong? You were fine this morning, laughing even." And now we're here, classic Rhett. The delay is over and we're back to full-on thunderstorm. "Cannon didn't get much and I *insisted* on paying for everything out of my own money."

"You don't have to explain yourself, Lizzie." Cannon rests a hand on my shoulder, moving in even closer, uniting his force, his body, his support to me. Tension is radiating off him, rigid leg muscles twitching against the backs of mine, erratic heartbeat timed with my own thumping on my back. He *had* to have felt my body tighten under his touch this time. Involuntary, undefined, but not subtle. I refuse to slink from it now, though, partly because Rhett's being a dick and it will give him satisfaction to watch me shun "new guy," but mostly because Cannon's doing it thinking he's protecting me, which is screwing with my sanity far worse than my touching phobia ever has.

"Lizzie?" Rhett scoffs, zoned in scarily on Cannon's hand upon me. "Does he mean you? And why the fuck is he touching you? Three days and he's your pet-naming, shopping together bodyguard? Fuck this!!" he screams and throws up his hands, storming toward his bunk.

Any second now....

"Bethy! I got fish, come see! Who's yelling? Where are you going, Rhett?"

Ummph. I fall back into Cannon's chest as Conner tackle hugs us both, as in together, at the same time. One big, suffocating, claustrophobic sandwich. "Bubs," I wheeze, lightheaded and seeing spots, the completely tangible contact on my back suddenly too much. "Bubs, let me out!"

Poor Conner is suffering major sensory overload, his head turning furiously back and forth. His voice volleys between panicked, anxious, and confused as he tries to address each situation in the room at once. "Sorry, Sister. Wait, Rhett, I wanna go!"

"EVERYBODY FREEZE!" I take charge, *demanding* control back. Placating Rhett, contemplating the effect of Cannon's nearness...it's all fun and games 'til you fuck with my brother's sanity. "Cannon wants to see your fish, Conner. Go show him while Rhett and I take a walk, okay?" I smile at my brother, softening my voice at the end. "I'll be right back. Everything's fine. Cannon?"

He moves into action, scooting out from behind me. "I'm dying to see those fish, Conner. Will you show me?"

Bubs instantly bounces back, heading to his room. "I got you a white one! Come on."

I wait 'til I hear them fully engaged in distracting conversation, then take a deep breath. Opening the eyes I've pinched shut, I fall in behind Rhett, who's been standing frozen at the open door, waiting for me.

CHAPTER *eight*

The Vegas strip is nothing if not aesthetically pleasing. You can walk and walk and never run out of things to look at, which is extremely handy right about now because that's all we're doing—walking and walking. Neither of us is speaking or sparing a glance at the other; a battle of wits at its finest.

We have a show to do in just a few hours, though, 'bout time for one of us to cave.

Any time.

Preferably in the time zone we're actually in.

*Fine.*

"We're alone, Rhett, please talk to me. What was that back there?"

"I shouldn't have freaked Conner out. I'm sorry." Shame is evident in his voice as he runs a hand down his face.

"Tell him that."

"I will."

We come to a crosswalk and I reach up to press the "walk" button, a perfect opportunity to start back the way we came. "That it?" I peek up at him, the anguish consuming his face and demeanor positively slicing into my heart. "Rhett, what else? It's only me here. Since when can we not talk to each other?"

The sign changes for us to cross, and as we do, his hand sneaks up to take mine. I instantly squeeze back, trying to tell him with that tiny gesture that anything involving him and me is always fixable.

"I've never seen you the way you are with him," he finally answers. "Since the first step in his direction, you've been different." The statement loses strength at the end, pain-filled words fading into the noise of the city.

"Who, Cannon?" I ask, his answer a "really?" look thrown at me haughtily. "Everyone's been different, Rhett. *He's* different. Of course there'll be adjustments when someone new joins. Even you. *Especially* you. One minute you're grilling him, the next you're telling him to write music. I turn around and you're throwing food and laughing with him and then in the next breath, you're starting fights over nothing. Honestly, of everyone, *yours* is the obvious head trip."

He drops my hand; guess we're back in defense mode. "You like him."

"He's all right, I guess," I shrug. "Nice to Conner, great musician, trying awfully hard to fit in. Having a pretty hard time finding anything wrong with him, not that *I'm* looking for it. But why do you *not* like him? I mean, half the time anyway?"

Both our steps have slowed, the walk back seeming much shorter than that away, still so much left to resolve. In fact, Rhett's not even picking his feet up, rather shuffling along noisily and biding his time. "I fucked a chick last night," he blurts out.

I freeze abruptly in place, sure I'd heard him wrong. If a gun was held to my head and a question posed, the only options get this right or die...*that* would have been my very last guess at what he'd say next. "Um, o-okay?" I stutter, not a clue as to how I'm supposed to respond to that.

"Random girl, no idea what her name was." He concentrates on the ground, tracing a crack in the sidewalk with the toe of his shoe. "I fucked her, cold and heartlessly, up against the wall in a casino bathroom."

"Why are you telling me this? What's that have to do with Cannon?"

He grabs both my shoulders forcefully and turns me to face him, the end of his nose touching mine. "I fucked her because she had short, bleach blonde hair and *you* want to fuck *him*!"

"Wh—" I suck in a deep breath and rub my forehead, searching for the right words, or question, or something. "I would never do that and you know it. He's hot, no lie, but that doesn't mean...I don't...fu—err!"

I shake off his hold, taking a seat right there on the sidewalk. Daylight's burning as fast as the time 'til our performance, but there's no longer a shit that I give. All I can do is try to sort through whatever the hell you call what's just been flung at me, some said, some unsaid, all of it deafeningly perplexing. How do I begin to process how I feel about it and form the questions I now have?

I spread my knees and drop my head between them, concentrating on breathing...fifteen seconds on the breath in through the nose, hold for five, fifteen on the exhale through the mouth. Long ago, I was taught this very helpful technique that gets me past hyperventilation, which I feel precariously close to right now.

"Hey, you're okay," Rhett soothes, sitting down beside me and rubbing my back. "I'm sorry for the way that all came out, Liz. But I'm not an idiot. I see the way you look at him. You may think you trust no one, but you already trust Cannon. I know a lot of it's because he's awesome with Conner, and he is, I can't take that from him. But a lot of it's about you. A you I don't recognize, don't know every single thing about. He thought he needed to defend you back there, against me!" He slaps a hand over his heart. "Me!"

"Okay, let's review. Basically, you're freaking out and fucking randoms because I think a guy is hot? Big deal! I do have eyes and a vagina! And if he hadn't stepped up, you'd be bitching about that too! Admit it, you'd think worse of any man who didn't protect a girl. Things are new to him too, and he wasn't sure, so he did the manly thing. And you screwed the girl *before* he did that. You're right, I do trust him, a little, because thus far he's proven to be nothing but trustworthy. I think he's hot because he is—ask Webster's Dictionary! But that doesn't mean I'll *fuck* him. I never, I mean besides..." I trail off, my voice and eyes filled with embarrassment.

He gently grabs my cheeks and lifts my head, holding it in place, forcing me to look at him. "Besides me?" he whispers, searching my face with his own glassy eyes.

"Well, yeah," I mutter. "You were there."

"You've never been with anyone besides me? Seven years ago?" He gasps out his questions, his shock blatant.

I shake my head back and forth in his hands. "You think I've been hiding some trustworthy true love from you? I'm a heterosexual young woman, Rhett, and some guys are attractive, but I'm safe controlling myself. You, on the other hand." One brow lifts, calling him out.

"I lost it." He chuckles, releasing my face. "I was mad and feeling insecure, and she was there. I don't know." He half smiles apologetically. "She was looking at me kinda like you look at him, so I pretended for a little while, with her."

"Rhett?" I whisper shakily, bracing myself for an answer I'm not positive I'm ready to hear.

"Yeah?"

"Are you in love with me?"

He sighs loudly, standing and offering me a hand. "I love you more than anyone in this world, except Jarrett and Conner, with whom you tie. I would die for you, kill for you, and kill myself if ever my life didn't include you. The time we were together will forever be the most beautiful, meaningful moment of my life, one I revisit in my mind often. But no, I'm not *in love* with you."

We're back to holding hands, our stride speedier. "Then why are you fucking my lookalikes and worried how I feel about Cannon?"

"Because I'm bi-polar, selfish, and codependent as hell." He grins at me sideways, a saucy flare returning to his navy blue eyes. "For seven years, I've always been the number one man in your life. I could still get some on the side—this is the selfish part, please forgive me—and never had to worry about anyone touching or taking you away from me. But now…"

"So you knew, earlier, that I've never—"

"Of course." He laughs, jiggling my hand. "I know everything about you. But it was nice to actually hear it confirmed out loud."

"You bastard!" I reach across with my far hand and slap his arm. "*That* was selfish."

"It was, totally, but it also told me what I already knew. I've never had to worry about losing you before. I knew you didn't want me, but as long as you didn't want anyone else, I was fine with that. But Cannon's different. He's got a shot. And if he takes it, I could lose you." He stops, pulling me against him. "You're my best friend, my medicine, my proof not everyone sucks. I don't want to lose you." He gulps, a choking, painful sound against the top of my head where his cheek rubs.

Resting my forehead on his shirt, I wrap my arms around his waist. Onlookers might see a couple in love, but we've just established *our kind* of love. "You'll never lose me, Rhett, ever, no matter who you sleep with and who I don't."

"About that." He shifts to catch my eyes. "No one will ever be good enough for you as far as I'm concerned, but whoever *you* decide is good enough for you, go for it. You're beautiful, and kind, and caring, and nurturing, with so much love inside you to give, just waiting for the right person to unleash it. Maybe that's him, maybe it isn't, but you deserve the chance to find out. You're overly worthy of someone whispering how magical you are in your ear and making you feel loved. Don't listen to me, Liz, my damage is done and irreparable, a cross I'll carry for life. But you," he trails a fingertip down my cheek, "are spectacular, and ready to live again. Ignore me when I try to stand in the way of that. This could be it for you—he likes you too." He laughs and kisses me softly, the lips of a beautiful friend, then pulls back. "How could he not?"

"We'll see, or not. I've only known him a couple days. I wouldn't plan a wedding just yet." I pop my shoulders casually, despite the anything-but-casual curiosity his speech has evoked within me. "But I'm glad we had this chat. I'm still not sure I understand it all, but I love you and I never want to hurt you, or lose you. Ever."

"You won't. And don't totally dismiss instant connections. We had one, and look how great that turned out? A spark ignites like *bam*!"

"Whatever," I brush it off.

"Love you, Liz, always."

"Of course you do! Now gimme a ride back and step on it!" I yell happily, jumping on his back and spurring him in the sides with my heels. I lean my head down to place a soft kiss on his cheek and whisper in his ear, "A therapist would have no idea what to charge you by the hour, my precious, crazy Rhett."

When we make it back to the bus, Jarrett has too, and is pacing, tugging at his hair in panic mode. His head jerks in our direction as we tentatively climb the steps, a look of relief flashing briefly across his face before a scowl sets back in. I don't know about Rhett, but I've had all the outbursts and drama I can handle today, so Jarrett better cool those jets of his real quick.

"Where the hell have you two been? And where's everybody else?" His arms wave frantically, voice three octaves higher than normal.

Wait, come again?

"Who's not here?" I ask, already en route to Conner's room, finding it empty. Panic creeping up, I fling open the bathroom door then the shades on every bunk—empty, all empty! "Where are they? Where the hell's my brother?" I scream, ripping my phone from my pocket. Dead.

"Both of you, check your phones. Mine's dead." My hand shakes so much that it takes two tries attaching it to the charger. "Well, anything?" I spit through a quickly narrowing throat.

Jarrett holds up a finger, phone to his ear. "Hey, Bruce, you with Conner?" He's nodding his head now, giving me a smiley thumbs up. "Huh, okay then. Yep, that'll work. See you then."

"What?"

"They went to eat. He and Conner will meet us at Fletcher's for the show. House Drums." He looks at Rhett. "Rest is fine, it's not far."

"And Cannon?" I ask.

"Don't know, he's not with them. What'd I miss?" He glances from Rhett to me, worry and suspicion a mixed cloud on his face.

"I'm getting ready," I muster, not up for a recap, grabbing my stuff hastily and slamming the bathroom door behind me.

*Fucking Rhett.* I adore him and have already forgiven him, but one person's volatile, sporadic, swiftly fleeting moods should not dictate the lives of everyone else around him. He runs off Cannon for no reason, taking it all back at his convenience, one walk too late later, and everything's supposed to just switch back to good. For some people, especially those who don't know him well, it's not that easy to forgive his crazy outbursts in a snap.

Now we're right back to square one—a player short.

But that's not all that's bothering me. One of us, the girl currently immersed in way too hot of water, scrubbing her scalp furiously, is *far* from back where she started.

Cannon has no phone to call and beg him back, which I'm not even sure I would do. I don't strike myself as a beggar, but then again, I didn't know I was a blusher before either. All I know for sure is I can't unhear the words Rhett said or unfeel the things awoken in me the last few days any more than I can unremember how much I enjoyed Cannon's company.

And Bubs? Yet again, my sweet, innocent, always kind and accepting brother comes out the worst. Confused and bereft, he won't understand a damn thing about the politics that surround him, only that he's lost another friend.

Is my father right? Am I dragging Conner through a maze of uncertainty and instability? Is my uncle miserable, faking wanting to be here only to make sure I don't destroy his nephew?

Too bad I can't simply say "things were better before, let's go back to that," cause that's certainly not the case. *Before* sucked colossally, no one happy or stable.

And now's not looking real great either. Which leaves only future…so I guess we'll see what happens.

Tonight's show is at Fletcher's, a skeezy, way too big and too questionable venue for my brother, so not only am I dismal from today's events and our wanderer having wandered, but I made Bruce and Conner skip the show, giving them free run of my credit card for a movie or something else fun instead.

With some last minute adjustments, Jarrett's got his bass in hand and I'm about to shred on the guitar strapped around my neck. I usually prefer to play piano, but tonight I need raw, soul-searing metal in my hands—and we need a guitarist.

"Who's already hammered out there?" I yell into the mic, pressing my boot to the foot pedal, ready to melt faces and ears alike.

The crowd roars and wolf whistles in response, feasting off my aggression. "Well good. After the show, I just might join ya. We're See You Next Tuesday, but I won't. Rolling out of here later, headed for some other bullshit. Anyways, this first one's a favorite of mine and grossly appropriate."

I lead into "Disarm" by Smashing Pumpkins, not found on our set list. The boys catch on seamlessly and join in, I knew they would, but cared nothing if they didn't. Even if by myself, it's my battle cry, to Cannon, Rhett, life…all disarming me, testing my strength.

Eyes closed, head back and whole world spinning around in my head, I leave everything in the song. Painfully personifying lyrics burn their way up my throat and damn near *cry* out my mouth, the words objectifying me so much so that I'm drained when it's over, yet tempted to sing it again.

"Well, look what the cat dragged in." Jarrett laughs into his own microphone as I fall silent, pulling my eyes open.

It's probably stupid and unrealistic, but I know who he means without the slightest movement of my head. Amongst the noise of the bar and the heat of the lights—more than anything, I can *feel* his return.

"Sorry I'm late," that seductively rich voice rings out. "I must've misplaced our schedule."

Frozen, losing my anger-fueled showmanship all at once, I fight to keep my focus straight ahead. Thank God Jarrett knows me so well, immediately commandeering the lead.

"Give it up for Liz on guitar!"

I use the break to unstrap and take the guitar to side stage, almost not wanting to walk back out. But I'm back, front and center, by the third bar of our original "Unapologetically," a ditty written by all three of us, featuring jovial, more on the country side, lyrics with a mean bass line. One of my faves. Rhett sings this one with me from behind his drum kit, the ray of sun returning from behind the clouds evident in his harmonious tenor.

With Jarrett at the helm, of course there's double meaning banter in between every song; he loves playing with the crowd. And his ornery segue to our fifth number seems to be a crowd favorite, judging by applause and raucous laughter.

"Say Cannon?" he asks with a chuckle.

"Say what?" the man to my right, who I still haven't looked at, answers.

"I believe you may be in the doghouse with our lead mistress, bro. What're you gonna do about that?"

My head flings to the left, shooting Jarrett a viscous scowl. How dare he broadcast band problems on stage? This isn't a stand-up routine, especially at my expense.

"Well, if she'd afford me so much as a glance, I'd ask if I could sing her a song." The audience, eating this up, cheers and whoops, loving Cannon's charm. Even men are grinning and clapping.

I can either go with it and be humiliated or crack his teeth and labeled the villain. Both glaring choices suck, but I concede to the first and ham it up, turning to him with a defiant stance, crossed arms and raised-brow. With an evil smirk, I ask, "What'd you have in mind, hot shot?"

He saunters over to me, the effects of his teasing approach devastating, and leans into my ear. "What was *your* song, Siren? The one sung *to you* all the time?"

"I-I—" Tears threatening, I gulp them down and manage a whisper, "I didn't have one."

"You do now." He winks, slowly moving backwards into place, mesmerizing eyes holding mine. "Grab somebody close," he instructs the room, "this is a slow one, for Lizzie."

Tunnel hearing, no clue if Rhett or Jarrett join in, I barely manage to remain standing and dry eyed as he sings "Girl," by, you guessed it, my beloved Beatles. Transfixed, the entire performance undoes me, but the parts where he hisses air in through his teeth, lip curling as he does so, right after he coos out "ahh girllll." Hot damn. Every feeling in my body is replaced with deliciously feminine longing.

He made that song his sultry bitch, never breaking our locked stare, carrying me away from the here and now to a place where only he and I exist, where I'm the "girl" who makes him hiss in a deep breath past a clenched jaw...in awe of the charge between us.

"I think you're forgiven," Jarrett laughs and razzes aloud when it's over, pulling me from the daze I'd fallen into. "Whaddaya say, Liz?"

Struck dumb, I bob my head, afraid to move any more than that, frozen stupid by the serenade. If you want my attention, play The Beatles...but newly discovered...if you want me tongue-tied and noticeably humid down south, sing "Girl" to me...*like that.*

"All right then, let's wrap 'er up. Go crazy for me people, this here's 'I Will Wait' by the almighty Mumford!" Jarrett shouts, fixing all the ladies with a sexy smile.

My role in this one is merely back-up harmony, a strategic choice by Jarrett since I couldn't lead a song right now if I tried. So much is changing at once, new feelings, friends and their startling revelations...I'm confused, but alive, excited but...petrified. I'm scared to death of all things over which I have no control. Management I've clung to, ensured, in every way I can.

"Thank you, good night!"

I vaguely comprehend Jarrett closing the show, I have no idea if we did two or twelve songs, and I robotically wave and smile, rushing off stage. Damn near running down the hallway, I crash open the back door and suck in the cool night air while I dig out my phone.

This, I *must* control.

"Hey, how was the show?" my uncle answers.

"Good, great, where's Conner?"

"Kidnapped by pirates, damndest thing."

"Is that supposed to be funny?" I screech.

"He's right here, perfectly fine. Calm down. We're in the penthouse at The Hayes, very swanky indeed, watching Pay-Per-View and pigging out on room service like the happy gluttons we are. And *you* are taking a night to be twenty-three."

"Let me talk to Conner, please."

"I mean it, Elizabeth Hannah Carmichael." Eek—scary stern uncle voice *and* the first name I hate. "We're having a great time and will see you tomorrow. Now here's your brother."

"Bethy?"

"Hey, Bubs, you having fun?" My question's immediately met with indecipherable ramblings of everything they've done, are doing, or still have to conquer. I know he's cared for and deliriously happy, but I had to hear it myself. "Ok, I guess you go ahead and stay and I'll see you in the morning," I agree with a trace of glumness, which is selfish, feeling unimportant instead of happy for him.

"K, bye," his voice drifts off as he drops the phone, which I hear hit the bed. I go ahead and hang up, looking around now with a snort. I'm worried about him in a hotel with our uncle while I stand alone in the dark back alley of a nightclub. *Shit.*

Interesting tidbit, the door doesn't open from the outside...and now I'm scared. My whole body instinctively trembles as I turn and face the looong walk from where I stand to the street. I have no choice though, better moving toward the goal than standing still like a target. Maybe ten steps out, something cracks under my foot and I scream, turning back abruptly, my eyes growing moist.

"Lizzie!" The door flies open as Cannon screams my name, searching around desperately. Spotting me, his body visibly jolts, starting to move in my direction.

92

"Hold the door!" I yell at him, running that way. I can't help it, don't want to, I slam into his chest and bury my face in the balmy smell of his shirt, fisting it in my hands. "Thank you."

"What the hell are you doing out here?" He holds the door with one arm, me tightly around the waist with the other. "We've been looking everywhere for you. Rhett may've called the police by now."

"I know, I'm sorry. I didn't realize, and the door closed and wouldn't open," I hiccup as I unhand him and back up. "I needed air, and to check on Conner. I'm," I look down, "stupid. Sorry."

Refusing my retreat, he pulls me back to him in a tight embrace, one I don't mind at all. It's actually welcomed by my frightened, frazzled nerves, and when he sighs against my hair, I join him.

"I'm just glad I found you, stubborn woman. I could've told you Conner's having a great time if you would've asked instead of running."

I lift my head up and back, my incredulous look calling out his hypocrisy. *"You're* gonna talk about running?"

"Yea, I am, to you. Later, though. For now, we're gonna go call off the search party and have a good fucking night." He locks his hand around my own and leads me inside.

"How'd you know about Conner?" I ask.

"I went back to the bus, but I'd already missed you guys. Your uncle told me where we were playing and why they weren't going to be there, so I gave him my credit card and told him and Conner to have fun."

"They already had my card," I laugh. "If they actually use yours, I'll pay you back."

"No," he stops suddenly, me banging into him, unprepared, "you won't. I wanted to do it, I did it, and it's done. Leave it. In fact, leave a lot out of your mind, where it belongs, and come have some fun for a change."

"Bossy," I mumble, but not low enough, since he cocks his head back and winks.

Rhett and Jarrett rush towards us, relieved at my reappearance yet full of seething questions, but are rebuffed immediately by one demandingly in control Mr. Blackwell. "She's fine, let's drop it. And she's off duty tonight. Think we can show her a good time?"

"Fuck to the hell yes." Jarrett beams, clearly onboard.

"Liz?" Rhett questions, holding out his hand to me.

To take it, I'd have to leave Cannon's side. I'm probably making it seem monumental in my mind when it's not, but something tells me, in my gut, not to choose. Instead, I turn and head to the bar, alone. "Find a private table, first round's on me!" I call out, bounding away, determined.

"What can I—hey, you're the girl from the band!" the handsome bartender gushes, leaning across the bar to me with a huge grin. "Whatever you want, on the house."

"Well," I look up behind him, confused by the lack of menu, "three guys, one girl, all night to kill and most of them harboring a lot of fury and resentment. What would you suggest?"

"That's a tall order." His brow creases. "Is this girl safe with the guys?"

"Absolutely."

He considers me a moment more, finally seeing enough in my resolve that he's assured of my safety. "Shots and beers then. Anything particular?"

"Surprise me." I smile, kinda excited. I've never done this, even when Conner's on "visitation." Awkwardly balancing a full tray through a rowdy crowd, I search for the boys far too long when a curly, red haired waitress takes pity on me.

"Hey, band front woman, right?" she yells over the music.

I nod, watching the teetering tray skeptically.

"Let me get that for ya." She takes the waiting disaster from me in stride. "Follow me, your group's up here."

Making a note to tip her well, I follow her up a flight of stairs, illuminated by purple light, into a raised level of much more private tables.

"I'll try not to put anyone else up here," she says, starting to set the drinks on the table.

"Shit, sorry, Mama." Jarrett stands, pulling out a chair for me. "I should've helped ya. But thank you very much…"

"Vanessa," she answers his unspoken question with a full, blushing grin. "I'll keep you guys hooked up."

"Thank you, really," I tell her. "The bartender said on the house," I scrounge in my pockets, never leaving myself without some money, and pull out a crumpled hundred, "but this is for you."

"Thank you. Enjoy. I'll be back."

The three of us all watch Jarrett track her retreat, hunger and intrigue oozing from his pores. "Nessy, Nessy, Nessy," he mutters, licking his lips. "Come into my web, said the spider to the fly."

I snap my fingers right in his face. "I dare you to have five lines of innocent, interesting conversation with her, *before* you find out what color her panties are."

"She's not wearing any," he quips back, eyes dancing.

"Wha—how?" I stammer in astonishment.

"You wanna talk with the boys, you drink with the boys. To breaking in Liz." Jarrett raises his shot glass, gesturing with his head to mine. "Come on, tough girl."

Cannon and Rhett, silent until now, both chuckle, their shots already in the air. *Well then.* I mentally scratch my pseudo-balls and raise my glass, sit straighter in my chair, and clink the cheers. "Bring it on, penis packers!"

We toss back in synchrony, me busting out on my own to cough and sputter afterwards.

"Easy there." Jarrett claps me on the back. "Here, always be ready to chase it." He hands me my beer, which tastes even worse than the esophagus-burning concoction I just consumed.

Now that the preliminaries are over, we've hit a block of silence, but the alcohol's already spreading warmth through my body and loosening my jaw, so I shatter that shit. "Good show tonight, guys. Thanks for making it, Cannon."

"Here we go!" Vanessa's back with a full tray. "We like these or something different next time?" she asks, setting a shot and beer in front of each of us.

"I think we're good?" Jarrett gauges the rest of us, all agreeing. "Yep, keep 'em coming. So, Vanessa..." We all stiffen in preparation for Jarrett to snare his fly. *This I gotta see.* "What do you do besides work here?"

Holy shit. That was a totally normal question.

"Why?" she retorts. *Atta girl.*

"Just curious." He shrugs, tipping his shot down the hatch.

"I go to school part-time for graphic design. Sometimes I run, read, stuff like that."

"And spend time with your boyfriend, of course." *Oh please!* Surely he knows that line was smooth as sandpaper.

"No boyfriend." She smiles at him and scoots closer! A-maz-ing!

"You should join us." He places a hand on her hip. "That doable?"

She smirks. "It is if the band insists on it to the blond-haired manager in the blue shirt at the north end of the bar."

"Be right back," he says to us and pops up, grabbing her hand and disappearing in a blaze.

"Did I not say five questions?" I ask them, still shocked how seamless that transaction was. "At most, being overly generous, that was three, tops."

"Not my sister, not my problem," Rhett blows it off, bringing his shot to the center. "To the three of us and clearing the air."

By saying so, you actually do the opposite, filling the air with awkwardness. Or so I thought.

"Amen," Cannon chimes in, turning to me for the last word.

"That'd be great," I manage, barely thinking before pouring the fiery cure down my gullet, grabbing my beer and guzzling immediately after. "Ahhhhh," I hiss out when quenched. "So now what? Surely there's more to this 'let go' thing than just getting plastered as fast as you can."

"Usually, people talk way too much and say shit they'd never voice sober. I'll go first," Rhett grins. "Hey, Whistle Britches, I'm sorry I jumped you earlier. I'm glad you're here, you're a helluva musician and pretty good guy. That shit earlier was me being an insecure asshole. I hope you'll overlook it and stay."

I smile at Rhett, full of admiration and pride, knowing how hard that was for him.

"I appreciate that, man, I do. No hard feelings." They tap beers, the shots long gone, and drink to seal the deal. "And I'm sorry about bailing for a while. I figured everyone could use some space, without me in it, like they're used to. I'd never quit without telling you," he says directly to me now.

I kill rest of my drink, giving him a quick jerk of my head letting him know I appreciate that. "Where'd you go?" I blurt out, forgiving myself of bluntness in the name of alcohol.

"Funny you should ask, cause there's stuff I probably need to mention, in case—"

Cannon's interrupted by the boisterous return of Jarrett, who slams down a bucket filled with ice and beers in the middle of the table "This is what's up!" he shouts. Vanessa, right behind him, unloads more shots than I can count, placing them in front of us too. "This should last us a while." He sits down and pulls her on his lap.

"Thank you, Vanessa." I smile, then turn to Cannon. "Continue."

"Well," he reaches back and does his neck rub thing, boring holes through the table with his eyes, "I went to an internet café, sent the family emails letting them know where I was, checked my inbox."

*And?* Surely there's more story coming, 'cause even nearing inebriation, that news was boring as hell and far from worthy of dramatic neck rubbing buildup.

"Let him finish," Jarrett nudges me with a snort.

Obviously we need to review the rules. First of all, no nudging me. I'm having balance issues and may very well fall right the fuck out this chair. Secondly, *self,* quit saying shit out loud! Crazy, I know, but people tend to *hear* you when you do that.

*So can't hold my alcohol.* Like, almost not even in my hand either, without spilling it.

"I guess people posted shots of our show on Facebook and tagged me?" Cannon says with a hint of question, clearly unfamiliar with the workings of Erbody'sBusinessBook.

"How'd they know your last name?" Rhett tilts forward, placing his chair back on all four legs, leaning his elbows on the table. "And *why* do you have a Facebook?" he goads jovially…like his ass doesn't have one. Uh huh.

Cannon lets out a long, frustrated sigh, spinning his beer in his hands. *I've seen that move before too.* "I guess Ruthie made the account, probably some sort of tracking device, which worked. I didn't even know I had it until I read Sommerlyn's email; she thought it was pretty funny, the brat." He grumbles, but the affection for his sister is clear in his slight grin. "Anyway, Ruthie's been emailing incessantly—she's sorry, misses me, whatever."

*Of course she does. You're incredible.*

Seriously, if I said *that one* out loud, I *will* smash this beer bottle and use the shards to slit my wrists. I wait anxiously, ready to claim alcohol poisoning, exhaling in relief when no one laughs or checks my forehead for a fever.

"Somebody fill me in," Vanessa chimes in, which oddly, I want to thank her for. Usually I'd hate a new girl buttinsky, but she's more than welcome to elicit the information I don't trust myself to ask tactfully. "What are we talking about? Who's Ruthie, your grandma?"

LOVE. VANESSA.

"Did you tell her to say that?" Cannon smirks my way.

"Nope." I casually take a drink of beer, hoping I look all Swayze in *Roadhouse*, 'don't give a damn cool.' "Didn't have to. I told ya, your chick's got an old lady name."

Sorry to any young, cool Ruthies out there. Just sayin'.

"*Ex*-chick," he corrects me indignantly.

"Can we get the whole story, bro? Not to be in your business, but last thing we need is crazy ex drama," Rhett, ever the voice of reason, tells Cannon. "Or worse, you thinking of splittin' on us?"

And there it is—my concern, eating away at me since this conversation started, spoken for me. Three hours ago, I thought we had lost him. Then he's back, singing me songs, and now he might be leaving again. I can't keep up with the vast array of emotions and uncertainty; I thrive on consistency.

"Whoa, sailor," Jarrett grabs my arm, stopping the shot to mouth progression. "We shoot together. Cunts," he picks one up and directs the rest, "to Cannon's bullshit drama and the strength to sit through this story."

Vanessa huffs, red faced and headed out, when Jarrett starts chuckling and snags her back by the waist. "Our band, gorgeous, See You Next Tuesday? I didn't mean anyone, especially you, was a c—"

"Don't say it again!" she shrieks, playfully slapping him on the arm. "I hate that word. But," she leans forward and kisses his cheek, "I get it, so you may live."

Five tiny glasses clink and we down them through our laughter, still amused at Jarrett's desperate explanation, then all eyes quickly fix back on Cannon. He's squirming, visibly uncomfortable, but I want to hear the details more than I want to change the subject and save him. I'm a selfish drunk.

"Ruthie and I met in college, dated a while, got engaged. We were supposed to get married next spring. Now we're not."

We all wait anxiously, glancing at each other, then back at him. That can't be it.

"You are the worst storyteller *ever*." I definitely speak aloud this time. "I vote for open Q and A or we'll be here all fucking night, none the wiser."

He laughs, dark eyes alight and pinned on mine as he ushers a hand toward me. "Fire away."

"Why did she dump you on the side of the road?" It's out my mouth before I can stop it, unleashed at long last.

"We had a fight."

"What was the fight about?" *Loving this*; the liquid courage coursing through me is the exact security blanket I need to ask unabashedly.

"She got her tubes tied without telling me."

And then there's *that*.

I had my mouth open, ready to spout off the next question...'til right about now. Vanessa's gasp and Rhett's "dayumm" pretty much summed up the stupefied shock of us all.

Except Jarrett.

"Wait, I don't get it. I mean, I get it, sorta. Why's that a big deal, though? They're *her* tubes, right?" He looks to each of us for an answer, truly lost.

Vanessa appears disgusted and ready to knock some sense into him via her hand upside the back of his head, so *him*, I'll save.

"Hold your fire, Vanessa, let me give it a shot. Jarrett," I start, taming the condescension in my voice, "they were *engaged*, like, going to get married." He nods like he understands, but I don't see his light bulb actually come on, so I continue. "Usually, people get married with the assumption it will be forever. No one else, for the rest of your life. I mean, not anyone we grew up around," I titter facetiously, "but other people do it all the time. So Cannon would have committed to *only* being with her, but she apparently decided he wouldn't ever be having kids, without telling him. Kinda a big deal."

"Do you want kids?" Jarrett asks him matter-of-factly.

"See how easy that was? That's what *she* should have asked him, *before* taking his ring *and* getting her tubes tied behind his back!" I have no idea why I'm screaming and banging my hand on the table. Maybe I just like making a valid point. Or, again, blame it on the al-al-al…you get it.

"Ahhhh, got it," Jarrett drones, his face twisting. "Damn, dude, what a bitch."

"Definitely not cool." Rhett raises his beer to Cannon, waiting for the proverbial "bump" back.

I'm studying Cannon, zoned in for the sign that tells me what he's thinking and feeling…an eye twitch, a turn to his mouth, maybe a sag in his broad shoulders. All I get is his brilliant smile and an absentminded jerk of his head, visibly dismissing spending an ounce of sadness on it. "Kinda what I thought, although I didn't call her a bitch, even if I *was* thinking it. I just asked why she thought I wouldn't want to be included on such a big decision, and I got back a screaming earful of how it was her life, her body, her being saddled down." He chuckles softly, shaking his head to himself. "Sounded pretty fucked up coming from the person who insisted I change my degree, work for her father, and detach from my buddies. I wasn't about to let her take away my chance of ever being a dad too."

"But now she's sorry and wants you back." It comes out a whisper, meant for only me, before I can stop it. Maybe they didn't hear me.

His head tilts my way, warm smile reaching out, sending my cheeks up in flames. "She's *sorry* that I'm getting some attention she can't bask in. She *wants back* the arm she can hang on, perfect couple façade, while she bosses me around under her breath. Not happening."

"What if she agrees to get them untied?"

"Not the point. She doesn't think in terms of 'we.' It's always been her first, then 'I'll convince Cannon.' Honestly, she gave me the out I'd been waiting for. I was miserable for more of our relationship than not and she just firmed up the fact that I was right. I'd been trying to hold on for the wrong reasons."

My brows are trying to cock, so many more questions fighting to form on my tongue, but my reactions are a little lazy from the drinks, resolving me to a dumbfounded, silent stare.

Um, letting loose is depressing. I don't feel like I've been missing out by not carousing now. Granted, I'd sympathize with Cannon's story even sober, but in my current state, it's as though I can actually feel the weight of his raw turmoil sitting on my shoulders.

"Nu-uh, no, ma'am." Vanessa jumps off Jarrett's lap. "Do that shot and come on, we're dancing!" She shimmies her hips my way and smiles. "I could've stayed on the clock to serve a bunch of sad sacks. Down it and let's go shake our groove things!"

I look up at her pitifully, alcohol-induced honesty spewing out. "I don't know how to dance and I'm positive I don't possess *a groove thing*. I might be the most boring, pathetic twenty-three year old on the planet. Except maybe Ben Stein's kids, I bet they're dull as fuck." I zone out, losing total train of thought.

"She's lying," Rhett smirks, "she can Roger Rabbit like a mofo. Go show her, Liz."

"What about that New Edition spinny-hop thing?" Jarrett hee-haws, slapping his own leg. "How many times did we have to watch that damn video? Go on, girl, show 'er your moves!"

"Do those count?" I ask her, looking down at the dance floor, no one exhibiting my type of *skills*. "It appears only dry-humping is allowed down there." I point and burp.

Right out loud.

I burp.

Not a little "scuse' me" Southern belle hiccup-like sound. No, I "The Man Likes Beer with His Super Bowl" all-out belch.

The laughter at my table is louder than the music. Jarrett's crying and Rhett's practically on the freaking floor, holding his side. If I wasn't so buzzed, I'd probably crawl under the table, and I definitely wouldn't look Cannon's way. But I'm halfway to plastered, which is why that's exactly where my eyes wander.

"You're precious." He winks then slowly stands and offers me a hand. "Come on, Lizzie girl, show me your Running Man."

*I know that one too!*

"Hot damn," Jarrett's slap on Vanessa's ass echoes, "we gotta dance off, hotness. Let's do this!"

"I'll judge!" I turn at Rhett's voice, my out-of-nowhere excitement dampened only by the thought of him being left out. Like a book, he reads me and smiles sincerely. "I'll judge. Go do the damn thing, girl. Make me proud."

# CHAPTER nine

"Are we moving?" Not daring to open my eyes, willing off the nausea threatening violently, I wait for someone to answer me. Which never comes. A tad more awake now, I can make out the distinct sound of traffic, so it's not just my own brain swimming around in my fuzzy head, we are, in fact, moving.

*Conner!*

I jolt upright, and oh shit does it send splinters of painful throbs through…my entire body. Too bad; I've got to find him. Jumping out of *Conner's bed?* I hit the floor running, flinging open the door. "Bubs?" I yell, cradling the side of my head in sheer agony.

"Bethy!" Oh Lord, not this morning…the lack of pummeling I was braced for causes me to peel open my eyes; where'd he go? Did he trip? Ahh, saved by Jarrett, snaring Conner around the waist, chuckling at my *condition.*

"On it. Figured you're in enough pain."

"It's all right." I hold open my arms. "Come love me, Bubs, *very soft.*"

Conner makes a show of hesitantly tiptoeing my way, embracing me as gently as he gets. "Are you sick?" he tries to whisper, which blares like Dolby in my aching head.

"No, I'm fine, just a headache. I missed you. Did you have fun?"

"Yep." His head bobs up and down decisively. "Hey, come do a puzzle with me and Nessy. She's good at them, better than you."

Suddenly completely sober, I glance around the bus, taking in all that'd escaped me until now. Rhett's in his bunk, laptop open and earbuds in, but attune as ever and eyeing me warily. Jarrett stands in the middle of the aisle, face shrouded in caution. Oh, and lookie there, Vanessa and Cannon are sitting at the table in front of a puzzle, both sizing me up.

And reconfirmed by the sway wreaking havoc on my equilibrium, the bus *is* moving, as in...*away* from where we found Vanessa.

Code. Fucking. Blue. I brace a hand on the wall, trying to hold my shit together for Conner's sake, but wiging out inside—pissed, sick, and confused simultaneously. Flashes of the night before start streaming into my consciousness, horrific scenes of me attempting to dance that I'm praying only happened in a nightmare, but not enough for me to piece together how we got to *here*.

Everyone moves at once; Rhett pulls out his headphones, starting a hasty descent from his bunk, Jarrett takes a step my direction, and Cannon sweeps past them all, placing himself directly in front of me. "Conner, will you go help with that puzzle?" he suggests, his voice soft. "I'm gonna get your sister some medicine for her headache."

"I'm better than him," Conner says conspiratorially, hiking a thumb at Cannon. "Don't worry. I got this."

I attempt a grin for Bubs, waiting for his back to turn before lifting furious eyes to Cannon's.

"Where's your aspirin?" he asks me calmly.

"Bathroom cabinet," I growl.

"Great, same place as your toothbrush." He winks, humor lost on me. "Let's go." He uses both hands on my shoulders to turn me and prompt me forward to the bathroom. Once he shuts the door behind us, turning the space from tight to claustrophobic, he holds me firmly by the shoulders and speaks in a rich, bottomless voice. "Take a deep breath in for me," he instructs, and, as though hypnotized, I do. "Good, now blow it out slowly, for you. Better?" *No*, but I nod to appease him, which he buys, sitting down and trying now for levity. "I'm opening a Q and A—go."

Funny man. I recall saying those exact words to him last night as I narrow my dry, aching eyes his way. "Where are we headed?"

"Oregon. It's 'bout seventeen hours according to your uncle. Hillsboro, I think."

"Why is Vanessa on my bus?" I ask around my brush and mouthful of paste.

"You invited her." He laughs. "Insisted, in fact."

Not possible. Spitting dramatically, I start the second round of scouring, worried this rancid taste will never disappear. "Let's pretend that *actually* happened." Spit. "Does she know she's headed *away* from home?"

I toss the toothbrush on the counter and rinse, gargling loudly as I give him a scathing glare from the corner of my eye. Spit. "Who does that? Hops on a bus of strangers one night? Doesn't she have a job and school?"

He raises his hand with a sheepish smirk.

*Oh, that's right.*

"Whatever, you know what I mean! Is she our new backup singer? No, she's just a tagalong! This isn't a goddamn Greyhound! And Jarrett knows better! I don't allow pussy on the bus with Conner. You *all* know that! He took advantage of me drinking, *for once*, and you guys sat back and let him, *knowing* I wouldn't like it! *This* is why I never turn my back!"

I have to calm down. I know they can all hear me out there, the only one of which I care is Conner. Turning on the cold water, I splash handfuls on my face, over and over, 'til there's no more. *Did he really turn it off? Guess I was done.*

"Here."

A soft towel is placed in my hand and I blindly use it to dry off.

"Here."

I open and look at the two pills in his hand. "What am I supp—"

A Coke magically appears and he pops the tab, which usually doesn't sound that loud. "Drink it all; great for hangovers. Now we're gonna go in Conner's room and finish talking rationally. You ready?"

I pull the can from my mouth, having had just about enough. "You are *not* in charge, Cannon Blackwell. You do not eat my pussy or pay my bills, so you don't get a say."

He busts into a fit of snort, choke, laughter, one hand on the counter to hold himself up. "Are you still drunk? Did you hear what you just said?"

I have no idea where that came from, undeniably the raunchiest words I've ever spoken, and I feel my cheeks heat immediately. I exude my best false bravado when I answer him. "Yes, and I'm serious, you're not the boss."

"I hear ya, *bossy*. Now do you think you can manage to walk from here to Conner's room without petrifying the entire bus?"

I'd like to reach up and yank down that sassy eyebrow of his.

"Of course, but *only* because *I* want to," I huff, stomping out ahead of him while I still have the upper hand. I climb on the bed, my back against the headboard, braced for a colossal discussion.

Cannon's right behind me and a tingle shoots up my spine as he shuts the door. At least he's actually wearing a shirt, albeit a tight one, perfectly outlining his torso, paired with jeans begging to fall from his hips and no shoes—he might as well be naked.

"Why are you shutting the door?" I squeak, cringing from the vulnerability even I heard.

He smirks. "To ravage you, of course."

It's official—I definitely have alcohol poisoning and may stay drunk for days.

"I was kidding." He sits at the end of the bed and jostles my ankle impishly. "I shut the door so you can flip out again and maybe they won't hear *every* word. Want me to open it?"

"It's fine." I force my eyes to roll and sigh as though inconvenienced. "She can't stay and I'm furious with all of you. And until we safely drop her off somewhere, she needs to pee in a cup. And where's my phone?"

"She passed the drug test and has no record. Ran 'em both last night. What's your next excuse?"

"I don't *need* an excuse. It's my fucking bus!" I rip my leg back, dislodging the hand he never moved from my ankle. "A big revolving door of bedmates isn't good for Conner. He gets attached and doesn't understand why people leave."

"How do you know? Who's the last *bedmate* he saw leave, the one who left and it hurt him?"

"Well, Cami left, or uh, got thrown out, but she was a band member." I cross my arms defensively, fearing I've made his point for him.

"So, not a bed buddy. And before her?" he challenges me, his face solemn minus the uncontrollable brow thing. His already very dark brown eyes turn almost black as he waits impatiently for his "told ya so" moment.

"No one. I get what you're doing and it won't work. I know my brother and what's best for him. She can't stay. That's final. Why do you want her here so bad anyway? Jarrett share?" I wince as it leaves my mouth; that's snide and unfair to all of them. "Sorry, I shouldn't have said that." I hang my head, fiddling awkwardly with the comforter.

"Lizzie, look at me," he demands me with a low, calm timbre that eliminates choice. "Stay with me for a minute without getting mad, okay?" I nod. "I don't care if Vanessa stays or not, and file this away while we're on it: I. Don't. Share."

My eyes flash up to his and the intensity I find there, mixed with compassion and sincerity, causes me to take a long, deep breath. I'm beyond shocked. I couldn't have placed more perfect words in his mouth myself.

"I want you to ask yourself, how do you know what Conner will do about anything? You're an amazing sister, and he's goddamn lucky to have you, but maybe you should let him have some room, even just a little."

I'm debating between crying with my head in his lap and slapping his know-it-all mouth when the door flies open.

"Bethy, are you okay?" Obviously forgetting about my headache, Conner leaps on to the bed beside me, barely dodging Cannon, screaming his greeting.

"I'm fine." I can't help it, I throw my arms around him and hug him tight. "Are you okay?"

He pulls back, stunned silent for but a second. "Of course. Why?"

If Cannon thinks I don't see his grin, he's wrong, but I concentrate on Conner. "Bubs, are you happy?"

"About what?"

Cannon joins my chuckle. "Everything. Are you happy with the band, being on this bus?"

"I wish it was bigger and I wish it had a bathtub," he answers quickly. "Why did you sleep in my bed?"

"I wish it had a bathtub too. God, I miss nice, long baths." I tip my head back, picturing it briefly before shaking it off; no sense torturing myself. "And I have no idea. Cannon," my turn to taunt with bouncy brows, "why did, or *how* did, I sleep in his bed?"

Conner's already climbed over me, murmuring to his fish, so Cannon answers me alone. "I thought you'd be more comfortable in a big bed, and it wasn't being used, so I carried you in here."

Nice try, mister. I lived years with a politician, coincidentally also the most full of shit person to ever walk the Earth; you will *never* hide your lies from me. And I saw it, a blink of half-truth flashing in those dusky pools. Holding his guilty eyes, I slowly dip my head to the second pillow, inhaling…pure, sweet Cannon. His head accidentally hit the pillow when he carried me? Nooooo, his soft brown locks scented it up when he laid beside me. In the bed. My skin sizzles at the revelation and I bite back my smile.

"Just for a little while, to make sure you weren't gonna be sick," he explains, unquestioned, his words hurried, wide eyes lined with apology.

"Sister?"

"Yeah, Bub?" Shamefully, I forgot he was there for a second, wandering dazedly through thoughts of Cannon's body lying beside me, taking care of me.

"Your fish died. Sorry 'bout your luck."

And still, I stare at one, yet speak to another. "No worries, Conner. I'm thinking my luck might be turning."

The room is completely black and deathly quiet when I wake up. The bus is still and the pillow I'm clinging to smells like Cannon.

We're stopped, it's nighttime, and I'm still in Conner's bed. The pounding in my skull has finally subsided and I have some semblance of clarity. Therefore, I'm able to recall falling asleep lying face to face after a long discussion on the meaning of life, music, marriage, and everything in between with Cannon Powell (his mother's maiden name) Blackwell. And certainly, I remember clearly, at Cannon's reassuring insistence, conceding a wee bit of control, agreeing to let Vanessa hang, for *a while*, but *not* in Jarrett's bed. She does seem nice, and although it's fuzzy, I remember instantly liking her, and she passed all the tests. Doesn't hurt that Conner thinks she hung the moon.

In a week, I've changed more than I have in the last seven years combined. In mere days, I've felt more than in a whole lifetime. Bland, disappointing, and heartbreaking is

110

starting to slowly but surely morph into "huh, maybe there's something to this clusterfuck called life after all." And today alone, I've opened my mind and heart to the possibility of a new, trustworthy friend in Cannon. Yes, I'm madly attracted to him physically, but it's not only that—he's actually a cool guy. He has a certain *vibe* oozing from him effortlessly that compels you to give anything he says credence. Much like when I first met Rhett and Jarrett, I instantly knew he was completely worthy of some good ole fashioned gettin' to know him time.

It's been a big week, and...I'm proud of myself, opening up to new ideas and possibilities, becoming more amenable. How many times have I been called inflexible? *My ass.* I'm a damn pretzel over here, bending to possibility every damn time I turn around! My *Pandora's Box...seems someone out there was holding the right key.* I cave much more and I'll be turning out backbends and splits, an open-minded contortionist of gold medal caliber. *That'd be something.*

Chuckling at the image, I slowly rise, making my way out to see what's keeping the boys so silently occupied, only to find an empty bus and note on the counter.

*We all went out to eat so you could rest. I'll bring you something back. Try not to trash the place while we're gone. –C*

Unless Conner's suddenly started writing me notes...C means Cannon. Hmm.

Now would be the ideal time for that long bath I've been craving. In the tub we don't have. I resolve to enjoy a hot shower, first taking Cannon's note, folding it four times, and then burying it in my underwear drawer. Why, I have no idea; it just felt like the thing to do. *Don't judge me.*

Only once I'm under the hot waterfall of the shower, loofahing myself with my favorite eucalyptus body wash, does it dawn on me. *They're out with Conner!* No one asked me first, told me specifically where they were going... I spring from the shower, only a hand towel to be had, and go angrily in search of my phone, dripping wet and barely covered.

Kneeling into my bunk, I search frantically, letting out an aggravated groan when I come up empty-handed and realize I just got my sheets all wet. That'll be comfy tonight. Ducking back out, I turn to go scour the table and shriek, stunned, barely stopping short of falling straight on my *naked* ass. "Holy shit!" I scream, fumbling to utilize the minimal square of cloth that I almost drop, for optimal coverage. "Cannon, I thought you guys were out? Where the hell is Conner?"

"At the restaurant." He rubs a hand over his mouth, failing to cover his smirk. His eyes, shaded playfully as perfect coffee with just a dash of cream, simmer tauntingly, taking one rapid scan of my exposed state and then politely divert, glancing around the room. "You need me to dig you up an actual towel?" he asks, shoving his hands in the back pockets of his deliciously baggy jeans and tilting his head to inspect the ceiling.

"There aren't any clean ones, thus the hand towel I'm trying to hide behind. You could have said something, like right when I pranced out here naked!" *Oh God.* I feel my whole body ignite in a mortified blush. *I was just bent over my bunk! Bent. Origin: English, slang for ASS STICKING UP IN THE AIR.* "Turn around," I grumble, mentally willing my own, immediate, death.

"Gimme options, Siren." It sounds like he's challenging me, but maybe he's joking.

"Cannon," I warn.

"You're no fun," he huffs playfully but does turn. "And you're not *completely* naked." I hear his snicker, tempted to rage on him, but more tempted to flee the scene of the crime against my dignity.

"Why are you here?" I start creeping backwards toward the bathroom, a flushing scarlet mess of fumbling hands and towel stretching. Maybe I should flip around and run for it; he's already seen my ass after all. "Why isn't Conner back too?"

"I brought you food; figured you'd be getting hungry. You haven't eaten all day. And there's an arcade in the restaurant, so they could be there all night. He's with your uncle and best friends in the world. If you can't trust him with them, give it up and handcuff yourself to him once and for all."

"Where are we?" I yell through the bathroom door, hurrying into clean clothes and refusing to acknowledge his advice.

"Bum fuck. I have no idea. Bruce says we have about nine hours left. Did you get some good sleep? Feeling better?"

"Yeah, a lot." I emerge, *covered*.

"You look good." He reaches up and runs a tender hand down the side of my face.

The touch itself may be soft and soothing, but my reaction is anything but...an embarrassed, uneasy heat enflaming me from head to toe. "Um, thank you," I wisp out in a staccato breath, quickly moving aside and away, out of the heated cloud. "Thanks for this." I open the Styrofoam container he'd brought me, picking out a few bites of nachos. "What'd you have?"

"Nachos," he quips with a smug grin, taking a seat on the bench and pulling off his boots and socks. "Are we okay? I kinda got all in your business today."

"Surprisingly," I glance over my shoulder, "yeah, we're fine. I may," I pinch my thumb and finger and grin, "find talking to you less than torturous." I rock on my heels aimlessly, finding myself in yet another completely unfamiliar situation—nothing to do. "What now? I'm wide awake just when they'll all be getting tired. This whole "Conner freedom" thing is throwing me off. I don't have a clue what to do with myself."

"We could work on one of your songs," he suggests daringly, his already taut body bracing rigidly for my reaction.

"My, uh what?" Suddenly famished, I stuff nachos in my mouth, my back to him, unsuccessfully warding off his intrusion into my every molecule.

113

"Your songs, the ones you write in the green spiral notebook, third drawer, under your bed. Any of this ringing a bell?"

*That little snoop!* I whirl on him, now sorry I can't get the gluttonous mouthful down quicker to start yelling.

"I didn't go hunting, Lizzie, relax. I sleep across from you, remember? Conner mentioned it once and your bed light hits me right in the eyes." He stands and walks over to me, voice gentling a hair's breadth from my face. "And when you write, you hum and tap your left foot. Which is odd, since you're right handed."

Should I keep fake chewing now that the food is gone? 'Cause words won't form and I feel dumb just staring in stunned silence. Who notices me or what I'm doing? No one, well, except my foursome, but no one else, ever. I'm the plain, blends into the walls chick with a loud bark, *if* you even take the time to corner her.

"I'm sorry," I finally reply, "I thought pulling the curtain would be enough not to bother you."

"Fun fact." He winks and leans in closer to my ear. "If you turn on a light behind a curtain, it actually illuminates a beautiful silhouette even more." He pulls back, gauging the reaction on my face, one I couldn't guess if I had to.

"Like ghost stories and tents," I murmur breathlessly, partly because his warm breath just husked in my ear, but mostly because I'm now thinking about how he watches me from across the way, from the shadows, my body outlined seductively for him. *I was completely unaware of my closet romantic, which I suspect is being drawn out of hiding by another certain romantic on the bus; maybe mine'll come all the way out and write some lyrics for me.*

"Kinda. And it doesn't bother me, at all."

"Good to know."

"You know what else is good?" His golden brown eyes dance sinfully and the right corner of his plump, enticingly close mouth curls up.

Never have I needed to hear a next sentence as badly as I do right now. "No," I shake my head, "what?"

"Collaboration. Will you show me your songs?"

I want to melt into a puddle. I want to, for once, let go and steal a taste of his mouth. I want to kick him in the shin for teasing me so, befuddling my stoic resolve and making me question all I thought I knew and controlled. He makes me want silly, whimsical things reserved for frilly girls, which I'm not. Or so I thought.

"Yes?" he prods, since I choose not to answer, again, adrift in my own head.

I shrug my shoulders and scoot around him. "You know where my notebook is, help yourself. I'll be back," I say, the bathroom door shutting behind me.

CHAPTER ten

"Bethy!" A knock pulls me back from wherever I'd gone. "I need to use the bathroom."

I hurriedly clean up my mess, no idea how long I've been in here, but relieved there's again a crowd on the bus. "Sorry, Bubs." I open the door with a smile. "You're back. Have fun?"

"Yes. Can we get an air hockey table? I'm the bomb. I need to pee bad." He fidgets uncomfortably.

"Oh yeah, sorry." I laugh, exiting for him. *Shit*, me and my figurative slang! *Please* don't let him think I said yes to the air hockey table.

But we're talking about my beautiful brother here, so I'm wasting energy thinking of anything other than...*where the hell am I gonna put an air hockey table?*

"You're very pretty, Sister!" he screams through the door.

My hand creeps up instinctively and finds my hair, his compliment reminding me. I'd been in there so long, I'd almost forgotten.

Jarrett whistles from behind me and I turn with a yelp, finding him smiling with one arm around Vanessa's waist, who's grinning as well, giving me an "okay" sign with her hand. "There's our girl. Welcome back," he says.

Rhett comes forward and wraps me in a hug, dropping a soft kiss at my temple. "I love it."

"For real?" My fingers fiddle with a strand, insecurity evident in my voice.

"Definitely. Been a long time. I almost forgot what color it really was." He chuckles. "God made you exactly right the first time, though. It's perfect."

"Thank you." My head falls on his shoulder, needing the brace, the support, the familiarity. And he thinks *he's* codependent? We're quite a pair, each other's matching mess.

"Hey, Lizzie, can you come 'ere a minute?"

Yes, I'm acutely aware of him sitting at the table, guitar in his lap. And yes, I won't even attempt to feign coy. I was waiting for his acknowledgement.

Oh shut up—you know damn good and well there can be a hundred people in the room, 99 of them rushing up to say they love your dress, but until *that one*, the one you wore it for, says something, you might as well be wearing a trash bag.

If nothing else, I'm real. The fact is, I *am* feeling it; I might as well admit it to myself.

"What's up?" I ask in my best attempt at aloofness.

"I really like this one." He gestures toward my notebook on the table—opened to "Lost & Found." *I really like that one too.* "What'd you have in mind for it? 'Cause I'm thinking either slow solo, kinda Jewel-esque, or it might make a cool duet."

Jarrett appears, taking a seat, bass at the ready. "Hit me with it."

"Hit me too," sweet Conner joins, tambourine in hand.

Cannon's nimble fingers start to play—*my song*—to perfection. I don't write music, only lyrics, but if I did, I imagine it'd sound exactly like the melody filling the air now.

"That B minor?" Jarrett asks and with Cannon's head bob, no break in playing, he starts to lay his foundation.

117

Barely audible over Conner's tambourine accompaniment, I hear what I think is…yep, I turn my head and Rhett's tapping out a beat on the metal rail of his bunk, the bob of his head keeping time.

Look at us—a jam session—minus the singer who's currently too overcome to sing.

"Should I video this?" Vanessa asks from behind me.

"Uh, sure, but on my phone, please." I run and grab it, handing it to her at the same moment they've stopped playing.

"So?" Cannon looks at me.

"The bridge needs a little oompf," I comment, distracted, trying to hear it in my head.

"That voice of yours will make the bridge. Let's do it again with vocals and see if I'm right."

"Yes, Bethy, you gotta sing!" I was hesitant, Conner derailed that with his gleeful encouragement.

"Ok, lemme see the words." I stick my hand out, drawing it back with a flush when Cannon calls me out—nail on the head.

"You know the words."

I flip him off with a saucy grin. "Fine, go."

This time everyone starts together, fusing flawlessly just that fast, as I square my shoulders, close my eyes, and let the words fall out.

*"The smile you know is gone,*

*My face now a lie,*

*And the long hair you loved is cut,*

*Maybe that's why.*

*You must have been searching,*

*Where else would you be,*

*Now you know what to look for,*

*Same ole', never yours, me."*

Shit, that's all I'd written, but the tune keeps going, so I do too, the story flowing out of me purely on its own—my heart singing before my mind even knows it's happening.

*"You don't get to decide,*

*Only she can do that,*

*The lost girl inside,*

*That I want to get back."*

Here comes the bridge. *That voice of yours will make it,* I remind myself. I clench my eyes tighter and dig deep, to a spot way down inside that I seldom revisit.

*Don't ask where she went to, you already know,*

*don't you dare come to visit,*

*you're not welcome no more.*

*When she passes by, go ahead and keep your head turned,*

*her face a reminder of bridges you've burned."*

*Fuck.* That felt good, time to bring it home. I drop my octave, almost speaking the rest.

*"Not sure where I go now, but sure glad it's me.*

*The face in the mirror, I'm happy to see.*

*She and I, her and me, lost and found, and finally free."*

No need to wait for a pin to drop, Rhett does a fine job with his drumstick, shattering through the awkward—for me, anyway—silence. Even Conner's statuesque and silent for a full ten seconds.

"That was very good, Sister. Very, *very* good."

"Thanks, Bubs. It's late, you ready to watch a movie?" I extend my hand, praying he'll take it fast and drag me from this spot; on the spot.

Like the best big brother in the world, still able to rescue his sister—he does. Charitably, no one says a word as we leave the room and shut Conner's door behind us. I just did all the talking I can manage for a while.

"Hey, Conner, can I sleep in here with you tonight?"

"I guess," he sighs, right before pouncing on me and smothering me in tickles. "Bethy?"

"What?"

"Are *you* happy?"

"Getting there, Bubs, getting there."

I check my phone for the tenth time. It's almost 2 am, surely they're asleep and I can sneak to my own bed. Sleeping with Conner isn't as fun as you might think, unless you think being caged with a wild animal sounds like a party.

As quietly as possible, I slink out of the bed and through his door, pulling it closed; *halfway there*. Sending up a silent prayer I don't meet any open, awake eyes, I turn, relieved at the lack of spectators, and scurry to my bed. After sharing my song tonight, I need some time to pass before I look them in the eyes—those lyrics, the tremor in my voice as I sang—I'm not ready for questions or commentary.

"Pssst."

Of course I didn't pull off the covert bed switch undetected. This bus—40 x 8 feet—might as well be a shoebox. I draw back the curtain, squinting my eyes against the dimness.

"Hey," Cannon greets me with a whisper and grin from his bed, curtain also pulled open.

Giving him back the smile I can't contain, I finger wave. Has he been waiting up for me? Was I secretly hoping he'd still be awake? Do I want to know either answer or what it says about me? *What planet am I living on that this is now an issue?*

"Here." He scoots to the edge of his bunk and hands across...an earbud? Eyeing him curiously, I turn on my side, facing his way, and put it in my ear. "Shhh." He puts a finger over his lips then winks and slips the other bud in his own ear, only breaking eye contact for a split second to tap the phone screen, then reconnecting in the muted light.

"Hello, Lizzie," his voice sounds in my ear and as my eyes pop in surprise. He once again does the "shhh" thing, nodding to me to just listen. "I thought about playing you 'You Are So Beautiful,' but surely you already know that. This, you may not."

There's a brief pause, then music starts... It's "Have a Little Faith in Me."

I know I whimper aloud, but I force my eyes to stay on his no matter how badly I want to hide them and the building tears. Through the entire song, I stare and he stares back, mouthing the words every once in a while. With the closing notes, his voice returns.

"Not too corny, I hope. Just...think about it. Sweet dreams, Lizzie."

Apparently picking up on the fact I've been rendered incapable of functioning, he reaches over and gently removes the earbud, taps the end of my nose with his fingertip, then closes my curtain for me.

I'll have the corny with a side of corny please.

# CHAPTER eleven

Hillsboro, Oregon, home of Jazzy's. Now owned and run by Jasmine and Lorelei, wonderful, young sisters who modernized their father's pub after he passed away a few years back, Jazzy's is a favorite of mine. Tonight makes the third time we've played here and I love the family feel, with baseball memorabilia and pictures of "old times" covering the walls. It's so comfortable in fact, that Conner joins us on stage at this one!

Or...Conner butts in front of me and talks in the mic at this one.

"My sister, her," he points, "wrote a song, the words. Me and my band did the music part. That's what we're gonna play. Your turn, Bethy." He kisses my cheek and steps back, tambourine up, waiting impatiently.

"You heard the man." I over-giggle, a bit nervous, since being "informed" we're about to debut one of my own...the words part anyway. "This is 'Lost & Found.'"

I look out beyond the crowd, searching for my focal point, a spot that screams "concentrate right here and no one will see you." I only use this trick for songs that *mean* something to me and it's usually dead center back of the room. But tonight, when I need it most, Bruce and Vanessa are *in* my focal point, both filming on their phones.

All right, then. The pay phone in the corner looks good, another piece of history the girls left intact. See—all this *focusing* and we're already at the chorus—I'm assuming

I've been singing on auto-pilot this whole time since no one's booing. *Worked like a charm.*

When the song ends, I snag a quick drink of water then intro a number with more of a country, upbeat vibe—suitable for Conner's tambourine.

And the next three songs as well. I love when he joins us, a happy glow never leaving his face. No matter what song I choose, he plays them all exactly the same way—perfect. What was I thinking before? Conner's on stage. *He's* the only focal point I need.

But by the time we're on number six, Bubs has had enough, simply walking off the stage right in the middle of the song. Thankfully, Bruce is way ahead of him, already waiting at stage right, so I keep singing to the end.

"Give it up for my big bro, Conner, on tambourine!" Waiting for the applause to die down, I strain to conjure up what song feels right, failing. "What'd ya'll wanna hear next? Any favorites?" I ask the crowd.

"I got one," Cannon pours smoothly into his mic. "Rhett, Jarrett, whaddaya say we do one for our beautiful *brunette* leader?"

*He did notice.*

"You mean a little something like," Jarrett fades out as the bass strums, unmistakable "My Girl" fading in.

"That's the one," Cannon chuckles. "Rhett?"

"Right behind ya, man."

Next thing I know, I'm forcibly plopped onto a stool that's mysteriously appeared at center stage, by Vanessa—*traitor*—and they start the song again.

Oh Lord, Jarrett takes the first verse, singing up close, right in front of me, while the other two stooges blend in backup harmony.

Their three voices, Rhett and Jarrett both tenors and Cannon clearly a bass, merge cosmically for each chorus. In a less tame bar, the women would be doing a lot more than swaying and swooning like the females at Jazzy's tonight; it's quite the show. I don't why they're all googly-eyed, though—they're singing *to me*—and if I ever say I hated it, you caught me lying.

When they get to the bridge, my loud laugh rings out as Cannon spins, in the most debonair way possible, then slides my way to serenade me, voice robust and sexy as he growls about needing no money or fame. He can *really* sing, goofin' around or not. They all can, but Cannon…does carnal things.

If sexy was a sound, it'd be Cannon Blackwell's voice caressing a song.

How they planned this whole act without me knowing is baffling—we live on a cramped bus together—but it's truly been one of my life's highlights. My face feels like it may split wide open by the time they're done and my cheeks are warm as I stand and approach the mic on unsteady legs.

"Those silly boys," I play it off, rolling my eyes and grinning. "They live to embarrass me. This next one will be the last tonight. Conner, where are ya?"

He waves his hand from the back where he stands beside Bruce. "Always for you, Bubs. We're See You Next Tuesday, thanks for having us. And he," I point to Conner, "is my 'Beautiful Boy.'"

The next three shows are in Boise, Idaho. We kept the same set list, despite my badly faked mortification of the "My Girl" addition, their "hamming" gaining grandeur with each performance. By close of the final night, we're all pretty tired, moods souring like the caged in, constantly moving, close quarter neighbors that we are. Everyone is out of clean clothes, the provisions from the shopping spree Cannon and I made are depleted, and I, for one, could use a break.

When the equipment's loaded, I waste no time clapping my hands to get their attention. "Is anyone opposed to a break? I'll spring for hotel rooms somewhere nice. Then tomorrow, I'll either do the laundry or the food shopping, but not both."

"Thank God," Jarrett lets out a relieved moan. "Nessy, baby, grab our stuff. We'll do the shopping tomorrow. What hotel?"

"Easy, playboy, let everyone else decide too," I razz him.

Yes, Vanessa is still with us, still not on my nerves in any way and Conner still enamored in a sweet, adorable way. And they respect my rules, Jarrett chivalrously taking the pull-out so she can have the bunk every night.

"Sounds good to me. How about I give the bus a good cleaning tomorrow while we're all off it?" See—even Rhett's cheers up instantly with a break and the prospect of a nice bed and bath tub.

"Thank you, Rhett, that'd be awesome. All right, that's four."

Bruce lumbers forward, holding his back. He definitely needs a rest from all the driving. "I'll stay with Conner and do no chores. Sound good, Con?"

"Can we get movies and lots of food again?"

"You bet! Grab your—" Bruce starts to say, but Conner's already running to do so before my uncle even finishes his sentence.

"That leaves you, Cannon, yay or nay?" I grin at him, knowing he's in.

"Hell yes, and I'll help with laundry. That'd take you all day by yourself."

"Sounds like we gotta plan. Bruce, can you get," I take count, "five rooms somewhere nice?" I hand him my credit card. "We'll get the dirty clothes bagged up."

We all shift into high-gear, one team all desperate for the same goal. I can't wait to sink into a tub of sweet-

125

smelling bubbles and spread across a huge, fluffy bed. It totally makes doing twenty loads of laundry worth it. Not to mention, I don't trust any of them with the task; I'd be stuck wearing shrunken, not supposed to be pink, clothing when they finished.

Thirty minutes later, we're parked behind a tall brown sky-rise, looking more like heaven than a posh hotel. Bruce trudges back on board and hands out all the key cards, adding to the wonderment by announcing in-hotel laundry, and we all cart the bags through the back entrance, *slumming it*, but I'm still thrilled I get to do it there instead of another trip to a laundromat.

"Bubs, you sure you don't wanna stay with me?" I ask him before we split up.

"Will you be sad if I stay with Uncle Bruce?" His worry spoils his sweet face so I squash it immediately.

"No, not at all. You have fun. I love you."

"Love you more!" he yells, alerting every guest in this hall as he trots away.

Most of our room numbers suggest nearness, except Jarrett and Vanessa, who have a 600 number on another floor. *Thank God.* They've respected my rules to the letter, merely eye fucking when Conner's not paying attention, so I do *not* want to hear all their making up for lost time through the thin hotel walls.

I get my door open and Cannon and Rhett bring in all the bags of laundry and dump them in a pile for me, then say goodnight as I push them out the door, flipping both locks.

*Dayummm*, this room is nice. I run and leap in the air, arms and legs spread wide, freefalling onto the huge, pillowy mattress. I could easily stay like this all night. Seriously, I'm five seconds away from falling into dreamland on top of the covers, fully clothed, when music jars me. I can't quite make it out, so I get up in search of it.

Well *shit*. I got one of those rooms with an adjoining door to the room beside me. How creepy are these things? I never quite know what's on the other side, or if I'm the one on the other side? Am I locked in or out, the sitting prey or the mass murder? I never know. Screw this. For two bills a night, I'll be damned if I'm robbed my peace and quiet, so I bang on the secret door with my fist. No one answers, nor does the music stop or even lower, so I pound again.

Nothing.

Maybe they're in the shower. I'm about to go ahead and take that bath I've been dreaming about and hope my rude neighbors settle down by the time I'm done when a knock at the door, the real door, startles me.

Expecting Conner, I open it with a huge grin. It's not Con, but I still smile at the surprise before me. "Ms. Carmichael?" she asks. "May I bring this inside, ma'am?"

"Oh, okay, sure." I step aside, making room for her to roll the cart in.

"I'm Renee, Guest Relations Night Manager. I've brought you an assortment of bath products, several sleeping garment choices from our boutique, and a basket of assorted drinks and desserts. Is there anything else I can get you this evening?"

"Where, why—"

She pulls a white card from under the basket and hands it to me. "This may clear things up."

> *Relax, enjoy and invite me over for a movie when you're done. –C*
>
> *P.S. I'm on the other side of the weird, misplaced door.*
>
> *P.P.S. I couldn't think of a cool code knock.*

"Shall I leave all this with you then, Ms. Carmichael?" Her polite question drags me back from Swoonville.

"Um, yes, please. Thank you. Let me grab you—"

"Everything's been taken care of, but thank you. Now, what laundry needs service?"

*Godsend say what?*

SE Hall

"You have laundry *service* here? I don't have to go down and do it?"

"Yes, the gentleman said six bags? Items will be delivered back by check out tomorrow. That pile there?" She points to the obvious heap.

"Yes, but…"

"Our pleasure, Ms. Carmichael. Now where shall I empty the cart as to load the laundry on it?"

"Let me help," I start, grabbing before she can professionally refuse, stacking goodie after goodie on the desk.

"Any special cleaning instructions?"

"Wear a hazmat suit when you get to their underwear?"

She gawks at me, mouth agape, her eyes large and rounding in shock, then we both break out in raucous laughter together. "Seriously, that's a weeks' worth of five men's underwear. You should definitely let me tip you again—*trust me.*"

"Girl, please." She blows her lips and waves a hand. "I don't do laundry. Save that sympathy for the housekeepers."

"If you say so. I'll leave them a nice bonus when we check out. And thank you again."

"My pleasure." She smiles warmly as I hold open the door while she grunts, pushing the loaded cart out.

I happily bounce over to the desk, checking out the array of bath goodies. I'm sure I groan aloud. Choosing the lavender dissolving salts and foaming bubble bath, I head to the bathroom, already feeling the tension leave my body.

When the sunken tub is full, steam vapors rising from the surface and beckoning me, I strip and ease down into the delightfully scented warmth. My head falls back and my eyes close, then pop right back open. I swear that friggin' music just got louder.

*He's gonna wake up the whole floor!*

128

But I don't think he cares, and quite honestly, neither do I. Cannon's sense of humor is invigorating and quirky and adorable. You can't help but like him.

Perfect example being now. He's blaring "Come Over" by Kenny Chesney, apparently his not-so-subtle way of telling me to hurry up so he can do just that.

Too cute. And obviously, he's gotten himself a new phone, apparently used more for music than calls since I haven't seen him make a single one.

As I soak a little longer, my mind drifts to what I do best—overanalyzing any and every situation until I've beaten it into the ground, causing myself ulcers. Cannon's frazzling my nerves, making me second guess all I thought I knew about myself. I have zip knowledge of "relationships" with men, and since anything with Cannon—*definitely* a man—is so different from anything I've experienced with Jarrett and Rhett—also men—I just don't quite know what do with myself. These days I'm confused anytime I'm awake, especially since he fills most those seconds with serenades, surprises, and a dozen other "Cannonisms."

He hasn't tried anything and our interactions, even if alone, are merely friendly, effortless, and fun. He does flirt, but I think it's just his personality, not specifically because of me. And as attractive as I find him, my fingers sore and the bus forever out of hot water because I've become a habitual showerer (the only time I get to take all the "Cannon" that day and release it, finding nirvana and some serenity), I honestly look forward to simply "hanging" with him. Okaaay, there's a "sizzle" no matter what we're doing, but not uncontrollably so.

When I hear the song change to the old Aretha Franklin attempt at a comeback, "I Knew You Were Waiting," I can't stifle my giggle and pull myself up and out of the tub with a sigh. How does *that* song even come to his mind? It wasn't worth listening to even *in* its decade.

But I can take a hint, however painful to the ears...patience of Job that man hath not.

I peek around the door of the bathroom; I wouldn't be the least bit surprised to find he'd broken in and was waiting in the room. But it's empty, so I scamper over to my pajama choices, picking a luxurious but comfortable looking pink tank and shorts set. Drying off and dressing in double time, I walk over and rap out a few hard, loud knocks on the adjoining door.

And the music stops.

"Ghost of Christmas Past, is that you?" he calls through the wooden barrier.

See—quirky and hilarious. Who thinks of stuff like that?

"Get your ass over here if you wanna watch a movie, DJ Not Kool," I simper back, taming my girly laugh.

"Then open the door."

Oh, so it seems I'm on the gate*keeper* side.

I open it and gulp, suddenly slightly lightheaded. Cannon's leisurely stretched out before me, his arms braced over his head on the door frame in only mesh shorts, the kind that tease you, all "will I hold on to these sweet hips or fall right off?" Come to think of it, all his bottoms say that to me.

"Glad to see someone's okay with me slacking at the gym lately." He winks, brushing past me into my room.

There, that—is that just his flirty personality or for me?

Embarrassed at being caught gawking, and called right out on it, I take my time shutting the door before I have to turn around. I know, as every woman knows, that my nipples are gonna be poking like sharpened pencils through this silky top when I face him. So I do the only thing that comes to mind, cross my arms over my chest, then turn and fly across the room all in one movement, babbling in hopes of distraction.

"Thanks for the treats; the bath was heavenly and long overdue. What movie did you want to watch?"

He chuckles from behind me. "Did you snort a line off the side of the bathtub?"

"What?" I spin around in indignation. "Of course not. Why would you ask that?"

He's made himself at home, leaning back against the headboard, long, muscular legs covered in a light smattering of brown hair stretched out the length of my bed. "You seem jumpy and you're talking fast." He tucks both hands behind his head and crosses his ankles. "What are you nervous about?"

"I'm not nervous." My brow creases. "Still amped up from the show, I guess."

"Lizzie." My name falls off his tongue in a smooth, husky tone, patting the bed beside him. "Come 'ere."

I hesitate, but when he holds out his hand to me, I glide across the room and place mine in it.

"We're friends, aren't we?"

"Yesss?"

"Have I ever done anything to make you feel uncomfortable?"

*Cha, yeah!* There's a permanent tingling throb between my legs that's pretty damn *uncomfortable*, Mr. Pretty. Not to mention my nipples' constant state of tight strain.

"No." I shake my head, answering according to what he actually meant.

"Do you trust me?" He peers up at me, him lying back on the bed, me standing over him, our hands still joined.

"I do," I whisper automatically, absolutely without doubt.

My easy answer makes his already devastating smile positively electric. "Okay, then hop your cute little ass in this bed and pick a movie to watch, *friend*."

"Question," he interrupts the movie yet again and I roll my eyes as I hit pause.

"What?" Could he really have this many questions or is trying to get me to turn it? Or he is actually this adorable?

"Aren't chicks always squawking about 'he can't possibly love me yet' or 'it's too soon to tell him'?"

"I believe you're referring to insta-love. And yes, according to the occasional magazine I stumble upon, it's a controversial point of bitching for lots of people, although, Rhett seems to be pro-insta. Why?" I ask, dipping into the bowl for another handful of popcorn, courtesy of the snack basket.

"So riddle me this, Bat Lizzie. This dude starts falling for her *inside a week* because she played with some opera glasses and slung a shrimp across the room?"

"It was a snail."

"What?" he asks, face adorably confused.

"She flung a *snail* across the room, not a shrimp. And it's those little things he falls for. She's charming and refreshing because he's so stuffy."

Could that explanation have sounded more familiar, albeit backwards?

"She's. A. Hooker," he deadpans, obviously thinking that speaks for itself, which it doesn't.

"Very good!" I praise. "You understood the first ten minutes of the movie. Now what's all the rest of your rambling mean?" I cock a brow, mocking him but anxious for a debate.

"Hear me out." He sits up, setting the bowl aside and shifting to face me. "So women don't buy the instant love stuff, and criticize it, but they'll watch this movie every time

132

it's on. It's a movie that sells you in a 'Yes, I take dick professionally from random strangers but I fist pump at polo matches so forget that and truly love me in a week' sort of way. That about sum it up?"

Holy shit—he's right.

"Ah ha!" He points at my dumbfounded face. "I nailed it. Horseshit, right?"

"I believe you just won your case, Mr. Blackwell. Congratulations." I give him a golf clap. "I probably shouldn't mention *Cosmo's* other coveted theory; 'don't sleep with him too soon if you want to keep him,' huh?"

"Women." He shakes his head. "You watch this show but gripe 'it's too soon, don't trust him, girl.' Conventionally hypocritical. Oh, and review—She. Is. A. Hooker. So stuff the whole 'hold out' theory for sure."

"May I ask why this is such a sore subject for you?" My mouth twists in a threatening snicker, amused at how heated and animated he's gotten over *Pretty Woman*.

He shrugs, picking the popcorn bowl back up and popping a few pieces in his mouth. "It's not. I just like to know I'm right and prepared to successfully argue any crazy, hypocritical, you-don't-know-what-the-fuck-you're-talking-about topic. You never know when someone might hit me with an insta-love debate."

Could he mean? No, don't be a dumbass, Liz…you're thinking with your vagina.

"Okay, well this movie's shot. Wanna pick another one?" I ask.

"Actually, I better head back through the wardrobe before that spooky half-goat guy comes looking for me. And you need to rest." He climbs off the bed, stretching his arms over his head mesmerizingly, then flashes me a wink. "See you in the morning, Lizzie. Sweet dreams."

And with that, he slips out, leaving me lying silently in bed, without words, even more mystified and hormonally unbalanced than before.

# CHAPTER twelve

The next morning, I wake as thoroughly rested as I've been in months. If I could fit this heavenly bed on the bus, I'd steal it, no questions asked.

My phone dings from across the room and I scramble out of bed to grab it. I'm not sure what time it is, but it's never too early for Conner to be up.

**Hot Hitchhiker: Come down and have breakfast with us sleepyhead.**

**Me: Who is this? IDK any hot hitchhikers. I do know a HACKER.**

**HH: Funny, now get up. We have a few hours to enjoy outside if u hurry. Btw…..HOT Hacker works for me too.**

**Me: Con w/ u?**

**HH: Yep, itching to explore the city before he's trapped on a bus again.**

**Me: Gimme 15.**

I rush through a shower, bumbling my way through hair, teeth, and getting dressed. Side note—the more you rush, the more you actually impede speedy prep by tripping over pant legs and losing stuff in the scramble. I throw on some jeans, a t-shirt, and Vans, gather up all my stuff in a neat pile, and hurry downstairs. Last to arrive at the smorgasbord, I find the other six putting a hug dent in the complimentary breakfast buffet. My stomach gurgles angrily when the aroma hits me.

"Morning, Sunshine, glad you could join us." My uncle leans down and kisses my head when I fall beside him in the feeding line. "Sleep well?"

I'm loading up my plate vigorously, not realizing how hungry I was. "Like a log. You?"

"Maybe not that well." He laughs. "Our room had one bed and Conner isn't the stillest sleeper. But all in all, pretty good."

When our plates are overflowing, we head over to the booth where the others are sitting. It looks pretty crowded and I'm definitely ravenous enough to throw elbows, so I take the booth directly behind them.

"Morning, Liz. I could have moved," Vanessa offers, eyes flicking down.

"No worries. I'm hungry enough to hurt someone in the attack." I smile at her and dig in, unashamed.

"Cannon said we have time to go to the zoo!"

Um, ouch. I jab myself in the gums with my fork, Conner bouncing me three inches off the seat with his greeting. Swallowing, I swipe my mouth and inspect the napkin; only a little blood. "He did, huh?" I cut narrowed eyes over the top of the booth to Cannon, already watching me with a knowing smirk. "Everyone wanna go?" I ask louder.

"Nessy and I are gonna take a pass," Jarrett declines into her neck as she giggles and swats him away.

"Rhett? Bruce?"

"I'd just as soon use the time to rest my back," my uncle says with an apologetic frown.

I nod. "Of course. Do we need to get you in to see somebody about that?"

"Pshhh." He waves me off. "Nobody's gotta cure for old. That's all it is."

"There's a spa here, Gramps. You oughta see if it has a masseuse," Jarrett suggests, earning him a swat from Vanessa for the sarcasm.

"Hmmm, worth a ty." Bruce stands, eyes gleaming at the possibility of a female-given massage, I'm guessing—and gagging. "I'll see you kids later."

"Maybe she'll help him *really* throw his back out."

This time *I* lean up and slap Jarrett on the head.

"Rhett, how 'bout you?" I look to him, my expression full of hope. The two of us seem to be growing apart and I'm not okay with that.

"Sure, I'll go," he answers instantly and I about fall over with happiness.

"Okay then. Let's go!" Conner jumps up and shouts.

"Con, let's go load the bus while your sister finishes eating," Cannon suggests, my stomach thanking him.

While the rest of them disperse, I shovel down a few more bites and throw some money on the table.

Bring on the zoo!

Is it possible to get kicked out of a zoo—a place specifically for wild animals, you ask?

Why yes. Yes it is.

See, when they post instructional signs such as "don't feed the animals" or "don't tap on the glass," they actually mean it. In all fairness, there wasn't technically a "don't climb the fence to join the monkeys" sign, but it was a deal breaker for them—the final straw—and out we were shown.

Despite the walk of shame out of the park, sequestered on all sides by zoo employees, we had a great time. Conner thinks he needs his own chimpanzee now, and as we approach the bus, Rhett and Cannon are still *acting* like chimpanzees, but it's been one of the best days I've ever had, uncontested.

"Lizzie, love, stop."

And I sure the fuck do, stopping cold when his deep voice demands it. *Love?*

"You have peanut shells in the back of your hair. Lemme get 'em," he murmurs lowly from right behind me, running one hand up through my hair. "Guess we missed the elephants a few times," he teases, long fingers gently separating and picking through the strands.

"Ya'll coming?" Rhett leans out the bus door and screams. "Bruce said we need to get moving. He already loaded everything over from the rooms, including clean clothes! Bonus!"

I hadn't realized they'd gone ahead, leaving Cannon and I standing alone under a shade tree. But now that I'm cognizant, my body goes taut, back ramrod straight and breathing staggered.

"I feel like one of those National Geographic specials where the monkeys sit around and pick at each other," he says, laughing softly.

My own forced chuckle sounds fake. "Are you done?"

"All done." His hands move to my bare shoulders, fingers grazing lightly over them. "You got a little sunburn today. Hurt?"

"No," I wisp out, trembling with each feathering pass his fingers continue to make on my skin.

"Good. If it starts to, we need to put some aloe on there, but I think you'll be fine. You ready?" He steps around in front of me, offering back his hand to lead me to the bus.

I pull up short on his hand, digging my feet into the gravel. "Cannon?"

He pivots, asking "what" with only his face.

137

"Thanks for getting the shells out of my hair and...noticing. And, uh, being so good with Conner, even Rhett. You're a great addition and I'm glad you're here."

He steps into me and lifts my chin with his fingers. For seconds that feel much longer, he remains silent, searching the depths of my eyes with his own. I almost think he might kiss me until he speaks in a whisper so soft and low, I have to tilt toward him to hear. "I'm really glad I'm here too. More and more every day."

I try to look away, needing reprieve from his permeating, consuming stare, but he now adds his thumb to hold my head in place. "Lizzie, if I kissed you right now, would even the slightest thoughts about it being too soon or rebounds run through your mind?"

I answer breathily, but honestly. "Yes."

"I understand." His mouth turns down just enough for me to notice, as though he's...disappointed? "Promise me one thing?"

"What?"

"You'll let me know the second your answer changes."

Biting my bottom lip and casting my eyes to the ground, I give a slight, affirmative shake of my head. Why *am* I always so damn honest? I could be tasting Cannon right now, finally confirming the flavor of my consuming fantasies.

Damn the whole taking the high road thing.

But I don't want to be someone's "too soon" or "maybe this will be better." I want all or nothing, and I'm sticking with the familiar and safe—nothing—until I'm certain I'm all.

"Come on," he entwines our hands, "they're waiting."

The three goobers who immersed themselves, literally, in the zoo desperately need showers once we're on the road. Conner's asleep by the time it's my turn. Oh, they all offered for me to go first—my gentlemen—but I like to be available when Conner's up and wanting to play games or watch movies. Which we did and he never once mentioned that I smell, perhaps because I didn't get up close and personal with every animal possible.

Besides, a cold, late shower never hurt anyone.

After the little speech Cannon gave under the tree about promises and kisses, coupled with him coming out from his shower glistening, donned only in pajama pants...a brisk shower seems imperative.

The water's almost lukewarm when I slink under it, a nice surprise, and after I've pre-gamed—body and hair—I make a conscious decision to change course. Rather than self-remedy away all my "Cannon frustration," the way I usually do, I decide to let it fester. After all, anticipation is the spice of life, and it makes me feel tingly and intrigued and *anticipatory*, knowing he's obviously thinking of kissing me. I'm going to let my raging desires build up for ultimate pleasure when, and if, we get our moment.

If anything, I should be kicking, not pleasuring, myself anyway—opening my big, honest mouth before! But it's true, Cannon's been with us for...thirteen days now, and that does seem a bit fast to go from planning to marry a girl to kissing another. I don't wish for time to fly by; I want to savor every single minute and conversation getting to know him, but part of me (okay, a lot of me) is ready for his rebound/too soon grace period to be over.

Feeling levelheaded now rather than robbed, I get dressed and ready for bed then step out of the bathroom to unexpected quiet.

SE Hall

I might not be a mother exactly, but I've developed a certain instinct via Conner that tells me if there's mischief afoot the minute I walk in a room.

My radar is currently beeping in triple time.

Hmm... Cannon and Jarrett are at the table, huddled together over a laptop. I pull open the curtain quietly and find Vanessa passed out in Jarrett's bunk, which is fine since he's not in it with her. Rhett is snoring softly from his own bed.

So then what tomfoolery is it I'm picking up on?

Approaching stealthily, I diagnose the cheesy disco and panting sounds coming from the screen far sooner than they realize I'm standing there. "Whatcha guys doing?" I whisper.

"What?" Cannon startles, turning a "cat at the canary" look my way. "N-nothing." He tries to slam the screen down but Jarrett holds him off.

"No way! I'm watching that! Conner's asleep; she can't get mad. In fact, Mama Bear," he pats the spot next to him, "come check this out."

"Jarrett Paul Foster, are you suggesting I watch internet porn with you two?"

"That's exactly what I'm saying. Now shh and sit down, I wanna hear."

Oh yeah—because the dialogue is *so* complex and intricate. It's a bewildering, often traumatizing, experience watching his mind work.

Shocked at myself, I do in fact take a seat, rolling my eyes. Cannon leans across and cocks his left eyebrow at me. "You want some popcorn, Siren?"

I glower back at him, then quickly turn my focus to the screen. "Okay, so catch me up on the riveting plot."

Jarrett jumps at the chance, pointing to the screen. "This girl called a maintenance man to fix her sink and his apprentice came along. Now they're, fu—uh, now they're—"

"Got it!" I hold up a hand to stop his enlightening, linguistically fascinating explanation. "All caught up."
140

The bench is shaking from Cannon laughing at my reaction, his head dipped and turned away, though it does nothing to hide his amusement.

"Um…" I cannot believe I'm about to ask this, but I know the curiosity will eat at me, so I gulp and go for it. "Why is head fix-it guy's penis two different colors?"

"What?" Jarrett booms, laughing like a hyena.

"Shhh!" I warn him, *not* wanting the others to wake and catch us in one of our least attractive moments. "Look, right where her mouth is, there's clearly a line where it goes from brown to pink. See," now I point on-screen, "right there, that line. That's freaky. Something's wrong."

Now they're both face down on the table, trying to muffle their boisterous laughter, and still not answering me.

"Cannon, you gonna take this one?" Jarrett snorts.

Cannon's head flies up, all signs of amusement gone, eyes wide and scared like roadkill in the headlights, seconds before the impending crash. "Not a chance in hell."

"Pussy," Jarrett goads. "Liz, lot of guys have lighter heads than shafts. Totally normal."

I scrunch up my face in disgust. "I would not put that *not normal*, deformed looking thing in my mouth. It'd be like unwrapping a cherry sucker and half of it's green. You know, something's just *not quite right*. Ergo, don't stick it in your mouth!"

"Oh no?" Jarrett challenges. "So you've already seduced him, and his dick's ready, in your face. You simply say 'no thank you'?" He laughs. "Awful harsh. Besides, you ever *really* looked at a vagina? Not exactly beautiful, all wrinkly and shit, like a raisin gone horribly wrong. Parts popping out of bigger parts, like that movie where the fucking alien is scary enough, then KAPOW, a baby one busts out his belly! "

"I have no idea what you just said, and I actually *have* a vagina," I mutter in a monotone response of complete abhorrence and disbelief while Cannon shields his face in his hand, his whole body shaking with tempered laughter.

"Your clit. It's all shrouded up in the wrinkles, then *surprise*, out it pops!" Jarrett thrusts out jazz hands and twirls them. "Talk about *not quite right*."

This may never happen again—I literally have no words. I just shake my head, scarily fascinated at his inner issues, and force myself to instead think back to the original point, *not* the eloquent vagina description, pondering if I *could* be that rude and make the guy feel bad. Hmm...my mind goes to work and I snap when I've got it. "I'd act like I fainted!"

Their wails can't be contained now, liable to wake the bus and the dead. I wait, knowing I'm brilliant, while they simmer down and regain the ability to converse.

"Fake faint?" Cannon asks with twinkling eyes, battling an amused grin. "Do you know how to do that?"

"Sure." I show him, letting my eyes roll back in my head dramatically, falling backward, arms limply out to my sides.

"Pretty good," he replies. "I'd buy it."

"Shit, me too," Jarrett says incredulously. "Women are so sneaky."

"Hey!" I come to life and shove him. "I'd do it to be nice, not sneaky. Now finish your dick flick. I'm going to bed." I shoot them looks of disapproval and pad off, crawling under my covers. It's been a long, but blissful, day and I am spent. "And Jarret?" I turn back with a saucy grin. "Thou protesth too much; dead giveaway. I'm sorry about your rainbow penis."

*What the hell?* Feeling like I *just* got to sleep, I come to, looking around in the dark, scared it's finally happened— pieces of Rhett's bed are breaking apart onto my head.

Then a wad of something hits me in the face, a subdued laugh from across the aisle following it. Ok, not the ceiling collapsing, just Cannon throwing things at me. My hands fumble around, finding two clumps and I switch on my bed light to see what they are. Unfolding the first crumpled ball of paper, I giggle out loud.

*Don't be afraid, Little Siren. At least 8 out of 10 penises are all one color. DO NOT do a field study, take my word for it. –C*

I open the second one, again tempted to snicker at the random thoughts keeping him awake.

*Rebound—to recover.*

*Recover—to return to normal condition, esp. after a setback.*

*Synopsis: Rebounding hasn't gotten a fair shake, the negative connotation thrust upon it unfair and incorrect. Getting back to normal after a setback is a good thing. A setback is not a good thing. –C*

If he's not the most witty, clever charmer in the world....

I reach above my head for a pen and turn the sheet over to reply.

*Why are you telling me this? In the middle of the night? –L*

Then I toss it back his way and go to the other one.

*Good information, thank you. No worries—no focus groups currently planned. –L*

Returning that one as well, I should really turn off my light and discourage further incognito, late night note passing—but my tummy's got acrobatic anticipation going on and my heart's thumping madly. No matter the time or method (*obviously*), I thrive on interaction with Cannon.

The wad comes flying back and my trembling fingers fumble to get it unwrinkled.

*Because I want you to understand—numb complacency wasn't "normal," just tolerable since nothing*

143

*else shined brighter. Only once a siren calls, do you recognize extraordinary from not too terrible. –C*

*Are you hitting on me, through a note? –L*

Throw.

Catch.

*Absofuckinglutely. –C*

*Oh Lord*, okay so that's hot and alluring and the best kind of charming. I pull back my curtain a smidge, enough to look out, his eyes are already locked right on me, turned raven and smoldering, just waiting for me to peek out.

"Hi," he mouths.

My heart patters swiftly as I jerk the sheet back in place, deciding notes are far safer for my sanity, not to mention my body temperature.

*You're a flirt. It's only because I'm here, convenient. And it's only been 2 weeks, my shiny and new will wear off, I promise. Mundane and bitchy should be resurfacing any time now. Or maybe the "movie" got you worked up. I thought we were "friends?" –L*

Throw.

Catch.

*I hate that we're doing this over 3ʳᵈ grade notes in too close quarters with an audience. I want to be able to see your eyes when I tell you things, so you can see the honesty in mine. We are friends, that's where it should always start. And you lying two foot away, all soft and sleepy, that works me up. Tomorrow before the show, may I please take you to dinner, just the two of us?–C*

*P.S. I haven't asked a girl out via note since I was 14.*

Even if I don't buy a word he's saying, except the part about not asking a girl out like since 14—that's hopefully, for his dignity's sake, very true—I always enjoy his company, so the answer is easy.

*Yes. –L*

Throw.

144

My curtain flies open and I gasp, scooting against the wall, stunned, as one sleepy yet forebodingly sexy Cannon looms over me.

"I can't wait. Come 'ere." He crooks his finger at me and with an echoing gulp, I inch toward him the slightest bit. "Closer," he says with a wink.

One more wiggle, that's all he's getting.

When he does, his head bends in and he places a single, tender kiss on my lips, then leans back to gaze at me. "You are definitely bitchy, in the most adorable, protective way possible. But if you ever call yourself mundane again, I will spank your delectable little ass. Twice. Until tomorrow, sleep well, my bewitching siren."

He pulls closed my curtain like he didn't just serenade my girly parts...and I guess falls asleep?

Lord knows I don't. Estrogen, femininity, and fairytale musings are currently running rampant within me, causing quite the "keep me awake" ruckus.

So I do what I always do and quietly sneak out my notebook to jot down the lyrics flooding my mind.

# CHAPTER thirteen

The next day begins with me on edge from the minute my eyes crack open. With my date with Cannon on the horizon, I'm anxious, but more nervous about the others' reactions when they find out. I'm dreading any buts or "are you sure?" skepticism; I want to enjoy this at face value, to blindly…have a little faith in him, it, this, us.

While everyone's busy with breakfast and showers, I sneak outside to join my uncle in his cloud of smoke.

"Morning, girl." He smiles fleetingly, turning to cough up a lung.

"I wish you'd stop smoking." I grimace, patting him on the back. "Why don't you try Chantix? I've read a ton of success stories on it."

"You know how expensive that stuff is?" he asks, strained.

"No, but I do know there's not a price I'm not willing to pay. So you'll try it?"

He tries not to look at me; I know he'll be unable to resist if he sees my pleading face. So I shift to stand right in front of him.

"When we get back home, make an appointment. Promise me?"

He ponders a minute then nods in defeat, stomping out his current stick. "That all you wanted?"

"Oh, uh, no." I conveniently take my turn to not look at him. I know it's silly, I'm twenty-three years old and actually "the boss" here, but nervous as a whore in church all the same.

I wonder if my mom would like Cannon, or if she really did send him to me *because* she likes him. If she saw him with Conner, undoubtedly she'd adore him, but what about *for me*? I'm getting too ahead of my whimsical musings—it's a meal with a man who two weeks ago was ready to spend his life with someone else, nothing more.

Oh, if I would just buy what I'm selling...but I'm quite possibly setting myself up for a hurt from which I might never recover. Because yes, it's been two weeks, but mine is an unquestionable attraction, no rebounds. I've never felt such things before; not with boys in school, not with Josh, our first guitarist, not even with Rhett, so methinks the little voice in my head holds merit.

Cannon's taken what he can't offer in return—my exclusive fascination, giving him both the upper hand and security, two things I try to always keep in my corner.

"Liz?" my uncle says, waiting patiently through all that mental rambling.

"Sorry. So," I turn on the charm, "I was gonna ask if you'd stay with Bubs tonight, before the show, so I could go to dinner? I'll bring you back something niceeee."

"With?" His tone drops suspiciously.

"Cannon," I say to the air beyond his shoulder.

"Elizabeth," he sighs, rubbing a hand down his face, "baby girl, I'd rather die than see you hurt. He was engaged not too long ago. And you, so kind and innocent. Do I need to kill the boy?"

I laugh. I can't help it. My sweet, worried uncle is so much more a father than my own ever was. "No need to load a gun yet. Just eating, do it all the time, with a guy who's easy to talk to."

He wraps me in a hug, speaking into my hair. "I worry, that's all. You play it off all you want, little lady, but I

147

know what a big deal this is for you, and hope it's not blasé for him. 'Cause I can be blasé about killing him."

"I'm a big girl; I can take care of myself, I promise. I'm well aware he was engaged, and I'm not naïve or stupid. Not lookin' to marry him, but I enjoy his company. And a man's never taken me out before." I pop my shoulders, hoping for casualty. "Might be fun."

He lets me go, stepping back to light another cigarette in silence, sucking in a big puff that he blows out slowly through his nose. "I'd be happy to hang out with Conner. You have a great time."

I stumble back, happily surprised at his sudden understanding and acceptance. "Thank you. I love you, Uncle Bruce."

"I love you too, baby girl, enough to maim him. Just say the word."

Turning to walk back in, I look over my shoulder. "You know, I'm not really *that* kind. You're biased. And worry too much." *Says the girl who worries about everything.*

Now to tell the other three. Jarrett's the one and only not concerning me.

"You hungry? I saved you a plate," Cannon asks when I enter.

"I could eat, thanks." I smile, taking a seat at the table, searching for the plate.

"I kept it warm." He pulls the missing platter from the microwave and sets it in front of me. "What to drink?"

"She likes coffee!" Conner yells as he plops down beside me. "Cannon said he's taking you to dinner, Sister."

The hairs on the back of my neck instantly stand up, and I turn to catch Rhett's look from the hall. Which look, for the first time ever, I can't pinpoint. I thought we hashed this out—he isn't in love with me and will never lose me—so what the current wave of tension is, I have no idea.

"He is." I turn to Conner with a cheerful grin. "Are you okay with that?"

"Cuz you're getting there to happy?" He remembered word for word the talk we had the other night...and applied it correctly. It's little things like this that always give me a boost of hope that he *can* recall things and make sense of them—maybe one day the really important ones.

"Something like that, Bubs. Did you eat?" I divert, taking a bite of omelet.

"Yes, and now I'm bored. When do I get to go see Dad again?"

I set down my fork, my appetite lost. It slices into my gut every time he asks to see the monster; pain, anger, despair all simultaneously. "Soon, Conner. We're a ways from home yet."

So now I've got Rhett boring holes in me about the dinner and Cannon doing the same for my reaction to Conner's request. But most disturbing is knowing Bubs will ask every single hour, on the hour, until I take him to our father.

Suddenly, I can't get a deep, full breath. My chest seizes and my throat narrows, stopping my inhales short. Panicking, my eyes water and spots cloud my vision and just as blackness creeps in from the edges. I'm conscious only of Cannon's voice.

"Stay with me, Siren. Look at me," he pleads, gripping my shoulders fiercely. "Breathe. One in for me," I mimic him, taking in a large, slow chest full of air, "and out for you."

Things start to get clearer, the oxygen helping, almost as much as his soothing but demanding instruction.

"Again, one in for me," he smiles at me, warm yet concerned, "and out for you. Good. Better?"

I manage a feeble nod, blinking away the tears, continuing the breathing pattern.

"You wanna go for a walk?" he asks quietly and again I jerk my head in agreement. "Okay, come on," he stands and holds out his hand to me.

Without hesitation, filled with trust, I take it and allow him to pull me up. "Conner, can you grab your sister's flip-flops, please? She and I are gonna take a quick walk while you get a puzzle ready, okay?"

"On it!" he cheers, scampering off. "Rhett, you wanna do our puzzle?" he asks as he passes him.

I can't hear Rhett's mumbled response, nor do I care. I also have no idea where Jarrett is, and I don't care about that either. All I want in the whole world right now is to take a walk in the wide open, fresh air filled vastness, with Cannon.

"Here you go, Bethy." Conner squats and helps guide my shoes on. "See you when you get back."

"Thanks, Con. See you in a little while," Cannon replies for me, then guides me to the door.

"Where you two headed?" Bruce asks, still outside.

"Lizzie needs some air. We're gonna go for a walk. Conner's getting a puzzle ready and Rhett's brooding like a little bitch. See ya," Cannon recaps, squeezing my hand.

"Baby girl, you all right?" Bruce says to me, voice and faced lined with concern.

"Fine," I mutter shakily. "We won't be long."

My uncle zeroes in on Cannon, a fierceness in his eyes, his next words a sinister warning. "They don't often come as good as her, young man, and some of us have been by her side for a long, long time. You start stepping in to take our place, you best plan on keeping the job. Otherwise, get the hell out of the way and let us handle it, 'cause we ain't going nowhere, ever. Not looking to start all over when you breeze out as fast as you breezed in."

I snap from my haze with a sharp, embarrassed huff. "Bruce, it's a walk! He doesn't have to commit for life in blood. Jesus Christ! Will all of you please stand the fuck down and let me breathe? I love you, but damn."

Cannon pumps my hand and scoots closer to my side. "I can only promise you this, sir. My awe and admiration of Lizzie is genuine and I'd die before I hurt her in any way. I didn't plan this road I'm on, nor do I know where it leads or ends, but I'm looking forward to finding out."

Bruce bounces his scrutiny between the two of us, once, twice, then unfolds his arms, a palpable acceptance setting in. "You guys don't go far. Date and show tonight, it's already noon."

I step forward and brace on both his shoulders, rising on my tiptoes to kiss his scruffy cheek. "I love you very much."

"Not half as much as I love you, kid. Go on now."

Turning, Cannon's hand is outstretched, waiting for me to reconnect, which I accept effortlessly. We walk in silence for a while, but his thumb never once stops caressing back and forth across my knuckles. Finally, he clears his throat and speaks, an easy, low rumble. "One thing at a time. What's bothering you the most?"

"You're a list maker, huh? Mr. Break it Down? A spreadsheet problem solver."

He winks my way with a light lift of his shoulders. "I'm a Virgo. Solid structure is the only way things stay standing."

"And I'm a siren?"

"No, well, yes," he laughs, "you are. But siren isn't your sign. My guess is that you're a Cancer. When's your birthday?"

"July 14th."

"God, I'm good! You're indeed a Cancer, could've told ya that ages ago."

"How'd you get so into that stuff? Do you own one of those Ouija boards? I'm not doing a séance, so don't even ask."

"Come 'ere." He pulls me to the side of our walking path and sits down, leaning back against a thick tree. "Sit down, stay awhile."

I take a seat beside him and fold my legs under me.

"My mom is a grief counselor," he admits. "She studied all possible facets of human emotion, what makes a person tick, develops who they are. One of the subjects that fascinated her most was astrology, how our sign may dictate our personality and habits. So growing up, she always talked about it, had charts all over her office. I thought it was kinda cool, so I learned about it too."

I could listen to him talk forever. His eyes brighten and he uses his hands when he gets excited, licking his plump lips every few sentences. If the Jehovah's Witnesses sent *him* to your door, they'd obliterate their "oh shit, they're here" rep, instead becoming the renowned "invite those mofos in for a while" bell ringers. I can picture housewives the world over in my mind, offering platters of cookies, all "No, don't leave. Here, read me this dictionary," and a giggle pops out.

"What's so funny?" he asks, poking me in the ribs.

"Nothing, I just thought of something silly. Anyways, that's cool. Your mom and you are interested in commons things. What about *your* father?"

"My father," he parrots my darkened tone, "is called Dad, and he's a Family Law Attorney. *And*, you're doing it again, Enchantress. I'm running off at the mouth and you've told me nothing, as usual. I gotta watch it around you, Witchy."

"Witchy, Siren, if you didn't throw in a 'Lizzie' here and there, I'd swear you forgot my name."

"I know your name, Elizabeth, but for reasons you've yet to tell me, you don't like it. But you do seem to like Lizzie, so that's what I call you."

I tilt my head and smirk. "I do, huh? Did you read that in the stars?"

He smirks, his eyes turning blackening, a sultry haze to them now as his mouth quirks at the corner. "Lizzie," he whispers.

My lips part, a feathery inhale tickling over them, my heart thumping wildly. "What?" I breathe out.

"*That's* how I know you like it. Every time I call you Lizzie, your body sings to me just like that. There are some things even you can't hide."

I dart my eyes downward, fidgeting uncomfortably. It's not only *what* he says, seeing me better than anyone ever has, but the *way* he says it—a deep, husky murmur laced with sexuality. It calls to the deepest recesses in me and begs the woman to emerge.

"Do I like when you call me Siren?" I whisper.

He laughs faintly, and in one movement, scoots closer and positions me in his lap. "You love it. You love that I call you that *and* you love knowing you have the definitive effects of a siren on me. *"

I remember the brief conversation we'd had about it before, but in this moment, and not just because I really could listen to him talk forever, I want to hear the whole story and why he appeals to me. A fishing expedition, admittedly...but still going for it. "Tell me the story of the sirens again, but really tell me this time," I purr.

The gentle touch of his warm hand on my knee draws me back, acutely aware of where I am right now, unable to meet his eyes. He lets me have that one defense and simply cups my head in his hand and pulls it down to rest upon his shoulder.

"In Greek mythology, sirens were the goddesses of the sea, irresistible female bodies who lured the sailors to their demise with their song." *That's the part he'd told me.* "What you do to me, Lizzie, your song, your smile, a look...you draw me in and I'm captivated, willing to sell my soul to know more. I can't wait to hear what you'll say next, what you'll wear each day, what will make you smile and laugh. I watch the way you love and take care of Conner, Rhett, and the others and all I can do is envy them, try to figure out how to get you to pour all that Lizzie love over me. Then let me give it right back." *That part he hadn't told me; glad I asked.*

No way is this real. I exude nothing that "lures" in a man, especially a gorgeous, kind, soulful, talented one. I've finally graduated to full-blown hallucinations, but I pray I never stop.

"Lizzie, look at me, say something. Please tell me I'm not alone and crazy." *I'm* crazy, doesn't he know that? I've never felt more out of control, confused and ready to jump from the highest cliff with him—crazy. "Lizzie?"

"You don't even know me," I mumble at the ground.

"I know your heart and your character. I know that anything you do gets your all, especially your love of someone. I know you long to be held and cherished, but you'll never ask for it. And I want desperately to know the rest."

"I don't like Elizabeth because that's what my father calls me, and I hate him. I don't want Conner around him, but legally, I can't stop it."

I have now, out of nowhere, shared with him more than I have in two years of therapy.

"You precious little thing." He nuzzles his face into my hair, inhaling rhythmically, slowly. "Now, big, deep breath, on in for me," we inhale synchronously, "and out for you." He curls both arms around my waist, not too tight, but telling me he's got me. "Why do you hate your father?" he asks calmly, like simply needing my pizza order.

Surprisingly, it comforts me into speaking the answer as easily. "He's a serial narcissist. A textbook sociopath."

I feel and hear his brusque intake of breath; yeah, it's a pretty heavy accusation, but sadly, true. See how precious he thinks I am now with so much hatred inside me.

"And why do you think that?"

Finally, I meet his eyes for the first time in most of this rendezvous. "Are you sure it's your mom who's the grief counselor?"

"Positive." He bows his head and kisses the end of my nose before I know it's happened. "Now continue, Witchy. I'm not falling for it this time."

"I like Siren or Lizzie better. Witchy sounds evil."

"Noted." He winks. "You do cast a helluva spell, though."

I adjust in his lap, getting more comfortable and he groans softly. "Oh, sorry," I mutter. "Am I hurting you?" I start to climb off him but he snares me back in a blink.

"You're not hurting me. But you gotta quit squirming around," he assures me, but his plea is strained.

"Why don't I just move?" I don't—"

"Lizzie, *please* sit still." He closes his eyes, titling his head to the sky and exhaling loudly through his flared nostrils. "Okay," he's instantly back, "go on."

I'm about to ask "what the hell?" when he shuffles us slightly and…oh! Blushing feverishly, I drop my head, biting on my bottom lip. He's rock hard against my bottom…and it's distractingly erotic. "I feel that," I moan, unable to stop myself.

He laughs, the shake of his body shoving his massive erection against me even more. "I'm sure you do. Much like I'm painfully aware of you wiggling your hot little ass all over it right now."

I peer up at him with my best flirtatious grin. "Sorry, I'll be still."

"Good. I finally got you talking, so please don't stop *that part*. Going for noble, not sainthood. Work with me." He slides a finger under my chin, demanding my eyes on him. "Now tell me more, without ass teasing my cock, Wiggleworm."

Once I stop snorting, finding his last statement funny as hell, I decide to take a chance, let him in a few more steps. What can it hurt? Actually, it might help; the more I talk to Cannon, the closer to whole I feel.

Oh good Lawd! I'm a cheeseball.

*But I'm a cheeseball that makes his dick hard!*

"My mother came from money, lots of it. When she married Lucifer, he built his social status and career while she built a home. He ran for office and basically became the King of Sutton, and we were all made to stand behind him like the perfect billboard family or suffer his wrath. Eventually, we literally became numb, ignoring his cruelty, absence, and indiscretions. Conner and I stayed busy with sports, music, and school while my mom self-medicated and drank like a fish."

He guides my head back down to his shoulder—*I think he likes it there*—stroking my hair, neither of us acknowledging the tears beginning to soak through his shirt. I bury my face in his neck, inhaling the glorious scent of soap, musk, and Cannon, embracing the wake of security coursing through my veins.

"One summer, I went to camp for two weeks. I was so excited to get out of that house, to go be around happy, functional people. Conner stayed gone more and more and my mother was a zombie," I choke, sobs building in volatility. "I didn't think anyone would miss me, need me. I just wanted to be free. But I shouldn't have gone! They needed me and I left!" My wails are incoherent even to my own ears, a screeching, slobbery mess, years of shame and regret flooding out of me in a landslide of guilty misery.

He'd done it, cracking the dam just enough for that one flaw to splinter, fracturing the whole wall I'd built. The collapse happens all at once, a torrent rushing forth, fierce and unstoppable. There's no air, my lungs burning in protest and my vision splotchy. I can literally feel the blood vessels in my head constricting. This is it—this is when I finally completely snap, murmuring and tracing shapes in the air for the rest of my life, broken, unfixable. I surrender, letting my head dangle loosely, landing where it may.

# CHAPTER fourteen

*"You're my little sis, I'd never let him lay a hand on you or Mom. He's not violent, just an ass. Now stop crying. I've got you."*

*"I will always take care of my children, Bethy. No matter what, I'm with you."*

*"Elizabeth, we need you to pack your things, honey. You're needed back home, a driver's on the way for you."*

*"What happened, what's wrong with Conner?!"*

*"Elizabeth, do try to calm down, your hysterics help no one. Go home with Alma, take care of your mother. I will handle Conner."*

"Lizzie! Siren, oh Goddamn, come back to me precious! Fuck! Lizzie!" His paranoid, crazed screams permeate my brain only milliseconds before a fiery hot shard of pain lights up the side of my face. I try to scream out to open my eyes, but everything feels heavy, like I'm trapped in a dream where the faster I run, the farther away my destinations seems.

*"What's wrong with my brother?!"*

*"Elizabeth, quit screaming at your mother, she knows nothing. Do I need to have the doctor get you medicine?"*

"Conner!" I think I hear myself say, trying to lift my arm, wanting to rub my throbbing cheek. *If you can feel pain,*

SE Hall

*you're not dead* is the one conscious thought that takes hold. "Conner!" I scream louder this time.

"Lizzie, open those eyes, darlin'. Lemme see you, come on, love. It's Cannon. I'm here. Look at me, please." His voice cuts out, so scared and filled with anguish that my chest aches and my eyes open, *for him*. "Oh, thank God," he sniffs, cheeks wet as he leans in and peppers my face with tender kisses. "I've never been so scared in my life. I'm so sorry, angel; you don't ever have to tell me anything again. I don't care; just never leave me like that again. Please, stay with me."

I'm not sure if I'm actually shaking or he's trembling for both us, but I'm compelled internally to comfort him. "Cannon," I brace a hand on his leg and push myself up, my mind fuzzy and my body lethargic, managing to wrap my arms around him, "I'm okay. Shhhh, I'm here, I'm fine. What happened, did I pass out?"

Now he laughs, his whole body jostling, the sound of relief pouring out of him more than humor. His head lifts as he discreetly swipes his damp cheeks. "Yeah, you were just *gone*. I couldn't get you back. I will never ask you to relive your past again, I swear. Please forgive me." He grabs the sides of my face, the seriousness in his eyes sending a cold shiver along my spine. "I slapped you," he gulps and chokes out, his eyes dropping shamefully. "I hit you. I didn't know what else to do! I had to snap you out of it, so I, I slapped your beautiful, precious face. I want to cut off my own fucking hand." He's inconsolable now, clinging to me, his face buried in my neck, wet tears splashing my skin. "God, Lizzie, I'm sorry."

"Cannon, it's okay. It was to help me, I understand. Hey," I whisper, nudging him, "what's that you're always telling me? Take a deep breath, then look at me."

When he finally does, my own exhale is a long, troubled sigh.

"Please don't let me ruin you," I say, keeping my gaze locked on his. "Please. You're magnificent and my ugly will only bleed over to you and taint that. I'm hopeless, Cannon, way too scratched and dented. Don't let me dim

158

your light. Tarnishing you in any way would be my gravest sin. And I don't know," my voice cracks, "I don't know if I can stay away, so it has to be you who stops it. *Please.*"

Without warning, his lips crash against my own in a gluttonous attack, stealing both my breath and sanity at once. He's brutal, unleashing his worry and fright into this kiss, a blatant message of his want, need, desire, and frustration. And I feast on it, letting him take his fill, reveling in the reward. He tastes of passion and power, his tongue swirling around and leading my own, but stoking every last inch of my being. All the other kisses in my life combined held not a fraction of this intensity, making me want to cry and scream at the same time, to crawl in the skin of my aggressor and get lost in him.

I whimper when he releases me, pulling back to gauge my eyes with his glazed own. "I'm so sorry, gorgeous girl. I'll never hurt you or put my hands on you in anger, but I tried everything else. Say you truly forgive me, please," he begs, a piercing sound that rattles me to the core.

"I do, I forgive you." I taste his mouth, soft and seeking, a timid brush of lips. "You saved me. I get it, I promise. Now shut up and steal my breath away."

"Ah, Lizzie." He leans into me, forehead on mine, both hands cupping and rubbing my cheeks. "If you were any fuckin' sweeter, I'd die from a sugar coma. I don't care if it's been two weeks or two decades, I adore you. I want you. I want us."

"Seriously? Like, boyfriend and girlfriend?"

Yes, I'm really eloquent and versed at this type of thing, not at all like a twelve-year-old girl.

"Nothing, never mind, errr…" I conceal my reddened face in my hands. "I didn't mean it like that. Ignore me, please. Of course you don't mean *that*, you were just engaged, I know."

Do I *ever* stop talking? Fucking ramblerrhea already!

"Love, one in for me," he rubs my back and takes an audible deep breath with me, "and out for you. Again." He waits. "Better?"

I nod, face still hidden until he gently peels my hands away. "Let's stand up, we gotta get back." He goes first, then helps me. My body feels burdened, exhausted, and I wobble a bit. Instantly, he swoops me up in a cradle hold, tucking me safely against his durable chest.

"Cannon, I can walk."

"Probably, but I wanna hold ya. You've had a rough day. I'm so damn proud of you though, for trying to open up and let me in. You can't know how much your trust means to me, Lizzie. So you keep taking baby steps and I'll carry you on the big ones."

"Tell me about Wanda," I rush out before losing my nerve.

"What about her?"

Ah, *finally* he agrees—all old lady names are the same! "Did you love her? *Do* you love her?"

He puffs out a long-winded sigh, perhaps the exertion of carrying me, or maybe in pondering. Either way, I wait silently for him to answer.

"I loved her fire and determination. In college, I just knew *nothing* was gonna keep that girl from her goals. She was smart, and sassy, and motivated, and being around her made you feel excited and accomplished. She ran her sorority and was always heading up fundraisers and charity events and collecting donations for something. I always thought she had such a giving heart. So yes, at first, there were many things I loved about her."

"And?" I squeak, afraid of the answer. I knew it was building, but after today, I don't want to think of him with anyone else. He lifts me up, literally; I feel like I can fly. He makes me hope for possibilities, that someday I'll be happy and normal and worthy of him.

"And then she changed. Nothing was natural, or easy, or given. Everything she did or said had a hidden agenda; a

160

means to get her one step closer to the caviar, country club, trophy wife status she would kill for. I wasn't her partner, I was her pony. She picked my clothes, my job, my degree, my friends. I became some mindless puppet who did whatever she said so I didn't have to hear her ear-piercing shrieks or answer to her daddy at work."

He's talking about another woman, but I'm drowning in the beat of his heart beneath my ear and the melodic cadence of his voice. And his strength—not remotely out of breath, carrying me as though I'm weightless, his grip as sturdy now as the first step.

"You fall asleep on me?" He chuckles.

"No, just listening. That all?"

"Well, you know what the final straw was about, the tubal thing. She wouldn't even hear my point, no consideration for my feelings. And she didn't even tell me—I overheard her telling her mother, who saw nothing wrong with it, either. Ruthie's not a bad girl, she'll make an excellent politician's wife, but she wasn't the one for me. Nobody's fault, just not meant to be. The End."

He takes a few more steps in silent deliberation, and by the time a devastating smile has worked its way back over his face, his voice has returned to "my voice," where his register deepens and the words pour out like silk. "Now, about tonight. I think we should cancel our date and the show so you can rest. You scared me so bad back there and I think you need to take it easy. We can tell the others you're sick if you want."

Actually, resting tonight sounds divine, but I don't know if I can do that to the guys. "If Bruce can get the venue to reschedule tomorrow or Sunday, fine," I concede. "The guys need the money and exposure. Or do it without me; you three sing better than me anyways."

"I don't need the money or exposure, so if you're out, all possible appeal to me is gone. I'll be taking care of you. I can see the bus ahead though, so you better decide."

"What do you think, send them or no show?"

He stops short, looking down at me. "You're asking me what I think?"

Confused, I must give him a look as such. "Yes?"

His face again splits in a beautiful smile, something tender amidst his amber eyes. "I think if they want to do a drum/guitar different kind of jam, let them. If not, try to rebook. And last resort," he winks, "fuck it."

"Will you lay it all out to them, tell them I'm sick? I wanna head straight to a hot shower. Especially since there'll be a million questions. I just don't have it in me right now."

"I got you." He bends his head and kisses my forehead, then nose, both eyes, and lastly my lips, where he lingers a hint longer. "Totally spellbound, Lil' Miss Not Witchy."

He starts walking again, so I chance it, needing still to put it out there. "Are you sure you're not—"

"Lizzie Siren Carmichael, if you say on the rebound, I will drop you on your ass then pick it back up and spank it. No, Goddammit, I am not on the rebound and what is with that fucking word around here?! And you wanna know how I'm *positive* that's not what it is, the ugly details? Fine! She and I hadn't made love in almost five months. Hell, we stopped using our tongues to kiss even before that. At best, I'd get a harsh peck immediately followed by instructions, *maybe* twice a week. Oh! And the last banquet her parents hosted for 'Blah Blah, we support blah,' a total act she went along with, I drank a bottle of citrate so I could pull off being too sick to attend! I slept on the couch because she said my snoring kept her awake. And I'm pretty sure she poisoned my cat because it shed!" He huffs, scrunching the forehead I know he wishes desperately he could rub if both hands weren't carrying me. "*Again,* and for the last time, to *rebound,* I'd be chasing that same ball. No. Thank. You."

"Then *why* did you stay?" I ask, tempted to laugh at the self-inflicted diarrhea part, but seeing how red his face has gotten, I think better of it.

"Because *my one* and I hadn't found each other yet and until then, I had nothing better to do. I know it makes me sound like a coward, but honestly, I was too damn disengaged to realize I was miserable. I functioned."

It reminds me of my mother, on a smaller scale, and I reach up to run my hand down the side of his face compassionately. "The absolute last word I would use to describe you would be emotionless."

"That's the last thing I am, now. It was like, why rock the boat if Katarina isn't in the water waiting for me?"

"Arturo," I whisper. *I love that movie. Twin, oh twin!*

"Yes, exactly," he murmurs, a pleased grin at yet another connection we've instantly made. "I didn't lie. We quit saying 'I love you' a long time ago. I didn't enter her body and act like things were fine just to get off. I cohabitated peacefully, same as she did. We're here." He sets me down easy, clutching my hips until I have my bearings. "You take a shower, I'll take care of everything else. And hey," he cups my cheek, his thumb grazing my bottom lip, "I'm so damn sorry about today. I had to get you back and I saw it work on TV once. I'd never hurt you."

"I know that." *As certain as death and taxes.* "Let's never talk about it again." I hold up my pinky and he promises, then I kiss where they connect. "And you don't snore." I give him a wink of my own and climb on board in front of him.

# CHAPTER
## fifteen

Jarrett had reappeared, a fog so thick around him it actually spelled out "don't fuck with me." Unbeknownst to any of us, until he got back, bottom lip scraping the ground, he'd taken Vanessa to the airport. She'd been gone from school and work long enough, so Jarrett paid to fly her home, and he's *not* happy about it.

So after hugging on him awhile, I head for that shower I urgently need and when I reappear they've all discussed and laid the plans for tonight. Here in the thriving metropolis of Douglas, Wyoming, the venue only holds about 60 max, so Rhett and Jarrett are gonna do an "unplugged" kinda thing.

Fine by me.

Rhett still hasn't spoken to me, even though he knows I'm ill or whatever, and that hurts. Bad. Conner loved on me, concerned, then offered up his bed as he and Bruce left to go bowling and out to eat, leaving Cannon to watch over me. I know they say let a sleeping dog lie, but I've never had a dog, thus my approach.

"Hey, Rhett, before you head out, can I talk to you?" I ask him.

"Sure, what's up?" It's stony and unfeeling, unlike our usual rapport, and I'm already prepping myself for a fight. But Conner's gone and this has been awhile coming, so

I'm down to do the thing if need be. Jarrett slinks off to the bathroom to get ready, but Cannon stays put, a hard set to his jaw and his arms crossed across his chest.

"I thought we talked everything out and agreed things were good?" I start, clinging closely to my bravery as he paces back and forth in front of me like a caged lion ready to roar. "Why are we back to angry, not speaking to me Rhett?"

"I'm not mad at you Liz, I'm mad *for* you. Have you by any chance been ignoring your father's calls?" he questions me, brows lifted.

"Of course, I always avoid that bastard until I can't put Conner's requests off any longer. You know that."

"Well, he's calling *me* now, incessantly. I thought it was too weird, so I answered." He comes and sits down beside me, throwing an arm around my shoulder and taking one of my hands with his other. Cannon hasn't moved, just watching in silence. "I'm not sure if this will be too much right now, I heard you had a rough day, so I was trying to hold off. But you need to know. Wanna wait before I tell you the rest or—"

"You know when people leave you a voicemail and say 'call me back, I have something very important to tell you!' All they had to do was actually *tell you*, right then, but instead, they leave you hanging, all worried. That's exactly what you're doing right now. Just say it."

"He's engaged, your father."

"So," I grit, failing to conceal my disgust.

"So, apparently this woman has children and your dad's running for some new office. I didn't listen to which one, but he wants his son home to meet his new brother and sisters. They're planning a family trip to Hawaii for two weeks and want to take Conner."

"OVER MY DEAD FUCKING BODY!" The windows rattle and Rhett jerks back, visibly shaken, while Cannon rushes forward, visibly in protector mode, at the same moment Jarrett runs in, confused.

165

Cannon has me scooped up in his lap faster than I can shove him away. "Lizzie, breathe for me," he pleads.

"Rhett talk to me, man," Jarrett demands, begging to be caught up.

"Go ahead," I grimace, waving a careless hand to give Rhett the floor. "I don't care, talk about it all you want; it's not happening."

*How do you sell "family" if only one of your kids is there?* And how does he convince someone to marry him once they talk about their pasts? He'd literally have to tell her his wife died in bed at 43, no autopsy, his son woke up one day with a cerebral hemorrhage that left him with special needs and his daughter hates him and plots ways to convict or kill him. "I do" would not be the next words out of a sane woman's mouth. Which means she's as bat-shit crazy evil as he is and NOT COMING NEAR MY BROTHER!

"Lizzie, right here, my eyes, love." Cannon turns my head for me, demanding I come out of my own head and look at him. "In for me," he pauses, "out for you. One more, in for me," he smiles at me, "out for you. Okay, now—"

"What was that hypnotist shit? Teach me, too, I've been wigging since I got the call." Rhett rambles, running a shaky hand through his hair.

"It's called breathing, bro. I'll teach you later, now shut the fuck up," Jarrett says, then turns. "Sorry, Cannon, please continue."

"I was gonna ask Lizzie, can your father do this? Legally, per agreement, whatever. Does he even have the option?"

"He gets 24 hours every other holiday, ten weekends, and a single two week block. So yes, he can. He's barely used any of his time and never cared before, he's just cashing in now to sell 'family values,'" I air quote harshly, blanching my knuckles, "in his campaign. And possibly, to show new wifey that *he* tries and *I'm* the problem. Doesn't matter, he's not taking Conner out of state for two weeks with some fill-in family, probably MANSON, that I don't know. I'll leave, take Conner, and run before I allow it."

"Well, we can't solve anything tonight," Cannon concludes and exhales, strained. "You guys go do your show. Lizzie needs a night of solid, peaceful rest, and we'll regroup in the morning. Sound good?" He looks to each of us, seeking acceptance or a better idea.

We all agree with half-hearted nods and murmured agreements and I trudge to Conner's room while they pack up and head out. "Have a good show, boys, love you!" I call back, faking enthusiasm.

"Watch her phone, he comes up as DIE DICK. Don't let her answer it 'til she speaks with her attorney," I hear Rhett whisper to Cannon. They forget I'm Conner's sister; that comes with werewolf hearing and a keenly developed sixth sense. He could have signed it and I would've heard him.

Unless, of course, they're planning top-secret on stage serenades. Then, somehow, I'm oblivious. That one still perplexes me.

Exhausted, mentally and physically, I fall face first into Conner's bed, fully clothed, legs hanging over the end, not giving a damn. When it rains, it pours. And this whole day has been a shit storm of epic proportions. I was *supposed* to be out on my first *real* date, with Cannon, no less, right now, then doing a show with my best friends, concluding with arranging the next *one* day Satan could visit with Conner. And look where I'm at instead, as far from said plans as possible without being on another fucking planet.

Why do I keep waking up in Conner's bed, having to piece together previous blocks of time and events? Wasn't there a movie like this—ignorant chick was being drugged, losing blocks of time, and it took her the whole flick to catch on? I remember thinking *what a dumbass*, yet look at me now.

Light cuts through the darkened room and I wince from the sudden intrusion, shielding my eyes with one hand.

"You need anything, babe?" It's Cannon, his voice hushed and kind, checking on me.

"What time is it? Where's Conner?" I start to rise, pushing back the covers, but he hurries to me and stops my progress with a gentle hand on my shoulder.

"Everyone's still out, you only slept about an hour. Just relax, I can take care of anything that needs it. Lizzie," his lips find my forehead, first a kiss, then rubbing lightly back and forth never breaking contact, "I know you don't trust easily, but I mean this. Any time you wanna treat yourself to a well-deserved break—nap, movie, whatever—I will make Conner my number one priority. So anytime you start to panic that you turned your head, just stop and trust. I picked up where you left off."

"Why?" It escapes a hopeful, but disbelieving, whisper.

The hand on my shoulder gradually slides across my collarbone, then up my neck to cup the back of my head. He inhales sharply, blowing it out warm on my skin, before his own forehead replaces his lips against mine. "I don't believe in magic or luck or fate. I know what you're thinking, but I only give astrology some thought because, well, God made the stars. And I do believe in destiny, because that's just a fancy word for what was planned anyway. But above all, I believe in instinct, the personal GPS you were born with. To me, instinct is the only tool you have when others try to mess up the ultimate plan already laid out for you. Don't let them pull you off track, just follow your GPS. And Lizzie," he cradles my cheek and tilts my head up, "all my instincts tell me to covet and cherish you fiercely, with each breath, and work harder to make you mine. Each and every time you try and push me away, to put that guard of yours back up, I need to hold on tighter, chase faster. Until my arms are the ones you want to run *into*."

Despite my struggle, my eyelids flutter, my mouth goes dry, and my pulse accelerates to dangerous speeds; he's more than lyrical...he's intoxicating. I stay silent, for no response I would utter could do justice for all the things he makes me feel, the most prominent of which is safe.

"Say something," he whispers on my lips, where his own now tease softly.

"So you don't really believe in sirens?"

His gentle laugh is contagious, and I join him, but more so because of all I could have said...that's what popped out...*and I actually write lyrics*.

"I do now."

I'm lying in Cannon's arms, my head on his shoulder as he strokes my back rhythmically, when Conner bursts through the bedroom door.

"Oh no, Cannon likes my bed too?" He frumps, stomping his foot.

I sit up while Cannon pauses our show, both us battling snickers. "No, Bubs, we're just watching a movie while we waited for you to get back. You wanna finish it with us?" I pat the bed beside me.

"No." But he sits down beside us anyway. "Bethy, is Cannon your husband?"

I snort with laughter; my brother and the things that come out of his mouth; the purest joy in my life. "No, Conner, he's my good friend and he's watching a movie with me."

"That's good. Because girls aren't supposed to be in bed with boys that's not their husbands. Mom said."

Warm blood in my veins stops, turning icy cold, racking my body with an eerie shiver. Cannon immediately senses my apprehension, twisting to make the conversation a circle and curling an arm low, subtly behind my waist.

SE Hall

"What do you mean, Con? When did Mom say that?"

He's probably just taking words of advice she'd given, probably something along the lines of "no sex before you're married," and repeating them in "his" version...but the little voice in my head coerces me to dig deeper.

"I don't know." He pops his shoulders and suddenly jumps up to go investigate his fish tank.

"Do you have your phone in here?" I whisper in Cannon's ear. "Record this without distracting him."

I'm running purely on *instinct* right now. I wait for him to dig the phone out of his pocket and wink at me that he's ready, then I try again with my brother.

"Conner, can you come sit down and talk to me, please?"

He sighs over-dramatically and drops back down on the mattress.

"Bubs, when did Mom tell you about husbands and beds?"

"She didn't tell *me,* Bethy, she told dad's friend. 'That's my husband and my bed, you tramp! At least have the decency to keep it out of my home!' She was mad."

Years—nothing—then out of nowhere, and on today of all days, he'd just literally mimicked an exact memory, quoting the words of my mother; he even changed his voice to imitate her. I'm vibrating with anger at watching almost firsthand what went on in that house, but more with anticipation, hoping greatly that the recollections continue, and lead me to conclusions I've suspected all along. "What happened next, Bub?" I peep, scared but longing for more of the story.

"And then I tried to hug Mom because she was crying. Dad was screaming at her. He made—" he stops, fists clenching as his face reddens. "Dad was making Mom cry. He was being mean to her."

Cannon scoots flush against me, his fingertips digging into my hip reassuring me.

170

"You're doing great, Conner. I love your awesome memory. You're so smart," I encourage him and take a deep, bracing breath. "What else happened?"

"I told him to leave Mom alone. I wanted to hug her, Bethy. Dad only had on his underwear." He laughs. "Mom said she wanted a divorce."

My eyes dart to Cannon's lap, making sure his phone is recording all this. Finally, some information, some clue what the hell I missed, the pivotal push to my family's demise. I could cry, but just as easily jump for joy, which seems deranged at first, but no...the not knowing has been the hardest part.

"Where was Dad's," *cringe*, "friend then?"

"She left, but not in her underwear anymore."

"And what did Dad say next, Conner, about the divorce?"

"He was very, very mad. He said loud stuff. He broke your pony picture on the wall. Are you sad? I'll get you a new one."

What is he...? It hits me like a bolt of lightning, kinda like his memories pick and choose when to flash in his mind. At the top of our grand staircase was a landing area, a central spot shaped almost like an octagon, with several doors to the various rooms. In that landing were two mahogany sofa tables along the wall, decorated with pictures, flowers, and such. The far left one held a picture of me, about seven years old, atop my pony, Dusty, in a black frame. I can picture it now as clear as if it was right in front of me.

"Did he throw the picture at the wall, Con?"

He gestures affirmatively, but I need the words recorded, so I clarify.

"Yes, he did?"

Peering at me with troubled, pouty eyes, he answers, "Yes, sorry, Sister. I'll get you another one."

"It's okay." I reach over and pat his leg. "I'm not sad, promise."

"Mom didn't want him breaking your stuff. She was even gonna call the police!" His face and voice become animated. "And Dad chased her over his dead body and then Mom went to Heaven."

Wait, now I'm confused. My mom died in her sleep, long after I returned from camp. I thought this fight happened while I was gone? I'm usually able to follow anything Conner says, but I'm lost here.

"Bethy, I'm tired. Can I have my bed now?"

"Oh, sure, sorry we'll get out of your way." I'd like to keep him talking, of course, but I don't need it sounding like I'm "guiding" him on the recording. And, I'm puzzled now, no idea what to even ask next. Cannon and I rise and Conner scurries to the middle of the bed, huddling under his covers. "You want me to watch a different movie with you?" I ask him warmly, somewhat worried this had been too much.

"No, I wanna go to sleep. See you in the morning. Cannon, can we cook breakfast?"

Cannon has to clear his throat he's been quiet so long. "Of course. Just wake me up when you're ready."

# CHAPTER sixteen

I quietly shut Conner's door and turn to find Bruce, who never stays on the bus at night, sitting at the table, the usual four lines of worry on his brow grown to six. "You heard," I state, his face telling me the answer. Taking a seat across from him, I prop my elbows on the table and let my head fall into my hands.

I hear Cannon set a cup, coffee no doubt, in front of Bruce then feel him scoot in beside me, our thighs touching.

"Thank you, Cannon," my uncle says politely, full of respect. "Elizabeth, ah," he holds up a hand to halt me, my head flying up to contest the use of that name. "Elizabeth Hannah Carmichael, your mama, my beautiful sister, gave you that name. All the time growing up," his voice cracks and he ducks his head, "she always said when she had a daughter, she was gonna name her Elizabeth. Every single one of her dolls, all named Elizabeth." He shakes his head with a chuckling smile, the reminiscing clear in his glossy eyes. "So instead of hating it because of him, try embracing it because of her."

Well, when he puts it that way.

"And quit holding back your tears, young lady. You're not half as hard and bitchy as you'd like to think."

"Agreed," Cannon throws in, squeezing my thigh under the table.

"What Conner told you, that's a big breakthrough, on the day you needed it most." My uncle smiles at me with a brow lifting in message. "My sister, your mama, has been at work here today." My flesh tightens, goosebumps breaking out over every inch of me. "Here's what we're gonna do. I'll stay on the bus with Conner tonight and you take my hotel room. Get a good night's sleep and in the morning, where he can't hear or be under foot, call your lawyer and tell him what that bastard father of yours is scheming. Let him know what Conner remembered tonight too. See what he says you should do next."

I nod resolutely, knowing it's the ideal plan of action. But one thing's still niggling at me. "I'm afraid the credibility of Conner's memory will be doubted, because something's not quite right. It couldn't have happened the way he said. I was home when mom died. There was no big fight, she just went to bed and didn't wake up. My d—my father wasn't even home when I finally went to check on her that morning and she was," Cannon curls me tight into his chest, "she was already gone; she was cold and stiff. So," I choke, "so cold."

"If I may," Cannon interrupts humbly, my uncle apparently urging him to continue as I don't flinch from his snug hold on me, face buried in the clean smelling shirt encasing his solid chest. "As an outsider and a new set of eyes, I have some thoughts, if you can help me piece some things together. But only if you're able to." He kisses the top of my head. "Just say the word and we'll wait. I can't see you like you were earlier again."

"How was she earlier?" Bruce barks in fury, causing me to flinch against Cannon.

"Easy," Cannon placates him. "Lizzie was telling me a little about all this on our walk and had a pretty bad panic attack. She blacked out for...well, for too long. And I'm not gonna lie to ya, I slapped her to bring her back." His head dips much like his voice and he runs a hand through his hair. "Nothing else was working." He lifts his head and looks Bruce in the eyes. "I needed to apologize to you, too, 'cause I told you I'd never hurt her." He returns his hold around me, more constricted, brooking no chance of escape. *Furthest thing from my mind.* "But I did, and I'm sorry. It wasn't in anger, only desperation, and I'll take whatever you hit me with like a man. It won't hurt half as much as having to touch her like I did." His chest rumbles against my cheek with his prolonged exhale.

"I appreciate that, son, for telling me, and for helping her. I've long since figured out I have nothing to worry about with you. You're a good man. And what I said before, well—"

"We don't have to rehash that," Cannon cuts him off, sparking my curiosity enough that I lift my head and eye him suspiciously.

"Rehash what?"

"Nothing." Cannon shakes his head and shoots Bruce "a look," attempting to pull mine back down to him.

"Nu-uh," I protest, holding my head firmly upright. "Tell me."

"Your uncle was concerned you might be a *rebound* for me," he mumbles, looking away.

There it is again, *that word*.

"*Pretty Woman*," I mutter absently and his head spins back, molten brown eyes studying mine.

"Instinct," he whispers back, dripping with seriousness, sensuality.

"Pretty Instinct." I sigh, thinking it's our perfect title. Maybe I'll write a song called precisely that.

My uncle groans and his bones pop and crack as he stands. "Let's get you to the hotel, girl. I'll come fetch ya in the morning after you've had time to make your calls.

"Um, Bruce," Cannon shifts me gently so he too can stand, "I'll take Lizzie, and," he refuses to look away from my uncle's critical scowl, but does scratch his head with an apologetic, nervous twitch to his mouth, "I'll stay with her, get her back in the morning. Do me a favor, though? I promised Conner we'd make breakfast. So can you do that, or hold him off 'til I get here?"

No way I'm looking up from my lap, the heat of my blush at what my uncle must be thinking fully aflame.

"Well," Bruce drawls out, surely to prolong my agony, "She's a twenty-three-year-old woman; done a fine job taking care of herself so far. All right, then, guess I'll go make Conner scoot over and see you kids in the morning. Don't be late. I don't cook and we're off to Lincoln next, eight hour trip with no stops, and three shows there. Big ones—Adamo's, Jenning's Jukebox, and The Fieldhouse. Need everyone in top form. Night," he says as he closes Conner's door behind him.

"He's gone. You can look up, my shy little Siren," Cannon whispers in a teasing voice.

"My *instinct* is telling me to kick your ass. I cannot believe you told my uncle we were gonna sleep in a hotel room together!" I pick up the nearest thing I spot, the box of Uno cards, and chuck it at his head.

He dodges stealthily and laughs, moving in fast to grasp my hand. "Come on, grab your stuff and let's go. I want you calm, rested, and confident to handle things in the morning. Together, we're gonna start eliminating all your burdens, worries, and issues one by one 'til we get you sublimely happy, and all mine, of course."

There he goes again with the "mine, happily ever after, do-da" junk. My reality isn't the kind found in storybooks, and as badly as I want to, I can't shut off the cynic in my head. Cannon's wearing it down, though; I so hope he keeps up the fight.

And our current location is another contender heavy on my mind. Ohio is sneaking closer and closer; home, a break. And what state's right before Ohio in our path? Indiana. Cannon made one grand sweep, had a good time, met some new people...but surely he'll want dropped off at his own home, back to stable ground.

Those storybooks all end in the same way...The End.

But while he's here, and delusional, I'm gonna eat it up with a spoon. I'd rather let go at least once and burn into my memory all I can—every word, every touch, each kiss and caress, his look, smell, sounds—to remember, to comfort me, once he's gone.

"Your phone's going nuts, it's Rhett. Want me to grab it?" Cannon calls through the bathroom door, slicing through the serenity of my bubble bath.

"Sure, don't want them worried and Bruce is probably asleep. My code's 1212," I answer, closing my eyes again and settling further down in the water, luxuriating in the satiny feel of my skin and ease in my muscles.

Luckily, it's but minutes before he knocks again, startling me awake seconds from my sleepy head dipping under water. Guess that probably would've woke me up too—but a "Cannon call" is better. "Had them bring up warm towels. I'm gonna set one with your pajamas on the counter, close your eyes."

Kudos on the nice try, but how out of it does he think I am? "Don't you mean, *you'll* close *your* eyes?" I giggle.

"That's what I said."

"Uh huh," I cover my chest with slick hands and cross my legs, turning to my side. "Okay, come in!" I call.

The door gradually opens and his head emerges around it—eyes closed. He puts out a hand, fumbling around seeking the countertop. "Left, up, getting warmer," I guide his blind venture through laughter. "Hotter, oh you're red hot, got it!" I clap when he lands the pile by the sink, a triumphant grin on his face.

"Thank you, Cannon," I purr...amply aware that clapping leaves my breasts exposed, swelling with longing from his close proximity. Even though he's being a gentleman and not looking, I feel wanton and electrified, the boldest opposite sex dealings I've ever had. No, there was nothing bold with Rhett and me, merely two broken souls clumsily (and *very quickly*) consoling each other.

"My pleasure," he hums, a raspy, tortured sound, revealing his battle with temptation as burdensome as my own. "You need help getting out?" His mouths quirks. He's adorable, standing there trying to be all suave tempter...with his eyes closed.

All he wears is gym shorts and a smirk. He sure is pretty...so I add the instinct. *Go for it.* "Yes, that'd be awfully sweet of you."

He jerks with his sharp inhale, igniting all my senses too. I can hear each deep, labored breath he takes as if they were my own, and the shifted, magnetic current in this small space zings along each nerve in my body. I watch his bared, hairless chest rise and fall once, twice, before he lets his eyes lazily open.

Accepting and emulating the siren he seems to think I am, I rise from the water with slow, deliberate taunting, and present myself to his now lust-filled, probing eyes. Never breaking our gaze, he licks his bottom lip and reaches back his hand to search out the towel. His greedy eyes devour every displayed inch of me, first down with long, leisurely strides of his eyes, then back up, even more intricately. "Do you want to hear the sweet thoughts or the 'me man, you...you version'?" he asks in a growl.

"Both," I whisper, bravely keeping my arms at my sides.

"I will never be able to pick a favorite part of you, each more flawless and beautiful than the last. You're absolutely perfect, Lizzie. Without a doubt, the most exquisite woman in the world, inside and out."

Dizzy, I teeter under the onslaught of those magical words. He's instantly there, holding me up, his large, strong, caring hands burning my skin where they touch. "Easy, I got you. I've always got you," he croons in assurance, wrapping the towel around me from back to front. "Hold on," he softly warns only seconds before scooping me up in his arms and carrying me toward the bedroom.

No, no, no…I was, I was practicing foreplay, getting used to…I'm not ready for *this* yet.

"You wish." He dips his head to me and winks. "Emotionally exhausted and worried sick isn't really a turn on for me, babe. Just gonna set you down so you can get dressed."

"I didn't say anything," I reply, but my voice is frail and pathetic, a poor attempt at denial.

"Didn't have to." He places me down on the bed softly and takes a step back. "But one day, you will. You'll have to beg me to stop because your body can't take another second of pleasure. Until then," he bends, chastely kissing the end of my nose, "get ready for bed. I'm gonna grab our phones in case they need us. I'll be right back to wrap my body around yours and hold you all night long."

He starts to leave, halfway through the door when I manage up the trepid words. "What was the other version you were gonna say?"

Turning, his eyes gleam and that smirk I've come to adore—that's a lie, I liked it the first time I saw it—is already in full effect. He stalks back to me and bends over me, hands caging me in at my sides and whispers smooth as silk in my ear. "I promise, I'll tell you the minute I slide inside you for the first time."

And with that—he's gone.

And so am I—totally, hopelessly gone over Cannon Powell Blackwell.

Know what else just dawned on me? Lots of those storybooks don't end with "The End"…they often close with the mystical, perhaps not unattainable words, "Happily Ever After."

# CHAPTER seventeen

Lying in bed, still awake despite the fact we have an early morning and monumental day ahead, Cannon almost makes me forget anything else exists. He's captivated me with tales of his childhood for hours, giving me reprieve from all but his soothing voice, taut arms around me, and hilarious retellings.

"So did you get expelled?" I ask in amusement. "Surely streaking across the field at a high school football game carries a pretty hefty punishment."

"Suspended two days from school and benched for four games. But it was the last game and I was a senior, so…yeah, they didn't think that one out too well."

"Did your parents make the two days at home miserable?" My father would have put Conner through hell for embarrassing him like that.

He chuckles so hard his eyes tear up. "Um, not exactly. They went to work and Lacy skipped school to *keep me company*," he wiggles his eyebrows.

"Lacy was your girlfriend?" He nods. "And she skipped school to come have sex with you while you were on punishment?"

He's laughing as he turns his head toward mine. "Isn't that what high school couples do? You sound shocked."

"I am."

"Why? You and your boyfriends never snuck out, figuring out secret trysts?"

"Had I ever *had* a boyfriend, no, I would never do anything like that."

His jaw drops, eyes bulging. "You've *never* had a boyfriend?"

Shaking my head, I don't trip up like I normally would, unafraid now of revealing too much. Cannon's had glimpses into my past, my family—dysfunction in all its glory. And more every day, I don't mind him involved, in my past or present...and maybe, just maybe, if I don't screw it up...my future. "First of all, any guy would've had to get past Conner, the most over-protective big brother ever. He's extremely large, as you know, and he played football then; he would've made the younger boys in my school piss themselves with just a snarl. And even if they managed that feat, there's no way I'd bring them around my parents or the house of gloom and doom. So, I hung out with Rhett and Jarrett, my angels placed right across the street."

"Conner played football?"

"Did he ever! He was awesome. So quick on the snap, he'd tackle three guys at once right off the line."

I see his confusion, creases around his eyes, mouth tightly drawn. I've never *quite* laid it out for him, nor will I now. If he wants to ask, let him, and *how* he asks will be a make or break moment.

"When did he stop playing?"

"After high school."

I give nothing more. His first question was fine, but he's got the rope now. I'm praying he doesn't hang himself. Not only would I be flabbergasted, completely misjudging him, but I'd be heartbroken, and my faith damaged irreversibly. I believe in Cannon's character, more, dare I say, than I do almost anything else in the world. I won't "guide" him through this; either he confirms my suspicions and takes the honorable path (I will be waiting at the end with open arms) or he doesn't.

He rolls to his side, facing me, lazily drooping his right arm over my waist. "Lizzie, please don't try to entrap me. You know what I'm asking, and you know I love Conner. There's no way I'd disrespect him, or you, with a badly-worded question. But you've never been on *this* side, and it's difficult to express it precisely how I want to and how you want me to, but still actually ask the questions. I know you're ready to bite my head off if I misstep, but I wish you'd trust me enough to meet me halfway. Please don't wait for me to screw up. Come to me and lead me *away* from the wrong words, and I promise to always do the same for you."

All this time, I've held the proverbial "right way, wrong way" lists in my head...and they were defensive piles of shit, because Cannon just taught me the unequivocal right answer. Humbling myself with a long, calming inhale, "now out for me," he whispers, I do exactly that and begin, chastened and amazed at his sincerity and open honesty.

"Conner suffered a cerebral hemorrhage. Basically, he took a blow to the head in his frontal lobe that was bleeding out. It happened the summer I went to riding camp. I was fifteen when I left and sixteen when I got home, because my birthday's in July, and Conner was only just nineteen. When I left, *that* Conner was an honor roll student, double sport athlete, in a band and well liked all through school. He was still living at home then, and about to start college nearby. He chose to stay close by rather than run as far and fast as he could because he was worried about Mom. She was..." Even before they're spoken, the words taste guilty, but if I'm gonna tell him, I'm gonna tell him the unabridged truth. "She was an alcoholic, and popped blue and yellow pills to go up, light pink and white to come down. She stayed in an unfaithful marriage and pretty much her bedroom, unless my father needed her to stand beside him and smile at a charity event. Some days she didn't even bathe, just took the bottle to her bedroom with her. Other days, she painted up her face and hosted brunches. You just never knew with her; it was a constant crap shoot."

His arm across me tightens and he pulls me in against his body, stroking my back, encouraging me to continue. "Anyway, like I said, when I left, he was fine. Then there was an emergency and I got picked up from camp early by the family driver and taken straight to the hospital. Conner was hooked up to every machine I think they could find. Doctors had gone in and stopped the bleeding and were keeping him in a coma until the fluid and swelling on his brain went down."

I have no idea why I sound like I'm reading from a script, monotone, when I've never once spoken these details aloud.

"He survived. He woke up, obviously, but he was never the same. He doesn't remember what happened, or blocked it, or won't say, who knows. What he said tonight...it's the most I've ever heard, either."

The story and silence settles over us as we stare at each other, unmoving or speaking for what feels like forever. Finally, amidst our private little pocket of safety, where it's only us, Cannon clears his throat and lifts my hand, placing a soft kiss upon it. "Thank you for telling me, trusting me with your pain. Can I ask some questions now?"

I bob my head yes and he proceeds.

"So, when Conner said your mom went to heaven, was he already injured? Was he in the hospital or back home? Where was he when she actually passed?"

"Home," I mutter, "from the hospital. It'd been a while."

"Maybe he's lost that chunk of time in between his injury and her death and...having trouble remembering." He chooses his words carefully, respectfully, and I snuggle closer against him for it. "Did he suffer the head injury on the day of the fight he was describing? And not to sound trite, but *who* could possibly take Conner out, especially from the front? I don't get it."

"I don't know anything for sure. Dead people don't talk, Conner doesn't know, and my father..." I toss my head with an evil chuckle. "Don't even get me started on him. All I know is I wasn't there for a big fight like that, but it could've happened any time. But if that's Conner's last memory between her alive and dead, it's pretty likely it was when I

183

was away. Other than camp and school, I was around, and more than Bubs. And *after* he got hurt, honestly, Mom practically *was* dead, a complete zombie, so I doubt she was up for a battle."

"And your father never told you what happened? Surely he at least made something up. He didn't think people would forget to ask, did he? What about Child Protective Services or your family?" He's talking fast, huffing...

*I get it, Cannon, been there, felt the same frustration.*

"Oh, there was an investigation. Not by Protective Services, since he was over eighteen," I give him a pointed look, "but definitely some questions. Bruce is all that's left of my mother's family, and he was taking care of my aunt. My father's parents? They're as goddamn naïve as everyone else who meets the motherfucker. So, that leaves...my mother, literally catatonic and unable to speak coherently, and my father, saying he wasn't there. No one could prove otherwise, and the sheep in Sutton backed my father and his political social status. It simply got swept under the rug, the unsolvable mystery that people simply turned a blind eye to. It wasn't even a few months later that my mother went to sleep and never woke up. Her death was ruled an overdose, a blood test confirmed that. She took the easy way out when she was alive and in death. She was weak, a coward, and left her children to fend for themselves in the mess *she* built. Oh, she padded us financially," I bark a laugh, which sounds even more sadistic than the last one, "but by that time, Conner couldn't even count money—the wrong kind of help and way too late. Huh," I wonder aloud, reaching a tentative hand up to check—yes, I'm crying. "I didn't realize until this very second how angry I am at my mother. I always thought of her as my angel."

She's gone, been gone, but the wound feels reopened, a fresh cut, like I just lost her all over again.

"Hey," he tilts up my head, "she *is* your angel. Lizzie, your mom loved you. Weak doesn't mean evil. Again, merely an outsider looking in, but it sounds like she got lost in her unhappiness and couldn't find her way out. She has my sympathy much more so than my anger."

"Maybe. I don't know." I close my eyes, my head still in his hands. "I'm ready to go to sleep now."

He slides down on his back and lowers me gently with him, guiding my head to the crook of his arm, easing it under my neck and unfailing kissing my hair again and again; it's the last thing I remember.

Only a few hours later, Cannon wakes me with soft coos in my ear and kisses on my face. Once he's convinced I'm really awake to stay, he grabs a shower while I call my attorney, Will Morrison. He's been with me since I turned eighteen and fought for custody of Conner, helping me win. Thankfully, his father had worked for my grandfather, on my mother's side, of course, so he was willing to go against my father's clout.

I give him the rundown of my father's plans as well as Conner's story, but his response is grim. He's gonna call me back after he makes some calls of his own and does some digging, but believes that as long as my father discloses their location and agrees to be receptive to communication while they're gone, he's within the legal guidelines of our agreement to take Conner. As for the memory, Conner will definitely have to be evaluated by an agreed upon mental health professional *and* recount everything to them in person.

Is he fucking joking? You can't just snap your fingers and expect Conner to recite on demand! Therefore, Conner's recollection is basically unusable.

Beyond discouraged, I get dressed and ready to head out, barging into the bathroom to tend my hair and teeth with no consideration whatsoever for Cannon's privacy. He's already out of the shower, a towel wrapped around his waist, droplets of water glistening on his chest, but a half-hearted once over is all I can muster.

"Bad news?" He steps behind me, squeezing both my shoulders and finding my gaze in the mirror.

"Conner's story won't matter, he'd have to retell it on command during a psych eval. Never gonna happen, and I don't even wanna put him through trying. They oughta *eval* the dumbass who thinks that's a reasonable idea."

"What about the trip with his dad?"

"*That* probably *will* happen. Justice system at its finest. So can you hurry?" I shrug his hands off my shoulders and walk out.

Why? Because I'm a bitch, my scars crusted over with skin so thick even someone as extraordinary as Cannon Blackwell can't permeate through. Once again—bam!—a rock fell right at the end of the tunnel, blocking any light.

"You ready, precious?" He strides to me, taking my hand in his.

I flinch, trying to pull away, but he only squeezes tighter. "Trust me with your pain, Lizzie, please. Trust me with your anger, confusion, resentment, fear, and all those feelings of powerlessness. Give it all to me. I will carry it, you, and us to the other side."

"Spare me," I mumble, relaxing my hand in his since it's futile to struggle; he's not letting go. "Have you seen your own resume? You skipped a huge level in between me and What's-Her-Grandma-Name. In the middle somewhere is a surplus of women who aren't clueless, heartless morons with an agenda, nor are they moody, baggage-laden, distrusting, wishy-washy misfits such as myself. You could have your pick, you know? You're *that* remarkable. I wouldn't mention the part about thinking you liked me, though, that may reflect badly on your sanity and taste."

"I'm sorry, all I heard was 'I'm having a really bad day, gorgeous man of mine, so please ignore everything I say until I'm back to your sweet Lizzie.' Which, the answer's 'yes, Siren, I can do that.'" He lifts our joined hands and kisses mine, treating me to a wink. "My brave, justifiably grumpy girl, you keep me in awe. So many others would run, give up, and curl into a helpless ball. But not my girl, she keeps fighting. This morning," he winks, "it just happens to be with me."

Oh for...I roll my eyes then gain the leverage, using our hands to pull him to me. "Even if you survive me, Mr. Blackwell, I'm still not sure I'll survive you. Maybe not in *that* way, but..." I peter out, petrified to speak such alarmingly liberating words out loud *to him*.

"One in for me," he inhales with me, "and out for you. Now tell me."

All right. With a few tweaks to the script, I can do this...with my eyes pinched tightly closed, of course. "I love who you are. I love how you find the exact words to reach inside and drag the real me out, kicking and screaming. I love when you touch me and the storm passes. Most of all, I love how you give me hope, hope that someone like you could sincerely see potential in me. In for you," I suck in a lungful, letting it roll through my chest, over my raw, exposed nerves, then let it, "out for me." I open my eyes timidly; meeting kind, rich brown ones smiling back at me.

"My precious Siren, say it again, without words."

One jump and he catches me, holding me close as I wrap my legs around his waist and dig my trembling hands through his silky hair. I kiss him like I do in every dream I've ever had about us—untamed, hungry, and confident—tangling our tongues in a battle of want vs. fear, need vs. brave enough to try. His forceful, capable hands grip my face and angle the way he wants, allowing him further depths into my mouth. He breathes in and out for both of us, his air my own, and I whimper, squirming my body against his, desperate to get closer.

"Gonna get it all fixed," he grumbles into my mouth, then pulls back after one last, chaste kiss. "And then, you're mine, all mine, for real and forever. Hear me, Lizzie?"

The grin that consumes my face unstoppable, I nod, squealing internally in anticipatory delight. "Okay, let's go fix shit."

"Finally Cannon is home!" Conner yells as we walk in the bus. "I am starving for us to cook breakfast. Hear that?" He comes over to stand in front of us, poofing out his stomach.

"I don't hear—"

"Shhh," he cuts me off. "My stomach's 'bout to growl."

Cannon and I both laugh, the former springing into action. "My bad, Con. Come on, let's get busy before you waste away."

I force my attention to the rest of the bus, both Foster boys watching me with loving smiles in place. When I meet eyes with Rhett, he crooks his finger and, without any hesitation, I rush straight into his arms. These two arms, always strong and manly, will forever make me feel safe and remind me of a time when only Rhett could reach my darkest depths, when he was the one who understood me best. But, they're not the arms I now seek out first, and that thought sends a little twinge of sad ache through my chest.

"Always be my girl," he whispers in my ear, "and now his woman. Looks good on you." My sob leaps from me, loud and blatantly pained, but he shushes me and kisses my temples. "He can't replace us, any more than I could replace him; it's totally different. Lots of different kinds of love, Liz. And I'm more than okay with our kind, and damn happy to see you find another one. Feel me?" He leans back slightly to look at me and amid bittersweet tears, I offer him a shaky smile. "Now, get cleaned up and let's figure out a plan. I'll wake Bruce and get us on the road."

"Already done," Jarrett interjects. "He's getting up now. Lincoln, here we come! Morning, lady." He holds open his arms for me, which again, I fall into wholeheartedly. "Just a rough patch, don't worry. We'll get it all fixed." He kisses my forehead and releases me, flicking my ear.

"I love you both so much." I glance between them. "I couldn't do it without you. I don't say it near enough, but thank you."

"Oh my God, Whistle Britches, you've turned our girl soft!" Rhett teases Cannon, who turns, a grin in his eyes, but a mask of determination over his face.

"*My* girl." He winks, focusing on me but a moment before turning back to breakfast.

"Did ya'll—"

"You're a shit whisperer, Jarrett, and mind your own fucking business." Cannon shuts him down, never looking away from the food.

"Andddd I think I'll go shower now," I announce dramatically. "Have fun, boys."

# CHAPTER eighteen

The trip is eight hours and the show's in twelve, so of course we stop for a leg stretch; to hell with being early for once. I'm not gonna bitch though, 'cause honestly, Jarrett's been on the phone with Vanessa the entire last three hours and I'm ready to stab out my own eardrums. Twice.

All four boys head for the door the second we stop, shoving and pushing jovially—Conner winning, tossing them out of his way like rag dolls. #teambro

Thinking it'll be nice to join them, a little fresh air a bonus, because one of them is hella gaseous today and not fessing up, I go hunt for some shoes.

I know no one will ever believe me, that'd be way too convenient, but I swear my mistake is innocent, at least at first. Digging under and around the bunks, then table, a phone dings and my heart leaps in my chest, my only thought that it's Will getting back to me.

ONLY. CONNER. Which is why it doesn't instantly occur to me that Will never texts, or that I'd grabbed Cannon's phone—until it's too late. From the second my eyes catch the name on the text, setting the phone down and backing away, minding my own business and his privacy is no longer an option.

**Ruthie: I see your phone is active again, about time my love. I'm sorry for our fight, not telling you,**

kicking you out. Cannon, I was angry and wrong. Please come home.

Cannon: I'm sorry too, that things didn't work out and things got ugly. I'd like to remain cordial.

Ruthie: Cordial?! Cannon, we're getting married.

Cannon: On what planet? You got a tubal without even talking to me. I want kids, a family. You don't and you think it's okay to decide that for me. You left me stranded in the middle of nowhere! How do you even have the nerve to contact me?

Ruthie: I'm sorry, okay? We can work everything out when you get home. I'm afraid for you, sweetheart. The band of misfits you somehow found are dangerous. I mean, look at them.

Cannon: You have no idea what you're talking about. Ruthie, please move on and leave me alone. I'll be by to get my stuff when we get near there, and I hope that transaction can be done with at least the semblance of two people who once cared about each other.

Ruthie: Is this about sex? Are you fucking that dykey lead singer? I forgive you, and I'm sorry I was cold the last few months, but I had to make sure there were no accidents before the procedure. It'll be hotter now.

Cannon: Quit calling. I'm not going to answer. I don't care that you hadn't touched me in MONTHS. I don't care that you're jealous. I'm done. Leave me alone.

Ruthie: THIS IS WHO YOU'RE GALAVANTING WITH. People wind up retarded or dead when they know that girl. I refuse to let her hurt you.

And then she sent a picture of one of the many news articles, which basically outlined everything I'd already told him with a few minute details I hadn't thought to mention.

Tunnel. Rock. Again.

It never fails.

SE Hall

"Elizabeth, what's wrong? Why are you crying?" *Shit*, totally overlooked the fact that my uncle was still on the bus.

I'm not sure why I'm crying. My fucking face just leaks these days. She didn't tell him anything I hadn't, but it's still embarrassing and shameful. Is this how it'll always be—friends and family he's know far longer than me, opinions he's had more time to value, reminding him what a disgraceful, risky choice I am? Eventually, he'll *have* to listen, fed up with the onslaught. Can I really saddle him with my bullshit?

"Nothing, just cramps." I turn around with an overdone smile and discreetly hide the phone behind my back all in one motion.

"Oh, um," he starts backing up, hands up in front of him, "well, do you need, or..." He looks at the door anxiously, his escape so close yet so far away. "Maybe I'll give you some privacy."

"That'd be great, thanks." Never fails—say period, tampon, or cramps and men run like you asked them to take a look at things down there. Except for Jarrett, who's oddly fascinated by periods, which we've discussed *way* too many times.

The good news is, dealing with my uncle gave me enough time to calm down and manage to mix some rational in with my crazy. Alone again, and since I've already snooped well beyond deniability, I sit down and read the whole conversation again.

With a second swipe at it, through saner eyes, I'm actually feeling better. Cannon said nothing "wrong." In fact, he reinforced every single thing he's ever told me—even when I wasn't looking—I *can* trust him, and pretty much already there before, it's infinitely solidified now.

I trust him, I want him, us.

I love him, I think. What I feel for him is definitely different than anything I've ever felt before—it's not what I feel for my brother, or for Jarrett, or even Rhett, who I've

192

actually *slept with.* Is this really insta-love? Is this the *Pretty Woman* thing? What did he say it was for us? Pretty Instinct?

I love him. I'm sure of it. This is it. He's it. The man I miss most when he's gone the least amount of time. The first one I want to see in the morning and last at night. If I think it's funny, he either said it, or will laugh with me. And sad, hurt, scared, unsure...that's when I long for him most.

And let them talk, drag my name through the mud, I *believe* in Cannon, he's more than man enough to tell them to fuck right off, he knows the truth.

Differently, of course, but as strong and unfailing, I love him as much as I love any other—a whopping four—person in the world.

I almost wanna run and scream it into his mouth right this minute, but...baby steps. No sense becoming a completely unrecognizable, romanticizing, gushing, cheesy idiot all at once.

I'm grinning like a fool when my phone sounds off, *knowing* things will somehow be all right. Optimism—unfamiliar yet welcomed excitedly.

"Hey, Will," I answer. "What'd you figure out?"

"Wellllll." His nervous cringing is tangible through the phone. "Liz, you have to let Conner go with him. If you refuse, your father could have you found in contempt, and that may carry jail time, or worse, a reversal of your primary custody over Conner. And because you're somewhat...well, because your father was concerned you might try something, he's already filed to have the two weeks start immediately and yours and Conner's names and passports flagged. You won't get a flight, Liz. I'm afraid you have no choice but to cooperate."

It's important that I stay calm, no inflection in my voice, no red flags waving, deep breath. "I understand. Give me a little while to think and talk to Conner and see how soon I can get back to Ohio. I'll call you back in a few hours."

"Liz, please," he pleads. "I know, okay? I understand. But if you go vigilante on this one, you will make things so much worse than merely a two week trip. I'm speaking as a longtime family friend here. I'm begging you to think your next moves through very carefully."

"Thank you, Will, I appreciate it. I'll talk to you in a bit, not long, I promise." I hang up, needing that fresh air worse than ever.

I'm going to take a cue from the best—I'm gonna take a walk and make a list, pros and cons, acceptable and not, counter-offers and compromises. Peeking out the door, I survey the situation, all of them preoccupied, either playing football or...rolling around on the ground together in a heap of man love. Bruce is filming them with his phone, back to me, so I hurry around the front end of the bus and take off. Stealthy as a giant flashing arrow with bells and whistles, I make it along the side of the bus, ready to make a mad dash behind the line of trees ahead, when I'm viciously denied by a large, sweaty, shirtless Adonis sporting an angry scowl.

"A lil' witchy, a tad bitchy, and five feet of beautiful Siren, you are. Sneaky, not so much. Where ya headed, hot stuff?" He widens his stance, effectively blocking my getaway, and smirks down at me smugly. "Oh, P.S., I'd ask how your cramps are, because I care, but great news, you're still eleven days out on your period."

What the hell is with the guys in my life and periods? NOT. NORMAL.

"*How* do you possibly know that, Creepy McWeirdasfuck? You need to stay away from Jarrett."

He leans in to me, his sweat an intoxicating, virile fragrance just as I suspected, and says huskily in my ear, "Fun fact, when you leave your birth control pills open on the communal bathroom counter and throw in some simple math, we all know when to prepare ourselves for LMS."

"Lizzie Menstrual Syndrome?" I take a wild guess and he nods. "Clever. *Anyway*, I needed some time to think, sort some stuff out, so I was taking a walk."

"Want some company?"

I give him the nicest declining smile I have. "I kinda wanted to be alone."

"No problem," he agrees easily. "Don't get too far though, okay? I've got my Lizzie tracking skills honed to an intricate science, but," he glances around, "I don't know where we are. We need to get back on the road soon, too."

"Understood." I make to the left, instantly floating backwards mid-air, my feet off the ground, one arm around my waist pinning my back against his front.

"Kiss me," he murmurs along my neck, moving my hair out of his way. "As soon as I make it up to your mouth." He begins to kiss, suck, and lick, with a few teasing nips, his way up my neck, using one hand to turn my head when he's reached my mouth. "Now, kiss me."

I do, squirming and twisting around, knowing he won't drop me until I'm facing him. "I love your mouth," I moan, nibbling his bottom lip, pulling it out then running my tongue along the inside of it. His body shudders against mine as a deep, feral growl rumbles from his chest, his hands sliding down along my sides to find and firmly squeeze my ass.

"You sure you don't want company?" he pants, pressing his hardness into my stomach.

"I said I needed to *clear* my head. The exact opposite of that happens when you're near me. But," I take my turn tasting along his neck, ending the trail with a gentle bite to his earlobe, "I will take a rain check."

"Uhh," he half groans, half pouts, setting me on my feet after one more hard, quick squeeze to my butt. "Okay, be safe and hurry up."

I salute and head off quickly, before he can distract me again. I can feel him still standing in the exact spot I left him, watching my retreat like a horny hawk. Sure enough, I toss a flirty glance back over my shoulder, and there he is, covering his crotch modestly with both hands, grinning at me.

I don't go far, I know what has to be done. Bottom line, I don't want to go to jail, delivering Conner straight into my father's hands. And I don't want to lose custody, which would yield the same result. Nor do I own a private jet or airport, so I can't get far enough away, fast enough, so that he wouldn't intercept us, thus revisiting the jail drawback.

So, first, I'm gonna talk to Conner, see what *he* wants, and then, I taste vomit just thinking it, I'm gonna talk to my father, mano y dickhead.

"I'm back." I climb on board, a little sweaty and winded. "We ready?"

"As ever, take a seat and I'll get us moving," Bruce says and heads to the wheel.

I go straight to the source, purposely avoiding the three sets of curious eyes cued in on me. "Hey, Bubs," I slide in beside him on the bench, "can I help you with your puzzle?"

"You gotta do the hard work too, Sister, not only corners," he warns, his tongue poking out in concentration.

"Yes, sir." I snicker, giving him a quick hug. "Con, I'm gonna talk to you about some stuff, and you just answer whatever you feel first, okay? You don't even have to stop doing your puzzle."

Radio silence.

"Conner, okay?"

"Okayyy," he does his inconvenienced drawl, "that's what I was doing what you said. My puzzle."

Ahh, my adorable little smartass. And all three spectators are doing a terrible job of hiding their laughter.

"Conner, Dad wants you to go stay with him."

"Okay."

"He wants it to be for a while, Bubs. Fourteen days. That will be the longest you've ever stayed."

"Nu-uh. I used to stay there my whole life, with you too."

"Not as kids, Conner, Mom was there then. He wants you to stay that long right now. But not in the house, he wants to take you on a vacation, to Hawaii."

His head pops right up at that, eyes bright, glowing even, as he starts clapping loudly. "I vote yes! Will you watch my fish?"

I'm not even sure if he knows what Hawaii is or if he understands how long two weeks is, but I guess my goal shouldn't be to talk him *out* of it. "Yes, I will watch your fish. And I'll call you every single day, Bubs, but I won't be right back to get you. You'll have a ride on a plane two times, *then* I'll come get you."

"You will miss me very much, Bethy."

"Yes." That comes out a garbled, choked back sob, so I stop and try again, about the time I feel the support of *his* hand on my shoulder, which I reach up and cover with my own. "Conner, there's something else. Dad is gonna have a new wife. And she has kids. They'll all be there too."

"Laura," he says, looking at his puzzle. "Her kids are little though, little as you."'

My hold on Cannon's hand turns quickly to a vice grip. "You've met Laura? And her kids?" I ask, every effort to taper my voice that wants to scream.

"All the time, silly. She's nice and pretty."

I look over to Rhett, then Jarrett. Neither of them have moved a muscle or made a peep since Conner said he wanted to go, taking all this in alongside me, much like they've done our whole lives. I know they're going through the same range of emotions I am, living it firsthand with me.

Rhett must sense the end of my road, that I have no idea what more to say, so he comes to sit across from Conner.

"Con, look at me buddy." Conner does so instantly and Rhett gives him a reassuring smile. "Do you like Laura and her kids?"

"Yes, a lot."

"And they're nice to you?"

"Very, *very* nice. Why?"

Rhett chuckles and holds up his hands in surrender. "Just wondering. And your dad, Conner, is your dad nice to you?"

I stiffen, Cannon squeezing my shoulder.

"Yes, but not nice as Alma and Laura. He screams in his phone and slams the door, but then he says he's sorry and plays *Monopoly* with us. I am the bomb. I always, always win."

*My father apologizes and plays Monopoly? Since fucking when?*

Since he's been luring in Laura, that's when.

I look up and instantly get angry at the pity in Rhett's eyes. I don't need goddamn fake ass family game nights—my family isn't all here, on this Earth—kinda impossible. If I even liked *Monopoly*, which I don't.

"Bubs," I touch his arm so he'll focus on me, "do you want me to call your dad and tell him you'll go?"

"Yes."

"On a long trip with—"

"Yes."

"Him and Laura and her kids?"

"Yessss!" he yells. "Want me to get you a present, Sister?"

"Sure." I stand, *daring* the sniffle I can feel to make a sound lest I kick its ass. "Okay Bubs, I'll go call him."

I reach back without looking for Cannon's hand and instantly he takes it, saying nothing as I pull him into Conner's bedroom with me. He shuts the door as I get situated on the bed, then he joins me, wrapping me in his arms, rocking us back and forth in soothing rhythm as he kisses my head.

# CHAPTER nineteen

"Tell me something you *need*, something that makes you feel weak to admit."

"Approval." His sigh brushes warmly along the back of my neck. "Even if I'm hell bent on an idea or plan, I feel better about it if my parents, my sister, you," he nuzzles further into me, "approve. It's actually scary in a way, being reliant on what other people may think. Luckily, it only applies to a select few for me. The rest can kiss my ass." He laughs. "Why do you ask?"

I turn to him, laying my cheek against his chest while I fiddle with the sleeve of his t-shirt. "I need you here, with me, while I call my father. But I've always done it alone before, so I feel stupid, weak. Now that I know," brave inhale, "how much easier things are when I have you, I don't want to go back." A frustrated, embarrassed howl escapes me as I try to escape his hold, to run and hide from vulnerable honesty, but he's faster. I'm instantly pinned to the bed, flat on my back, a heavy breathing Cannon looming over me.

"Love when my Lizzie comes out," he growls, something sinister yet tender flashing in his darkening brown eyes before he dips to my neck. "Gonna be right here," he drags his tongue up to my ear, tracing the outside with its pointed tip, "nowhere I'd rather be. But I sense you're wound a little tight, maybe you should release some tension first, on me," he teases, his voice a sultry, deep taunt.

"Come here," I whisper, luring him to my mouth with only my request, since he has my hands captured.

"What is it, beauty?" he asks against my lips.

Slowly, I outline his plump mouth with my tongue, looking him dead in the eyes. "I'm not gonna get busy on my brother's bed, Horny Henderson. Down boy." I laugh, declining both him and the pulsing erection poking me.

"I am gonna love making you pay for that, Siren." He nips at my chin and rolls off me, both of us then sitting up.

I'm ready to make the call, my spirit floating adrift on Cannon; nothing or no one can bring me down. I press my father's number, on speaker, holding Cannon's silent, supportive gaze as it rings.

"Elizabeth," he answers in his ever dignified voice.

"Richard," I respond as stoically, using his first name for perhaps the first time ever.

"His name is actually *Dick*?" Cannon sorta mouths, more whispers, with wide, laughing eyes.

I nod and slap a hand over my giggle.

"Elizabeth, I assume you had a reason for calling?" *Ugh*, he's still there.

"Yes." I clear my throat and reaffirm my confident posture. "I understand you've got a new family of *Monopoly* connoisseurs and want Conner to partake in two weeks of *Leave It to Beaver* Hawaiian bliss with you?" I couldn't have summed up every resentment better if I tried. Even my sophisticatedly bitter tone was perfection.

His sharp, hissing inhale is audible over the line, as tangible as Cannon's flinch beside me. "Elizabeth," he drones, something weird, unknown happening in his voice, "honey, I think it's high time you and I had a sit down."

I barely have the wits about me to pull the phone away from me and stare at it, double checking I have the right number. Who the fuck is this "honey" of which he blathers? "Richard, if you're high right now, I can call back."

"And she bites," he mumbles. "I don't have a new family, Elizabeth, I have *more* family. All of whom would be delighted to get to know you, along with your brother. Would you like to join us on the trip? Anytime? Dinner, perhaps?"

"I know what you're doing!" I scream, my hand shaking so badly that Cannon peels the phone from me one clenched finger at a time and holds it, his free hand rubbing up and down my back. "You need your campaign banner picture, that's all! Speaking of pictures, did you throw mine against the wall, when mom caught you with some whore?"

Fabulous—I lost my temper and showed my hand.

"I probably did. I won't claim to be a good husband, Elizabeth. I was unfaithful, many times, and I will forever be sorry. And I was a shameful father, absent and emotionally distant. For that, I'm even sorrier. But the other *ideas*, the resentments you harbor? They're unfounded, and frankly, far crueler than my shortcomings."

"You're a fucking demon! You hurt Conner, tried to kill him, ruined his life, *and* drove my mother to suicide! On what planet is my hatred worse than that?"

I flinch, hearing the door bang open from behind me, and snap my mouth closed. When I dare turn my head, I meet the frightened, worried eyes of Conner, Rhett, and Jarrett, all huddled in the doorway, Cannon doing his best to reassure and shoo them away.

"Did my son just hear that outburst?"

Cannon takes it off speaker and hands me the phone, a look of pity and disappointment on his face.

"Let's go." He ushers the others out and pulls the door closed, leaving me in shameful isolation. I can't mourn the loss; I'd forced his attention to bigger *needs*.

"Yes," I croak, "but he's gone now."

"Elizabeth, all I've done, or haven't done, right or wrong, I have *never* laid a hand on your brother."

"THEN WHO DID??"

He's back. The lock clicks seconds before I'm wrapped up from all sides, his strong arms, long legs, broad chest each doing their part to protect me. "In for me," he whispers, "come on, big one in for me."

"Conner? Son?"

"No sir, not Conner. She needs a minute," Cannon tells him. "Now out for me, love," he once again says softly, only to me.

"Rhett? Is she all right?"

"I'm sorry I left, had to settle Conner. But I'm back," he kisses below my ear. "I'm here."

I heave in and out, my breathing labored with anger, yes, but also fear—have I gone from irrationally self-sufficient to helplessly reliant on Cannon? Fuck that. "Richard," I compose myself, "are you going to answer me?"

"No, Elizabeth, I'm not. Never let it be said that I speak out of turn."

I saw that cop-out, talk out the side of your mouth bullshit coming before I was done asking the question. I roll my eyes, exhausted, as I always find myself talking to him. "Conner would like to go with you. We're in Nebraska. You can come get him, *you*, with Alma, or I'll bring him to you when I can. And Richard? If one hair on his head is out of place, or you don't bring him back to me on time, there'll be no safe place for you."

Cannon nudges me, a disapproving frown and shake of his head.

"When will you be back in Ohio?" he asks with an inconvenienced huff.

"When's your trip?"

"We're supposed to leave Tuesday."

Five days from now, three of which we have gigs, doable... "Probably not gonna happen," I tut back, my inner brat fist pumping. *Inner.* Lord knows Cannon would chastise me with that scowly brow of his if I actually did it.

"Where in Nebraska?"

"Lincoln."

"I'll head out as soon as I can. Please answer your phone, Elizabeth. I'll need your exact location when I get there."

I can hardly speak past my utter astonishment. "You're actually gonna come get him, all by yourself?"

"No, per your instructions, Alma will be accompanying me. If it's all right with you, I could bring Laura as well. Perhaps you'd like to meet her?"

"Hell no, I don't want to meet your f—"

"We'll wait for your call, sir. See *you and Alma* soon," Cannon interrupts me, hitting "end call" the second he finishes the sentence.

I'm about to give him another *Pretty Woman* lesson—the "I saw when" part! "What the hell do you think you're doing?" I say, my voice as scathing as I can manage, scooting away from him.

He demolishes that space in one fell swoop, plastering his body to mine, bracketing me in at my sides. "I'm stopping the incredibly sad display of you making an ass of yourself. I get that you're angry, and resentful, and scared," he glides his knuckles down my cheek, "and all that's understandable. But you're not hateful and venomous, so stop trying so hard to act like it. And," he lays his fingers across my lips to hush my retort, "I will gladly eat your pussy and pay your bills, so I *do* get a say." He winks.

I couldn't now tell you why I was mad at him only five seconds ago if my life truly depended on it. His scandalous turning of my back on me have a direct, searing link to the currently throbbing spot between my legs. I lick my lips, searching for how to respond, when he leans in and wets them for me. "You like the thought of that, don't ya?" he hums, a deep, delicious sound.

I must nod, or maybe I answered, who knows...certainly not lust-crazed me, because he laughs softly and kisses me. "Me too, angel, me too. Soon, I promise

204

you, very soon I will cherish every single part of you with every single part of me."

My gulp echoes in the room, giving away my nervousness. The only thing I'm certain of is that my three-minute tryst with Rhett years ago did *not* prepare me for Cannon Blackwell, and I will surely disappoint him. "Let's, uh," I squirm back from him, "let's go tell Conner and get ready for tonight's show."

"Hey," he latches onto my wrist, halting my exit, "what just happened?"

"Nothing," I say to the door rather than him.

"Nooo, it was definitely something. I look forward to coercing it out of you."

The talk with Conner went...loud. He screamed and jumped around, absolutely thrilled, at which I plastered on a grin.

I feel like Sybil, one version of myself relieved and truly happy to have such obvious reassurance that he enjoys being with our father, completely unafraid, one of the other Lizzies worried sick and still not trusting the sperm-donating asshole any farther than I could bury him in the ground, and yet another one of my personalities confused and kinda jealous...without a father to love.

I've been hiding in the bathroom long enough under the guise of "getting ready," so I suck it up, squashing all Lizzies, and join everyone in the common area.

"This cannot possibly be the right place. I think I spotted Boo Radley on a porch back there," Jarrett glances out the window, skeptic frown.

"Just because his name was Boo doesn't mean he was scary," Cannon comments with a chuckle. "Quite the opposite, in fact. And they lived in a nice neighborhood."

I catch Cannon's eye and give him a flirty smile; by now I'd be more surprised if he *hadn't* read my all-time favorite book. I've also quit tracking "points." He wins the whole Lizzie enchilada—if he wants it.

"Bubs, you don't need your bag tonight. Dad won't be here yet; it's a long drive from Ohio. How about you put it back in your room?"

Even though I just finished analyzing myself and told all the voices in my head to shut the hell up, one observation and all the questions are back full-force. Cannon's taught me so much about instinct and intuition, opened my eyes to optimism and daring to dream, that I simply can't keep it turned off. So, as I look at Conner, clutching that bag like a life vest, giddy with anticipation at our father's arrival...I wonder.

Admittedly, I consider Conner my ace "people reader," my gauge of people's auras that somehow Bubs always sees. He doesn't hate our father, not even a little bit, and he's far from afraid to be with him—that's trying to tell me something, an option I've been resistant to for years, now an inkling that I need to follow. I have to put my finger on this lest it drive me insane.

"You said he was coming," Conner pouts, puffing out his bottom lip.

"He is, just not tonight. We'll do the show, go to bed, and maybe late tomorrow, he'll be here."

Bruce finally manipulates the huge bus into the back parking lot of the venue. After a quick glance out the window, I find myself agreeing with Jarrett—it gives off a serious heebie jeebie vibe. "This is it," Bruce says and emerges from the cab, volleying his gaze between Conner, gloomy mood palpable, and the rest of us. "Con, what's wrong?"

"I'm not getting off this bus 'cause my Dad can find me here." He crosses his arms on top of the duffle in his lap. "Sister told him too long cause she screamed at him. I heard her."

"Conner, look at me." I'm in front of him in a flash, on my own knees, my hands on his. "I swear to you, Bubs, I didn't tell him wrong. I know you're excited to go, and I want you to have fun. I promise, I didn't tell him too long. Con?"

"Did she, Cannon?" he asks *him*, needing verification of my word. That's *never* happened and it hurts worse than anything I can remember.

"Conner, has your sister ever lied to you before?" Cannon challenges him kindly.

"No," he mumbles.

"So why would she lie to you now, bud?"

"Cause she hates my dad."

"She loves you, very much. She wouldn't lie to you."

I wipe my tears, grateful for Cannon's support but crushed all the same. The other three look on in silence, the tension in the air almost as thick as the lump in my throat. "Time to go," I stand and mutter, pulling down my skirt that'd ridden up. "Bruce, can you stay on the bus with Conner?"

He answers only with an affirmative jerk of his head and I grab my stuff, heading to the door.

"See you after, Bubs, love you."

His lack of reply twists the knife in my gut deeper.

# CHAPTER twenty

"I'm sorry, Sister." His apologetic, sweet little face pops into my bunk, waking me.

"No worries, Bubs." I push the covers back—obviously time to get up. "Wanna do something just me and you today, before you leave?"

"Yes, I do. Can we eat Cannon's pancakes before we go ice skating?"

I laugh; guess I'm going ice skating after some delicious pancakes I now smell. "Sure we can. Lemme get up and run to the bathroom. Meet ya there."

"Everyone, we're going ice skating!" he screams and I cringe—needing coffee urgently *and* I wanted it to be just him and me. He's about to leave me for *two weeks*, eons longer than we've been apart for close to a decade. My heart aches just thinking about it. I miss him already.

"I got a cab for you guys in thirty minutes, so eat up." Cannon winks at me as I sit down and pushes my plate in front of me. "So, a buddy of mine tracked me down. Wants to know if we can fit in a stop at his bar when we pass through? He just opened it, needs promo or whatever." He pops his shoulders and pours me a coffee. "Told him I'd ask."

I'm still stuck at "we pass through." That didn't sound like plans to jump ship to me. Swallowing down pancakes and anxious hope, I muster up aloofness. "He in Indiana? Whereabouts?"

"Yeah, in Brownsberg, right by my hometown. I figure we'll be there by Monday night. We could do it then, or Tuesday, if we don't have anything else booked. Might help him bring in business. He's a good friend, it'd be cool to be able to help him out."

"I'm a good friend," Bubs interjects through a mouthful of pancakes.

"You sure are." Cannon gives him a fist bump, which Conner "blows up" as animatedly as possible, pieces of breakfast now flying out his mouth.

"We're open Monday or Tuesday!" Rhett yells from his bunk.

Cannon's gaze drops down as he kneads the back of his neck with one hand, rubbing nervously at his bare chest—I have long-since 100% decided never to buy him a shirt—with the other. "Can we do both nights? Don't you have to get home to Ohio?"

"For what?" I ask. "Conner'll be gone."

"I don't know, your house, pets, whatever. Don't wanna pit stop?" His brow creases more by the second, clearly perplexed.

"No home, no pets—"

"Hey! We got fish!" Conner reminds me.

"Oh yeah," I chuckle, "the fish. Okay, so just no home."

"You don't have a 'home base,' an apartment, nothing?"

Why is this so bothersome to him? "I have a car. I keep it at my uncle's house. But no, I don't need a 'pad.' I'm on the road more than not. And if I *did* get a place, it would *not* be in Ohio."

A horn beeps outside, the cab, so I down another huge swig of coffee and hustle to go grab my stuff. "Conner, shoes! And wait for me, please."

"Will you be all right today? Sure you don't want me to go?" Cannon asks quietly from behind me, pressed up against my back.

"That's sweet, but we'll be fine. I need a day alone with Bubs before he leaves. Tell Bruce where we're at when he shows up, please."

Rushing, eyeing Conner bouncing up and down at the door, I think I grab everything and head out right behind him, yelling bye to everyone.

"Ice skating place, please," Conner tells the driver with sheer glee in his voice.

Bubs is a natural, whizzing around the rink like a pro. I, on the other hand, am watching from a booth in the concession stand, sitting discreetly on a bag of ice, which is no different than my many failed attempts at skating—my ass is magnetically attracted to the ice.

He waves frantically each time he goes by and when I drag out my phone to snap some pictures, I see missed texts from Cannon.

**HH: Bruce confirmed we're free, I booked Mon + Tues at Sark Pit.**

**HH: Get your laughs out now—his last name is Sark...he thinks it's clever, like Shark Pit**

**HH: Where are we headed after that?**

"Sister!" Conner bellows, sending me into action, tapping buttons like a madwoman to snap multiple pictures.

"I got your picture, Bubs, great job!" I yell back, watching him for a minute. It's no surprise he's doing great—like riding a bike—Conner always had athletic prowess. Seeing he's fine, I return to my texts.

**HH: No apt, huh? Do you sleep on bus during break? Where would you get a place if u were gonna? Indiana is beautiful country.**

That was the last one. He could have asked Bruce, since he's there with him, where we went next. I think he sent it to me to make it clear—he's staying onboard, *with me*, thus the "we."

Feeling spunky, I text him back. No, do over. I'm feeling downright Sirenesque, so I call him.

"If you're being held hostage and can't talk, beep once," he answers.

I have got to start writing some of his quirky stuff down.

"No hostage situation," I chuckle, "weirdo. What possibly made you say that?"

"You haven't answered my texts in almost two hours. I was standing outside holding up tinfoil so the aliens would abduct me and take me to you."

"Oh my God." I laugh harder, and there may have been a snort thrown in as well. "You don't believe in luck, but you believe in aliens?"

"Nah, not really. Besides, ten minutes of your sassy mouth and they'd drop you back off. So what are you guys doing? Having fun?"

"Conner's having a blast. I'm the stoked spectator with the sore ass. Not much of an ice skater, it would seem. Oh Lord, hold on," I cover the phone and pull it away from my mouth. "Bubs!" He looks at me and I shake my head no. "He's too little, Conner, no spinning him!" I wait, making sure he listens, then get back to Cannon. "He's got five little boys huddled around him, waiting for their turn to be spun around. Surely their mothers," I glance around, looking for them, "know that's a bad idea."

"They wearing helmets and knee pads?"

"No."

SE Hall

"Then yeah, stop him." He laughs heartily. "When ya'll coming back? Jarrett's in the midst of a Vanessa telethon and Rhett's still in bed. I'm bored as hell."

"Feel free to clean," I joke.

"Already did—spotless. I was thinking about using your laptop to look for an apartment if you don't mind?"

"I don't mind at all, you know that. Just don't delete my porn. Wait, that's no longer funny; don't *add* any porn."

"That was all Jarrett, I swear."

"Uh huh, whatever, perv." I snicker. I have no doubt whatsoever that Jarrett was indeed the mastermind of that little escapade. He always is.

"So, where should I apartment hunt?" His question is asked in a not quite seductive, but infinitely suggestive, tone.

"Why, oh, hang on." I check the screen. "Cannon, it's Conner's dad. Lemme call you back." I quickly switch over, now paranoid of messing up Bubs' plans. "Hello?"

"Elizabeth, it's your d—it's uh, Richard," he says.

"Yeah, I know. Where are you?"

"About two hours out." He either drove all night or started very early, again shocking the shit outta me. "Where should I go exactly?"

I direct him accordingly, hanging up to go wrangle in Conner, which isn't hard since he's ecstatic when I tell him about the call.

A short cab ride later and we're back at the bus, Conner flying up the steps and crashing through the door when Bruce opens it.

"Whoa, slow down, bud," Bruce says. "Where's the fire?"

"My dad is almost here! I gotta get my bag!" He sails past him toward his room.

"How long?" he asks me solemnly.

212

"Less than two hours," I mutter, slumping down on the bench seat. "Where're the boys?"

"Went to grab something to eat; hoping they hurry. I'm gonna disappear until your father does, for your and Conner's sake. I know my limits and you kids don't need an ugly scene."

"Is he here?" Conner wails, running back in, bag banging into all in his path.

"Not yet, Bubs, little longer," I giggle at him. "Give Uncle Bruce a hug bye, he's gotta go do some stuff and it'll be a while before you see him again." I end on a slightly hoarse note, melancholy creeping in.

Conner swallows him up in a hug and I catch my uncle's slight flinch. I hear ya; maybe he'll pop your back and actually make it feel better instead of just squishing the life out of you.

Bruce takes off and the boys show back up about thirty minutes later, to find what must resemble a circus sideshow. Conner's bouncing off the walls, quite literally, in uncontainable excitement and I'm a coiled up, ready to hiss, ball of anxiety.

"You probably won't believe me, but I missed the hell out of you," Cannon greets, hugging me to him.

"Yeah, right," I scoff, fighting off his embrace. "And don't try the 'breathe in' thing, it won't work. Go," I gasp as a tear falls and duck my head, "go say bye to Conner."

"Precious girl," he pities me, pissing me off further, "let's go with them, fuck it! I don't want you miserable. Let's go to Hawaii, you can watch Conner and I'll watch you." He caresses my temple with his warm, soft lips, talking quietly to me. "If it'll make you feel better, I'm in."

"Liz, a little help here!" Rhett hollers from the back, giving me the excuse I need to walk away from this asinine, no-win conversation.

"Wha— Bubs, what are you doing?"

SE Hall

"Taking my fish," he states, looking at me like I have two heads as he attempts a stealthy slide of the net behind his back. "Dad likes fish. He's got a big tank!"

"I know, Con, but um…" Well shit, what do I say here? "I'll miss 'em if you take them. It'll be my piece of you while you're gone." Not a lie, the last part anyway.

He's gnawing on his lip, serious debate evident in his shuffling feet and flittering eyes. "Okay, Bethy, but do good taking care of them."

My chuckle holds the hint of tears, which I force back. "I promise."

The knock from the front and my back into the edge of the bedroom door—ou-motherfucking-ch—both happen simultaneously, Conner's body slamming me harshly aside as he barrels to answer it.

"Shit," Rhett rushes to me, "you all right?" He helps me get my footing and peeks around me, lifting up my shirt in the back. "No blood, but you'll feel it tomorrow."

"Lizzie, your—" Cannon stops, either panicked or confused why Rhett's lifting my shirt—no clear call. "What's…uh, can I help with something?"

"Conner slammed her into the door when he ran by, hurt her back," Rhett explains.

"Lemme see." He pushes Rhett's hand out of the way to survey it himself. "You need an ice pack, love?" he asks against my skin, where he kisses the, I'm assuming, either red or already black and blue spot.

"I'm fine, let's get out there before he just takes him," I grumble, walking past them both.

"Elizabeth," my father, standing *in my bus*, greets me.

I ignore him and move straight to hug Alma, another mystery—wonderful person—who for some reason stays with him. "Alma," I hug her, tearing up despite myself, "how are you?"

214

"My precious Elizabeth," she coos, squeezing me back, ouch again. "How are you, my darling girl? So beautiful." She leans back to pet my hair the same way she used to and I have to suppress a sigh.

"I'm fine. Miss you though. Are you joining them in Hawaii?" I shoot straight, locking on my father from the corner of my eye. Surely he knew I'd verify.

"I am." She bobs her head and does a little clap. "I can't wait! Finally a vacation." She laughs and elbows Richard in the ribs.

"Mmm," is his only response. "I said hello to the Foster boys, but I don't believe I've met the young man standing guard behind you, daughter. Care to do the introductions?"

"I do care, actually. You don't—"

"Cannon Blackwell." He steps around me and offers his hand, but not without shooting me that "shame on you" look of his. Gonna have to work on that, we are indeed.

"Nice to meet you. Richard Carmichael. And this is Alma. She's been with us since Conner was in diapers."

"Pleasure." Cannon smiles and takes her hand—and my sixty-year-old once-nanny blushes.

"I am ready!" Conner loudly demands back everyone's attention. "Hug me, Sister, we're outta here."

If I don't, does that mean he won't really leave? I dismiss the silly thought and turn, wrapping myself around my brother. "I'll miss you so much, Con. Please call me and send me pictures, okay? Stay close to the others and wear a life jacket if you swim and tell Alma if you need anything, and—"

"Bethy, I know!" he huffs good-naturedly. "I got my Bubcuff on, don't worry. But don't sing my song 'til I get back, though, 'cause it's mine. And don't kill my fish."

"Got it." I discretely sniffle and wipe my nose on his shirt—couldn't be helped. "I love you more than anything in the whole world, Conner. Come back safe to me, soon."

"Love you more, Sister." He kisses all over my face, one last squeeze, then he's bouncing off the bus. "Bye, Cannon!" he yells, meeting up with Rhett and Jarrett, who'd long ago slinked past the reunion and been waiting outside.

"Give me a hug, Elizabeth, I need to hurry after him." Alma laughs, holding open her arms. "He will be fine, I give you my word," she whispers in my ear. "I'm so proud of the woman you've become. Please do some living for you."

I can only nod, soaking up the comfort of the hug that I've missed for too long. I feel so much better hearing from her mouth that she's going and will take care of Bubs. *Her*—I trust.

"I best go follow him. Nice to meet you, Cannon." She waves, leaving the three of us alone.

"Here's all the information on where we'll be staying, flights and times, contact numbers." He extends a file folder to me as if this is all a business transaction. "I appreciate you allowing this peacefully, and I give you my word, Elizabeth, that he will be well cared for and have a wonderful time."

Cannon's hand finds my shoulder and squeezes, letting me know he's there, and instinctively, I reach up to hold it—my father's eyes widening at the gesture.

"I meant what I said, too, about us perhaps sitting down and talking sometime. I am your father, and I do love you very much."

"Will you be saying that after the ballots are counted?" I bite out, earning a harder squeeze from Cannon.

"If I drop out of the race right now, will you join me for dinner? Explain some of that hatred?"

"No."

"I assumed as much. However, my answer is yes."

# Cannon

If I could rewind but an hour, I'd have checked all Jarrett's hiding spots and dumped the liquor. My little siren is two shots in and not taking kindly to my attempts at cutting her off, though getting shitfaced *after* the gig seems like the better plan.

In fact, if she doesn't come out of the bathroom in the next five minutes, I'll have no choice but to assume she passed out while getting ready and go in after her.

I know she misses Conner; hell, I miss him, too, and it's only been a few hours, but she can't spend two weeks in paranoid, self-destruct mode. I won't let her. I'll give her space, room to analyze, brew and boss all she wants…but other times, when she may not even realize it's what she really needs, I'll take her to the place where she doesn't have to think, decide, solve—that will be *my* job.

"You got her?" Jarrett asks me, hitching his bass up higher on his back, kit bag in hand. "We're gonna head on over."

"Yeah, we'll be right behind ya."

Rhett hesitates, considering me with a heavy, assessing stare, before finally shaking his head slightly, a charitable grin taking over. "Good luck. She worships her brother. She might as well have lost her arms and legs—that's what it feels like to her right now. You're either man enough to handle her or not. But I'm betting on ya, Whistle Britches," he sighs, patting my shoulder, "because I love her, and *she's* betting on you too. She wants it to be you."

"I got it," I quip, though it comes out meaner than it should have. I'm glad she's always had Rhett, but his work here is done. She's mine now. Mine to love, fret over, console, and support in anything she needs, and the sooner he concedes, the smoother things will be. He can *say* he's betting on me all he wants, but I can't say as I believe him...until I do.

Jarrett graciously, subtly, coughs, drawing mine and Rhett's thoughtful scowls apart and I turn my head, the air audibly whooshed from my body.

All of a sudden, there she is, emerging from the chrysalis that is apparently the bus bathroom, pushing all other thoughts to the wayside, the intoxicating creature that she is.

"Fuck me," I manage past the barrage of emotions lumping in my throat, something not really meant to be spoken aloud.

"Not even with Rhett's dick, but thanks for asking." Jarrett slaps me on the shoulder with a chuckle. "But I hear ya. She's something, all right."

Her saunter toward me is tantalizingly, all the sexier because... I don't even know. All I know is that I couldn't look away if I tried, the mesmerizing sight of her redefining beauty. Her hair, back to a natural golden brown, is curled at the ends, pulled back from her sweet face to show off those huge, curiously vulnerable brown eyes. There's some new smoky, dick beckoning thing going on with them tonight and her lips shine a little brighter with each slink closer.

She's a short little thing, no doubt, but the black boots that *may* have a heel are as magical as they are bewilderingly mind-fucking because I swear her legs now go on for miles before sneaking under that barely there matching

218

black skirt. I already knew she had glorious breasts, but that white tank she has on is seriously toying with my chivalry on dangerous levels, and the hot pink bra underneath, obviously meant to vibrantly tease all that God used to make a man a man is working like a charm.

Lizzie Carmichael's a showstopper.

Words would undoubtedly fail me, so I crook my finger, begging her closer. Her eyes flick away briefly, then back, seeking mine out in unspoken need. The sound of the door closing confirms we're alone, the Foster boys mercifully turning tail and giving us a moment.

Her little pink tongue peeks out and glides back and forth nervously as she slowly makes her way to me and my fingers twitch in my clenched fists, begging to snag her up and never let go. But I deny them—she has to come willingly, on every level.

"Too much?" she asks in a soft whisper once she's in front of me.

I shake my head, raking my eyes across every inch of her. "You're beyond radiant. Exquisite. There's no word worthy of you, really."

"I, uh, well," her sweet heads dips only just, "tried a little harder tonight, maybe. I don't know." There it is—the tiny, vulnerable peer up at me from underneath her lashes that sends shockwaves of protective, primal instincts through me. "Felt kinda free, sassy."

That sweet pink glow spreading across her cheeks...damn. I'm gonna keep it there always, constantly reminding her she is coveted and adored. "You ready? I'm thinking ten seconds to say yes before I devour you right here."

Her delicate, shy laugh bolsters everything male about me and I growl without conscience, stepping in to her.

"Need a little nibble," I murmur, and unapologetically steal a few along her jawline, ending at her earlobe, then painfully force myself to pull away. "Let's go, gorgeous." I take her hand and intertwine our fingers, hers short and dainty, mine warm and strong, all trembling. "I'm only so strong."

The show tonight is infinitely our best. See You Next Tuesday is on point, blowing the roof off the place! While Lizzie sincerely misses her brother, the liberation positively radiates off her. Without having to worry where Conner's at every second, she transforms into this carefree spirit, relishing *her* time, the siren I've seen all along embracing it for herself…alive and captivating on stage tonight. Lizzie shines like her very own constellation, her voice heady and seductive, delectable little body swaying with an exotic energy that steals every set of eyes in the place. Especially mine.

I decided acting suggestively in any way on the first night Conner left might seem tacky and insensitive, but she's more than welcome to come to me. And I'm picking up what's she throwing down—long looks and subtle, sensuous brushes of her skin along mine—either I've lost my intuition or she's receptive, *ready*. So the sooner I can tear her away from this table, celebratory drinks with Rhett and Jarrett, the better. I'm anxious to see how far she takes it. No matter what path she decides tonight holds, I want her to take the path all the way to the end, give me her all of anything, even if it's just holding her (I pray all night), whispering all her stories on my chest, telling what she liked when she was a little girl, what she wants to name our children.

"I've never understood this song," she says, pointing a tipsy little finger up in the air toward the music sounding from above.

I perk an ear… "High for This," by The Weekend. I can't wait to hear her insight, constantly fascinated by our in-depth discussions on all things music…throw her shot count into the equation, and this is set to be noteworthy.

"Whaddaya mean?" I ask, tucking a strand of hair behind her ear, wanting a clear shot of that stunning face.

"Don't get me wrong, it's got a solid, unique beat, but the words?" She scrunches up her nose. "Call me crazy, but if a guy has to warn you, 'excuse me, ma'am, you're gonna want to be high to get through this'? I'm thinking warning bells don't ring any louder than that. Do not start undressing or lay yourself beside him! Run, screaming 'help me!' the entire way!"

Delighted by her mind, sarcastic and always engaged, I laugh and lean in to thieve a taste of that clever mouth. "Excellent point. You *are* a lyrics girl after all. So I'm guessing 'Informer' drives you crazy?"

"Right? What the fuck is that dude saying?" Jarrett the Eavesdropper yells. "Is he even speaking English?"

"It wouldn't matter what language it was, the natives of any country couldn't understand him. I think it *is* English, and we don't." Lizzie giggles, then stretches back in her chair, arms reaching for the sky, and yawns.

"Looks like I need to take you home," I hiss in her ear.

"Mmm," she closes her eyes and hums, the mewl throbbing in my ears louder than the music. "So ready when you are."

"Gentlemen," I stand, offering my siren a hand, "we're out."

"Heads up, I *will* be having Skype sex on the bus tonight." Jarrett consults his invisible watch. "Soon as Nessy's off work, it's on. Plug your ears, close your eyes, whatever you need to do, but it's happening. Maybe two or three times."

"I'll be plugging *that*." Rhett gestures with his head and we all turn to track his crosshairs. Cute, tiny little blonde, not bad, but my foremost thought is how much she looks like the old Lizzie. I'll give him the benefit of the doubt on this one—maybe he simply prefers blondes—unless he forces me to cure any hang ups in the form of my foot up his ass.

"Bus is all yours, boys, just sterilize. I'm bathtub and room service bound tonight." She clicks the side of her mouth. "See ya."

She leads, her grasp on my hand unyielding as she weaves us through the horde of bodies. I should probably take over and commandeer control, but damn it all if I can't pull my eyes off her ass in that skirt, salivating just imagining all the things I wanna do to it.

But not tonight...the greatest test of willpower I'll ever endure. I have to keep reminding myself—let her come to me, set the pace and limits. I can't scare her off when I only just got her...if I've really got her.

In the bustle, a hard blow into the side of my body knocks me sideways enough that my hand loses Lizzie's. I'm quick to gather my bearings, my only concern reconnecting myself to her, but it's hard to spot her, much shorter than all the others around us. "Baby!" I yell frantically, then shake my head—like she's the only *baby* in here? "Lizzie!" I scream again, louder.

Relieved, I see her little hand pop up amongst the sea and wave madly, and I instantly know it's not a good wave, she's scared. Growling, *now* a ruthless man, I shove and toss people aside like limp rags, fighting to get to that hand; the only thing I see. But when I make it there, I'm no longer relieved.

Some punk, about an inch shorter than me, but say, 20 pounds heavier, has my Siren wild-eyed and pinned against the wall. From here, I can see the pulse in her neck racing, and all I see is red, crimson, the color of blood when it first leaves a body. Yanking him by his shoulder, I pull the fucker back and spin him to face me. "I believe you may be too close to what's mine," I sneer, fists already locked and loaded at my sides.

"I didn't see your name on it," he drawls, wreaking of cheap whiskey, teetering slightly.

"You don't know my name, dumbass." I hold my hand out to my side, around him. "Come to me," I tell my frightened girl and she does so immediately, curling her hands, face and whole body into my side snugly.

"Just wanna go," she mumbles.

I snatch dude up by his collar and growl in his face. "When they're shaking and waving their hands in the air, they're scared, not into you. Try picturing your mom or sister next time, asshole." With that, I shove him back hard enough his ass finds floor and sweep Siren into my arms, cradle style, marching us the hell out of there.

# CHAPTER
## twenty-two

I confess, tonight scared the shit out of me. Before I knew what was happening, I'd lost Cannon and been trapped by a stinky, obviously too drunk to decipher right from wrong cowboy with bad teeth and a worse approach. But seconds after the fright set in, it was as quickly replaced with assurance…I knew only death would keep Cannon from finding me, and immediately.

*Safe.*

Even with masochistic Marlboro Man hovering over me, I felt an overwhelming sense of safety. The douchebag would be lucky if it was only Cannon that found me and not the rest of my cavalry.

I hated needing to be rescued (I'd always thought myself smarter than this whole damsel in distress shit), it turned me on, crazily so. As "tough" as I try to be, independent, self-sufficient, I am woman hear me roar, the thought of a strong, powerful, domineering man swooping in to claim and save me…well, judge me *after* you've experienced it for yourself.

Speaking of my beautiful barbarian, what is he up to out there? Those big feet of his clomping back and forth frantically, the clanging noises… I can't help but shiver in anticipation, pretty sure he's "setting the mood" while I enjoy my luxurious bubble bath.

I could have saved him a lot of trouble had he asked—no frills are needed, I'm beyond ready. No more lurking pitifully in angry shadows for me. I *will* move forward, into the sunlight, where Cannon waits, hand extended to capture mine.

I've been so worried about becoming "dependent" on him I cut off my nose to spite my face. Everyone depends on something, even if it's their hell-bent *independence*...the idealistic view of themselves they *cling* to; dependence by definition.

My anger, insecurities, snarky armor—those are mine, my go to safety nets I allow to define who I am and justify my hesitance to ever take a risk. But infinitely, the crutch I lean on the most is Conner. It's laughable, really. I'm so much more dependent on him than he could ever be on me. Sometimes I'm not even sure he *depends* on me or if I'm just the person he's most comfortable with. Bubs is gonna do whatever he's got planned regardless of what I'm doing. But me...I have no idea who I am when I'm not worrying about him, clueless as to where he ends and I begin.

So I'm kidding myself, I'm *already* dependent...just perhaps not on the right things. I'm still Bethy/Sister and Conner will always come first, but I'm gonna start watering the other parts of me too and see if they can't blossom.

And by water, I mean have sex with Cannon Powell Blackwell.

Silently, I observe his efforts about the room before speaking with soft conviction. "I don't need candles or music, Cannon. I only need you."

With a satisfied smirk on his face and tender honor in his eyes, he spins to face me. My heart starts thrumming in my chest as he prowls across the room to take my cheeks in his hand. "And I will only ever need you," he says softly, "but I wanted to help you relax tonight. I know it's a lot for you to—"

SE Hall

"It's not my first time." Damn there I go, talk first, think later. "I mean, it will be special because it's with you." I lean up on my tiptoes to kiss him, met with stiff lips set in a grim line. Sighing, obviously failing at my attempt of smooth recovery with no one to blame but myself, I drop back to flat feet and address the elephant that just barged in the room with us. "Why are you upset? You're not a virgin and I'm not mad."

"I meant help you relax because you're stressed out about Conner leaving. I was trying to be sensitive," he grumbles, a primitive edge resounding. "But thank you for the insight. It gives me a whole new realm of concerns."

I move to embrace him, this conversation feeling like one best had when touching, but he balks, stepping back, worry lines straining his forehead.

"This isn't what I thought tonight would be about." His stare is firm, the conviction within eliminating any doubt of his words. "But now it is, so here goes." Heady exhale. "You've never had a boyfriend or a protective older brother and no secret rendezvous; you flinched if I so much as brushed elbows with you the first two weeks. I'm just trying to figure out how I misjudged all that in my head. I admit, I would've bet my life on you being a virgin, so I don't like the two possible conclusions plaguing my mind right now."

I narrow my eyes shrewdly and prop my hands on my hips. "Which are?"

"Were," his Adam's apple bobs quickly, "were you a-assaulted?"

"No." My defensiveness instantly vanishes and I wrap my arms around his waist; this time he accepts. "Nothing like that."

"Rhett." It's not a question, and that's not my Cannon's voice. I squeeze his waist tighter and nod into his chest. "How long?" His menacing growl makes me flinch.

"Only once," I whisper.

"*How long ago?*"

226

"Years." I calculate mentally. "Almost seven. Seven years ago, one time, after my mom. I just...he was consoling me and..."

"That all? Just him, just once?"

"Yeah." I tilt my head, needing his eyes to tell me what this frightening new tone of his means. And now I see...it means he's jealous and can't stand the thought of it. "Cannon, don't be mad. It was two kids, friends, hurting. Hugging and comforting turned into curiosity, that's all."

He expels a long, tedious breath and runs a hand over his face. "Of course I'm not *mad*, that'd be asinine. I'm uncomfortable. If I was leery of your relationship with him before, the looks he gives you, his comments...now I'm, well, I'm justified."

*So not how I saw this night going.*

"No doubt, I love Rhett, always will. And he the same. But not *love*, not in a way that should bother you. In fact, he and I had a conversation clarifying the difference."

He shifts away from me, and for a fleeting second, my arms long to tug him back, but I force them not to. If he wants to have this conversation, we'll both think more clearly if we're not touching. Now he paces, scrubbing his hands manically through his hair, huffing and puffing like he's fully dilated. If it wasn't so funny, it'd be hot.

Scratch that, it's still hot.

"You 'bout done?" I tease him, perched now on the end of the bed, leaning back on my hands, brow cocked in challenge.

"Not quite. I'm gonna take a walk." He grabs his boots and heads toward the door. "I don't wanna say things I don't mean."

"You go make your spreadsheet," I tease. "I'll be waiting right here. But I want you to keep a couple things in mind." He turns back to face me, silent, receptive. "You slept with your ex-fiancé a lot more recently than seven years ago, and until just now, I'd forgotten...but I know she's blowing up your phone. I grabbed it by mistake, I swear, and literally

227

forgot about it until right now. But, you were gonna marry her, and she's still in your life. Seems more like something to worry over, wouldn't you say?"

*Ah, my stoic, strong Cannon.* Again, my eye's far too trained by the life that's been mine to not pick up on the split-second wince and pupil dilation, but he forces that chiseled jaw of his to just as swiftly lose the tick and square the broad set of shoulders I know would carry me all their days. It's one thing I respect of him most—when he says he won't get caught up in the moment and say something he doesn't mean—*that*, he means.

We both know my own question was rhetorical, and once I see he refuses to counter-engage, I continue. "Jealousy is only macho and flattering if it comes from a good place, *not* if it's really just a lack of trust. I'm not asking you to trust Rhett, but I'm demanding you trust me. You have mine, and giving the same is the only way you'll keep it." Letting that soak in, I rise and take a walk of my own, toward the bathroom, the only option of escape, then say over my shoulder, "See ya when you get back."

Just finished brushing my teeth, I turn off the water at the same time I hear the door shut.

He's back; gone fifteen minutes at most.

Even still facing the door, he knows I'm behind him—the moment I turned the corner, he froze, spine straighter, muscles flexing visibly through his t-shirt—but he says nothing, waiting.

Slow motion at its finest, he turns around, the ravenous, masculine hunger in his eyes blatant. "If you break a mirror, they say 'seven years bad luck.' A background check or tax audit both go back seven years. And did you know there's a movie called *Seven Year Itch?* That doesn't sound fun."

228

Um… "Okay?" I sputter, a bit lost.

"It *is* okay," he prowls toward me, "very okay." His right hand slides up my arm, cupping the base of my neck as his left slinks around my waist and pulls me flush against him. "Seven years is universally the 'do over' point, gone, vanquished, never happened. And," he kisses the end of my nose, "seven is a lucky number."

"I am so confused right now," I breathe, tilting my face up in invitation of more nose kisses.

He chuckles in understanding, smooching my nose once more. "I don't like the whole thing because it's him. When I look at him, which is inconveniently every damn day… Well, anyway," he smiles, not hiding the lingering discontent, "it doesn't count, so never mind."

Cannon's analytical, logical, highly intelligent, and doesn't believe in luck. This is obviously his quirky little way of accepting the fact that yes, the man across the table was my first…so whatever, I'll go with it. Not to mention, that's impressive research in fifteen minutes. God bless Google.

"Doesn't count," I coo, going to my tiptoes to wrap my arms around his neck and nip at his chin. "Now show me what does."

He holds strong, my honorable gentleman, waiting for me to make my exact intentions perfectly clear. And while my pulsating parts are screaming at me to jump him, my heart is telling me to savor each second, each flash of control slipping in his eyes, to show him that the journey to get me *here* was worth the wait.

Refusing to break from his wanton stare, I will my hands to stop trembling and slowly untie the belt on my robe. Licking my suddenly parched lips, I pull open the sides, offering my still damp, overheated body up for display. With one roll of my shoulders, the robe falls to the floor behind me and I stand unabashedly bared.

"Lizzie," he growls, "tell me what you want, gorgeous girl. May be the only time I let it happen this way, but tonight, you call all the shots."

SE Hall

Sucking a deep, fortifying breath in for him, I blow it out for me and answer in a husky, aroused whisper, "I want to see you too."

His eyes flick from my face to my body, then back again, his labored exhale tickling, goosebumps rising on my skin. In an explicitly sexy move, he reaches back and pulls his shirt over his head, tossing it aside. I love his chest, tan with a light splattering of dark hair, outlines of muscle and those dents at his hips that make angels weep. He reaches for my hand and places it at the waist of his jeans, rubbing his thumb on the underside of my wrist.

"You want it, you take it out," he rumbles, pulling his hand away to leave me totally in charge.

My tongue pokes out, stiff in concentration as I work open the five buttons and pull the jeans down over his hips. He helps me get them off and steps out of them, leaving him before me in only black boxer briefs...the ones we bought together.

A whimper defies my valiant efforts to not do so and I then divest him of the briefs too, again him helping me until they're kicked away. I feast, more accurately blatantly gawk, at the naked specimen of man, close enough I can reach out and touch him. He far surpasses my wildest of dreams, virile, large and foreboding in the most sensual of ways. And his dick? Magnificent. Long, thick, and hard, protruding up and out, *all one color*, with minimal hair surrounding it. His thighs are wide and solid, and before I can stop myself, I stroll around him in a lazy circle, gulping loudly at his high, tight ass. Oh yeah...he's the epitome of what a guy should look like.

Coming back around to stand in front of him, with nervous, anxious eyes, I tell him what's in my heart, actual words, knowing body language will soon take over. "I want you, Cannon, because I love you. And I love you because I never want to feel any other way than the way I feel when I'm with you. If I'm scared or sad, no arms but yours will do. When I fall asleep, the thought of you, your quirks, laugh, kindness, and companionship ensure my sweet dreams. I want you inside me because that's when I'll truly be whole. I

230

don't want to be strong by myself anymore. I want to be *stronger*, because I have you."

Barely having collected my breath, I'm hoisted in the air, powerful hands gripping my thighs, directing my legs around his waist. His erection nestles perfectly against my slick center as he attacks my mouth and moves us toward the bed. Together, he lays us down and kisses along my neck, across my collarbone, then pulls back to gaze at me.

"You have a way." He chuckles, shaking his dipped head. "Good thing you write the words, my love, 'cause I can't explain it, what you do to me." He rests his forehead between my breasts, kissing between every few words. "It's like this *pull*, a force bigger than me. I couldn't fight it if I tried."

"Me too." I sigh, tangling my fingers in his soft brown hair. "I know exactly what you mean."

He lifts his head, his smile lighting up the whole darkened room as he holds my eyes reverently with his own. "I love you too, Lizzie. Pretty sure since the minute I met you, and certain I will forever."

Done with professions of the spoken sort, I grin devilishly and crook my finger, at which a primal groan rumbles out of him and he crashes into my mouth. He kisses me with his entirety...tongue demanding my surrender, hands finding mine and pinning them above my head, hips rocking his erection through my wetness, the broad head bumping my clit with every up slide, sending tremors scorching through me.

I'm overwhelmed, turning my head to catch a breath, grinding back against him brazenly, my pulse thumping loudly in my ears. "Cannon," I pant, "I can't take it."

He *laughs*, pulling his mouth off my neck. "Oh, Lizzie my love, we're just getting started. This is the part where you let go; no decisions, no planning, not a thing to worry about, and let me take care of you. You're always in charge, always stressed. Turn it all off and trust me. Can you do that?"

*Can I do that*? Completely abandon my post? I can't even comprehend it.

He releases my hands and trails a fingertip down each arm, across, tracing a circle around each of my nipples. They tighten into aching points and he hums low in his throat, licking his lips, his carnal gaze upon them. "Beautiful," he whispers, still circling, antagonizing me.

"Cannon," I whine, squirming under him.

"Hmm?"

"I—d-do s-something."

"You haven't answered my question, Lizzie." His mouth pulls up in a grin but his eyes stay on their prize while I try to remember the damn question.

*Oh.* "Yes, I can do that."

"That's my girl," he murmurs, lifting his eyes quickly to throw me a wink, then captures my right nipple in his mouth.

A gasp rips out of me and my hands fly to him, anywhere, I have no idea, running wildly over his body. He sucks harder, flicking the point with the tip of his tongue, using his bodyweight to keep me still.

His dick never stops sliding against me, teasing my clit mercilessly, hinting at my opening every few glides, and as hard as I try to manipulate, to guide it in me, he keeps my body trapped, thwarting all my attempts at taking control.

"Not even close to time," he denies me, now treating my other nipple to his hot, wet mouth.

Fuck this...I *am* gonna explode, shoving a hand between us and grabbing said huge, hard dick before he can deny me. "Ah!" I squeal when he bites my nipple, not hard, but noticeably. "My mouth, Cannon," I beg, "come 'ere."

He breaks with a "pop" and kisses me as I've asked, soft and deliberately, and I match the speed of my hand pumping him up and down.

"I want you," I plead into his mouth, giving his shaft a squeeze.

232

"You have me. God, do you have me." He trails down my torso, both hands groping and squeezing my breasts as he licks and sucks his way to my navel. "Lizzie, move your hand…you gotta stop."

I audibly pout but do what he says, his kisses moving lower. "Gonna have to think of a new phrase, baby, cause I'm about to eat this pussy," he croons, hands pushing apart my thighs.

An embarrassing squeak barely has time to sound before becoming a desperate mewl, his mouth latching on to the center of me. *Oh my sweet…* "Cann—oh my God, Cannon!" I squeeze shut my eyes, head thrashing side to side as his thumbs spread me open and a hard tongue slides inside me. "Ah, fuckkk!" It's one long, drawn out howl, his tongue fucking me, his finger pressing my clit in circles. "Never stop, never ever stop," I beg, my knees bending, legs gripping the sides of his head, hands pulling his hair. "Oh, I'm—"

"Fuck yes, you are," he growls carnally, "all over my face, now!" And then he's back with almost painful suction, spearing that wicked tongue in and out, pinching my clit as he plays with it.

I'll never know where my orgasm starts or ends, only sure it's the most phenomenal thing I've ever felt in my life…absolutely no comparison to the ones I give myself. Once the spots quit flashing behind my eyelids, I slowly open them, sated and boneless, as relaxed as I may ever get.

Here he comes, kissing his way back up to rumble in my ear. "Feels good giving me the reins, huh?"

"Mmm."

"That's my pussy now, baby, and it tastes perfect."

I turn my head to him and giggle. "Not quite the gentleman I thought you were, huh?"

"Sometimes I'll be gentle, other times not so much, but I'll always give you exactly what you need," he kisses me chastely, "I swear it."

SE Hall

I nod, as sure that's true as I am of my own name, and latch on to the back of his head, initiating a carnivorous kiss, pulling away when I realize...

"Get used to it, love." He traces my lips with the tip of his tongue. "Gonna eat ya, a lot, and always gonna kiss ya."

I don't feel bad about my whole Sybil thing now, since Cannon's clearly made up of different layers himself. As amazing as his chivalrous, gentlemanly side is, I'm quickly finding I thrive on his inner sexual heathen just as much.

No way I'm discouraging his feasting upon me, and I'm damn sure not going without his kiss...resolved, I delve into his mouth with every ounce of passion and abandon I possess, whimpering each time his hands find a new spot on my body to caress and command. No part of us left untangled, he rolls, placing me on top of the sweaty, writhing heap we've become and I take to it naturally. It's now my scandalous movements that control the glide of him through the middle of my wetness, until he grips my hips fiercely, halting me.

Glistening chest heaving rapidly, he releases my mouth and lays his head back to take one methodical scan of me astride him. "I promise to tell you when you're not naked too, but damn, babe, you're flawless." He places both my hands on his pecs. "Lift up," he instructs and pats my ass. When I do, he treats me to yet another fatally sexy maneuver, wrapping his hand around his erection, eyes fastened on the place we're about to join. "Take me in, baby, slow and easy. We only get this moment once. Savor it with me."

For a split second I think of the lack of condom, but dismiss it just as fleetingly. We both know I'm on the pill and I trust him; I know he'd die before hurting or putting me at risk in any way. I take a deep, brave breath in for him and exhale it gradually as I take him inside me. A pained hiss accompanies my wince and his whole body tenses under me.

"Dear God, Lizzie, love, snug as—" His hands at my hips lifts me up some. "Gonna have to work it in, little at, ahh," his head crashes back on the pillow and his eyes roll up

234

in his head, "at a time." Adam's apple bobbing frantically, he directs my body, up, down some, up, and downward again as more of his rigid, pulsing length eases inside the depths of my body.

Honestly, I liked his mouth better. This is as pleasurable as a steel rod being forced in a pinhole. But each time, our union becomes wetter, silkier, until my ass finally rests flush on his thighs.

It's not as painful anymore, merely noticeably full, and I can't prevent the tears that spring to my lids. Not from discomfort, but from gravity of the overwhelming sense of unity. Cannon's *inside* me, physically catching up to where he's been mentally and emotionally for a while now.

I belong to someone, wholly, on every level I have to offer.

"I love you, Cannon," I whisper past the deceiving sob.

He lifts a hand to wipe the tears that broke free. "I love you too, beautiful girl, forever. Come 'ere," he says, nestling me against his chest. "You okay?" he asks warily, placing a kiss on my hair.

I shake my head, sniffling. "Just love you, feel loved."

He grunts, rolling us over again as one, staring down at me. "Wanted you to take it yourself and you did. Now I'm gonna show you just how much I adore you. I want to *make love* to you."

"Please." I fidget and flash a tiny grin in anticipation of what this beautiful man can do to me—give life to the deepest buried and untapped piece of who I really am. His eyes stay on mine as he begins to slide in and out of me, taking frenzied breaths through his nose, his waning control shining in our stare.

"*This* is where I belong. You feel so right, Lizzie," he groans, eyes pinching shut as his thrusts increase in force and speed. "My Eden."

My hands know no boundaries or agenda, touching all of him, my fingers gliding across his sweat slickened skin and coiled muscles, eventually seizing his taut ass.

"Pull your legs up, knees bent," he snarls, my body immediately complying with his demand. Rising on his own knees now, he slides his hands under my ass and tilts my pelvis, driving into new depths, rumbling over my moans. "You tight little witch, feel what you do to me. Need you there too, baby, use your fingers. Hurry." His pants, words, and grunts combine into a magnificent chorus of masculine, satisfied reverberations that ignite a fire within me.

I do his bidding, flicking my clit feverishly as he pounds into me with reckless abandon. Refusing to close my eyes despite their best efforts, I absorb the sight of him relishing in my body and brace myself when both mental and physical switches in me flip. "Cannon!" I shriek, my inner muscles flexing and contracting around his hardness in a gush of ecstasy.

"Oh fuck, ye-yes," he hisses past his clenched jaw, then hastily pulls himself out of me and comes all over my stomach. Still pumping long after he's done, his eyes finally open, seeking mine that never closed. "Don't you move." He winks and blows me a kiss, climbing off the bed.

He's back before my pulse has time to decelerate, toting a warm washcloth that he uses to gently clean between my legs, then my stomach. Tossing it on the nightstand, he lies down and drags me against his warm body. He tucks my head under his chin, kissing my hair delicately with a drawn out sigh. "I should've asked about a condom," he says softly. "I'm sorry, baby."

"Don't be. You know I take the pill and I trust you." I snuggle in closer, lavishing in the large, solid body encapsulating me in comfort beyond my dreams.

"Well, if you're not mad, then may I just say, now that I know...I'm quite sure I'm allergic to condoms."

I chuckle at the hopefulness in his voice. "Is that right?"

"Absolutely. And I shudder to think what might happen if I'm expected to pull out while you're pulsing around me ever again. I may never recover."

"Cannon?"

"Siren?"

"Go to sleep."

# CHAPTER
## twenty-three

If I wasn't already well aware he hadn't fallen asleep either, the heavy weight of his stare, even at my back, and the tender bites on my shoulder definitely gave it away.

"Know you're awake," nip, "need a nibble," another tiny bite. "You, my love, are the Patron Saint of Posers."

I try to roll over, but he stops me with an unyielding hand on my hips. "What's that supposed to mean? I *was* asleep."

He chuckles against my skin, stroking his foot along my calf. "Not just sleep posing, which you were, but everything. You try on so many masks Lizzie, to intimidate, hide, lots of reasons; you don't have to do that anymore. Just as you are, anyway, any time, I'm right here with you, loving *you*. You're my tough little nut, but I cracked ya. Any further hiding or guising on your part would be futile. I'm so locked in, I'm not even sure I'm a separate entity any longer."

"You pillow talk pretty, Romeo. Calling me a posing nut will *not* get you anywhere," I reply grouchily. "But the rest of it? Hmmm," I moan groggily, euphoric and free-falling into the security of his potent, lovingly reverent words, "I *might* like it."

"Liar." He moves my hair aside and places open-mouth kisses down my neck, his lips finding rest between my shoulder blades. "You love that I call you out, refuse to let you hide. You need my rational as badly as I thrive on your ferocity, admit it."

"I admit nothing." I attempt to scoot further away, triggering the exact response I was seeking—his carnal growl and reeling me back in, eliminating so much as an air pocket between our bodies.

"My sweet Lizzie, so stubborn and guarded, a legendary badass in her own mind. I knew it the minute I met you." He tests my will, trailing his tongue down the length of my spine.

"Knew what?" I beg on a whisper.

"Shh, I'm counting your pulse. If it breaks 150, I'll be forced to take drastic measures."

Oh Lord, his left hand leaves my hip to slink down and across my stomach, hinting at my curls. *That will not help my pulse, I assure you.* "Cannon," I husk breathily, pushing my bottom into him.

"137. I can do better," he proclaims in a stern, confident voice and flips me over and under him. "I knew we'd be perfect, timeless. Your pulse sped up every step you took my way, till it finally matched how fast my heart was beating in my chest watching you from afar."

"Cannon." My eyes water happily as I lift a trembling hand to his cheek. "Thank God opposites attract. Which means I'm officially nothing," I choke up on a sob, "because you are everything. Everything."

"Not sure I like you calling yourself nothing," he grasps both my hands and pulls them over my head, "but I do adore the sentiment. I love when my Lizzie's heart talks," he murmurs, burying his face in my neck and with one false bump, slides gently inside me.

He traps my hands, but not my legs, which I wrap around him, digging my ankles into his ass, forcing him deeper, closer...never close enough. "Kiss me," I plead, hopelessly addicted to his kisses.

"Tell me." He runs his nose along mine, puffs of restraint hot on my lips.

"I love you, Cannon. I need you, I *choose you*. Oh God." My murmurs turn to a scream when he...honestly, I have no idea what the hell he just did but, ohh...

"Don't squirm, baby, you want me on *that spot*, I promise."

*No need to sell me, Magic Man, I so believe you.*

He lets my hands free to scoop under and dangle my knees over his forearms, reaching a place deep inside where scarily good things happen. He turns his head and takes his nibble from my ankle without letting up in the rhythm of his powerful thrusts. "You haven't," surge in and pant, "missed a pill, right?"

"N-no," I somehow answer.

"Fingers, baby, I'm coming in ya, want you with me."

I don't need it this time, truly, he's hitting some mystical "easy button" in me, but Bedroom Cannon brooks no argument.

I'm coming before my hand even gets there, exploding and wrenching around him from such an elicit, vulgar...sexy command. This one's much different. I can't get a deep breath, getting dizzy, barely conscious of his single, hoarse wail filling the room.

Later, I wake, the heat and light of the afternoon sun fighting through the blinds, in a cocoon of Cannon's arms and legs, snaring me from every angle, as though clinging for dear life—one false move and I'd disappear. I know the fear all too well. Not wanting to disturb him, I ignore my bladder for as long as possible, gaping in awe at his beauty, quiet and peaceful under the shroud of his sleep.

I could lie here and study him all day, dark hair unruly, a smirk hinting at his mouth even in slumber, but

nature calls incessantly, like a telemarketer jacked up on Dew.

"Cannon," I whisper, trying to rouse him gently.

"Mmm," he hums sleepily, reaffirming his hold on me.

"I'm sorry, but I need to use the bathroom and you seem to be holding me hostage." I giggle, peppering his cheeks with soft kisses.

"Come right back," he groans, easing his bondage clutch.

I climb from the bed, intensely aware of aches and tingles in swollen parts far too long neglected and grin at the reminder.

Surely he fell right back to sleep, which means I can take a bath, desperate to soak away the soreness. I make quick work of lowering myself into the warm, soothing water, certain areas overwhelming grateful.

As soon as I'm nearing sated comfort, the door opens. I flinch. While my aches are gloriously earned and far from regrettable, I refuse to go another round...at least until I've been cleared by a holistic hoochie healer. "My vagina is on a twenty-four hour sabbatical, if that's what you're huntin'," I deadpan, not opening my worn out eyes. Every part of me is exhausted; even my hair hurts.

"I wasn't huntin', 'til you dropped the v-bomb. Is this one of those reverse psychology things where you say you don't want what you're actually jonesing for?"

I let my head fall his way and pry open one eye. "Not even a little bit. But if that's for me, I might have a kiss in me somewhere."

"It's for you." He hands me the tall glass of orange juice. "Kiss me hard on de lips and I may have a couple of pain relievers in my other hand." He bends over, lips puckered adorably.

"Closer," I whine, refusing to meet him halfway, which would require actual movement.

SE Hall

He destroys the gap, grazing his lips on mine whisper soft, holding his hand out and open with my relief. "Thought you might be sore, and I'm sorry you're hurting, but—"

My phone ringing from the other room cuts him off and he rises to go grab it, while I swallow the pills, not stopping 'til the glass is empty.

"Really? That's awesome, Con." He walks back in, his whole face beaming at whatever tales Conner's weaving on the other end of the line.

*Now* I move, climbing out and swiping two towels off the rack. I wrap one around me, the other over my hair, and shove my hot little hand toward the phone. "Gimme."

"Con, your sister's dying to talk to ya, so I'm gonna give her the phone," pause, "miss you too," he answers solemnly, corners of his mouth turning down just a bit.

"Bubs! How are you? I miss you so much!" I practically scream, all in one breath.

"I am very, very good, Bethy, very good. I miss you. How are my fish? There are so many fish here, big ones, but they don't swim by me."

I clutch my chest and bite back tears, an actual twinge in my chest. I miss him badly, but more so, I'm overcome by the sheer happiness in his voice. "Your fish are good, Bubs." I shoot a look at Cannon and he bows his head to veil his laugh—I haven't checked the dang fish once, and they're not known for their sturdy, long lives. Shit!

"What have you been doing?"

"Nothing, we just got here, Sister, except swimming one time. My dad wants to talk to you, bye!"

"Conner?" I yell to catch him, unsuccessfully.

"Conner, stay by Laura!" my father pierces my eardrum with his yell. "Sorry about that, Elizabeth, he's far too excited to be contained. I'll be sure he calls you back when he's settled down."

"I'd appreciate that. So, you guys made it there fine. Everything else all right?"

242

"Actually, I did wish to discuss with you the phone call I received from my attorney. If now's a good time?"

I glance around, at or for what I have no idea, but Cannon's right there, arm around my waist, and he leads me to sit on the bed, climbing up beside me. "Yes, now's fine," I finally reply, forcing a stoic tone.

"Wonderful. Well as I said, Damian phoned me regarding a call he received from Mr. Morrison."

Silence.

"Elizabeth?"

"Yes?"

"Did you hear me?" he asks, irritation obvious. "Well?"

"Well what? Was there a question in there I missed?"

He sighs loudly and then clears his throat. "Elizabeth, I understand Conner had a memory of some sort and you'd like to have him subjected to a monitored psych evaluation?"

"No," I bite, "no, I would not *like* to do that to him. Honestly, my attorney's call was premature and without my go ahead. I hadn't decided anything for sure, yet." As quickly as my back had gone ramrod straight, Cannon's hand is there, rubbing it, relaxing me somewhat.

"Calm down," he leans in and whispers in my free ear, kissing my temple. "In for me," he waits as I inhale, "out for you, baby."

I wheeze it out and nod chastely, telling him I'm better…'cause I know without a single doubt, that question was coming next.

"But," I speak once again to my father, rationally, "yes, I'd like to know more about Conner's memory and that would be the only way."

"The only way for him to remember?" he scoffs, brimming with condescension. "Rubbish. You mean it'd be the only way to use it against me. Elizabeth, I know you don't believe or trust me, I dare say you hate me, but for Conner's sake, I must implore you to not subject him to such

243

invasiveness. I give you my word, daughter, nothing Conner might remember will reflect badly on me. You will have traumatized him for no reason."

I grip Cannon's thigh, flexing my hand repeatedly, like I can milk some strength out of him to seep into me.

"Elizabeth, tell me this, what is it that you want? What's your ultimate goal with the fact-finding mission?"

"Easy," Cannon mumbles beside me, touching my hand with his own. Apparently he can hear my father through the cell; not surprising, but shocking how I'm actually going to take his advice.

"I'd like to know how Conner got hurt and make sure the person responsible doesn't get near him ever again. I'd like to know why my mother checked out and make sure the person responsible dies a slow, painful death." I turn to Cannon, expecting a smile of approval, instead getting a frown.

*What the hell? I said it monotone and calmly!*

"Would you consider a compromise, Elizabeth? If you'll agree to halt exposing Conner to lab rat type examinations, I will agree to telling you a bit about your mother's condition, and to a sit down with you and your brother so we can speak with him together, upon our return."

"Why would you do that? What's in it for you?" I throw out harshly.

"Perhaps some peace, finally. I'm tired, Elizabeth. Tired of fighting with one child to see the other. Tired of knowing you despise me. Tired of bestowing any love I have to give on Laura's children because my own are never near. But above all else, daughter, I'm tired of the thought of you hurting, going through life angry and bitter. You're grown up now; you can handle more."

"Are you dying?"

"Lizzie!" I jerk at Cannon's reprimand.

"Sorry," I murmur in the phone. "I just meant, are you, I mean, you're different, like trying to borrow back time or something." I peek at Cannon and he winks.

244

"Like a fine wine, people tend to get better with age. My father," he sighs, "everyone thinks him the kind, distinguished, level-headed gentleman, which he is, *now*. But when he was younger, when I was younger, he was the meanest son of a bitch you'd never want to meet." His laugh is facetious. "Elizabeth, I admit I was a horrid father. I was so busy chasing status and wealth that I forfeited my greatest treasures. And I was the worst possible husband a man could be. Your mother—" his voice cuts out and I hear a loud, sharp throat clearing. "Anna was a fine woman, her greatest fault her overly soft heart. The more I was gone, preoccupied, the deeper into depression she fell. I watched her spirit slowly die and I did nothing, hoping she'd get drunk or sedated before I had to hear the nagging and crying. And when she was finally broken, I chose to use it as my justification to seek the company of other women rather than to save her. I was a cheater, a louse, and the sole cause of your mother's demise. I will forever be sorry, Elizabeth. I robbed you of a happy family, and your mother."

It takes me a minute to realize he's stopped talking, or that Cannon is cradling my head to his chest as the tears pour freely. I've just had the longest conversation with my father ever, and it's more of a glimpse into my past than what I got actually living it. I almost don't know what to say, how I feel, anything…but my spirit finds a voice.

"T-thank you, for the um, talk. Have Conner call me. And," I sit up, needing my own support, "I would be agreeable to the three of us having dinner, or whatever, when you get back."

"Elizabeth, I—"

*If he says "I love you," this phone and the wall are gonna make fast friends.*

"I'll see you soon."

# CHAPTER twenty-four

Tonight's show, wrapping up our stay in Lincoln, went great; everyone in sync and seemingly high spirits…until we were all once again packed together on the bus.

The current tension in the circulated air couldn't be penetrated with a chainsaw wielded by Mike Myers even if today *was* the 13th! Problem is, I know precisely what's eating at each of them and can't do a damn thing about any of it.

*Silly me* misplaced my magic freakin' wand again and can't make Vanessa suddenly materialize to appease Jarrett. Nor can I simply walk over to Rhett and politely ask for my V card back, vanquishing the jealous, pensive vibes radiating off Cannon. And Rhett? Huh, rewind, 'cause there's no telling what crawled up Rhett's ass, if anything at all. He quite literally could be farting happy bubbles ten seconds from now; there's a questionably large gamut of mood swings all trapped in one great guy.

No wonder Bruce blazes a hasty trail between driver's seat, venue, hotel, and back to driver's seat without fail. You wander one inch off your path around here, and you're liable to get chewed up and…swallowed. Case in point: the clueless hiker who stumbled into this foreboding den of angry bears.

"As much fun as this is," I slam both hands flat on the table and rise, "I'm gonna take a shower. If you actually kill each other while I'm gone, clean up your mess!" I chirp sardonically and walk away, not daring to glance back.

I listen against the closed bathroom door for any sounds of an ensuing blood bath. After a few minutes of hearing only absolute silence, I turn on the hot spray, stripping and immersing myself in a steamy jet of blessed sanctity.

Maybe it's time for a real break off this merry-go-round. *I never did like those things.* The initial rush of adrenaline is enticingly deceptive, 'cause after a while you're disoriented, nauseated, and can no longer decipher anything specific, everything around you just one big blur.

And this traveling tin can of dysfunction is starting to feel a lot closer to that nightmarish ride than fun, or its original purpose, escapism.

*"Fearing change is a sign of ignorance, Elizabeth. It shows one's lack of confidence in their ability to decipher and maneuver any situation by using their intellect."*

One conversation, even remotely of substance, and I'm recalling his idealistic "lessons," with which I don't agree, in my head?

Talk about a change I don't like…

But it's already blowing and strengthening in gale force, a new wind sweeping through my life a smidgen more every day.

The big questions I need answered will ultimately be what decides if this is fleeting pessimism or the path I should travel. But I won't ask or beg. No, these answers must *come* to me, willingly and blatant.

"It's bad enough we're sleeping together in Conner's bed, so don't get any big ideas, Mr. Perky Penis," I warn him and the obvious erection poking at my back.

SE Hall

"Can we fake some moaning at least? Or, just scream my name a couple times and I'll be happy." He laughs, tickling my sides.

"That to inflate your ego or *deflate* Rhett's?" Yeah, I called him out. "Don't be a dick. Rhett's no threat to you. No sense in fucking with him for no reason."

"You're right." He sighs, pushing aside my hair to nuzzle his face in my neck, his arms circling my waist and firming their hold. "I just need him to know you're mine now. I'll be the one seeing to *all* your needs. No more 'Rhett's my rock' missions. I'm who takes care of anything you crave, want, or require. You cry, *my* shirt gets wet. You scream, my eardrums bleed. You come, *my* dick's squeezed. All of it, everything."

I have to snort in laughter. He goes from sweet and poetic to crudely sexy in one breath. I love it. "He knows that *and* supports it, so be nice. I'm serious. I care about him and won't play mean mind games. Just like I know you care about Ruthie, at least fundamentally, which is why I didn't shoot her back a nasty text. By the way," my tone dips shamefully, "I really am sorry for creeping your phone. I *did* grab it by mistake, but once my eye caught her name, I was hooked. I'm sorry."

"I don't care. Read my phone anytime you want. And send her any text you want. If I had something to hide, I'd probably have a password." He playfully nips at my earlobe. "I love you. Mi business es su business. Promise."

"I'm not going to attack her," *I would love to*, "that's ridiculous. She didn't do anything to me personally."

"Probably best you don't go at her. That'd be like her showing up to a dog fight carrying a rabbit; she wouldn't stand a chance against my tough little nut." He chuckles on my neck. "So glad I get to see your sweet center, though. My favorite piece of candy, hard on the outside, decadent on the inside."

"Oh, brother." I roll my eyes even though my back's to him. "Go to sleep, Walt Whitman."

"He was brilliant. I'll take that as a compliment."

248

Agreed, and none surprised he's read another of my favorites. But I remain silent, actually quite tired, ready to cease the sonnets and go to sleep.

"Baby?" he whispers.

"Hmm?"

"Are you okay after the talk with your father? You haven't mentioned it."

My exasperated lament bounces off the walls of the small room. "Surprisingly, yes. Now I know why my mom got weird, and while I appreciate him finally admitting his role, his fault, it was still on her to be stronger. She stayed, tolerated it, and found ways to block it out and accept it. Conner and I didn't have that luxury. We had to live through the dysfunction, sober and trapped. They were both equally selfish, if you ask me."

"I did ask you, and I think you're right; your feelings are valid. So what're you gonna do now?"

"I'm gonna eat dinner with him and Conner and see if I can't get some more answers."

"Want me to go with you?" he offers in an empathic, kind tone. Another part of me melts, soft and pliant to *let him in*, thus rolling over to face him.

"I appreciate that, babe, more than you know, but I think both of them will talk more if it's just us. You understand?" I peer up at him, hoping he does.

"Absolutely." He nods, resolute. "You called me babe." His smirk appears, my favorite look on him.

"Yeah?"

"Liked it. You've never pet named me before."

"Well, Siren was taken." I shrug with a soft giggle, suddenly feeling cheesy and embarrassed.

He in turn growls, diving into my neck once more. "Oh yeah, Siren is definitely *taken*. By *me*, mine, forever."

When I wake, the bus is stopped and peaceful. "Where are we?" I grumble in a froggy morning voice.

"Brownsberg, Indiana," he answers with a smooch to my forehead. "Your uncle went to a hotel to sleep since he drove all night. Not sure where Rhett or Jarrett went."

"You call your friend?"

"Sark? Yeah, told him we'd come check out his place in a couple hours. You ready for coffee?"

"God, yes," I moan, then whimper before I can stop it, when he releases his hold on me and rises.

"I'll meet ya in the bathroom with a cup. Grab a shower, sleepyhead."

*Why is he in such a hurry?* I wanna lay here and relax, devour my caffeine fix, and drag myself up gradually.

"Up, baby!" he yells from the other room.

*I am not a dog.*

"Please," he adds in sugary taunt, earning himself reprieve from the chastisement I had on the tip of my tongue.

"Hmpthmph," I grumble, peeling myself from the warm, much comfier than my bunk, bed. When I dawdle to the bathroom, he's waiting with coffee and a smile—*only*.

*Now* I know why he's rushing me. Empty bus, won't give him play in the bed... I should've realized it sooner, really, but I just woke up. Slow on the uptake.

"Did you know you're naked?" I cock a brow and reach for my coffee.

"Did you know you're not?" He wickedly leers back, pulling the cup out of my reach. "Get naked and have a sip."

Holding his hungry stare, I grab the hem of my shirt and suggestively lift it up and off, tossing it aside. "Drink," I demand, holding out a hand.

He steps forward and tilts the cup to my lips, giving me time to blow on it before pouring some in my mouth. I try to slurp fast, needing my sunrise crack like a twitching junkie, but too soon he pulls it away.

"The rest," he drawls, looking down to my shorts, intense and assertive.

"This is blackmail," I jeer, not genuinely aggravated, and shimmy my pj shorts over my hips and down my legs. I step out of them and use a toe to fling them in his direction, my mouth open. "More."

He complies, once again offering me a drink. "You hold it," he instructs, going to turn on the shower when I do.

I'm appreciating both my coffee and him, naked and glorious, his lengthy, hard erection jutting up and out from his defined, leanly sculpted body. He steps under the waterfall and holds out a hand to me. Audaciously, I set aside the mug and hasten to him, anticipation flushing through my whole body...more evident in certain tingling parts than others.

He draws me in and very impressively, since this shower wasn't meant to fit two (I don't mind the tight squeeze), pivots me directly under the spray, running his hands up my neck, using his thumbs to tilt my head back, saturating my hair. When he's satisfied it's good and dowsed, he curls his long fingers and brings my head back upright. "Turn around," he demands, a baritone overtly brimming with arousal. He lathers in shampoo, his care thorough and methodical, no strand left untouched, individually gliding each between his fingers. "I love your natural color, baby."

"Oh yeah? Took you a while to say something," I goad, glancing over my shoulder with a coy grin.

"I noticed the second you walked out. I just wasn't sure it was okay to profess it publicly back then. I notice everything about your gorgeousness." He's moved on to soaping up my back and butt, distracting me beyond further conversation. "Okay, turn around." He takes me by the hips and guides me around, exuding complete control. "Lean your head back and rinse that out."

I'm about to ask why he's not doing it when his hands answer, roaming down my torso, fondling my breasts far more than what's required in the mere interest of cleanliness. Then the devilish mitts slide lower, washing my belly, before he's *thoroughly* washing my most intimate place.

Completely at his mercy now, I moan, my head thrown back, fingers tangled in my own hair. Exhilarated and in real danger of combustion, I push myself against his hand. "What are you doing?" I shriek, jerking my head up, eyes popping open. "Oh my God, that tickles." I giggle. "*Why* are you kissing my armpits?"

"Because I'm guessing no one ever has, and that's a damn shame. Your little pits are precious and deserve love too." He lifts his head and winks before moving to the other one. "Okay, baby, turn around again so I can do your conditioner."

"No need. That's two in one shampoo. Not the greatest, but saves time with five people showering on one hot water tank." I shrug. "My turn to wash you," I say, and it comes out in a sexy purr.

I lather soap in my hands, my eyes sweeping over every part of him, deciding where I want to start—not that there's a wrong choice. My foam-filled hands worship the brawny muscles beneath them, fingers digging in on the definitively outlined pecs, hip indents, and rippling abs. Blushing fiercely, I take intricate, methodic care between his legs; first his heavy sac, rolling it in my hands, then his light smattering of closely trimmed hair, finishing the job by stroking my firmly clenched hand up and down his rod-hard length...multiple times.

He groans when I squeeze, grunts when I tug, and utterly *hisses* when I perpetrate a twisting motion. "Baby, enough," he begs in a breathy huff and takes a step away, turning around. "Finish washing *me* before I finish, please."

I re-lather up and start at his shoulders, dipping down into his pits, finding them almost as ticklish as mine, then caress over every rigidly flexed muscle in his back. Licking my lips, I grip both his butt cheeks and rub my palms and fingers lasciviously; this taut, delectable ass is definitely one of my favorite parts of his body. I can't wait to test my theory of its buoyancy later.

"All done," I pant, backing into the spray to make sure I'm completely rinsed.

"Hardly." He turns, stalking me the few steps until my back is against the wall. He spins me around, seeking out my hands and forcing them flat against the tile in front of me. "Leave 'em there," he growls in my ear, partaking of a nibble while he's there. I feel his piercing grip my hips, tugging back on them 'til he has me poised at the angle he wants me.

I shiver, scarcely able to stay braced and upright as he runs a single finger through my moisture, mockingly sliding that single digit inside me, then just as swiftly out. "Love the way your body talks to me. I want you too, my little Siren," he says at the same time he spreads me open and plunges his thick hardness all the way into me.

I moan/scream at the tight fit, the stretching fullness bordering on stinging pain.

"Easy, baby, relax," he coos into the back of my neck. "You little minx, quit flexing or this won't last long."

I'm not doing it on purpose, my center is literally protesting the intrusion on its own.

When his dexterous fingers find my clit and strum it in perfect harmony, I do relax, every muscle in me going lax with glorious euphoria. "There we go, melt around me, baby, tight but eased wet, just how I like it," he murmurs as his thrusts pick up speed and force. He tugs at my hips, bringing me up on my tiptoes, then pushes down on my lower back, effectively popping my ass higher in the air.

"Fuckkk yeah," he rumbles, reaching a whole new *that spot* inside me. "Right there, perfect."

It feels so damn good, the friction of his head hitting my upper wall, his fingers relentless on my clit, and his sounds—*God, his sounds*—the quivers within my walls come on quick.

"That's my girl." He bites lightly at my shoulder, immediately covering it with an open mouth kiss. "Give it to me, Lizzie, drench my cock. Now."

His ministrations grow more urgent, pressing down and around, rolling my clit like his toy, his pounding into me maniacal, and I do... I see black, then flashes of white, my head falling forward limply as I clasp and pulse around him. Nothing else exists, just the two of us locked in a bubble of pure ecstasy where I float, only aware of the sweet sounds of our slapping skin and his pleasure, piercing but unable to penetrate my blissful daze.

He comes, body going motionless, hands compressing down mercilessly on my hips, dick twitching inside me. I embrace it, mind, body, and soul, basking in what we make each other feel.

Having yet to reclaim my breath or bearings, he slips from me, the hot evidence of physical domination coating the insides of my thighs. Instantly, he's there with a washcloth, soothingly cleaning me before twirling me back around to face him.

"Making love to you is the only perfect thing I've ever known." He kisses my forehead then beholds my eyes. "I love you, Lizzie Hannah Carmichael, and I always will. Completely."

"I love you too." Overcome, I lay my cheek to his chest and count his heartbeats thundering beneath my ear.

"We better get ready." And with one more kiss to my hair and playful pat on my ass, we do just that.

# CHAPTER twenty-five

"Sark, my man!" Cannon and his friend bro hug, complete with sharp slaps on the back.

"How the hell you been, Cannonball? Traveling man now, huh?" his handsome, charismatic, blond buddy asks.

"Something like that." Cannon chuckles. "Hey, I want you to meet someone." He reaches back to where I'm trying to blend in behind him and snares my waist, catapulting me forward. "Kasen Sark, this is Lizzie Carmichael, my *one*."

A confused visage crosses his face briefly, but he's quick to recover. "Pleasure, Lizzie. Thanks for doing some shows here." He initiates a handshake, mine cold and clammy from a stranger's touch.

"Pleasure's mine, and thank you for having us," I muster, my head dipping marginally. I can't help being a bit apprehensive...he's wondering where Ruthie is, obviously. Do I measure up? Does he already hate me? And I care why?

*Because he means something to Cannon, who means everything to me—that's why.*

"What, uh, happened to—"

"Why don't you show us around, Mr. Tactful," Cannon interrupts him, knowing, as I do, he was about to ask about Grandma Fiancé. *Told ya.*

"Oh. Yeah, sure." He changes directions of conversational topic *and* to show us around the place, suddenly spewing off every fact about the bar, "his new baby," he can think to tell.

The place is very sleek; red, black and yellow leather seating, along. L-shaped bar and a ginormous dance floor, which is white, but obviously made to glow with the right lighting. Upstairs is a plush VIP area, same color combos and its own, smaller bar as well. Sark tells us as we tour that there's a full kitchen somewhere that serves until 11, then finally takes us down a different set of stairs to show us the stage and tombs. He has a state of the art drum kit, sound board and stage lights, and asks if he can run for us.

*Fancy schmancy.*

Cannon looks to me for how to answer and I just shrug. We've never done all the bells and whistles, so even if Sark does it wrong, I'll never know.

"Just don't shine anything bright up in our eyes," I say, jovial.

"You got it. So you guys wanna go ahead and sound check or do you need the others?"

"We don't have our instruments," I answer. *Did he not notice that?*

"I've got some backstage. They should work to get things set."

*No, that's not how that works.* But Cannon's way ahead of me.

"I'll check bass and drums, you do guitar on my side and the front mic." He winks at me, proud of his solution.

"Okay," I agree, though skeptically. Not only will it be a half-ass check, we'll just have to do it again when the boys join us. But then it hits me, and my heart threatens to burst; Cannon's doing this for his buddy, who so obviously wants to show off his new gadgets, full-out running to the sound booth.

Once we're set up and strapped at our first stations, I lead in a song that's been brewing in my head (and heart, if I'm honest) since Cannon and I got on "our" page.

Cannon's whole face beams in recognition. I sing *for* him, *to* him, "Wild Horses," my favorite version by The Sundays, entwining all my emotions into the lyrics, tone, and look in my eyes as I gaze at him. It's the perfect song because the wildest of horses have no chance of dragging me from Cannon.

When the song's over, I unstrap the electric and only just have it set down before I'm swallowed up by my man. "I loved it, and ditto, Siren, ditto. I love you so much, you sexy thing," he says, all while placing kisses on every inch of my face. "Need a nibble," he murmurs, already buried in my neck, collecting his fix.

"We'll do one more run to test lead and drums!" he yells out to Sark when he comes up for air.

Sark answers with a thumbs up high in the air, enthusiasm bright on his face.

"My turn?" Cannon asks, his playful brow raised.

"By all means," I bow and fan out my arm.

"Sing harmony, though, gotta test the mic," he calls, climbing behind the kit.

He beats out lightly on the heads the part that's normally a piano in the song—somehow making it seem even more suitable. And then he sings—a tender bass, infiltrating the soul, my soul anyway. I pluck the mic from its stand and turn to him as I sing accompaniment. He chose "Have a Little Faith in Me," which he's played for me on his iPod, but today *he* tamps it out, his sultry voice making love to it *for me*, unambiguously pleading with me to do exactly what the lyrics ask.

Too late—I already do.

We grab lunch at a sidewalk café, and he holds my hand on top of the table as we wait for our food. When it arrives, he dishes half of his on my plate and vice versa, without me having to ask—which I was totally planning to.

"So I was thinking," I throw out absently, looking down at my food.

"Uh huh?"

"Well, maybe I should finally get a house or apartment, somewhere to land when a break seems necessary. I could decorate it, cook in a real kitchen, be crazy and sleep in a real bed…"

"And where were you thinking for location?" he asks, then pops a bite in his mouth, chewing slowly, awaiting my answer with focused, curious eyes.

"I don't know." I pop my shoulders in nonchalance, hoping he buys it. "Where are you getting your apartment? N-not that I like w-wanna move next door and stalk you or anything," I stammer like a crazy person. "Just making conversation."

"Hey." He sets down his fork and speaks, his voice mellow. "Give me your hand." He offers his once again atop the table, upturned to clasp onto mine, which I lay in it willingly. "I know it's fast—well, not as fast as the hooker movie, we've tripled their one week, and living 24/7 in a cramped space together adds at least a month. We already know each other's annoying habits and that we can live together and be around each other constantly, right?"

I'm still dwelling on the "annoying habits" part, quite sure I have none. In fact, neither does he, really.

"Lizzie, I wanna be where you are. Speaking of stalker tendencies, I took the liberty of mapping the halfway point between your father's house, for Conner's visits, and my family.   That's Richmond. Population 36,000, great schools, lots of outdoor parks and activities; all in all a nice town to raise a family."

*Can't breathe.*

*Cold sweat.*

*Throat constricting.*

*Stomach revolting.*

*Whose family does he plan on raising?*

"Lizzie, no, ma'am, look at me right now. Big one in for me," he mimics the motion, "and out for you, slow and easy."

"Not better!" I choke out in panic.

"One more then, in for me," he simulates again, "and out for you." His eyes search mine, waiting several minutes to proceed, until apparently he sees what he needed to. "I'm just saying, if you buy a house, it might as well be one you can see fitting your long term needs, right? Moving sucks." He grasps my hand more snugly, rubbing his thumb back and forth across the rapid pulse in my wrist. "Do you ever want children, Lizzie? Not tomorrow, but ever?"

"Yes, definitely," I affirm with no hesitation.

"Well then. Why not plan for that?" He raises the right, analytical brow in question.

"It's sudden, scary," I mutter, almost inaudibly, knee jackhammering under the table.

"Have you *ever* felt what you feel for me?" I shake my head no. "Me either. Not for anyone, not even down on one knee for the wrong reasons. My whole life, my heart beat half this fast, no fire in my belly. With you—it's like an inferno, every part of me burning, alive and excited. I can't wait to wake up every morning to spend the day with you. Three weeks, three hours—I'll still feel this way in thirty-three years. I know it like I know stars will always fall and it will always rain, somewhere, every day."

"But," I almost don't say it, feeling like a broken record, "you were engaged not a month ago."

"I didn't ask you to marry me. I asked that we try living together, or at least side by side. House, apartment, treehouse, box in an alley, Alaska, New Guinea. I don't care. Hey," he snaps, "we could live in a tent and do the ghost stories/shadow thing you went all dreamy about. Anything, baby, for a chance."

I offer my best placating smile. "I'll think about it."

"You do that." His head droops the tiniest bit as the light burns out of his usually unfailing vibrant eyes.

We finish eating in stiff, uncomfortable silence, him releasing my hand and not taking it again when we walk out.

# Cannon

The Sark Tank is packed; definitely gonna be a profitable night for my buddy. With the mass of bodies, it's odd that I'm able to look up during "When You're Gone," by The Cranberries, which Lizzie *kills* at singing, like instant too-snug crotch kills, and spot...*Ruthie*, sitting and playing family *with my family*. I wrack my brain, wondering if Lizzie knows what any of them look like, a wave of nausea rolling through my gut.

I glance at my Siren, but it does me no good, her expression's been a mix between tense and dread since our little talk. I'm without a clue on if she knows who they are and that they're here or it's just residual.

"Thank you," she says faintly, half-heartedly, at the end of the song. "This next one is a classic that I don't have near the voice to pull it off," she funs, ducking her head but a second before finishing. "Not even sure my boys know it, but Imma sing it anyway. Gotta get it out."

Her voice begins alone, a cappella and hauntingly vulnerable. "Lying beside you..."

I recognize and lend her a rhythm to "Open Arms" by Journey. I chance a subtle, corner of my eye glance at her and she's already zoned in on me, her eyes brightening with each word, telling me here what she either just decided or couldn't manage to confess face to face before.

"Nothing to hide…" Rhett brings in the beat.

"Come to you, with open arms," Jarrett strums a deep groove, "hoping you'll see…"

I'm glued to her face, watching every nuance and inflection, praying, elated at what I think she's telling me.

"Thank you so much, you've been a great crowd!" She waits for the raucous noise to settle. "This will be our last of the night, chosen by our own Cannon!"

Oh, she's putting me on the spot, seeing what I'll now sing to her in answer. Hmmm, nothing like a little pressure. "This is a newer one; hope we all know it," I chuckle, "and you all like it. Hold somebody tight. This is 'All of Me' by John Legend."

I sing it as deliberately and sensuously as I can, never breaking my own loving gaze away from hers. It says everything as though I wrote it, for her—"your smart mouth," "your mystery ride"—perfect, from me to her.

I've hardly finished before I'm strolling to her, my Lizzie, distantly hearing my name shrieked above the noise. I'd know it anywhere, a flashing reminder of how much time I'd wasted, beckoning me. Lizzie's eyes search the crowd for the sound and when they land on the provocatively dressed, boobs-pushed-to-her-chin redhead quickly approaching, I feel her body go rigidly tense from here.

"Ruthie?" she asks under her breath.

"Yeah." I sigh, running a frustrated hand back through my hair.

"Who are those people she was sitting with?"

"My parents and sister. As soon as I blow her off, I'll introduce you."

"No, no, they're here with her. The girl you were supposed to be with, to marry. Take your time. I gotta help load the bus." She turns and walks away as fast as she can without all-out running, leaving me stranded to handle Broom Hilda alone.

"Hey, baby." She sidles up, fakeness dripping from her blood red lips. Lizzie never wears that ugly crap, masking her real taste, getting all over me and my collar. Ugh. I shiver at the thought.

"Hello, Ruthie." I bend my head to her level. "What are you doing here?" She waves dismissively at me, still wearing her engagement ring. I don't like it at all. Sure, her father picked it out, brought it to me and told me exactly when and where to propose, but still, she needs to take it off and move on.

"Gorgeous brother of mine!" Sommerlyn bounces up, leaning across the stage to wrap me in a hug. "I missed you, and boy, were you fantastic up there! The girl kinda made you all look good though," she jests, but she's completely correct.

Now my parents approach, tentatively, rounding out the party. For Moms, I jump down, giving her a big hug and smooch on the cheek before shaking hands with my father and giving him a one-armed hug.

"Thank you, guys, for coming out. You didn't have to."

"Nonsense! My handsome son's living adventurously, a rock star. I wouldn't miss it," my mother gushes, patronizingly squeezes both my cheeks.

"So," Ruthie intrudes, "why don't we all go out to dinner now? I doubt Cannon will want to drive tonight, so we could eat, find a hotel, and all leave in the morning together!" She bounces and falsely glows, like a yippy, nervous show poodle. I can't decide which part is making me sick and which is causing the pounding in my temple; probably a combination of her totally debilitating, pathetic state.

"Yes," Sommerlyn shoots her sinister eyes, "I think a private place to discuss things is a great idea."

My parents look trapped in a grueling tennis match, their eyes flicking back and forth between the cattiness.

"Well, I should probably go help the band," I explain, already backing away.

"Let's go help *and* tell them where we're going." Sommerlyn loops her arm through mine. "Wait here, we'll be right back," she chirps to our parents, and…

"What are you doing?" I growl under my breath as we walk away, leaving two confused parents with one deranged ex.

"Giving that bitch what for, as soon as possible. Playing all nice with Mom and Dad like she didn't get a tubal on the DL then dump you on the side of the road. Oh, hell no. You just leave it to your sister, Bubba, I got this. So, are you in love with the precious little lead singer or just wanting in her panties?"

I stop short. "Look at me, Som." She turns like a whipped pup at my harsh tone. "I'm madly, forever in love with her. Don't ever speak of her like that again. Okay?"

"Yay!!" She claps and bounces up and down. "I knew it! White hot chemistry. I could see it from out there. She's beautiful but doesn't know it, though, huh?"

"Sommer, zip it. We're here." I frantically search the tombs, then out back, for them. Nowhere, nothing. The bus is no longer out back. They're gone, leaving me here, marooned. Why the hell are people always doing that shit to me? I whip out my phone and call Lizzie—straight to voicemail, so I bang out a text, angry fingers on fire.

**Hot Hacker: Where r u & why'd you just leave me? Not very fucking cool.**

Usually I get an immediate response, but after staring at my phone like a hopeless loser for endless minutes, I decide to curb it for now. Gonna teach her a lesson first chance I get.

With a guilty, exhausted sigh, I guide Sommer back to our parents…and yes, she's still there too.

"Ready to go?" Ruthie smiles (if snakes smile), sidling up to me and looping her arm through mine, definitely feeling my flinch. When I try to pull away, she just keeps that fake ass face unaltered and subtly digs her cat claws into the inside of my arm in warning.

"Ready," I mumble.

"Fabulous. How about the sushi bar I saw about three doors down?" she suggests.

All the Blackwells just agree for the sake of peace and shuffle in behind our fear*ful* leader.

Well, tonight's show went *swimmingly*, but not the good version, nothing like a relaxing lounge in crisp, blue water on a hot summer day. No, I think it was more like paddling for your life in shark-infested tidal waves! Yeah, *that* kind of swimmingly.

Of course, I should have figured on Ruthie showing up; she lives close, knows Sark, and, you know, stalks my Facebook I never touch, so why I was surprised, I know not.

Why not shut down my Facebook, you ask? That'd be because I didn't make it and don't know the password.

Sommerlyn and my mom gave her what for tonight, the likes of their rancorous venom I've never seen. My father remained silent, as did I. When three women bear their claws, you step the fuck back and cover your balls.

I'm not a *ruthless* man…but Ruthie had it coming. Surely she didn't think my family would appreciate her leaving me abandoned in the middle of nowhere without a phone to call for help? And yes, my sister spread the gospel to my mother…the *other* part of Ruthie's treason. And trying to deprive that woman of grandchildren? Not wise, rabbit, not wise.

But no, ever the exalted, faultless princess her father's convinced her she is, Miss Ruthie showed up thinking I'd kept her dirty little secrets and would play nice in front of my family.

*That's what you get for thinking.*

Bright side? Something tells me she won't be back for tomorrow night's show.

But *none* of that matters. The only thing that does is the fact that I've just arrived back to an empty bus...a bus which I *finally* found, moved from behind the bar to the RV Park up the road by whom and for why, I don't know. I was just grateful I finally found the hard to miss monstrosity. Until I found it empty. It's after one and no one's here, no note...

Where. The. Fuck. Is. My. Siren?

I call her again, perhaps the tenth time since the Ruthie sighting, and like all the other times, it goes straight to voicemail. I then try Rhett, which should speak volumes of my desperation, but he says he left right after the show, assuming she'd be with me. And Jarrett? Well, he's so drunk all I could make out was a slurred "not with me."

Searching the bus again, I stoop to look under the table, beneath Conner's bed, even pulling back the shower curtain...could she fit in one of the kitchen cabinets? She is pretty tiny. Nope, she's not here. At. One. In. The. Morning! That's when the big hand's on the twelve and the little hand's on the one, for those of us who still know how a clock works (technology often sending us *backwards* in full brain development). Moral of the story—it's waaaay too late not to know where my woman is.

She probably got a hotel room, so I pull up a list of the choices on my phone—five—and call a cab. *Oh sweet, sweet Siren...Cannon's coming for ya, and he's not bringing kisses and candy.*

No, your man is mad as hell!

I run to the cab as soon as it pulls up, and spout off the directions before I've even closed my door.

I'm pissed, I'm scared, I'm—*fuck*! I feel helpless. What if she's hurt? And like an answered prayer, my phone rings. Why the fuck is Sark calling me?

"Hey, man, what's up?" I try to shroud the sheer panic in my voice.

"You tell me." He chuckles. "I gotta close soon and get home to Cyndi, but your little pixie is forehead down on my bar."

"Lizzie?" I breathe out.

"Yep, not exactly drunk, more like a whipped dog who gave up and found a place to fall."

"Sark, I need a *huge* favor, man."

"Name it. You helped me out five figures tonight."

"Meet me at the back door with your keys. I'll lock it up, I swear." I hear, but can't even attempt to squash, the desperation in my voice.

"You got it. Text me when you're here. And lock it, fucker! I mean it!"

After the handoff, Sark heads to his car and I lock us in, then slink quietly through the kitchen. Through the circle window in the door, I see her, chin resting on her folded arms, staring off into space, a full bottle of beer in front of her, not a single sip gone, from the looks of it. Hell, from the far-off, vapid aura she's casting, I doubt she evens knows it's there.

I spot a staircase to my left and follow it up to VIP and down the other side, stopping only to program a track to play later, 'til I'm approaching her from behind. Oh, she's not a bit drunk; when I'm still five feet away, her head pops up and her spine goes stiff. Her breathing picks up in speed and velocity, shirt actually rippling with it. She's acutely alert, and aware that I'm in the room.

Before she can turn her head, I advance, trapping her in with my hands braced atop the bar on either side of her and my chest pressing into her back with authority. "No nibble for you, my love. What I *need* is an explanation," I growl, restraining as much anger as I can.

"Lemme guess, after family dinner, you all loaded into the Griswold family truckster to go home, you fucked Ruthie against the back bumper, then helped her in and with her seatbelt," she sneers, spewing jealous, ridiculous malice. "Please, enlighten me on the plans for Thanksgiving."

I lean as close to her ear as possible and hiss, "You open that smart mouth again, and I'll damn sure keep it better occupied...with my dick shoved in it."

"What?" she gasps, but not before she shivers. "Fuck you, Cannon." She tries to turn her head, but I use my chin to nudge it back in place.

"Don't turn that head. You shut up and listen, *very* carefully." I'm not *exactly* trying to scare her, but *damn*, am I boiling on the inside. My voice is adamant and sinister, the restrained fury evident. "I've never been so worried or scared in my life. Something could've happened to you. Putting yourself in danger just to punish me is immature and selfish!" I slam a hand on the bar. "Now tell me, what'd you think you were doing?"

"Not playing house with my ex!" she screams, voice quivering, fighting off tears like the tough little nut she is. "I can sit at a bar if I want! I wasn't hurting anyone," her bravado loses some oomph, insecure sadness peeking through, "just hurting."

"What'd I ask you to do? Have a little faith in me? Was that just too damn much?"

"What? I'm not in the mood for mind games, Cannon, say what you gotta say," she snips unconvincingly, because for the first time ever, I hear hopelessness in her voice.

"I didn't know Ruthie was coming; neither did my family. She crashed their table, which was a *bad* move. My sister and mother tongue-lashed her up one side and down the other. I tried to find you to explain before I left with them, to take the scene *elsewhere*, but you'd already tucked tail and run."

"I was helping load the bus," she pathetically makes the excuse.

"Cause you didn't think three grown men could handle it without you? Or was it the totally unreasonable assumption that I wouldn't want to introduce you to my family?" I pull her up under her arms, leaving her facing away from me. She comes pliantly at least.

"With Ruthie there?" she scoffs.

"*Especially* with Ruthie there. Sooner she knows my end-all finally found me, the better." I take her hands and pull them up, laying them flat on the bar, then gently kick her ankles apart, prepping her stance to bear the brunt of what's clawing its way out of me.

"Jealousy is only flattering if it comes from someplace good," I mock her one time words to me, "not from lack of trust."

*Finally*, the music I'd set starts to play around us, my man, Anthony Hamilton, "Do You Feel Me." Ideal lyrics, asking her all I need to know for sure.

I slide my hands up her legs, and, reaching her hips, I make quick work offing her skirt. That delectable ass, curved and firm, *almost* tempts me to go feral on her instantly, but I maintain. "When you need me most, you'll find me right by your side, not slinking off in doubt, leaving you to bear hurts or fight battles without me." I leisurely side her thong down her legs, stomping a foot down in the center to remove it completely.

"When I feel threatened, I'll fight that much harder for you." I shred her t-shirt, pulling it apart, right down the middle, with one rip.

"When a man tries to snake his way in, I'll dip you in front of him and show him exactly how your man makes you wet with one kiss." Thumb and forefinger pinch in, bra's loose, and I push it down her arms. "Any questions?"

She shakes her head, but not as fast as her legs are shaking beneath her. The musk of her arousal glistens just inside her thighs and the sweet scent fills my senses.

"Turn around."

Timidly, bottom lip clenched in her teeth, she spins to face me, but her eyes stay down.

"Look at me," I grind out starkly, guising my want, her perky breasts and taut nipples calling to me. "Why'd you run and leave me to fend for myself? I thought we were a team. I thought you loved me?"

"I do." She flinches, then adjusts her defensive shriek to a more docile tone. "I do love you, Cannon. But I saw her with your family, smiling, so sure she'd won. I was scared. I thought maybe your parents wanted to help settle things between you. She's very glamorous; long, shiny hair, perfect make-up, and were those *pearls* she had on?" She laughs softly, shaking her head for herself only, stirring up doubts in her mind. "I'm a mess. No way would a mother want her son with me over Pollyanna." Ashamed, unguarded and self-doubting, she wraps her arms around her waist and drops her chin to her chest. "Why am I naked?"

"Because," I flip open one button of my fly, "the only time you're truly *with* me," second button, "is when I'm inside you. So I'm going to fuck you 'til you're back to certain," number three, "and remind you," four, "we. Are. We."

All five buttons now agape, I push my jeans below my hips and pull my cock out. "Not you, me, sometimes us, not quite sure—WE. If someone gets in *our* way," now I step flush against her and pick her up, hands gripped on her sweet ass, "you stay right beside me until we've defeated them, together. Understand?"

"Yeah," she whispers, a lost light slowly beginning to re-emerge in her brown jewels.

"Now, I realize you went crazy tonight, but you think you can manage to guide my dick home?" I wink at her.

She nods anxiously, reaching between us and wrapping her precious little hand around my throbbing cock.

Guiding it to her center, with just the tip in, I manage to speak. "Lean both hands back on the bar and hold the fuck on, Siren."

Then, in one purposeful thrust of my hips, I seat myself fully in her snug, warm heaven. "Whose dick's in you?"

"Yours," she groans, head tilted back.

"Name," I bark, pulling almost all the way out.

"Cannon's."

"Goddamn right." I plunge back in with a savage moan. "Whose pussy is this?"

"Cannon's, yours," she whimpers now, grinding against me.

"Do I love you?"

"Y-yes," her pants choke her up.

"Do you," I gyrate my pelvis in a lazy circle, looking for my target, "love me?"

"Yessss," she wails—*found it.*

I sink in and out, seeking the same destination with a swirling rub every time 'til I feel her pussy start to clamp and quiver around me, sparking the warning fire in my balls. "Never doubt me or us again. You hear me?"

"Yes, God, yes, I hear you. I promise." She lifts her head and locks molten eyes on me. "Now make me come."

"Always." I pucker my lips, which she leans into, kissing me with the fervor and passion of a siren about to explode. "Fingers, baby, play with my pussy for me."

I feel her maneuver a hand between us, so I tilt her only just, driving into the deepest part of her. Sweat beads on my forehead and my knees quake; I close my eyes, relishing in every single pulse of her tight sex around me.

SE Hall

"Fuck me, Lizzie, love you, inside you, nothing close," I babble incoherently, the relentlessly flexing and contracting of her tight heat around me telling me she can't hold out much longer. "Now, baby, come with me."

"Ammmm!" she cries, tightening her legs around my waist painfully, pulling the shit out of my hair as she tries to swallow my tongue.

I unload shot after shot into her luscious, tiny body, marking her as all mine.

We're frozen, a sweaty mess of tangled limbs and heavy breathes. I drop my forehead between her boobs and gather myself, the scent of sated, well-fucked, all-mine Lizzie damn near enough to set me off on her again. "Love you," I murmur, kissing her slickened breastbone.

She pets my hair methodically and giggles softly. "Love you more. But you gotta move, I'm pretty sure my back is broken. Andddd," she giggles, a breathy, magical sound, "don't be surprised if you get a call from Sark. Pretty sure that's a camera in the corner there."

# CHAPTER
## twenty-seven

No Ruthie in the crowd tonight, which is almost too bad—I could go for another "we're a team" fuckin!

His parents and sister *are* back, third table to my left, and no matter how hard I try to keep my gaze elsewhere, I'll be damned if I haven't looked at them 100 times squared. What they must think...not only is her past um, colorful, she's a staring freak and in a band with two guys. Okay, three guys. One of whom is their son. And she's most likely fucking him. Or maybe all of them.

*Yeah, I'm every mother-in-law's dream.*

Almost *during* the closing bars of "Cloaked," our original, Cannon's on his mic. "How's everybody doing tonight?" he rasps, laughing while he waits for the pandemonium to die down. "Yeah, me too. Sark, the owner of this shack, is an old buddy of mine and it's an honor to grace his stage. Sark, where ya at, brother?" He shields his eyes from the stage lights, searching. "There he is, the handsome gent behind the bar. He happened to tell me," he cups his mouth, as though telling a secret, "two dollar select shots 'til the next song ends!"

I hoot brashly when Sark flips him off, then turns, face white as a ghost, to the sudden swarm at the bar. Cannon was mindful enough in his jeer to specify "select" shots, so hopefully no one expects a two dollar shot of expensive stuff, not that I have any idea what would qualify.

"I'm also pretty damn happy that my parents, you can call them Moms and Dad, and my beautiful little sister, you can call her *never*, are in the crowd again tonight! Wave hi, familia!" he embarrasses them…or nah, since Sommerlyn stands up and curtsies, blowing random kisses to the crowd. "And last, but as far from least as possible, which would be *foremost*," he jests with the crowd, "is the fact that I share this stage and every single day, with my gorgeous, talented as she is kind, girlfriend, Lizzie." He turns to face me, the love and respect glimmering in his eyes stealing the breath from me. "Now, my Siren *loves* her Beatles, and *I love her*, so hear me out."

Ah, clever segue, my sweet Cannon, for my toes are already curled, rewards being mapped out in my head before the first word of "If I Fell in Love" slides sexily from between his luscious lips. Not to be contained, I join in for *help me understand* and *if I gave my heart*, then again at *would love to love you.*

Rhett joins in with a soft, mellow beat and I glance back skeptically, afraid of what I'll find. Needless—all I get is an air kiss and a quick thumbs up from an endearing friend, happy for the other.

I'm a blubbering mess when he finishes, so Jarrett, like a champ, closes the show and I scurry off stage. The heat is right there behind me, filling the air with a heady weight of protection and adoration. I'd know he was in the room if I was in a coma. My nipples perk, my knees shake, and my breathing accelerates…my body attuned…like it's other half is near.

"Thank you," I whisper, back still to him, mostly to hide my hasty wiping of my sniffling nose.

"Always my pleasure, love." He glides up closer, wrapping his monstrous arms around my waist. "Need my nibble." He doesn't move my hair this time, rather just maneuvers his face under it and nips at my neck, licking the spot after. "Let's go introduce you to the Blackwell clan."

"Huh?" I squeak, tensing.

"You heard me. I figure you wanna walk to them, but I'm okay with throwing you over my shoulder. Your call, baby."

I can *hear* his smirk. *Throw me over your shoulder, my ass.*

"Walk," I acquiesce grumpily. "Do they know?" I twirl around, nervous moisture pooling in my mouth, tongue threatening to swell beyond capable speech.

"Know what? That I love you? Yes. That you're amazing and selfless? Yes. That you sometimes poot in your sleep? No." He grins a devilish, ornery goad.

"I. Do. Not. Poot. And even if I did, how hateful of you to mention it! You hump your mattress in your dreams." I cross my arms and prepare for battle.

"Sometimes." He shrugs, grabbing my hand and pulling me to the stairs that lead to the gallery. "And sometimes you poot."

Lightening the mood to keep me from hyperventilation was his tactic, I know. But now I'm even more self-conscious...*I fart in my sleep?*

"Siren," he peers back, "if you were walking any slower, you'd be going backward. Come on, sassy girl, you got this."

And with thirty-two more steps, not counted by me of course, we're standing in front of his family.

He squeezes my hand and pulls me closer in to his side. "Moms, Dad, Sommer. *This* is my Lizzie. Elizabeth Carmichael."

Of course, his mother's the first to approach, but not with the handshake I'd dried my clammy sweat off for. No, she has me secured in a perfumed hug before I can blink, then pulls back, spreading my arms out, and looks me over. Remember that scene in *Sixteen Candles*, the "Oh, and Fred, she's gotten her boobies!" one? It's racing mortifyingly around in my mind until she takes a different route. Thank God.

"You are the most precious thing I've ever seen! So beautiful and collected. And that voice? You have a wonderful gift, Elizabeth. I'm honored to meet you."

So much better than I'd expected. There might actually be one of my heartstrings wobbling a bit right now.

Next is Sommerlyn, a supermodel blonde with glowing green eyes. "Hi, Lizzie, nice to meet you. I'm Cannon's sister, Sommerlyn." Niceties first, *then* she takes her hug. *How fortunate Cannon has helped tremendously with my touching phobia or else this family of huggers would be freaking me out right now.* "My brother is smitten," she whispers in my ear. "He's fabulous, you'll be happy, I promise."

"Damn right, she will." He chuckles and kisses the top of my head. Sommerlyn needs to work on her whispering, 'cause you could cook meat well-done on my flaming cheeks right now.

Then there's his dad, who honestly, I already like. More than obvious where his son gets it, he's very handsome and well kept, with a smile that instantly invites you in. "I'm Marshall Blackwell, it's very nice to meet you." He shakes my back to clammy, vaguely trembling hand. "Could we treat you kids to a late dinner?"

Respectfully, Cannon leaves the decision up to me by stealing a subtle glance and squeezing my hand.

"Are you hungry?" I ask faintly.

"I could eat." He shrugs, giving me no hint on which way he's leaning.

"Lizzie," Sommerlyn kinda whines, "please?"

"All-All right," I stammer and offer an uncertain smile. "Let me just check with the rest of the band." This was the last show and we haven't even really talked about anything... I'm practically running backstage, crashing open the door.

Thankfully, they're still there, waiting on Uncle Chimney to finish a smoke. Everyone looks up at me when I burst out.

"Hey," I speak to the ground, "what are the plans?"

"We were just talking about that. Technically, we're at the end of this leg, and pretty close to home." Rhett laughs.

"Well, home is figurative. Anyway, your uncle could rest up while we regroup."

"I'm going to see Nessy," Jarrett says, his face lighting up.

"Rhett, where will you go?" my question sounds worried, and accurately so. I never know what Rhett's plans are, and I feel the tiniest bit guilty that he's gotten bumped further down my priority list.

"Dunno." He shrugs. "But I've saved every dime I've made, plus the grandparents' trust fund that my parents don't know about. I was thinking of looking for an apartment for when we want to go home to an *actual* home."

I don't mention I was thinking of doing the same. "So why don't we do this? Jarrett goes to Vegas to see his honey—kudos on the monogamy, by the way." I give him a high-five. "Rhett and I find places, and Bruce heads to the home he already has and rests up?"

"You can drop me at the airport," Jarrett tells Bruce as he bounces foot to foot, rubbing his hands together.

"I'm straight. I'll find a way to get there when I figure out where there is," Rhett says. "And I assume you're sticking with Cannon?"

I nod and grin. "I am."

"Okay, sounds like we got it. Everyone can call or text, see where we're at after the break," Rhett says optimistically but glances over at me, his eyes telling me—*he knows.* "Hands in," he offers first me, then the others, a poorly faked smile and we make a pile of mitts. "New path on three, one, two, three," he chants and we all yell it and throw our hands up like the band of dorks we are.

Jarrett hugs me first. "Be seeing ya soon, Liz. Call me if you need me, or when you're ready to head out. Tell Con Man hey for me."

"Will do. Love you." I kiss both his cheeks.

"Back at ya, lil' bit." He smiles and flicks my ear.

Next Rhett and I have our moment, which leaves us both crying, my tears far sloppier than his. "I'll miss you," I sputter into his shoulders.

"Me too, Liz, me too. But you're gonna be fine, I have no doubt. He's a good one and he loves you. I trust him with the most precious thing in my life—you. Maybe I'll go find someone that lights me up like that." He kisses my forehead, one last lingering embrace. "Call me and be good." He starts to walk away and stops, not immediately turning to face me, every breath an obvious effort through his shirt. Finally, when I'm seconds from rushing to him and embracing him in the hug of a lifetime, he turns to look over his shoulder. "Even if it's not next Tuesday, I'll always be seeing ya. I love you, Liz."

I nod shakily, biting my lip enough to hurt, the pain counteracting and keeping the tears at bay. "Always," I mouth, and hold strong as he walks off, giving Bruce and me some time alone...or maybe himself.

My uncle, kind but rough around the edges, gives me a knuckle rap on my cheek. "Go fly, baby girl. Just remember your way home. Let me know when you need me."

I nod, reaching to hug him fiercely. "I love you."

"Not half as much as I love you, angel. Go live. You know where to find me. And don't you start feeling guilty," his brow furls at me sternly, "those boys will be fine. Your turn, Elizabeth."

I watch as the bus fires up and pulls away, then stops, Jarrett jumping out and running back to me with Cannon's duffel and guitar case, the actual instrument still inside the venue with him. "Phone's in the bag. Anything else, I figured you could grab from your uncle; I wasn't about to carry all of everyone's crap out here," he laughs. "Love you." He kisses my cheek and disappears again.

About that time, Rhett's cab pulls up, he, himself unmoved from further down the sidewalk where he'd retreated. Once he's committed to it, inside the cab and it moving, he turns, glimpsing back to find my eyes. "Wipe those tears, Liz. I'll see you soon!" he calls through the open window with a reassuring smile.

And then he's gone.

All I can do is stand there, dazed. It shouldn't have been that cordial and effortless to part ways with three of the most important, day in day out, companions, friends, in my life. Maybe for them it was "Have a great summer, see ya when school starts," but for me, there's an air of finality gnawing at me, festering in my subconscious in the most sensible, but undoing, voice.

I simply can't remember the actual moment I last made a fresh start. Maybe because it was on the heels of misery and I've chosen to block it out…I don't know. But this time, it's different; exhilarating, exciting…but not less off-putting.

"I could've sworn we'd decided against you standing in dark alleys alone," Cannon says behind me.

"They all just left; hasn't been five minutes."

"Where'd they all go?" The ground coverage crackles beneath his steps closer to me.

"Bruce and the bus went home. He needs a rest. Jarrett's flying to Vanessa. And Rhett wasn't sure."

"And what about Lizzie? What's her plan?" he asks in a soft, seeking voice, chin resting on my shoulder.

Turning, I burrow into his chest and suck in his calming elixir. "I was hoping you had a plan."

One hand cradles my head, where he kisses, the other my waist. "Want me to plan it? Do you want me to ease your mind and take care of things while you lie back, all lovely, and relax?"

I'm not sure what's up with the Boss, Bitch, Defensive, and Always in Control Lizzies, but every single one of them just took a unanimous vote. "Yeah, that'd be wonderful. Just keep Conner in mind, prioritized."

SE Hall

"Of course." He smiles, I know without looking. "Now let's go eat with my family before they think we fled out the back door."

# CHAPTER
## *twenty-eight*

I know it's silly and dangerous to get attached too early, but you haven't met Cannon's family.

They're *amazing*, kind, accepting, open-minded, and huggers…Lord, are they huggers.

His father, I'm sorry, Marshall, (which he insists I call him) is just amazing. Not once all night did he criticize, scowl, raise his voice, or disappear. And it was him who suggested Rock-n-Bowl after our smorgasbord at IHop…where he had the Rooty Tooty meal. If he's the leader of the family, I'm following!

And Libby, his mom—she's loving, nurturing, and absolutely enjoyable! At the bowling alley, they played "Cha-Cha Slide" and she was all up in that, spanking it! I may love her. By the end of the night, I was *leaning* into her hugs.

Sommerlyn. Where do I start? First of all, she *vocally*, like six towns over can hear vocally, hates Ruthie. We were best friends immediately. And when she fawned over my hair and complexion, and called me adorable, repeatedly, I actually believed her.

Cannon sat back and watched mostly, a content smile on his face, though we dragged him up to teach us how to Dougie, even though we already knew. And may I just say…Cannon Blackwell can gyrate his hips and call it whatever the hell dance he wants, any time he wants; it's a wonderful sight.

When we finally parted ways with his family, around four in the morning, I truly didn't want to see them go and can't quite wait to see them again.

After Cannon and I trudge to our hotel room door, we crash in bed fully clothed, less shoes, and I personally fall asleep in a happily, delusional haze, drifting off to a tranquil place where I dream of family picnics and mother/sister/me day trips to the spa and lunch. It's a dream, so never having been a "spa girl" doesn't matter.

His family makes me long for things I've never had, things I couldn't have. I bet Christmas at their house is the bomb—at least, I hope so, since I'm invited!

The next morning, in this case, morning meaning noon, I stretch and groan, my arm immediately finding empty space. No noise, no shower running, where is my man? *My man*...I like it.

I roll out of bed, literally catching myself on one arm short of eating floor, and wander into the bathroom. I don't wake up pretty, I rise a zombie killer. If my hair and big ass eye boogers don't make one keel over in fright, my breath and dried drool trail will.

Wasting no time, I brush my teeth twice, then jump in the shower. I'm halfway through the fancy hotel conditioner rinse when the draft of the open door hits me.

"Morning, Siren."

"Morning, babe." I'm all giddy from last night and I know he loves it when I call him that, so I humor him. "Where were you?"

"Out getting every newspaper I could find. Not only to make sure Somm and my mother hadn't published an engagement announcement," he chuckles, "but so I could look for a place."

"Fun fact," I smirk over at him using one of his favorite phrases, "newspapers are on the internet now. Will you hand me a towel?"

"But do online newspapers have these handy dandy brochures with pictures and specs of the properties?" He spreads out several glossy booklets and fans himself with them. "Plus, what fun is it to circle rental options on a screen?"

"He shoots, he scores. Touché. Well done." I tap the end of his nose lovingly.

"And he hasn't scored yet," he growls, scooping me up, landing me on my back, bouncing off the mattress in seconds, "but he will."

He comes down over me, wrestling away the towel and lavishing kisses over my face, throat, and collarbone, until he latches onto my right nipple, sucking and nipping until he has it an aching point. "Perfect, it loves me. See? Pointing straight at my mouth." Then he moves to the left, giving the same sensuous treatment as I pant and writhe beneath him, tugging at his hair to keep him close.

Abruptly, he stands, relieving himself of his gray t-shirt with one yank over his head, then a few so sexy moves to lose his jeans and briefs.

"Don't move," I croon, soaking up every bit of him.

I'm ruined. No one will ever look this good, an intricately laid plane of cut lines and dents, just the right amount of hair in just the right places, golden skin with slightly darker nipples and a long, thick, turgid cock that seems to reach for me. And I know behind him is the broadest, most sculpted back and taut, risen ass in the history of mankind.

He's perfect; perfect for me, anyway. And when he looks at me, loving reverence in his dark brown, smoky eyes, I'd do anything to keep that gaze on me forever.

"All right, you may proceed." I giggle, repositioning longways on the bed.

"You feeling adventurous, baby?" he asks, timbre and whiskey-brown jewels smoldering.

"Maybe," I drawl.

"Stand up." He gives me his hand, then takes the spot I had on the bed. "Lie down on me backwards, head at my feet."

"W-we're not gonna—"

"Oh yes, we fucking are. Been craving a taste of you, and my cock really wants to meet your mouth."

I awkwardly and as unsexily as possible, get positioned, which he has to assist with, until a huge boner is twitching at me in 3D.

"Cannon, I've, uh, never—"

"Good," he snarls possessively. "That's the dick you'll suck for the rest of your life. Get friendly. You can't do it wrong, Siren, promise."

As I'm still staring, running measurements, analytics, and trying to remember what I learned about the esophagus in Anatomy, he clutches my hips, tugging me backward, and takes one long, silky lick of my dripping center. *Holy fucking shit.*

"Hmmm," he hums, the vibrations of that single sound making my entire body shiver in delight.

Without mind or planning, I take him in my mouth, testing out his taste and texture with my curious little tongue. Then I start at the bottom, playing with his balls in my hand, and lick all the way up, my tongue stiffened to a point.

He grunts from behind me, digging his fingers harder into my hips, and starts spearing his tongue in and out of me, mixed with a harsh suck in between each poke. No part of my pussy goes un-worshipped; he soothes his tongue up each lip, in between every crease, and uses his teeth to pull at my clit...I guess I should get busy cause right now I'm just selfishly fucking his face with no idea where his dick even is.

"Sorry," I moan, then fumble around until I've got a strong, clamping hold on his length. I take in the head, sucking, teasing the hole with my tongue, then I take a little more in my mouth. I practice open-mouth smooching-like sucks up the back side, swirling my tongue in no particular pattern on the down slide. He tastes salty and he smells divine, musky and manly, but he's far too big to ever feel completely tended to by my mouth, so I key into his sounds, noting what feels best, 'cause special tricks will have to get it with this big boy.

As he works me further, I go all carnal cat like, shoving as much as I can of him in until I feel him bump the back of my throat and I swallow instinctively.

"Ahh, God, Lizzie, fuck yes. Like that," he howls.

*Okay, he likes the deep swallow. Noted.*

"Play with my balls too, baby. Press down and rub the spot right behind them."

*Man, lots of steps to remember.*

But pretty soon it's coming naturally. With my right hand, I master ball-rolling with my index finger pressing his spot, while my left squeezes around the part that *is not* fitting in my mouth, sucking until my cheeks hollow, my tongue a constant tornado on the part that can. And when I get him in deep, I swallow.

*Definitely his favorite move.*

He's close. I can tell because he's ten times harder and leaking on my tongue, his clasp on my hips bruising. Also, he sounds like a springtime animal in rut back there.

"Fuck my face baby, *hard*. Wiggle that sweet ass for me any way you like it." He shoves maybe two (maybe more) fingers in me, stroking, not reaching "my spot," but close, and widens his mouth to cover all of me, then licks all areas around his fingers, and bites my clit.

*Game over!*

My vaginal walls flex ruthlessly around his fingers over and over as hot jets of his cum coat my mouth and throat. Not sure what to—ah, fuck it—I swallow it all, popping off and licking the perimeter of my mouth to make sure I got it all. Then I collapse, forehead to balls. *Sublime.*

"Tell me the part again about not knowing how to suck a dick?" He chuckles/grumbles pretty much to my ass.

"First time's a charm?"

"Never read up on it? Asked your friends, Google, nothing? Just. Like. That?" he teases, or really asks, not sure.

"I promise, never will I google 'How to give a Blowjob.' You have my word." I rise to my knees and again, ungracefully, pivot to face him, settling into his neck, my cheek and hand on his chest.

"Now that I have you all creamy and cooperative, let's talk about living arrangements."

"Hold that thought." I scramble out of bed and dig through the pockets of his jeans. "Roll over."

"What are you—"

"Just roll over." I dance giddily in place until he does as I say and turns onto his stomach. "Don't move, but flex your ass."

Oh Lord, he complies, making my mouth water. I take the quarter I'd scrounged up and—sure enough—right back in my hand.

Let the record show you *can* bounce a quarter off my man's ass.

He laughs into his pillow. "I can't believe you just did that."

"Yes, you can, that's exactly something I would do." I crawl up him and straddle his back, massaging his shoulders. "I love your booty."

He rolls over beneath me and grins up at me, eyes brighter than the sun through the window. "And I love you. And your booty also." He winks. "So we have eight days until Conner's home. Let's go get my car and drive to Richmond. Population 36,000—"

"You already gave me the stats, Mr. Salesman." I snicker.

"Schools test in top 10% in the state, lots of nature and a historic district, average price of house $150K." He just keeps right on going, adding a few new facts, really wanting to sell me on Richmond.

"That was quite the pitch," I tickle his sides, "*again.* You should apply at the City Welcome Center. I'd buy."

"No," he reaches up and taps my chin, "I'll buy. But you pick it out."

I gulp loudly, parched and panicking, hastily making to dismount him.

"Nu uh, better twitch that nose, Witchy. It's only way you're escaping this conversation," he taunts. "In for me," his eyes flare, brooking no argument, "now out for you." He runs both hands up and down my thighs in satiny caress. "Better or you need another?"

"Better," I mumble, his happy trail my focal point.

"I'm almost twenty-eight years old, Lizzie. I want a house. I want to re-paint the fence and change light bulbs and decorate nurseries and host Thanksgiving and hide Easter eggs."

"What about the band?"

He traces a circle around my navel. "You tell me."

"I was actually already thinking." I bear down on my bottom lip, searching out my nerve. Saying it aloud makes it real. "Conner could use some stability and he seems to like spending time with Richard and his new family. There's kids, and living fish," I titter, swiping away a lone tear.

*Oh, you didn't get the memo? Bus fish=all floaters, flushed to the ocean in the sky.*

"And my uncle's back can't take much more. And Jarrett, if he's actually serious, for once, about a girl, he needs to see it through. And Rhett—"

"Baby," he jostles me, "breathe. Our life, figuring it out...it's not a sprint, it's a marathon. Okay, now you were saying?"

"Rhett. The only thing missing between Rhett and I was smushy love. I found it and he needs to as well. Which he may not do if I'm around."

He strains not to laugh, which produces a sneeze through only your nose type thing. "Smushy love?"

I impishly slap his abs, all eight packs of them. "You know, romantic, not friend love. You and me love."

"Come 'ere to me," he beckons, crooking his finger, and I lean down over him, hands braced on either side of his head while he tangles his in my hair and pivots my head. "What's smushy love taste like? Show me."

I kiss him softly at first, each corner of his mouth, then roll my eyes and get up. "I will be at the curb, getting in a cab, in ten minutes. Hope to see you there, Scary Sex Drive."

I jump away from his reaching hands and run, locking the bathroom door behind me.

# CHAPTER twenty-nine

Once in the cab, Cannon assures me that the drive is about forty minutes. Now, I'm no mathematician, but I still slept in a Holiday Inn last night…so no way can that be right *and* be a halfway point.

"Forty minutes to Richmond?" I ask for clarification.

"No, to Lawrence, where I lived. We gotta grab my car."

*Keep breathing.*

"Is your car at your parents' house?" The hopeful optimism in my voice is a farce, but worth a try all the same.

He sighs, so of course I shudder, braced before I even asked. "Love, my car's at the house I lived in with Ruthie. I need to get it." He shrugs. "It's mine and we're here."

"So we're going, me and you, to the house you shared with your ex-fiancé, to gather your things? And you planned on telling me this *when*?" Now my voice is raised and unattractively nasal.

"Lizzie," *don't you condescend me, mister,* "where'd you *think* my car was?"

"I don't know, your parents' maybe? Cannon, I don't want to do this." Shaking my head adamantly, I let go of his hand and scoot across the seat.

"I've got the keys with me. We'll hop in and drive off. She won't know we're there, if she's even home." He slides across the vinyl, refusing to allow space between us.

"I'm not going in and dividing assets." I mock gag.

"Not a thing there I want or need, except my car." He forcibly raises my hand and kisses each knuckle, then my palm. "Five minutes and we're home free."

Still not happy and about thirty minutes left to burn, I ask some simmering questions. "If you lived together and were engaged, why's it only her house?"

He laughs, head tossed back. "Wait until you see it. I couldn't afford her lifestyle, so Daddy bought her a show castle."

"But you have money to buy yourself a house in Richmond?" I perk a curious brow.

"No, but I've got flawless credit and a good down payment saved, plus a degree with five years of experience under my belt. I can take care of us comfortably." He lays an arm around my shoulders and leans in to kiss me on the cheek. "I *want* to take care of us."

"I have money, Cannon. I don't *need* taken care of. I *need* a partner, 50/50. The troubles are ours, the good times are ours, and chores are most definitely *ours*."

"That sounds like," he gazes off, to where or at what I'm lost, but he's back soon, "everything I've ever wanted. Imma need a nibble for that one," he grunts, taking his fill in the crook of my neck.

The cab driver shifts loudly in his seat at my squeal, so I push Cannon off.

"So does this mean you'll live with me? I mean, somewhere other than a tour bus?" He smirks, knowing it's his power card, most valid argument.

The truth is, we have cohabitated, a hell of a lot closer than in a house, for quite a while, with not one fight. No, our one disagreement was in public, and ended very well, if I do say so myself.

So myself.

"We'll see. A house seems premature, a big investment to split unmarried," I naysay, despite the mental reasoning I only just finished.

"If you just proposed, my little Siren, the answer is yes!" He dive bombs me, crushing his arms around me, smothering my face and neck in kisses.

"You're scaring people in public again." I giggle. "Heel. And *no*, I was not proposing, I was thinking apartment, maybe a condo?"

He falls dramatically across my lap, looking up. *Please don't let me have any boogers in my nose.* "Hey, how'd you get that?" He touches the scar under my chin.

"It's a pretty gnarly story, think you can stomach it?" I tease, my smile devious.

"Try me."

"I fell down our stairs, running late for school, and went splat on the floor...and my pencil. Jabbed it straight up and through."

"Damn," he shudders, "ouch. I bet you—"

*"Mom's in Heaven now, Bubs, watching over us."*

*"But she was careful on the stairs. Not me."*

"Lizzie? Come back to me, love, breathe. Lizzie, it's Cannon, look at me, gorgeous. "

I blink, then blink again, my heart's pumping blood deafening in my ears.

"Lizzie? Where are you?" He's sitting up, shaking me by the shoulders, but his voice sounds like it's in a bottle.

"C-call my dad. He's in my phone, under 'Die Dick.' Call him! Call him!" I scream, the cab stopping so abruptly my head flies into the seat in front of me.

"Hey, motherfucker! What the fuck are you doing? Lizzie, right here," he yanks his shirt over his head and off, "hold this tight on your nose, head back, pinch it hard." I can hear Cannon's frantic, loud threats of physical violence to the cabbie, while I blindly, with one hand, dig out my phone.

Maneuvering it to where I can actually see it, I pull up my father's contact.

"Here, babe, I got it." Cannon takes the phone from me. "Lean back and apply pressure."

After several minutes of the cab driver grumbling in Idon'tknowwhatyou'resayingnese, Cannon speaks. "Mr. Carmichael, hello, sir. I'm sor—no, she's fine. Well, the cab driver busted her nose. No, no, she flew into the back of the seat when he slammed on—I don't know, hold on."

He moves the phone from his mouth and leans forward. "What's your cab number?" he snarls at the driver, then talks into the phone again. "Huh, yeah it's a Yellow Cab. Hey, you, driver, what's your fucking cab number?" The man, now an ashen color, hands back a card. "Ha!" Cannon rings out, "it's 5810666. Go figure. Don't worry; I'll kick his ass in about ten minutes. No, no, I don't agree, I think he needs a good gowlering. A gowler? A hit, like 'fuck, I didn't see that coming.' Hang on."

Well, if that wasn't the most confusing bout of incoherent rambling, some to the cab driver, some to my father, I don't know what the hell was. My head's throbbing as bad as my nose from it.

"Lizzie?"

I glance over at him out my good eye; is he talking to me or about me? One look confirms, he's worried, angry and doesn't know which problem to tackle first.

"Are you okay, sweet girl? Pull back my shirt and lemme see."

"Good news or bad new first?" He strives to grin for me. "*Not* you," he chastises in the phone, "uh, sir," he recovers. "Her. Lizzie, baby?"

"Good," I mumble.

He does a cursory examination and gives me a wink. "It's stopped bleeding and I'm confident you'll live."

"Bad?"

"You look like you face planted a car seat. But in the prettiest way possible," he gushes in hindsight.

I roll my eyes and groan, throwing my head back. "Hey, Evil Knievel, why aren't we moving? Andale!" I say, though he's no more Hispanic than I am. *Oh well.* I know what I mean....so do it. "Gimme that phone," I growl, yanking it away. I'm about to gowler (I also had no idea what it meant) the hell outta every one of these disorganized, hazardous men.

"Conner fell down the stairs," I state into the phone.

"Elizabeth, are you all right? Do you need to go to the hospital?" my father asks, with what sounds suspiciously like concern.

"Yes. No. Conner fell down the stairs. You put up rails and changed the flooring below. I'm right, aren't I?"

There's an extensive silence and finally he sighs, a painful, agonized sound. "Yes, he did."

"Why didn't you just tell me that?" I'm screeching— *no sudden movements, cabbie.*

"Like I said, you were young. Your mother was despondent. Your brother suffered a major, life changing injury, your father stayed gone like a coward, and then your mother died. As your father, however miserable of one, I thought your adolescent psyche'd had enough. I couldn't ruin the last beautiful, healthy, strong one of us left."

"He fell and hit the front of his head?"

"Yes."

"Were you there?"

"Yes."

"You said you weren't. Why'd you lie?"

"Elizabeth, we will sit down and talk when I get back, I promise you. Right when we get back. Please, go spend this last week of ignorant freedom with that fine young man. Don't hesitate to have your nose looked at. And for God's sake, make sure you have Conner's fish ready when we get back." He chuckles lightly. "I'll send you a list of the ones he expects to be there."

Chuckles. My father. Wouldn't have believed it if I hadn't heard it firsthand.

"How's your band, daughter?"

"Do you care?"

"Very much."

"Disbanded for now."

"Ah, prayers do get answered. See you in eight days."

"We're here." He looks out the window anxiously, rubbing what I assume are sweaty, nervous palms on his thighs. "Hey, driver, here's the deal. You apologize to my girl and hang for a few, call 911 if there's trouble, and we'll call it even. Or, I report you and kick the shit out of you now. Whatcha think?"

"I very sorry, miss. Ball roll in street, child might follow. And I wait, ten minute."

"Agreed," Cannon says, opening the door, giving me a hand, and digging out his keys. "Go around, babe, hurry," he almost whispers, pressing the unlock button. Fun fact— they beep. We both look at each other with wide, worried eyes, realizing the mistake, then scramble frantically into the car.

Don't even *try* to deny you'd do the same thing, even amongst panic...I take inventory. Pictures on the dash—nope. Pull down visor like I own it—nope. Backseat glance— nothing. Big whiff—all man, *my* man. Glove box—nada.

This car...is clean. No signs of her anywhere.

He starts it and throws it in to reverse, then slams on the brakes and jolts me forward, knee slamming into the glove box. WHAT. THE. HELL?!

I'm gonna invest in a top of the line, fully padded bodysuit. I mean, come on!

I really should have caught on sooner, and I would've if it wasn't for my recent head injury, but one look at Cannon's face in the rearview and I know.

Chancing a glance behind us, there she stands, Grandma Scorned. Hands on hips, pursed lips, eyes shooting daggers…blocking our path.

Oh, and shocker…cab dude bolted like lightning, long gone.

"Want me to call the po?" I ask.

"Nope." He exhales dejectedly. "Her dad would paint it like Picasso and make it our fault. Somehow, I'd end up in jail and you'd be a home wrecker. Just stay in the car."

"What?"

"Please, Lizzie, for me. Stay in the damn car. This isn't a fight of who's scrappier or has the sharper tongue, this is a battle of power. She has it."

He affords me one long, last glance, like he's off to war and never coming back, and gets out. His shoulders are slumped, his head down, his steps sluggish, and all I want to do is jump out and love him back to better.

# CHAPTER thirty

We've established, through Cannon's extensive "shock me with your love and understanding" therapy, that my bark is worse than my bite. I'm his favorite candy—hard on the outside, smushy on the inside, and I love far fiercer than I hate.

But even the fucking Easter Bunny couldn't just sit back and watch discreetly thorough her side mirror as the man she loves gets scratched, slapped, pushed, and screamed at. And since I'd used his shirt for the nosebleed, he's totally unprotected from her nails...which I've decided need ripped from the nail bed and shoved square up her ass.

Nope. Miss Priss 'bout to learn how "ladies" (especially those who wear pearls) should act.

She hears my door slam and jerks her head my way for a split second, before she's back at him, arms flying and screeching like the dirtiest sailor on the ship.

Cannon keeps her in one eye line and me the other, tight, tense lines of worry around his mouth and eyes. "Siren love, get back in the car," he grits pleadingly.

"Nah, got my dog for the bunny fight," I spit, staring at her. As I wave to her, she circles the other way *and* runs a key through the paint of his car, one endless scratch down the entire side. A nice car at that, one of those extended, luxury BMWs, the *only* thing he asked to take with him, and she just keyed the sumbitch.

"Was she always psycho?" I ask him as though she's not even within earshot.

His mouth curls up adorably. "Little bit. Easier to stay, I told ya," he shrugs.

"You buy this car with your own money?" I lift a brow in some sickening way, a tingle with anticipation, sort of flirting with him.

"Every cent."

"The house?"

"Her daddy."

"Her clothes?"

"Daddy."

"She work?"

"Not a day in her life."

"I'm right here! I can hear you, you dykey bitch!" she screams at me in the voice of a debutante who lost her tiara and can't handle it.

"Babe?" I ask and I think he knows what's coming.

"Yeah?" He lights up, the smirk I covet in his expression, from being called babe. I'm not sure if he's more pleased about the upcoming main attraction or the fact I'm "fighting for us" most, but it doesn't matter, pick one.

"You go wait in the car," I tell *him* now.

He salutes me, gives Ruthie a snarky finger-roll wave, and slides into the driver's seat.

"Now, Miss Ruthie." I make my way to her leisurely, biding my time, thinking of the most untraceable causes of death. Arsenic or air embolism—and me without the poison or a needle, dammit! "Why you backing up, badass? You were all yelling and shouting and keying cars like a prize fighter, so why you backing up?" I keep my voice deceptively calm, toying with her, stalking her like the scary flaming dyke she thinks I am.

"This isn't any of your business. This is between me and Cannon, my fiancé!"

So sneaky, my man, I hear him slide open the electronic window; he wants to hear his witch—I mean me, the *good* witch *without* a house on her—go to work.

P.S. I'm suddenly embracing the nickname with pride.

"Here's the thing. He's not your fiancé anymore, at all, not even a little bit, ever again. You used and tricked him then dumped him off like trash. I scooped up your trash, and it's my treasure. And *nothing*, comes between me and Cannon. He's mine. So it *is* my business. Now, you can either hand me your phone so I can block and erase his number and write me a check for the damage to his car," I roll my shoulders and suck in a calming breath for him, "or, I can change his number and put him on my plan," *should of thought of that a lot sooner, really*, "and take the damage out of your ass." I spread out my feet, cross my arms and cock my head to the side. "What's it gonna be, Princess?"

"C-Cannon! Do you hear the way she's talking to me?"

"Why'd you key my car, Ruthie?" he yells through the crack in the window.

"I was mad! I'm sorry. Daddy will fix your precious car, geez." She rolls her eyes.

"Then yes, I hear her talking and can tell you, after that admission of yours, I'm loving it and recording it!" He grins ear to ear and holds up his phone, waving it from side to side gleefully.

*And...he's smiling, having some fun now, keyed car and all! My work here is almost done.*

"You!!" she whines/growls/shrieks (in reality, I have no idea WTF that sound was), and lunges at his door, smacking into a wall—a tiny wall, mind you—of overly protective, pissed off Siren. Cannon's Siren.

"What's the password?" I taunt her, straight-faced and cool as a cucumber. His phone's as good as changed, at this point, I'm simply toying with the bitch, like a little ball of catnip that I enjoy batting back and forth between my paws...like she did with him, all that time, in so many ways.

"You are such an evil, low class lesbian," she sneers, an inch from my face.

"Evil is kicking people you supposedly love enough to marry out in the middle of nowhere and fucking with their future behind their back. Low class is keying cars and begging your way back when you're not wanted. And a lesbian wouldn't have sat on his face, screaming around his big dick in her mouth while she came. Guess what I did this morning, Twinkle Toes?"

*Kill shot.* Cannon snorts in full appreciation of that one.

"Have I mentioned lately that I love you and you're the coolest person I've ever known?" Cannon's praise is muffled through the window behind me.

"Yes, babe, now zip it. I'm busy schooling a bitch at the moment." I can't quite tame my grin fully, but I do manage to school it and turn my attention back on her. "What's it gonna be, Bad Root Job Barbie? Your phone and a check, or my exercise—well, besides this morning—for the day?"

"You lay one finger on me and my daddy will ruin you," she warns, crossing her arms.

I *cannot* believe I'm about to play this card.

"Cannon?" I call over my shoulder, not taking my eyes of her.

"Siren?"

"Whose daddy is more powerful?" I ask, literally tasting vomit, but taking one for my team.

"Yours."

"Richer?"

"Yours."

"Thank you, babe. So…" I give her the old "how ya like them apples?" eyebrow. "What now? My patience is running thin. I gotta go house shopping with my man."

"Fine, how much?"

*Ah, I just love it when everyone gets a happy ending.*

"Cannon, how much?"

"I'll take care of the car and change my phone plan and number. I'd rather she stay out here while I go in and grab my clothes, golf clubs, pictures of my family…"

She heard him, so I stare her down, waiting for her answer. I may also have my fist locked and loaded if it's the wrong one. I've never punched anyone in my life—well, I beat on a few guy's heads for being mean to Conner—but she doesn't need to know that. *If* I punch her, she'll think I'm a pro.

"Fine," she huffs, "I'll let you in."

"No you won't." I put a stiff arm straight out to block her. "You'll stay right the fuck here. Ten minutes, babe. Go."

"Tell the truth, was I more *Training Day* badass or like, say…*Laura Croft Tomb Raider?*" I ask, turned and childishly ecstatic in the passenger seat.

"You were Training Laura Croft, a hot and nasty all your own." He glances from the road briefly to wink. "I adore you, you know that, right?"

"Please, you just want free lessons." I giggle and swat his arm.

"You stood *by* me, *for* me. You don't know what it meant Lizzie," he says. "But you will, because I damn sure plan to show you. In multiple ways."

"I do know. Pretty sure I still have the edge of the bar imprinted on my back to remind me," I joke, looking out the window at our stopping point, empty desolation. "Um, if we *build* a house, where we gonna live in the meantime?"

"Not building a house," he grunts, turning off the car, shoving the seat back violently. Like a blur, several things apparently happen at once, each one more evasive to me than the last.

At some point, in what order I wouldn't chance a guess, he's turned on, or up, or both "Give me Love," by Ed Sheeran, and gotten his jeans and briefs past his hips, smoldering eyes watching me as he strokes up and down his hardness.

"Come 'ere," he rasps with a sinful cocked brow and come hither chin.

I'm turned inside out by the chin beckon, the cock in hand, the song, and the chance of being caught in public—a heady, deadly mixture setting me unrestrainedly aflame. I scramble over the console like a jungle cat in heat, licking my lips as I sit astride him.

My plaid, cotton skirt easily fluffs out and over his thighs, and my thong doesn't stand a chance as he yanks it to the side. I hear the rip of fabric, at least even to allow some "give."

"I've never wanted anything in my life as badly as I want you right now. You make me crazy in every way, Siren. Ride my dick, gorgeous, *please*, now." He sounds pained and desperate, a dying man that can only be healed by being buried inside me.

He watches, head dipped, ravenous brown eyes concentrated on my glistening wet center as he stretches what's left of my thong aside. Using his shoulders for balance, I take him in, so lubricated with desire it's not at all painful, but noticeably a perfect fit.

I watching him watch me and decide, since no one can hear me but him, to see how undeniably senseless I can make him.

"Does that feel good, Cannon?" I purr.

His head flies up, like quite possibly injured his neck fast, first with a look of astonishment, but the dawning of "oh, she wanna talk dirty" visually moves over his face and his smirk emerges, but with a predatory, primitive edge to it; his eyes go black, bathed in debauchery.

"So fucking good, Lizzie love. You were made for me." His breathing is heavy; I can't look away as he licks along his bottom lip invitingly.

"You like it fast and hard," I show him what I mean, "or slow and savvy?" I speak in a seductive taunt, clasping my muscles as hard as I can on the slide up, flexing in and out and circling my pelvis on the way down.

"Uhhh, my sweet—damn," he groans, head falling back on the headrest. "Any way, so good, anything you do. I can't, ah baby, fuck me however you want."

"Watch, Cannon, watch me ride your big cock." I grab his hair and yank his head up.

"I love when you're like this. Finally using that naughty mouth to talk to me. You're feeling like a bad girl, aren't ya?"

I nod, continuing my unhurried, velvety strokes up and down him.

"Naughty girls," he grabs both sides of my shirt and rips it open, buttons pinging off the window, dash, where ever, "get their tits sucked." He pulls down the cups of my bra, pushing my breasts up and out. He stares his fill, gradually taking them in his hands, full mitt gropes, then pinching the nipples. "Hell yes, need more than a nibble," he growls, opening wide to take one breast all the way in his mouth.

I ride him through "Don't You Wanna Stay," by Jason Aldean, but by the closing chorus of "Uhh Ahh" by Boyz II Men, he's grunting and moaning the exact sounds in the song, his forehead covered in sweat, his teeth searing into my nipple harshly, past the point of restraint. He lets go of my breast, purely to breathe, I suspect, his thighs shaking under me.

"Feels too Goddamn good, love." His hand finds its way between us and he gathers moisture off his dick as I rise, using it to slicken and manipulate my clit. "Nobody, never, only me," he gasps. "Never stop fucking me, Siren. Never." He makes brutal demands on my clit, holding down my hip with the other hand as he powers up into me. His dick must not reach my throat, although it feels like it, 'cause I'm able to scream.

"Fill me, babe!" I beg, falling into his face. "Mouth, kiss me. Kiss me 'til I'm empty."

And he does, penetrating me in glorious rhythm, harmonious with his clitoral stimulations, synced with his tongue wrapping around and wrestling mine.

Unsure if he supports me or I melt into him, I fall against his chest for the most loving, intense orgasm of my life, the rapid thumps of his heart beating on my cheek.

"Love you," I hear myself mutter…maybe.

He runs a hand up underneath my hair, massaging my neck with his thumb. "Not sure that does it justice anymore…I worship, no, I live, because you make my heart beat."

# CHAPTER
## thirty-one

Once we finally gather ourselves, we're back on the road to Richmond. Adrift on a cloud, Cannon has to comment several times and finally pat my leg for me to acknowledge that my phone's ringing.

"Hello?"

"Hi Bethy! This is Conner, your brother," he says adorably.

Sated to crying in seven words—I'm a sap. "Bubs, how are you? I miss you so much!"

Cannon keeps his hand on my thigh, soothing rubs constant, and shoots me a beaming smile.

"I'm good, better than Bryson." *Laura's son?* "Some bug bit him and his head's big as a melon, Alma said."

"Oh no, is he gonna be okay?"

"He better not be faking 'cause now we're leaving. Hope and me are mad, very mad. Dad wants to talk to you, bye, Sister!"

"O-oh, okay, bye," I say to no one, kinda sad.

"Conner, son, stop and look at me." There's a pause in my father's voice, now the one in my ear. "Please do not throw my phone in the sand when you're done speaking, *hand* it to me. All right?"

"Okay, Dad!" I hear Conner yell from far away.

"Hi, daughter," he chuckles, "can you hear me through the sand?"

"Yeah, just fine. So, Bryson, is that Laura's son?"

"One of them, yes, he's thirteen. Vaughn is her other son, fifteen. Then there's Hope, she's eleven and your brother's shadow, and last is Lisa. She's twenty-one and not here with us, busy with work and school."

"You're marrying a woman with *four* kids, three still young and in the house? You're no spring chicken there, Dad." I laugh, then go still, saliva pooling in my mouth. *I called him "Dad."* It just sorta came out.

Oh, he noticed. His returning laugh is as jovial as I'm sure it gets, a warm kindness to his voice—that I put there! Even Cannon's affected, the hand on my thigh doing a "good girl" pat thing.

"So, uh," I clear the frog in my throat, "what happened to Bryson, was it?" I have the memory of an elephant free basing ginkgo biloba, who am I kidding with the nonchalant pseudo-amnesia? Not Cannon, over there snickering.

"We're not sure, he got bit by something; high fever, sore muscles, vomiting. As soon as the doctor clears him, we're flying home. Conner's not very happy about it, but I've managed to bargain his cooperation for his own ultra-large saltwater fish tank in his room."

"He does love fish. I don't remember that fascination before, do you?"

He thinks, a low hmmm sound. "No, I don't imagine I do."

"All right, well, call me when you land. I'm actually sitting on the Ohio line right now, house hunting, so I'll be close by."

"House hunting?" His interest perks audibly.

*Shit*! Think, then talk. I'm gonna have to get it tattooed on my freakin' hand.

"Um, yeah," I look to Cannon, all Mr. Pride and Sunshine. "The band, we're, ah, taking a break, and I figured I probably needed a place to you know, *live*."

"I think that's an excellent idea, Elizabeth. What town are you researching?"

*Easy, big guy,* you've already gotten more information that I'm completely comfortable giving.

"Exactly halfway between Cannon's family and Sutton, so Conner can visit regularly without a long drive. Maybe I'll get him a damn dog."

"Or a regular dog might work fine, too," he jokes dryly, but his version of humor all the same.

"I'm sorry about Bryson, but I'm glad you're coming back early. I miss Conner so bad it hurts," I admit, my chest aching.

"I imagine you do. As against the bus life as I was, you're an exceptional sister, Elizabeth. When he had no one else, he *always* had you. I'm very proud of you for that, among many other things."

"Ugh," I groan, eyes rolled clear in the back seat. "Just get here, let's have our talk, and we can progress from there. These coded, half-assed, sweetsy-yet-non-informative talks are grinding on my nerves," I snap.

"Yes, all right. I'll call when we land. And good luck with the house hunting."

Remember that part about Cannon having OCD and being a perfectionist? Okay, now use an egg as the object of that description and then beat it and smash it over and over again with the biggest, heaviest cast-iron skillet you can find.

Feel me? The real estate agent does too.

Well, house #4 was my fault—I walked in, spun on my heel, and cruised on out. NO. STAIRS. It's one of my only stipulations and one on which I will not budge.

Numbers 1-3, who knows, I honestly suspect that with half the "issues" Cannon found, he made up a quarter of the words he used to explain his dislike.

In fact, he's being persnickety about everything.

"Jennifer, will you give us a minute?" I ask the friendly, young, obviously new and desperate for a sale agent, then drag Cannon outside.

I grab his chin off the ground and make him look at me. "Holy Grumpy Guts, what is your major malfunction?"

He just shrugs.

"Really? Mr. Walking Thesaurus in there and that's all you got? Bullshit. Spill it."

"Yeah?" He crushes me with just a glance, eyes trying to hope, but doubt weighing that down.

"Yeah, babe, yeah." I hug him close. "What is it? Talk to me. It's like a rain cloud moved in out of nowhere, with a vengeance."

"When you told your dad *you* were house hunting because *you* needed a place to live and *you'd* maybe get a dog, it was pretty loud and clear, louder than you never answering me, that I'm not in your immediate cohabitation plans." He shrugs, breaking my heart as he kicks a few rocks around.

"Amazing. You're not just being a passive-aggressive bratty ass man, it's actually true. I've never had 'a man' before, so I didn't know, or think about it. I'm sorry." My turn to study the ground and pester a few bits of gravel with my toe. "But it's no urban myth, it's actually textbook true." My mouth drops agape, eyes now up, wide and laughing.

"What is?"

"You can tell a man step by step, numbered even, instructions and all he hears are the last three words of step eight. But you talk off the cuff and he dissects and analyzes that shit like Cut Up the Frog Day in Biology. Have *you*," I poke his chest, "told your parents, who you actually *like*, that *we* are housing hunting?"

My arms are already folded, hip fully cocked out, 'cause I know the answer.

"Yeah, I have. Even asked Moms if I could have Grandma's ring. It's vintage, you'll love it."

Arms limp at sides, tucking hips back in now. *He asked who what?*

Certain kinds of tears, the ones that start down deep inside you and bubble their way up through your soul, actually make a "splat" noise and noticeable wet marks on the sidewalk, did you know that? That's how he knows I'm crying—*not* from the snotty sounds I'm so gracefully making.

"I don't need you to look at me, Lizzie. I need you to *hear* me. I love you. I won't ever *not* love you. I want to move in with you and build a home, a life…a family. And just as soon as anyone whose opinion you give a fuck about quits making a sour face with their whole 'he was just engaged' worn out fucking bullshit, I want to marry you. Now what's in here?" He lays his hand over my heart. "Their voices or mine?"

He really should write lyrics, but this isn't the time to mention it.

"House? You sure? Don't wanna start with an apartment or condo?" I gnaw on my lip, hopping from foot to foot.

"Conner would be miserable in a tiny apartment, so would the dog. Condos are not for families, they're for snowbirds and retirees. Families need a house."

"Then pick a house." I smile, heart decided, and threatening to burst…or flat line…shocked how easy and natural this feels.

He laughs from deep in his finally not worried gut and scoops me up to spin me round. "I've liked 'em all. Especially the yellow one with the wrap around porch and three acres. Back off the road, huge backyard, no stairs."

"That was my favorite too," I whisper, scared to share my brain with someone else.

"Jennifer!" he yells, and wouldn't you know, out she pops, Cheshire smile, sprinkles and cupcakes dancing in her eyes.

"Yellow ranch, Victorian, porch, got it. Asking price $205,000, already vacant," she spouts off from her supersonic, eavesdropping memory.

"My Siren and I would like to put in a cash offer." He turns to me and whispers, "I've got about 85 liquid," to which I nod. "Cash offer of $175,000 today. Let us know!"

And he carries me off into the sunset—meaning to the keyed car at four in the afternoon. Close enough.

Two hours later, Jennifer calls to tell us the owners countered the house at $180,000, which we jumped at. We sign papers and take possession Tuesday. Three days from now. Only that quick because I shelled out behind Mr. OCD's back for a rush inspection, Jennifer giddy to facilitate.

Funniest thing you've ever seen—two pretty well-off (especially for our age) people sitting in a hotel room in stark silence. We have nothing to move, no utilities to switch, no pets to board, no jobs to take off from, no mail to forward.

We could move in yesterday, fully prepared.

Without words, 'cause he still shares my brain and refuses to give it back, we bust out in gut-wrenching, side-splitting, obnoxious laughter at the exact same time.

"So, I guess we chill and fight over paint colors for three days?" I ask amidst suppressed laughter.

He settles too and kicks off his shoes, climbing up on the bed beside me. "You know my favorite part of the house?"

SE Hall

"I know," I sigh dreamily, "the in-law quarters, right?"

He nods, snuggling me closer, lacing our fingers of one hand, the other cupping my neck. "How cool would it be to unplug the stove," he snickers, "and give Conner some stone's throw independence?"

"You need to turn off the gas to the fireplace too, but yeah, I hear ya. Very cool." I tear up, 'cause that's all I do these days, at the thought. Conner—his own place, how he wants it—his domain to decorate and boss around whomever enters.

I love it, and more, I love that it was Cannon's first thought too.

He truly loves my brother.

# CHAPTER thirty-two

Cannon took me out for some fine dining, which I know we'll grow to love, at Hildebrand's Hickory House. Although, right across the street is Not Short on Steak House, where, before you even have your menu, you're briefed in a whisper out of the side of your server's mouth, like they'd rather lose their tongue than have to tell you, that they'd "never say an ill word of the owner's copycat sister-in-law and wish her all the success in the world."

I love small towns.

If Aunt Bea waltzes in and asks me to quilt a few squares for the town bazaar, I do believe I'll say yes.

After dinner, we stroll hand in hand down the infamous historic district. Everything's closed, but the window shopping is nostalgically—says the twenty-three year old—delightful. At ten sharp, all the streetlights come on and a sense of homey security fell over me, Cannon too, if his wink and hand squeeze are anything to go by.

When we finally collapse in the hotel room, I just know, sure as I know I'll have grandbabies with this gorgeous man across the room; it is time to make some calls.

The first is to my uncle, who didn't answer, because he goes to bed with the sun.

Then I try Jarrett, who answers on the first ring, sounding happier than I've heard him in a long time. "You at Vanessa's?"

"Yep!"

"Can I dial Rhett in and talk to you guys a minute?" I ask timidly, getting more nervous by the second.

"Sure. Hey, how are you, Mama Bear? How's Conner, Cannon?"

"We're all great, you?"

"Never better, truth."

"I'm so glad. I miss you, though."

"Me too, Mama, me too. We'll be back together soon, though. No worries."

Here goes. "Hang on," I bite off a nail, "let me connect Rhett."

Cannon stands and points to his chest, then out of the room. I shake my head no and hold out my hand, pulling him to sit right beside me.

Rhett answers in what may be a carnival and screams in my ear. "Liz, my girl, what's good?" he slurs on a high decibel.

"Lots, actually. Can you go somewhere quiet and I'll patch Jarrett in?"

"Ut oh, conference call." He laughs. "Yeah, hang on."

I flip over, get Jarret, and then have all three of us on by the time Rhett's found the cone of silence.

"All right, that better?" he asks.

"Much. Jarrett's on."

"Hey, bro, what's new?" Jarrett asks cheerfully.

"The pussy I just pounded. Never had her before." He snickers, a poor disguise for pain-induced self-destruction, but that's another call.

"Okay, guys, I want to tell you something pretty heavy, and I pray you're happy for me, and Conner, and use this as a stepping stone." In for me, hold, out for him. "I bought a house, with Cannon, right in between our parents. It has a house in back for Conner too, his own place. I've been learning a bit from Richard about the past, and I'm feeling a lot lighter."

Jarrett's first, although still stalled, surprisingly quiet for a moment before speaking. "That's great, Liz, for all of you. The only thing I want is for you all to be happy. I mean it. So, no more See You Next Tuesday?" His tone turns sad, jabbing at a part of my foundation, my one steady.

"Not necessarily," I hem-haw, and Cannon ducks his head to gauge my expression. "Rhett? What say you?"

"I'm of course happy if you're happy, always. But I'm waiting for the punch line, or kick in the gut, whichever." I hear him blow out...he *smokes* now? Only tobacco, I pray, though that's bad enough.

"I'm giving you both my bus, free and clear. It's yours, equally. And all the instruments, except Cannon's," I add quickly. "Go be big boys, brighter than all the lights. And always keep a ticket at will-call; you never know when I'll pop in. It's all yours—bus, equipment, song rights—hell, you can even have my notebook." I'm weeping, but chuckle into the phone. I don't want them to know I'm crying. "Just promise me you'll do it right, and *sterilize*. Hire a new driver, though. Bruce's days are over."

"I don't...I don't know what to say, Mama Bear. You *sure* about this?" Jarrett sounds leery and I understand, we're not practiced in too good to be good...only to not be true.

I lean my face into Cannon's chest and inhale a big whiff of content cotton and musky man who loves me, letting it infuse my soul slowly. When it hits my heart and saturates it, when he understands and wraps me tighter in his arms and buries his face in my hair, I answer.

"I'm sure, more than I've ever been of anything." It comes out a romantic whisper.

"Thank you, Lizzie, sincerely. Goddamn, girl, thank you. I'll pay you back," Jarrett whoops.

"No, you won't. My payment is the last two decades of my sanity, thanks to you. And as for money, I never needed that, and it hasn't changed. Just maybe swing by for Christmas, superstars." I *really* weep now, no laughing anymore.

"Well, talk about losing your buzz, Liz. Put Romeo von Whistle Britches on the phone," Rhett demands, which Cannon heard, hand already out.

This has me concerned...defining understatement.

"Hello? Hey Rhett, how goes it?" Cannon starts off nice. "I understand, I'd ask the same thing. More than my own life. Yes, yes, yes, definitely. Soon, you know she's stubborn."

I assume Rhett is grilling him or preaching because he's quiet for a long time, running a hand back through his hair, then laughing, then holding me desperately tight against him.

"As long as I breathe, with every breath. Absolutely. I'll even let you tie my hands behind my back." He laughs. "Good lookin' out, man, here ya go." He hands the phone back to me with a chaste kiss on the lips and a wink, then leaves the room.

"Hello?" I say softly.

"All right, Liz, you're good to go. Let him love you, and love him back, every day, hard. And have a guest room ready when I need my best friend ever fix."

"Hey, Rhett, that was really good, *not my best friend ever either*. But I had a few things to add, ball hog, so I call dibs when we have mini-Liz nieces," Jarrett, my sweet Jarrett, says.

"Noted; it was on the fly, man. We'll work on it." Rhett barks out a laugh lined with bittersweet goodbye.

In your life, you get five, *maybe* ten, if God thinks you're *super* special, people you call "home." I have two of the best on the line right now and I love them like fields love rain, birds love tiny, loose twigs, and campers *love* breakfast ('cause let's face it, you *know* it tastes better there).

And *when* did I do all this camping I'm always spitting poetic about?

314

"I love you boys so much. You need me, *ever*, for *anything*, I'm one call away. Go be happy too. Bruce has the storage and bus keys. I have the title. And you—you both have everything else you need inside you. Let other people see it too; I've been selfish for far too long." I hope they understood my snot-sucking ramble.

"Love you, Mama Bear, talk soon."

"I love you, Liz," Rhett sniffles non-discreetly, "forever. Any woman I think twice about, will be run down a checklist. Of you."

*Sob.* "Bye, boys."

Two things happen the next day.

First, gloriously first, I wake to the soft pitter-patter of a rainstorm outside and Cannon inside me. No words, no music, just our mouths making love, our bodies reverently doing the same.

He runs his hands over every part of me; toes, ankles, fingers, even his precious, ticklish armpit kisses. Forehead, elbows, navel, the two dents right above my butt, *definitely* my butt, shoulder blades…no fraction of my skin isn't physically assured it's adored and cherished.

And then, in a deep, lazy morning rumble, he whispers in my ear, "When I'm inside you, can you remember anything that happened before we had each other?"

Unequivocally, immediately, I'm able to honestly answer. "Nothing."

His face beams and his eyes water, a glistening haze over gems such a rich chocolate you can imagine them melting in your mouth, when he says, "Me either, Siren, me either."

With that, we remain locked in each other's gaze as we come together, in and around each other in an act too beautiful for even song lyrics.

The second wondrous event—Conner is coming home!

I swear I could run the thirty-five miles faster than Cannon drives them. And when I see him? Well, I teach Bubs what a full-body tackle *really* is!! Like, 112 pounds of me knock 240ish pounds of him on his ass, then suffocate him in slobbery kisses and tears.

I missed him.

I love him so damn much.

And I'm super jealous of his tan.

"Cannon, help!" He laughs and pleads. "She's crazy for me, get her!"

"Oh, please, you can take her," Cannon encourages him. "She missed you, Bubs, let her have her lovin'."

He's instantly still under me, his blue eyes bugging out the size of saucers. "Cannon called me 'Bubs,'" he whispers—which means like a seven on a one-to-ten scale of volume.

*Hmm, so he did.*

"Is that okay with you or not?" I *actually* whisper back.

He bobbles his head with a goofy smile. "I like it. He loves me."

"Yeah, Conner, he really does."

"Uh hmf." My father clears his throat, breaking up the loving, yet Wrestlemania-esque, undignified spectacle we're making in the foyer, and I spring up, embarrassed, straightening my attire.

He's smiling, scratching his chin. "Elizabeth, don't fret. I think it's fabulous you can pummel your brother. It lets me know I needn't worry about you taking care of yourself, should you meander up on a," he ponders, "street fight? Turf war? What is the lingo these days?"

Obviously he "took something" for the long flight and it hasn't worn off. *Turf war?* Maybe the in-flight movie was *West Side Story.*

"Mr. Blackwell," he steps to Cannon and offers his hand, "nice to see you again. Will you be taking a hiatus from the band as well?"

"Yes, sir, as long as Lizzie does. She was the only reason I was ever there in the first place."

"Bubs *and* Lizzie?" He perks his overly bushy eyebrows and restructures his stance to what he *thinks* is intimidating. "Seems you're rather close to my children…"

Cannon nods, not biting, no defensive shift in his demeanor. "I'd like to think so. Working on getting closer every day. In fact, you may have to start calling me Cannon soon."

"That's his name, Dad."

"Thank you, son, I'm aware." He grins at Conner. "Well, Lord knows, Conner's an excellent judge of character. And that one." My father indicates me with a head gesture. "If you've won her over, you've *certainly* earned the right to be called Cannon."

"Whaddaya say, Lizzie, have I won you over?" Cannon asks, all cocky.

"Shut up." I roll my eyes.

"Oh yeah," Richard slaps him on the back, "she likes you."

Okay, well *The Brady Bunch* was only a thirty minute show, so it's time to G-O. "Conner, where's all your stuff?" I ask.

"In mine and Vaughn's room," he beams.

I turn venomous on Dick—fair, sociably acceptable form of Richard—and prop my hands on my hips. "You gave half his room to someone else? There's nine of the fuckers and he was here first. Why the hell—"

I'm brutally rebuffed mid-ballistic tirade by...Conner. "I want to share with Vaughn, he's fun. It was my great idea, huh, Bethy?"

Done, overloaded, I rub my temples and pinch my eyes shut. "Bubs," I soothe as calmly as possible, "please go get your stuff. It's time for us to go."

"Lizzie, maybe you should—"

"Butt out, Cannon! Not your brother, not your nightmare! I. GOT. THIS."

"Sir?" He looks pleadingly to my father, whose lip twitches as he extends a "by all means, be my guest" arm and slight bow.

"I'll grab a couple scotches and meet you in the study." He points. "Third door on the right."

And then I'm hoisted up by a nosy Neanderthal, thrown over his shoulder, and carted down the hall of my childhood home. I hear Conner titter, then yell, "I'm going to play too, Sister! Bye!"

He's probably off to find Laura's spawn, no doubt locked in the attic, surviving on cookies sprinkled with suspect white powdered sugar.

Cannon throws me down unceremoniously on the leather sofa and makes sure to stand between me and the door. "You," he points a menacing finger at me, "are being an ass. I love you, and I'm not mad at you, but Goddamn, you witchy, mood swinging, sexy girl, *for once*, shut the fuck up and listen! Look around, my love, everything you need to stop hurting is right in front of your face."

"You're going to need this." Dick strides in, shuts the door, and offers Cannon a tumbler of amber liquid and ice. "Elizabeth." He takes his domineering, self-vindicating seat behind the overly large, compensating-for-something desk

Pretty Instinct

and crosses one ankle over his thigh. "At first, you were young and fragile. Then you were angry and confused. Next you went to bitter, defensive, and downright hateful. Now, now you're just complacent, scared to death to have to live every day without your staple defense mechanisms. Well, grow up, young lady!" he barks, slamming his hand on the desk. "You're young, beautiful, talented, wealthy, responsible, loved," he glances at Cannon, who nods brusquely, "and wasting it all on blatant stupidity. I've apologized for every role I've played in that and would *kill* for a chance to make up for it."

Cannon gains some mercy, or maybe empathy, and comes to sit beside me on the couch, grabbing my hand twice since I denied him the first attempt.

My father pulls open his desk drawer and rummages about, then shuts it and approaches me. "This is the key to your mother's safe deposit box at Federal Bank downtown, intersection of Patty Boulevard and Warne. Has the bronze statue of the horse out front." He sets the key in my palm, after prying my fingers back. "I'm not sure of the box number, as I've never been to it, but the password is 'Dusty.'"

*My pony.*

"What's in it?" I speak, not worthy of even being called a whisper.

"Like I said, I've never been to it. But as her only daughter," he chokes up and pulls out that handkerchief I hate, dabbing under his eyes, "I would imagine jewelry; hers, perhaps your grandmother's, I don't know. What I do know is I've changed my mind on our compromise. I've spent eight years biting my tongue on stories not my own. I've repented and confessed, both to God and you, and I'm done. Conner's at a good, healthy place in life. He loves me, he loves Laura and her kids, but above all, no contest, he loves *you*, Elizabeth. Now let him, and me, live as peacefully as we can and go fix yourself. It's time."

"You think a few necklaces are gonna fix me?" I snap, glaring at him like the man he obviously is, the one who lost his mind.

319

"Elizabeth," he sighs, tugs at his hair, and heads for the door, "shut up. Conner and I will be here when you get back, but only *I* will answer questions, away from him, and not at the dinner table Laura and Alma will have set."

I must seem deranged, glancing from the door he shut to the bronze key burning a hole in my hand, to Cannon, then repeating the cycle all over again.

"No more excuses. You scared?" he asks.

"No!" I snap. I'm not. I've been waiting for this opportunity. For some closure. Right?

"Oh, I think you mean yes. You know, even when you hide and build walls upon walls, I still find you, see you. So you might as well come out and let *everyone* see your beauty." His soft smile is more love than pity, so I spare him and fling myself in his arms, never going to admit I'm petrified. He kisses the top of my head. "I'm right here."

# CHAPTER
## thirty-three

Like I needed the name of the bank or the streets—the bronze horse is…noticeable.

I ask Cannon to keep the car running, in case I just say "fuck the secret box" and rob the joint instead, but what do you think he did?

Turned it off and linked his fingers with mine, opened the door, and let me walk in first with a whispered "I love you" behind me.

Of course.

The beautiful, dark-haired woman who greets us wears a nametag that says, "Riza, Branch Manager," and has us welcomed two steps over the threshold. *She'd better*, since they need all the customers they can get to pay for that horse monstrosity out front.

Why Cannon curls up his adorable nose at me I know not; I didn't say that part out loud.

"Nice to meet you, Riza." He shakes her hand and her loins (again, *if* we women have those) with his high-voltage charm and toe-curling voice. "This is Elizabeth Carmichael, and her father sent her with a key to see about a lock box?"

Riza's good, so professional and polished, in fact, that standing even an inch further back, my practiced, cynical eye would've missed the slight pupil dilation and lip twitch. But alas, I'm right here. And I caught it.

"You're Anna's daughter?" she asks.

"Was." I cross my arms. "If you knew her, you'll know she's dead. Seven years. It was in the paper and everything," I sneer crudely, "so that'd be a *was*."

"Knock it off," Cannon growls at me, smiling even wider at her. "You can imagine it's a rough day for her." He shrugs and apologizes on my behalf.

Riza nods, fucking pity in her eyes. "Right this way. You said you had the key?"

"Yes," Cannon hastily pipes in for me, obviously fearful of giving me an opening to speak anymore.

I am admittedly, undoubtedly, being a bitch. I know it, yet I can't stop it. Conner and Richard home and all chummy, secret boxes, buying houses…the jagged, rocky edge of overload is right in front of me.

"Please," Riza ushers to two chairs in front of her desk, "have a seat. Can I offer either of you a drink?"

I huff audibly, crossing an ankle, acting as impatient as possible.

"No, thank you," Cannon sing–songs, laying a demonstrative and quite directive hand on my leg.

"I just have to pull up the account." She taps away, then papers spit out from a printer at her right. "Elizabeth, your middle name?"

"Hannah."

"And do you have some identification please?"

I dig out my license and fork it over, hand still up and waiting while she makes a copy and returns it.

"Last thing. Do you know the password?"

"Dusty." This one gets me, a strangled croak my answer. I loved that pony. He was sold when Mom became "unavailable" to get me to my lessons regularly. *I wonder where he is now…*

"That's it. April?" she calls across the room and a curvy, young redhead with, uh, endowments in all the right places appears. I watch Cannon like a hawk on a fluorescent rabbit with a broken, fragrantly bleeding leg, but he either plays it well or sincerely doesn't care she's right beside him. "April, please show Ms. Carmichael to lock box 71276." She hands her a post-it with what I assume is the box number on it. "The gentleman may accompany her if she chooses, locked door, one hour."

"Yes, ma'am," April answers and begins to walk away.

Cannon rises and looks back for my hand, taking it with a supportive wink. "Want me to stay or not?" he asks.

I nod and we proceed.

"One hour, and the room is under surveillance," she instructs curtly. "If you're done sooner than that, press the green button on the wall and I'll be back." She slams the large silver door, locking us in what creepily feels like a mausoleum, or King Tut's tomb, you pick.

Nice of her to point out the actual box, since there are thousands. I try to get a tracking system when Cannon boasts, "Got it! Right here, 71276."

I hand him the key, nervous enough to undoubtedly break something. He unlocks it and slides out a long, slender box, setting it on the table in the middle of the room. Then he flips the key over and unlocks the box itself, holding the lid just ajar.

"Look at me," he demands softly. "In for me," his eyes do that big 'do it' thing when I'm uncooperative, "now out for you. Good girl." He leans in and kisses me once, then again, on the lips. *"I'm right here."*

He pulls the lid open to lay back against the table. The first thing that catches my eye is my mother's cameo broach and its ivory profile of her mother. I always thought it hideous and outdated, but today, it's beautiful and majestic.

"Set it to the side, please," I whisper, not ready to actually touch anything.

Next is an array of precious gem necklaces, rings, and earrings. "I'm sure they'll give us a bag," he comments, setting them in a pile on the table.

SE Hall

"Hmm, that's it? Weird." I shrug, standing.

"Lizzie," he grumps, "I know you see this envelope with 'Bethy' written on it. Will you read it here, or later?"

"Musta missed it." *Caught,* I look away and sit back down. What if I blubber like a hot mess in front of him? Or worse yet, what if I don't react at all, showing him heart of stone girl? "Here's fine. You wanna read it to me?"

"I can, or I can sit here and hold your hand while you read it. Or, I can even leave the room and give you some privacy. What do you *really* want?" He pulls the envelope out with some difficulty; it's kinda stuck at the bottom, the edges caught, a little too big for the box. "Dig deep, love. What do you want?"

"What would you do?" I beg him, lids rimmed with moisture, knee bobbing up and down, heart hurting and beating alarmingly fast.

"Oh, Lizzie, I can't answer that and you know it. Close your eyes," he gently whispers, leaning in so our lips just brush. "Closed?" I nod. "All right, in for me," I suck in loudly, "now out, what's your choice?" he says quickly, not giving me a chance to think.

"Read it to me," I answer automatically.

He doesn't second guess me and opens the envelope, eyes on mine. He sniffs, and I smell it from here, her scent. "Nice handwriting," he says to settle me.

"Eh." I shrug and motion with my hand for him to get on with it.

"Dear Bethy, my beautiful, strong girl." He clears his throat and rises, walking over to press the green button.

"All done?" April chirps.

"No, we'd like a box of tissues if you have them, please."

*Damn traitorous leaking face.*

Two minutes later, the door opens and she shoves a box inside then sequesters us in with another slam.

He takes his seat again and pulls out a Kleenex and hands it to me, then shockingly, takes one for himself! He must see my shocked face, as his mouth turns down. "Your pain is my pain, Siren."

I find my focal point, box 41002 right in front of me, and begins to tap out "Girl," with his foot. "Okay, I'm ready. Read it."

"Dear Bethy, my beautiful, strong girl. I'm writing this completely unencumbered by a drug of any sort, so every word is true, unexaggerated or molded to make me feel less guilty, and straight from my heart. I am weak, I always have been. The thing is, when you're born with a silver spoon in your mouth, you don't have to learn how to feed yourself. When balls are thrown in your honor and $10,000 dresses ensure you're the prettiest in the room, you don't have to dig deep to find you're pretty. When everything is done, fixed, or manipulated in your favor, and everyone exalts you because they have to, you never develop *instinct*."

We both *freeze*. Even in foresight, and now from the grave, she just spoke to both our hearts, in our language.

Inappropriate? No fucks to give. "Mouth, Cannon, now, kiss me."

And he does, extensively and delicately, telling my soul he's there for whatever I need.

"Continue," I breathe heavily. "The letter, I mean."

"Enough of my excuses," he continued, "and please, daughter, as you grow into a fine young woman, try not to make them. If you know the bottom's safe—jump. If you know it's returned—love. If you really want it—*fairly* take it. If you run, do it till your lungs burn. Laugh until your cheeks ache. And forgive, as you'll always want to be forgiven. I didn't say forget, and certainly your spirit won't *allow* for you to be a doormat, but forgive. Ask yourself, always, if they die tonight...was I really that mad? The answer will almost always be no, so act accordingly.

"At this bank, in your name, is more money than you will ever spend, beyond what you'll have already been given. Your father forfeited it all freely. I only ask that you take care of my beautiful boy. Take care of my Conner. I suspect you will have long since been doing that before you ever read this. Hire help if need be, but *promise me* that he will never spend one night in a special home. The day we brought *you* home, he made a fort under your crib and slept there for months. 'My baby,' he always called you. Love him, protect him, and keep him with you.

"If you've ever wondered, I gave him a song because I doted on you so, the baby, a girl, that I wanted him to feel special. Never more, never better or more loved, he just needed it. He resented you not one day; please return that unconditional love. Perhaps if I'd had a big brother...I digress, Bethy.

"Your father is a good man. He only knows what he was taught—work, provide, your way is law, then work some more. He got angry hands rather than hugs, whippings instead of kisses. He didn't have a clue how to reach, console or 'fix' a person of fragile makeup. I quit him long before he quit me, and at the end of the day, it was up to me to force *myself* to fix myself.

"If you're over 21, you can read this part. If not, skip to the next page."

We both pause and laugh. Part of me wishes I had found this letter and read it sooner, but part of me knows this time in my life, this moment, is exactly right.

"Bethy, men have primal, inbred, chemical needs. If not met, they will find it elsewhere, just as a male dog will leave the yard, despite the shock collar, if the poodle next door is in heat. It's nature, procreation, God's different design of Adam and Eve. Sex with me would—I can't believe I'll say this, but I need you to understand—sex with me would have bordered necrophilia. Forgive him. I did."

Cannon stops and blows out a long breath, eyes bulged. "Did not expect that," he comments, but his light laugh is false. "Want me to go on?"

"Yes," I say. "Surely it doesn't get worse than rutting poodles and necrophilia." I laugh softly even as I wipe my eyes, a mountain of wadded, soggy tissues in front of me, no longer able to breathe through my nose.

"Need a nibble first, baby." He leans into my neck, and I know he's actually checking my pulse, gauging my ability to continue, but I play along with the façade. "Okay," he exhales and continues.

I squeeze his hand. I'm ready this time.

"Yes, daughter, we're nearing the end, and *this* is the hard part. When I sign this letter and place it where only your father will find it, I will take measures to go to sleep and never wake. I will never see you or your brother's beautiful faces again, but to the villain goes the punishment. I am leaving not because your father cheated or because I'm weak anyway, or even because I live every single day in a fog of depression that none of the twenty-three medication/therapy combos I've tried have worked. I'm leaving because I'd rather die than replay that scene in my head even one more time.

"Your father came home late and wreaked of perfume, with sparkly lilac lipstick below his right ear. For once (I was drunk, no doubt), I still had my faculties about me enough to meet him on the landing. We fought and said some awful things. I actually spit in his face, which is beneath even a lush, and slapped him. He tried to leave, didn't touch me back, begged me to calm down. Your brother, a Mama's Boy to a fault, bless his angel heart, tried to break it up. Even then, your father kept his hands in his pockets and turned his pleadings to Conner, to leave and he'd take care of it. They both started down the stairs. I flew at your father, I SWEAR I was aiming for your father. The only time his hands left his pockets was to try and catch Conner.

"Accident, misaim, or not, I am the sole reason Conner, my precious, perfect, athletic, artistic son will never be the same. *THAT* I not only can't, but *refuse to* live with every day, asleep or awake, over and over. I love you, Bethy. I love your brother, and I love your father.

"But I am also your biggest burden, and ultimately, the literal instrument of your near demise, for I hurt you perhaps most of all. Forgive me, I beg you. No matter age, race, culture, anything…one of the only things in the whole world that is almost always universally alike is a mother's heart. It will always put its children and what is best for them first. This is what I feel is best.

"You and Conner will slowly rebuild, and recover, him never fully, but some. The gnawing cut of my selfishness will scar over; some days you may not even think of it at all and you most certainly will go on to find happiness. I will not. Ever. And would only lessen all of that for you. Goodbye, my beautiful princess. Love, Your Mama."

He gives me a moment to process the last words I'll get from my mother, a brand new harsh reality filled with ache since I thought I'd lived that moment years ago.

"Lizzie?" he whispers.

I hold up a hand, needing a minute, already well versed and in the middle of the *in for him* breath through my mouth. My nose may never unclog, my eyes unpuff, my hands stop trembling, my mind not spin.

"Love, there's more in here. One small note and another key."

"And?" I sob, staring at the table.

"The note says, 'if your true love has found you, bring him with you to use this key on box 112284. Or, if he's with you now, as a true love should be, send him over to it.'"

"November 22nd, 1984, their wedding day," I mumble. "Well, true love," I glance up at him, "what are you waiting for?"

"Lizzie, if you've had enough for today, we can come back." His effort not to frown or let me see the sympathy in his eyes valiant but futile.

I scoff, and since grace waved bon voyage the minute we walked in this place, I go ahead and honk my nose too. "Chicken," I tease him, my voice sounding close to normal again. "Go!" I point.

With his best loving smirk, he rises, one cautious eye on me, the other searching out the number. He finds it, gets the box, and sits back down, a nervous shyness emanating as his shaky hands open it.

Inside are two things: a ring, which somewhere in the farthest recesses of my mind, I think I remember, and a sealed white envelope, addressed to "The Man Trusted with my Bethy."

"Want me to read it out loud?" he asks, so chivalrous and thoughtful, thinking always first of my feelings.

"You know what? She went to all the trouble of not writing it in my letter and getting a separate box. I think she meant for that to be between you and her. If she was here, I'm guessing she'd catch you alone, to say it, so how 'bout we let her have her 'motherly moment'?"

# Cannon

*To the man my sweet Bethy deemed worthy of the letter to her true love,*

*I already like you. She's only a teen, but I trust her taste impeccably. She's wise, strong and all-seeing beyond her years. Even in her crib, the mobile had four little ponies: yellow, blue, pink, and green. She'd kick her little feet at them like she was riding a bike, but never at the green one for some reason. She'd stop, wait for it to go by, then she was off and motoring again.*

*She's picky, tasteful, and true to herself. If she says she loves you, then not only does she mean it, she will always mean it.*

*I can only imagine the young woman she'll turn out to be. I'm sure you know, but you are one lucky young man.*

*Bethy is artistic and soulful, a denied romantic; she dreams of dreams and slays dragons wherever they present themselves.*

*Be good to her. Appreciate her. Embrace what makes her the girl who got your attention in the first place.*

*When she cries and pushes you away, she's screaming "hold me closer!" on the inside. When she says she doesn't need your help, she means she believes in you enough that she shouldn't have to ask.*

*Never go to bed angry and never let her go to bed angry, even if that means you have to keep her awake all night.*

*Point out sunsets and falling stars to her. Slow dance. Write your own poem in the card. Carry her picture in your wallet.*

*Take her camping; she loves best the stories I tell about when my dad took me.*

*Tell her everyday she's loved, beautiful, and that it's not a sign of weakness to forgive.*

*I am handing you the one thing I wanted most in my life, for as long as I can remember—a daughter.*

*This ring, if you haven't already bought her one, was my mother's. She handed it to me the day I turned 18. I'll miss that, so I ask that you do it for me, whatever her age today.*

*Don't ever spank my grandchildren; two wrongs don't make a right.*

*And remember this always—"A daughter's your daughter for the rest of your life. A son's a son 'til he takes a wife." Do not EVER side with your mother over her. Defend your wife above all; right or wrong, her feelings are valid and the only one you need to protect.*

*Good luck, son!*

*Love,*

*Your mother-in-law*

What truly saddens me the most? The woman who wrote those two letters was obviously intelligent, humorous, prophetic, and filled with love. *Why* would such an amazing person, with so much to give, take her own life?

Because she couldn't forgive herself.

If their family would have just *communicated*, Lizzie would have forgiven her. I know my girl, she would have. And Conner, that guy can't stay mad, a ball of pure, innocent joy. It sounds to me like the minute Conner fell was the minute Richard, too, opened his eyes.

Such a waste.

The only thing I can do now is vow to honor every single one of her requests in that letter, keep her advice close to my heart, my mission, in her honor, every day I walk this Earth.

I tuck the ring in my pocket, even though I know my Siren saw it, for the right time and the perfect plan. Then I fold the letter, put it too in my pocket, and slide the empty box back in its hole; the same with 71276. I press the green button on the wall to tell April we're done and ask for a bag, then turn back to Lizzie with what I hope is a comforting smile. "Ready, my love?"

"For what?" Her voice is as clueless and hollow as her eyes, lost and overwhelmed. Everything she thought she knew, the founding blocks of the person she's become over the last seven years were wiped out in a tornado of discovery—no warning bell.

April, who needs to quit disrespecting my girl with her blatant flirting, opens the door and hands me a clear bag, fingers fondling mine as she pulls away. "Look at her," I motion my head back to Lizzie.

"Yeah?" April sneers, pushing her boobs closer to me.

"Either you're blind and can't see what I see, or you like losing. Now knock it off. We need another minute, and this time, send Riza to get us or I'll report you. Clear?"

"Hmpf." She spins on her heel and *really* slams the door this time.

I give Lizzie a minute, carefully placing all her items and letter in the bag, then finally squat down in front of her, hands on her thighs. "With me?"

"Always." She nods without question, her voice soft and childlike.

"You hear me then, so please *listen*. You've been rocked at the core, babe, I get that. But your past doesn't decide your future, and your future was with me when you walked in and it's with me when we walk out. I will *never* not protect you, love you, or be with you. I will *never* hide things from you or lie to you. When we walk through that door, *our* life starts. *Our* plans, goals, home, careers, kids, IRAs, pets, what the hell ever, belongs to only us. And Conner. And the new fish, which you know he'll ask about. Agreed?"

It takes a minute of swiping tears, sniffling, pushing hair behind her ears and straightening her posture, but finally, she looks at me...and through it all, she emerges, the light fighting through in her gorgeous brown eyes, my girl is back with me here in the room. "I need a nibble," she whispers.

*And I need to hear her whisper those sweet words to me every day for the rest of my life.* I lean in and let her take a whole damn meal. Riza clears her throat and blushes when she comes to get us, our hour lapsed.

Lizzie jolts and the sound, rushing to stand and walk toward the woman. "I'm Lizzie Carmichael, Anna's daughter," she extends her right hand, "and she raised me better than the way I treated you before. I apologize."

"Of course." Riza smiles kindly and shows us out.

We walk hand in hand out into the fresh air, not stopping to ask about the other account—it'll be there when we need it.

Once we're in the car, engine purring, I turn to her at the same time she looks at me. "Seriously, what now?" she asks.

I'm going for the long ball at the buzzer. It'll either swoosh in or bounce off the rim and beam a spectator in the crowd. Such is risk, though. "I believe Conner's waiting, and didn't your dad say something about dinner?"

In for her, out for me. *Please don't let her aim for my balls.*

"He is, and he did. Guess there then." She shrugs, leaning forward to turn on the radio.

"Should I," she nervously stammers, "ring the doorbell, or…"

She's precious; with everything shifted, she's not sure how to act. Fangs bared, guns blazing is the only way she knows how to walk in this house. So I press the bell, then take her tiny, sweaty hand in mine.

"Sweet girl, just walk in." Alma greets us with a smile and disbelieving shake of her head. "Mr. Cannon, how are you?" She goes up on tiptoe to kiss my cheeks.

"Call me Cannon, please." I take her hand and give a kiss of my own to the back of it.

"Alma, he's taken. Cannon, quit encouraging her." She shakes a joking finger at us while jovially narrowing her eyes.

I love her like this, light and happy, cracking jokes. I'm not ungrateful, but a bit shocked how it's so closely on the heels of everything she just learned. Gift horse though, ehh—I don't want to look in its mouth.

"Come in like you've been here before, for heaven's sake." Alma ushers us in and I squeeze tighter on Lizzie's hand.

"Where's my dad and Conner?" Lizzie asks, and Alma's step falters, astonishment plastered on her face.

"Conner's playing with Bryson and Vaughn somewhere. And your f—*dad*—well, let me check."

"I'm here," his voice sneaks around the corner. "Daughter, why don't you and your caller join us in the kitchen?"

I glance at Siren, who bites down a smirk. "Am I a *caller*?" I whisper.

"Gentleman caller," she nods and whispers back. "Very *Gone With the Wind*, right? He always talks like that. Ivy League raised and graduated. Come on," she drags me toward the kitchen, "don't be scared. Everyone knows those preppy guys can't bite worth a damn." She snickers.

"I heard that." Her father grins, chomping his teeth together demonstratively.

"You must be Laura." My girl, very friendly-like, not a hint of snark or sarcasm, turns to the attractive blonde woman sitting at the kitchen bar, white as a ghost. Seems rumor's out that my Lizzie *can* bite.

"I am." She stands, offering a hand. "It's nice to meet you, Elizabeth."

"You too, and please, call me Liz, if you'd like." Her poise fumbles. "I like Elizabeth too…whichever."

Saving her, I step flush to her back and lay my left hand on her shoulder, waiting until I feel her relax under my touch, then extend my right over her other shoulder. "Hi, Laura, I'm Cannon Blackwell. It's nice to meet you."

"Very nice to meet you as well, Cannon." She smiles sincerely, seeming to relax a bit herself. "Will the two of you, and Conner, be joining us for dinner? We're having manicotti, garlic bread, and salad, if that's all right?"

I'm not about to answer for us, and Lizzie is just staring at her father, either ignoring Laura or in a trance. I see where she gets it—more than just her piercing eyes and color, jawline and chin—he's not budging either, intimidatingly stubborn just like my Siren.

"Where's Conner?" Lizzie caves first, quizzical brow lifted.

"In his room with the other boys; Minecraft marathon if I'm not mistaken."

She stews, chewing the corner of her lip, inspecting the ceiling, Laura's…outfit maybe, then back to him. "Still got a deck?"

SE Hall

He chuckles. "Last time I checked, yes."

"Got beer?"

He steals a peek at Laura, who nods. "Yes."

"Figure we'll need," she ponders, "'bout six; three apiece. Meet *you*," she says to him, clearly uninviting me with a sweet smile but eye message leaving no room for doubt she doesn't want me to join them, "out there."

And she's off.

# CHAPTER thirty-five

"Can't say I ever thought this would happen." He hands me an ice-cold bottle of beer and takes a seat in the patio chair catty-corner to mine.

"You got any cigars?"

"Have you ever smoked a cigar?" he asks, clearly as amused as he is doubtful.

"No, but this feels like a cigar moment. Never mind," I slump in my chair, not feeling as DeNiro as I did five seconds ago.

"Here you go!" Laura chirps as she appears, two cigars in hand. "Elizabeth, if you feel green, lean over the railing." She grins, then walks to the intercom box on the wall and hits something. "*Now* you have privacy, carry on! We're eating without you, by the way." She waves over her shoulder and shuts the door.

"I don't hate her," I mumble around my stogie, leaning forward for the light he's holding out.

"I'm glad to hear that." He leans back, leg crossed at the ankle as he puffs out a perfect smoke ring. I'm just holding mine now, way away from me, the smell and that one taste enough to make me sick. "Elizabeth..." He shakes his head, taking it from me, and snuffs it out, *thank God*.

"I don't hate you, either." I speak softly, staring off in the distance.

SE Hall

"I'm *extremely* glad to hear that. What changed your mind, if you don't mind me asking?"

"Mom wrote me a letter, that's what was in the box at the bank." I turn at the sound of the door.

"Here, love." Cannon hands me a full plate, silverware, and a napkin. "You good?"

I nod and he winks, kissing the top of my head and retreating. I feel rude eating when this detour was my idea, but my father waves a hand absently, telling me to enjoy. "Mmm," I moan around my mouthful. "Did Laura make this?"

"She did. She loves to cook; used to own a restaurant I frequented. That's how we met." He gets a faraway look, remembering those early days of courting I suppose.

"She's very good. What happened to the restaurant? You said *used* to own."

"Her husband was killed in a motor vehicle accident, hit and run. She sold it to pay costs and support her four children."

"Only the one marriage? One dad for all four kids?" I pry.

"Yes to both."

Not only do I not hate her, I respect her. "Good kids?"

"Very. Vaughn's fifteen," he chuckles, "so sometimes he tends to have a smart mouth, but Laura has no qualms lining him out, I assure you. Hope's a little doll, Lisa's away at college, and Bryson is quite shy. All different, but yes, all good kids."

"Do you love them?" *In for me.* I wait for his reply, no idea what answer I'm hoping for. On one hand, it'd be nice to hear he has the capability to, but on the other…

"I love *you*, Elizabeth." *Out for him.* "And Conner." He leans forward, stinky cigar gone, forearms resting on his knees. "Do you want to discuss your mother's letter?"

338

I shrug, trying to seek out the moon through the heavy cloud cover. "You already admitted your wrongs; shitty, but I forgive you. She admitted hers, shitty and irreversible, but I would've forgiven her too. So I'm angry with her, yes, but mostly I feel sorry for her, and fortunate I didn't inherit such hopelessness. Was she on medication? I mean the right kind, for that depression?"

He sighs and tears up, obvious even in dusk. Running a hand through his still thick and dark hair, with the tiniest bit of gray hinting, he speaks painfully, as though he's living it over again. "Every kind they make, trials, combos, you name it. Nothing worked, not that it's supposed to when you skip doses, then overuse, then swallow it with liters of alcohol. It's excusable, but I didn't cheat for almost 20 years, Elizabeth, and it wasn't any better. That's why you never had maternal grandparents around this house; they loved you kids, but gave up on her long before I did. But no matter what, look at me," he barks and my eyes snap to compliance, "she did *not* mean to hurt your bother, and it's the one thing she couldn't find a pill cocktail to forget."

I don't mind the handkerchief now, he needs it badly, his whole body convulsing with wracking sobs. Seeing a man cry is startling enough, but one you've barely even seen smile? Witnessing his utter emotional breakdown, which I have no doubt is sincere, penetrates a part of me...I've never met.

"Why'd you do it?" I open my third beer, taking a long, therapeutic swig. "Bring a date to the funeral? Fall on your sword? Let me treat you like shit, blame you, investigate you in hopes of keeping your son from you?"

He ticks them off on his fingers. "So they'd frown upon me instead of her. Lots of people had formed opinions and whispered grumblings; I couldn't allow it. And yes, I was sleeping with Cheryl, so it served its purpose well. I let you hate me because you were angry, understandably so, and I'd rather have borne the brunt than have you in bar brawls, jail, or worse...in bed and despondent. And Conner...you couldn't have really kept him away for too long. If forced, he knew the truth; I just hoped it'd never come to having to hypnotize or medicate him to remember. I kept you both as secure as I could, exactly where you both needed to be, with each other. You're so good with him, Bethy, and his unfailing adoration of you tells me all I've ever needed to know. Sometimes I bit back, and I'm sorry, but it hurts," he clasps a hand on his chest, "to know your baby girl hates you and you can't say anything. I would rather fall on my sword, as you say, than disparage your mother when she can't defend herself, or make Conner relive it. After all, for anything nasty or cruel people could say, she gave me you and your brother, and nothing can take that from her."

He literally collapses back in the chair, wailing, shoulders visibly shaking. "This isn't what I wanted for my children." Then he snaps, turns a complete 180, and leans across to tap his beer bottle to mine. "We really should start old and get young, or for fuck's sake, at least get two chances. Cheers!"

"Um, cheers," I mutter, sipping my drink as he throttles his in one guzzle…after saying fuck and calling me Bethy. Should I cut him off? Are you allowed to cut your father off?

Seems we all have "crazy" in us, most often hidden, but sometimes, in our own ways, it comes out full force. To be human, which it turns out he is, means some crazy; maybe he's just crazier than the rest of us. What's the heavier burden to bear, knowledge with silence, or not knowing?

"BETHY! COME FIND ME!" The windows shake as Bubs screams inside, sending delightful fire to my heart.

"Does he have another volume?" My dad winces and rubs his temples as I die laughing.

"Sorta. I'll show you a few tricks." I stand, sliding open the French doors. "On the deck, Bubs!"

Oh Lord, glasses shake in the cabinets and the overhead light sways as the thunder gets closer and closer. "*Soft* love, Bubs, you hear me?"

He slides to a stop around the corner, big ole' body trembling with restraint. "Medium?"

"Okay." I giggle and hold open my arms. "Humph," I grunt. "That was not medium, stinker." I pinch his nose. "Where's Cannon?"

"Asleep on the couch. That's not his."

"Son, don't be rude. He's welcome to rest on the couch. Come out with us and sit down. *Soft* sit down." He sneaks a smile my way, getting the hang of it, and pats the spot beside him. "Conner, tell me about Cannon." My dad eyes me teasingly across the way.

"He loves me. Bethy more, though. He sings good, good guitar, really, really good at breakfast. Bad at puzzles. His fish is the white one."

*Damn fish*—will they never be forgotten?

"Are you okay with him always around?"

"Yes, very, very good."

This makes my father beam and shoot me a thumbs up. Which I didn't realize he knew how to do.

"Bubs, go get Cannon. *Soft* wake him up. And ask Laura to come out too, please. Hell, bring the whole gang if you want."

"You'll meet them soon, but they're young and self-absorbed in kid stuff," my father comments, dismissing the idea. "Just Cannon and Laura please, Conner."

Laura's first to appear a few minutes later, with a leery smile and glass of red wine, and she takes a seat by my father. Conner's next, bouncing in one move from inside the kitchen to right in front of me.

"Sit, please." I point to a chair. "Big news, but only if you chill."

"Chilled, Sister." He nods, folding his hands politely in his lap.

And last out, there drudges a sleepy, wild-haired Cannon. "Sorry, Siren, I tried, I swear, but that little girl had *The Sound of Music* on. Have you seen it?" I nod with a shiver. "Cool, you understand then. Hop up," he says and I do so he can sit and pull me down on his lap, doing a quick

341

survey of all occupants on the deck. "Everyone's alive, no bleeding, good stuff." He kisses my cheek. "Proud of you."

"So, we're gathered here today to begin Operation Lizzie's Informed and Wants Her Life Back. Dad, I love Cannon more than anything in the world, and he and I have bought an adorable house in Richmond. It's perfectly placed right between you and his parents. And," I turn to Conner, "it has a secret special house in the back that will be all yours."

"In-law suite," I mouth to my father and he nods, swiping at tears.

"Okay, okay." Conner flails his hands like Flappy Birds. "Okay, Bethy, okay. So I get my own house?"

"Yes."

"With a door and bed and TV and fish tank and shower and lawnmower and fish?" He's screaming, jumping up and down and clearly holding in his need to pee.

"Bubs, go pee and come right back."

Zoom—Flash Carmichael out.

"Bethy," my dad worries aloud.

"It's ten steps away and it has an alarm. The gas stove and fireplace will be disconnected, *Cannon* will mow the lawn, the yard has sensors and windows and doors are included in the ADT Security. What else?" I quirk both brows and cross my arms.

He looks at Laura and she simply snickers. "She's her father's daughter. Give it up," she says, giving him a comforting pat on the leg.

"And I thought I could hire Alma part time, if she'd like? I'll pay her well, of course, in case Cannon and I want a vacation or break, and maybe to check in two weekdays and nights, so he feels like it's company and not an overbearing sister?"

"Definitely. You and I can speak with her tomorrow. And the band, done?" he asks, his optimism sounding through loud and clear.

"Yeah, I'm good. I gave the bus to Rhett and Jarrett. They're the rock stars, not me. I don't need it."

"And Cannon, how long do you propose I allow you to 'shack up' with my only daughter?" Dad presses his lips together, eyes cold*er*, but not exactly *cold*.

"As long as it takes to get her to marry me, sir. You ready?" he asks me with a wink.

"Not yet," I whisper, blushing.

"Little longer, sir," he says, my dad throwing his head back and...laughing? I've never seen it before, but yes, I think he's laughing. Or having a seizure. Possibly choking, but Laura doesn't seem concerned.

He recovers quickly, smiling at my love, whose neck I wrap my hand around and rub. "Anything I should know?"

"Yes, sir, I was engaged for two months, only two months ago. She tied her tubes, lied, and dumped me on the side of the road. I never looked back and wasn't sorry. I stayed because her dad was powerful, my boss, and I had nothing better. I won't speak ill of her, so I'll just quit speaking of her."

"I will," I jump in. "She's a manipulative bitch. She keyed his car and threatened to sic her daddy on me. She sent him stories about us from the internet and called me a dyke *several* times. I hate her and adore him, end of." I bob my chin, daring argument or further scrutiny.

"Do you work?" Richard asks.

"Not yet; her dad had his thumb on that. But I will now that I know where I'm going to be living. I have a degree from IU. I'll be fine."

"I could—"

Cannon holds up a hand and stops him. "No offense, sir, and I appreciate it, but I'd just as soon do things myself this time."

"Very well." My father nods, pleased and impressed, Laura also bobbing her head in respectful agreement. "So when do you move in to this place?"

"Two days. Well, that's when it's ours. We have absolutely nothing *to* move in," Cannon answers and we laugh together.

"And you're staying where until then?"

"Four Seasons," Cannon answers.

"Nonsense, you'll stay here. Honey, could you ask Alma to make up a guest room?"

"Of course." Laura immediately stands, only to get trampled by Conner.

"Sorry, Laura-mom, sorry. Sister! I'm ready!"

"Con, house isn't ready for a few days. We're all going to stay here until it is, but tomorrow, I'll take you to pick out stuff for *your house*, okay?"

He's stunned silent—no, really—looking frantically between our father and I. "You don't hate Dad no more?"

"No Conner," I smile briefly in my dad's direction, "I don't."

"AND I get my own house?"

"Yes." I snicker, my favorite look of pure glee radiating of him.

But then, he gives me a new favorite. He lifts his head to the sky and folds his hands, and in a *legit* whisper, says, "Thank you, guys; I mean you, Mom and God."

Men, women, old, young, usually stoic or not…there's not a dry eye on that deck.

# CHAPTER thirty-six

The next two days, while we wait to take ownership of our house—*our house!*—were what I now refer to "coming home days." Obviously, because that's exactly what we'll be doing, but more over because that's what I did. I came home.

My mother, in death, set me free to love, forgive, smile, laugh, and live with as much fucking happy as I can possibly pack in one day. And with Conner and Cannon by my side, that's *a lot* of happy.

The real estate agent graciously agreed to let us in real quick to take some pictures so we could start planning. It felt intoxicatingly like *Ocean's Eleven,* as if we'd just pulled off a master caper—get in, snap pics, get out. Conner wanted to drop in from the ceiling and squeal around in a van to make it more authentic, but that just didn't sound like a good plan to me.

Now we stand in Mears Home Makeovers & More and Conner has filled four carts—for one room. I don't think he understood the dimensions of said bedroom.

"What's the wood for?" I ask, puzzled by the planks in cart three.

"The fort," he answers with a dumbfounded stare, clueless as to why I'm clueless.

"Bubs, you can't build a fort in your room, sorry."

He rolls his eyes and waves his hands, clearly unable to "deal with me" and starts to walk away. "Cannon, handle Sister. I give up!"

I spin around to find my man red-faced and suffocating on his laughter. "Deal with me, Yoda," I snap.

"Not to make light," he tries to harbor his chortling ridicule, "seriously, not at all. But honestly, Conner is the coolest person. On. The. Planet." I frown, feigning miffed. "Except you, Siren, except you."

"So you think it's *cool* to build a fort in his room? Actual wood, Cannon? Whatever happened to blanket forts?"

"Backyard, baby." He winks. "The fort goes in the *backyard*."

*Oh*. Well, sure it makes sense, when you tell it right.

"Where'd he go?" I frantically search the store. "What else could he possibly need?" I spread my arms, indicating the four carts.

Cannon sticks both fingers in his mouth and wolf whistles (since we're not in public or anything) and Conner screams from somewhere, "Row of paint!" Since we're not in public or anything.

"That's *if* we're done. Get him and meet me at the checkout." I duck my head and take an alternate route to the registers.

That evening, Laura and I both insist Alma take some "her" time and make dinner together. I can't help the nagging devil on my shoulder telling me I'm moving too fast, caring way soon, but…it feels nice to have "a family," or at least the atmosphere of one…and maybe if I start looking for the good, I'll find it.

At around seven, all eight of us sit down to eat. This is the first real amount of time I've spent with Laura's three children still at home and my opinions are formed immediately.

Hope is precious, 11 years old, with white blonde hair, grayish green eyes, freckles across her nose, and the voice of a chipmunk. I think she may be just as enamored of me as she demanded the chair next to mine and kept her chubby little hand on my arm most of the meal.

Bryson; he's a 13-year-old boy, so there's not much to say. He's a handsome young man, very quiet and extremely polite when he does speak, but that is truly the extent of what I know of him so far.

Vaughn? His days of sharing a room with Conner, when he visits, are over. This kid is ANGRY...like hurting animals in a sure sign of future serial killer angry. Not that I've seen him drown a kitten, *yet,* but he needs some serious help, stat. He's only fifteen and I've seen mug shots that scared me far less than the scowl this kid wears.

"Vaughn, honey, why aren't you eating?" his mother asks him.

"I'm not eating shit she made!" He points at me with his fork—a weapon in his mind, I'm sure of it.

"Va—"

I plead with my father's eyes to let me handle it. "And why is that, Vaughn? I'm unaware of anything I've ever done to you?"

"You treat everyone like shit and waltz back in here like nothing's wrong? Fuck you!"

I hold down Cannon while Dad holds down Conner. Laura and Hope start crying.

"Vaughn," I say calmly, setting down my fork and wiping my mouth. "What's my full name?" He shrugs defiantly. "I'll take that riveting answer to mean you don't know. When's my birthday? Favorite color? Best subject in school?"

"Don't know, don't care," he mumbles.

"So is it fair to say you know nothing about me?"

No response.

"You're angry, and if anyone in the world understands adolescent anger, it's me. Why I'm the chosen target for yours is what I don't get. You've been in this house a minute, a fraction of the time I *was*. You're the visitor, not me. I lost a parent, too, so if you're gonna have a pity party, you should at least invite me. And since you seem to draw power from curse words," I look at Hope and ask her to cover her ears before I address Vaughn again, "get the *fuck* over yourself. You know *dick* about my life or why I wasn't or am now in *my* home. You ever talk to me like that again, the only thing you'll be eating for dinner is your teeth, which I'll have knocked down your throat. You feel me, angry boy?"

"I love you." Cannon beams. "*Gotta* have me a nibble after that," he growls and leans in to nip and kiss my jaw.

"And I," my father places his hand on my shoulder and grins, "am damn proud of you. Any chance you'd like to write campaign speeches?"

"None whatsoever." I chuckle and shake my head.

"I'm not your friend anymore, Vaughn. You are very mean, very, very mean," Conner chastises, getting worked up until Laura puts an arm around his shoulders and cuddles him to her.

"Go to your room, Vaughn. Gather all your electronics in a pile and I'll come collect them when the family is done with their meal. While you wait, I want you to write down all the things you're really angry about and we'll discuss them later. You're excused." Laura finishes with him and faces me, eyes still moist. "I'm very sorry for that, but thank you." She laughs and pats Hope's shoulder. "You can uncover your ears now, honey."

"I'm sorry for cursing at him, Laura, but that's the language that empowers him right now. I had to take that power back."

She nods. "Understood."

Bryson waits until my eyes shift to him, curious how he'll react, and he blows me a kiss and *winks*! Always the quiet calm ones, I tell ya—look out, ladies.

Maybe I was out of line, but I'm looking at a lot of grateful faces around this table. My guess is they've all had enough of Vaughn's crap and were happy to see him knocked down a peg.

"May I be so bold to say, my girl did the cooking, so ya'll have fun cleaning while I steal her away." Cannon winks at me. "Gotta surprise for her."

"Of course. Laura, sweetheart, my surprise for you is, I'll do the dishes. Isn't your Housewives of Crazy Country show about to start?" my father teases her, rising to stack plates together.

"Come on, Siren." Cannon stands hastily and pulls me from my chair. "Be back later, Con."

No qualms following him anywhere, I giddily trek behind him to his car. Which reminds me, I should probably retrieve mine someday. "Where we going?" I ask once we're loaded in.

"You'll see." He flits a coy smile at me, a husky, secretive quality in his answer.

I turn on some tunes and settle in for the ride and surprise, softy singing along to one of my favorites, Bon Iver's "Flume." Cannon reaches over and links our hands, then sings with me. Four songs of the phenomenal album later, we pull into the driveway of our, as of tomorrow at noon, new house.

"Babe, this isn't ours yet, we can't be here."

"Lil' faith, love, yeah?" He comes around and opens my door, sliding his arms under my legs and behind my back, scooping me out and kicking the car door shut.

"For the next 15 hours, this is trespassing," I hiss quietly in the night, even though the closest neighbor is at least two miles, minus perhaps a family of field mice or maybe a nice cricket community.

"You open that negative little mouth again, and you know exactly what I'm gonna fill it with." He moves around to the back corner of the house, sets me down and pushes open the very small, very high off the ground guest bathroom window.

"Wh—how?" I utter in shocked sounds only dolphins can hear.

"Crawl through, close and lock it back, then go let me in the front door." He stoops, making a step for me with his locked together hands.

The longer I stand here bewildered, or argue, the greater our risk of arrest, so I place a foot in his hand and boost myself up, regretting my love of chocolate as I barely squeeze through the window. Luckily, all the windows are naked of curtains or blinds, so the country moonlight guides me through securing the window and making my way to the front door.

He's knocking when I get there, and I can't help but snicker at my quirky love.

"Who is it?" I coo.

"Maytag Man calling. Heard you needed something serviced."

"Is that so?" I open up with a saucy grin, which fades when I see his arms loaded down with a blanket, pillows, and that may be a candle? "Cannon Powell Blackwell," I take some of his burden, "what? When?"

He chuckles and closes the door, the slide of the lock an echoing, erotic sound through the empty house. "Loaded the stuff in the trunk. Unlocked the window when the agent let us in before." He taps his temple. "Kiss my brain, you know you love it."

I stand on the tips of my toes to lay a smooch at his genius temple. "Lemme guess, staying at my dad's is wearing on your libido?"

"Not at all." He fluffs out the blanket, laying it on the floor of our soon to be living room. Then he scatters the pillows and walks over to light the candle that he sets on the mantle over the fireplace. The room fills with an iridescent glow and my heartbeat quickens.

"I want move-in to be special for Conner, but I want one special, first moment in our new home with you." He kicks off both shoes, eyeing me hungrily in the candlelight. "We may have many homes, but this will always be the first memory. You good with that?" He smirks, now reaching behind his neck and pulling his shirt over his head.

"Yeah," I answer in a fluttery breath.

Any "first" forever memory with Cannon is one I'll treasure, guard in my heart and head always, and replay in my mind any time I gaze at him, or use to mend myself when angry with him…needs music; this is me we're talking about.

He thought of everything else, so I'll maestro the soundtrack. I flip through albums on my phone haphazardly, settling on a song only to change my mind a second later. It hits me like a swarm of angry butterflies—I can't believe I'd never thought of it before. If there's *one* song that says precisely what I say mentally to him every single day, this is it.

I remain still for now, savoring his tauntingly gradual strip tease, until he's splendidly naked and beautiful in front of me. Then I take my turn, peeling each article from my wanting frame, tears building behind my laden lids for reasons I can't begin to explain. He defies everything I thought I knew, the epitome of what I feared but desperately wanted, didn't need yet lived empty and amiss without.

When I'm brazenly bare for him as well, I grab my phone at my feet and press play, then toss it back down and beckon him to me with a seductive crook of my finger, wetting my lips.

He stalks toward me, primal and masculine, stopping short when he recognizes my confession, "The Woman in Me," by Shania Twain. Understanding and acceptance of the plea consumes his deep brown eyes and he advances, pulling me down on the floor with him.

In his lap, facing him, he wraps my legs around his muscular waist and drives his hands up through my hair. "Always got you, Siren. You have me," he promises me in husky reverence against my neck.

SE Hall

Without words, he angles my head to sink his hot tongue as deeply and possessively into my mouth as possible and I lift, finding his hardness with my hand, and place the tip at my core. Little by little, I tease him, taking him in only just past the head and flinching around him, then relaxing.

His eyes flare open and he emits a carnal, animalistic growl into my mouth, warning me with the unharnessed passion in his darkened eyes that he's about to take over running the show. But the song and lyrics are tender, so I decide to be so also, and lovingly ease down his entire length, stilling a moment to fully stretch around the base, the thickest part of him.

"I love you, Cannon," I moan on his lips, rocking back and forth on him, grabbing around his neck for anchor, letting my head fall back and my eyes close as I make slow, sweet love to him.

Together we writhe and gyrate in flawless coherence, his up and my down, my grind to his thrust. In this position, straddled in his lap, I need not his hands, the short, crisp hairs at his groin tantalizing my clit dreamily, and way too soon, I'm coming around and down him as he groans around my breast in his mouth.

"So sweet, my Siren, more perfect every time. Love me forever, swear it." He kisses me now, flat tongue licking after each puckered nip on my breast and collarbone, then up my neck. "Fuck me hard when you're mad, soft when you're not, bite my dick when I won't listen, and deny me until I beg when I'm late or forget something important. But always, always love me?"

I nod as tears begin to fall and I whisper, "More than my own life, promise."

"I believe you." He leans his head back to smile at me, which quickly morphs to a sinister, domineering smirk. "My turn," he grunts, gripping my hips and holding me flush against him as he thrusts up and into me with brutal, deliberate force, throwing his own head back, a feral howl escaping as he releases into me.

352

# CHAPTER
## thirty-seven

At 12:17 pm, we co-signed on our house, $180,000, half me, half Cannon, bought free and clear. God bless the vapid housing market, because tons of acreage, in-law quarters and over 3,000 square feet of living area when it's worth almost twice that much. Who buys a house in full, no financing? A girl with mama's family money and a man who stockpiled since his money couldn't buy daddy's princess anything good enough, that's who. And we won't mention it, because I'll replace them the first chance I get, but I may be privy to the fact that Cannon sold two guitars and an amp that he somehow carted out of Ruthie's in his ten minute time allotment. I also highly suspect my father slipped him a check for "Conner's house," because he knew damn good and well I wouldn't dip a dime into his actual account for it.

Sneaky ass men.

From the signing to our pad, 1222 Erin Drive, took 36 minutes, so knowing we signed at noon, and bureaucratic things, much like doctor appointments, *never* happen on time, I was more than stunned to see everyone we value in the driveway…or parked in the grass. *It is Indiana after all.*

And since I'm so tough and all, I'm equally surprised that my face is mysteriously, yet again, leaking of its own accord. Charming and a sign of being humanized at first, it's starting to get on my damn nerves now.

The first to attack, all at once, are Libby, Sommerlyn, and Vanessa, Jarrett's lovebird with amazing longevity and an even longer way from home and school, and Laura, who's not the evil stepmother I'd feared. Oh, and little Hope, holding Sommerlyn's hand.

"Sweetheart," Libby says pitifully, worried face, wringing her hands, "you have nothing. I'm not exaggerating. Sommerlyn, tell her I'm not overreacting. I mean, it's absolutely barren. I'm right, aren't I?"

"Mother, we talked about this." Sommer gives me an apologetic grin. "They've owned it for five minutes, it shouldn't be filled with their things."

"Oh," Libby clasps her chest, relief washing over her. "Thank God, so when will the moving trucks be here?"

"Libby, I lived on a bus for five years. I've never even had an apartment. And nothing from his house with," I shiver, "She-Devil is allowed inside. So," I rub my hands together optimistically, "there are no trucks coming; there's nothing to bring."

"*OH*," totally different inflection in the word this time, her chest clasped now in horror, not relief. "Wh...I don't...um..." She's flabbergasted, eyes flitting to everyone individually for a possible solution.

"Who likes assigned tasks?" I ask in as chipper a voice as I can, a reassuring hand on Libby's shoulder. "Trust me, I got it."

All hands go up, and I pounce into action before they have time to change their minds. "Who's got paper?" Of course, Libby whips out a yellow legal pad and pen from her purse. "All right, let's see." I close my eyes, picturing my new casa—gotta get a pattern room by room. "You first walk up to the front porch. Who wants it?"

"We'll take it," Sommerlyn raises her and Hope's joined hands and Lil' Bit nods enthusiastically.

"Sommer and Hope, porch," Libby says aloud as she titles the page. *Yeah, cannot fathom where Cannon got the list making thing.*

"I'd say we need," this will be a challenge eons away from my forte, "welcome mat, porch swing, paint for the front door cause eck, peephole cause uhh scary, pots and plants and maybe a pretty flag. Anything else?" *Maybe I'm not so bad at this after all!* "Oh, and a table for by the swing for drinks and stuff. And a rocking chair!" I finish, wistfully picturing it.

"Daddy!" Sommerlyn yells and Marshall trots over. "I need your truck keys. Hope and I have big items to get." He digs them out of his pocket agreeably and smiles down at Hope. "You ladies need help loading stuff, or money?"

"No, no!" I bust in, holding up a hand. "Cannon and I will pay for everything, let me go grab a card out of my purse. And the men at the store will load them up. There are lots of jobs, so we've gotta spread our troops thin." I giggle.

"No, no to *you*," Marshall kindly contradicts me, pulling an envelope out of his back pocket. "Me and the Missus thought money'd make a great housewarming present." He hands the envelope to Sommer. "Just what she asked for and bring *her* back the change, Saks Fifth Sommerlyn." His brow crinkles.

"Daddy, you wound me. Oh wait, Liz, what color for the rocker and front door?"

See—here I was thinking I nailed it...curveball.

I glance around and find Cannon watching me from across the yard with a look of sweet adoration. I chin nod him and he saunters over, Levis and boots making the simple act pornographic. "Siren?"

"What color rocking chair for the porch and front door?" I ask.

He glances over his shoulder at the spot, debates, then turns back to me. "White rocker, maroon or royal blue door? You pick."

"Royal blue," I instantly tell the girls. "And," I subtlety elbow Cannon in the ribs, "your parents are paying with our housewarming present." I regard them both with a huge smile. "Thank you."

"Thanks, Moms." He hugs and kisses her. "Thank you, Dad." One-armed man thing.

"Come on, Hope! See y'all!" Sommer calls over her shoulder, and they're off.

One project down.

"Jarrett!" Nessy hollers this time and I swear I don't recognize the man who sprints to her side. I repeat, Jarrett Playboy Foster *sprints* to her side. "You got any money?"

He shrugs. "Couple hundred, why?"

"Our labor is our housewarming gift. We're gonna need the card," Vanessa says to the ground, ashamed. "We're taking the master bedroom, since a bed may become a priority, unless you like sleeping in rocking chairs." She snickers. "What color you want it painted and stuff?"

Cannon wraps his arms around my waist from behind. "You pick this one, love."

I lunge, gripping my waist. "I don't feel so good," I croak.

"Lizzie?" He dips his head to look at me, worried.

I shoot up and point at his eyes. "Ness, see that color right there, that light, bronzy molasses? That color."

"Gotcha!" She smirks.

"So getting it for that later," he grumbles in my ear and I lean up to kiss him soundly.

"Sorry, had to nail it. Love you."

I quickly google furniture types and colors on my phone to show Vanessa, hand her my credit card, and Libby passes them their list.

And we're two down.

And so it goes—Dad, Conner, and Bryson take Conner's house, all possible things needed purchased since he mostly bought supplies to make a fort—and a treehouse—last time we tried shopping. *Who needs a bed and what not when you can just live like Bear Grylls, right?*

Libby takes the kitchen; we decided on a muted yellow and whatever color dishes and small appliances she liked...which oddly, seems to make her day. Alma takes the

356

flower beds since she loves that sort of thing. And in a mind altering twist, Vaughn appears before me, sullen and apologetic, and offers to mow, weed-eat, and trim hedges. I thank him with a hug and a ruffle of his hair and tell him that'd be great. Marshall takes to meeting the fence and security team at the end of the driveway, coordinating and overseeing both projects.

Just when things seem sublime, Rhett and my Uncle Bruce pull up together and make it that much better. As they get out, Bruce's face is hesitant and cautious, but I square up and walk fast to embrace them both. "How?"

"Cannon called," Rhett explains.

"Told me everything," Bruce adds. "Loved my sister, proud as hell of you, and plan to have a beer with your dad later. End of. Where you need us?"

"How about the living room? Cannon?"

He chuckles. "Right behind ya."

"Why don't you give them specs on couch, chairs, end tables, TV, rugs? Kinda a man thing. I'm going shopping with my soon-to-be stepmother for my bathroom and guest room. Thank you both for coming, and helping." A slobbering sap, I hug and kiss them both then run to search down Laura as fast as possible so I can hide my happy display of threatening waterworks.

"I'll do back deck and walkways and clean the flues for fires, babe!" Cannon yells, getting a thumbs up over my shoulder.

Maybe I dreamt it, because I wake up in a new, fabulous bed practically identical to my request, décor all around, including pictures on the walls, which are painted the exact shade of Cannon's eyes that I kinda shamefully captured…but I have an image of actually collapsing in the hallway from exhaustion in my head.

Imagine what the rest of them must feel like.

What feels most like Heaven is the lean, hard body draped across, around, and under me. "Morning, babe," I whisper in his ear, lavishing kisses up his thick, corded neck.

"Morning to you my love. Your turn for coffee delivery or go back to sleep," he says croakily and swats my butt.

"Did you happen to find me in the hall and carry me to bed, oh brawny man of mine?"

"Guilty." He chuckles softly, a morning rasp making it an even sexier sound than usual.

"Thank you. I love this house," I sigh happily, "everything turned out so perfect. We'll have to host a barbeque or dinner to thank them all."

"Sounds great. Just as soon as the discs in my back slip back to their normal positions," he mumbles into his pillow.

"Roll on your stomach," I nudge him, then straddle his back and start massaging. Either tight with strain or shear physical perfection, his muscles are hard against my fingertips, making it difficult to really penetrate.

"Feels great, babe," he moans. "Thank you."

"Of course." I dip my head, placing kisses intimately across his back. "I should probably check on Conner," I suddenly worry.

"Alma stayed the night with him and an alarm sounds in here if any of his doors open."

*He thinks of everything.*

"But feel free; a hard-on against a mattress isn't exactly comfortable."

"Then roll back over," I hum sexily.

He does with a sleepy smile, none the less seductive. "Gonna have to do all the work, Siren, I'm sore as shit."

"I think I can handle that." I take off my shirt, pull my panties aside, and glide down on him in one motion, all the way home.

"Mhmmm," a deep growl rumbles in his chest. "You feel so sweet and snug, Lizzie. Give it to me good, babe." He props both hands behind his head, smug smirk in place as he watches me ride him gently, but effectively.

When we're both depleted, glistening in sweet sweat, kissing every spectacular part of each other, I make a breakthrough decision, my love for him infinite and never-ending. As we lay tangled in *our* bed, I roll to my side, propping up my head in one hand and taking his left in my other. "Cannon Powell Blackwell, will you marry me?" I propose.

"Anytime, anywhere, as many times as you want," he raises our joined hands to his mouth and kisses mine, "but I will be asking you, my beauty. Be ready for a grand display of romanticism." He tsks and smiles, shaking his head. "Look at you, you witchy thing—trying to take my glory. What am I gonna do with you?"

"Love me," I whisper. "Do every single thing the best couples in the world do, with me, at least once, and pretend you like it."

"Let's hear this list." He pulls me back on top of him, my head sneaking into its spot under his chin, both his hands finding their spot, one on each cheek of my naked ass.

"Well, I don't have the whole list ready right this minute, but I'll be compiling it. You just have to agree to do it." I giggle and kiss the end of his nose.

"I promise, Lizzie love, anything you want."

"Oh shit, wait!" he panics. "I don't want to hang from a Ferris wheel until you agree to date me." He puppy dog frowns, begging me for a pass.

*Geez, I thought something was on fire.*

"We're already long pasting dating, and watching *The Notebook* with me was enough. Free pass on death hangs at carnivals." I wink, staggering off him and up to get dressed. "But you are so orchestrating a band and singing your way down the bleachers to me while I pretend to be a high school girl on a soccer field."

"Please," he rolls his eyes, "at least challenge me." He stalls, one finger in the air. "I'm not drinking any poison, though, my Juliet. That's all; those two are kinda biggies."

Six amazing months after *that* night, there's a beige and red rug in the spot Cannon and I first christened our home, which is where I'm sitting and folding laundry when Vaughn knocks on the edge of the screen door.

"Come on in." I smile, waving him inside.

He drags his feet, head down, shoulders strung tight as a bow. "Need any help?" he mumbles at the floor.

"No, but thank you." I love Vaughn. After our "Come to Liz," we've made giant strides, developing a pretty close relationship. He's a good boy, a little over sixteen now, and he's worked through a lot of misplaced anger. "Vaughn, what's up?"

"Is, um, Cannon here?"

"He is, down in the studio." The studio is our basement, which we converted when we felt the need to still collaborate. "Head on down, unless there's something I can help you with?"

"You're kinda my sister now, right?"

"No, not kinda. I am your sister, Vaughn, and I love you. And I changed my mind, I could use some help." I pat the rug beside me. "Let's figure it out over laundry."

He lifts his head now, a relieved and grateful smile peeking through the uncertainty. He plops down beside me and digs in folding. "Promise not to tell my parents?"

"Nope, not if it's illegal or harmful. They need to know about that, and I'll go *with you* to tell them, but tell them we will. Other than that," I nudge his shoulder with my own, "then yes, I promise."

"What, uh about…" he looks out the window on the other side of the room, "sex?"

I should remind him Cannon's in the basement. I should pierce out my eardrums, or…be a good big sister and keep my shit together. I mean, *I was his age when I did.*

"If you'll listen to the very important parts, then this is one of those conversations that can stay between us."

After six minutes of silence and him refolding the same washcloth the entire time, I clear my throat and steel my spine. "Vaughn, was there something specific you wanted to talk about or ask?"

"How do you know, when it's okay? How'd you know? How old were you? Where were you?" Man, he really went for it—and all in one breath.

"Okayyy," I drawl cautiously. This is one of those moments where I can truly mentor him into a fine young man or severely fuck it up. And we know my problem with the *think first, talk later* ailment. "I'm going to be honest with you, Vaughn, because you're mature, intelligent and I know you can handle it. All right?"

His head bobs frantically, eyes eager for some help, honest information, and most importantly, to be treated like an adult instead of a child.

"I was your age when I did it the first time. It was only once, in my bedroom, with a dear friend that I trusted completely, and still do. It wasn't really sex—I can't, and won't, explain…but it was more two friends who shared everything else. Make sense?"

"Yeah." He looks away and then back, biting the skin at the edge of his nail, which I raise a hand to halt.

"As for the other question, I think if it doesn't smack you in the forehead that *this. Is. Her,* then it's not. Ya know?"

"Like you and Cannon?"

"Yes," I tap his nose, "exactly like that. Can I ask you some questions now?"

He pops his shoulders and grabs a towel to fold this time. "Sure, I guess so."

"No, not guess so. Yes or no, Vaughan. I will respect your boundaries."

"Yes."

"Have you already had sex?" That actually hurt my throat to ask. He shakes his head and I can breathe again. "Is she your girlfriend?" Shoulder shrug, next towel grabbed. "Would you feel weird looking at her the next day?"

"Yes," he spouts instantly.

"If she got pregnant, could you take care of her? Would you be happy knowing you're connected to her for the *rest of your life*?"

His face turns a pasty white as his jaw hits his knee. "No freakin' way!"

I hold my face straight, unchanged. "Have your answer?" I ask.

"Yes," he stands, "cold showers it is. Thanks, Liz. Can I ask you other stuff when I need to?"

"Always, day or night. Love you, smart guy."

"You too. Going to Conner's, see ya!" He rushes out the back door.

"You're going to be the best damn mother in the whole world."

I jolt, jerking my head back over my shoulder to find Cannon tucked back in the hallway, leaning against the wall, arms and ankles crossed.

"You couldn't have done that any better. I love you, Lizzie. Every day you find new ways to impress me, even when you don't know I'm watching."

I feel my cheeks heat with a flattered blush. He starts to make his way to me, but chaos finds us first.

362

"Sister! Bethy!" Conner rushes through the back door. "Some of those darn fish smashed the tank and wet got all over my floor!"

"Put shoes on, love," Cannon suggests as he heads out to clean up tank takedown number…I think this makes three.

# CHAPTER thirty-eight

As I stand before the full-length mirror, I don't say yes to the dress—it's actually way too long and lacy for me—but I say absolutely to having a piece of my mother here with me today.

The ring she left Cannon, my grandma's, is back in the safe deposit box. I never even met the woman, so I felt strange wearing it. Instead, my finger is adorned with a ring Cannon designed for me, a beautiful princess-cut solitaire on a thick, white gold band, "My Siren" inscribed inside.

So the dress is old *and* borrowed. My ring is new. And blue? A ribbon, the color of Conner's eyes, a piece of his tie he wears today, is twined through my still brown hair that now graces the swell of my shoulders.

Cannon proposed, because he's as stubborn as he is chivalrous and just *couldn't* let mine stand alone, under "our" tree in our backyard and that's where we're getting married today. His father and Conner are his best men, then my father and Jarrett will also stand with him.

On my side, my Men of Honor, Rhett Foster and Uncle Bruce the Moose. Beside them, Libby, Sommerlyn, Laura, and Vanessa.

Hope is my flower/ring girl. Bryson and Vaughn are the handsome ushers in their gentlemanly suits, and my dear, wonderful Alma will marry us; determined *not* to have a small role, she ran out and got ordained.

Still haven't met Lisa, the missing link daughter, but I'm sure Laura keeps her apprised of everything that happens at the crazy Carmichael house.

My father knocks on the door, prepared to give me away, even though he's only just gotten me back, before taking his spot in Cannon's line.

I laugh in the face of conformity. *My. Way.*

"Come on in, Dad." I turn and smile. He's very handsome, and yes, I look as much like him as I act, which is becoming a point of pride for me more and more every day. The salt and pepper growing around his ears now looks distinguished to me, and there're no signs of Botox in his aging, yet still debonair face.

"Oh, my Elizabeth, you are a vision." *Out pops the handkerchief.* "A vision of a strong, courageous, gorgeous young woman who clawed her way to the finish and got exactly the happiness and adoration she deserved. There is no one more deserving in all the world, and I'm so proud of you, daughter. I find any words to try and tell you just how much inadequate."

"Thank you." I hold open my arms for a hug. "I love you, Dad. I missed you. I miss her, too, but I *respect* you for sticking around and waiting on me. Thank you."

"Hush now." He laughs, wiping his eyes. "I know you don't want for money, so here is my gift to you on this special day." He pulls two envelopes from his breast pocket. "Go ahead, open them."

The first one, well, I falter, stumbling backward, and he helps me sit on the chaise. "Oh Dad." I swipe his hankie from him before I cry all over the documents for a center he's having built in Sutton, "The ACC Guidance Center," full counseling, psychiatric, and medical services for people dealing with depression and/or addiction, as well as their loved ones.

"And yes," he gives a soft titter, "it will be filled with huge, colorful fish tanks."

"Life goes on," I whisper.

"So it does, my lovely daughter, so it does." He clears his throat, abruptly handing me the other envelope. "Should've given you this one first, a measly two weeks in Tahiti, ta-da."

We enjoy a *long* overdue, hearty laugh together, until finally, it's time. "Shall we?" He offers his bent arm, which I rise and take. "You, nor he, could have chosen any better, darling. Cannon is a fine man, as close to worthy of you as one will ever get. I'll tell you what I told him, Elizabeth. Never give your body to another. It's a fleeting, hollow replacement and the guilt and pain lasts much longer than the tryst. *Communicate*, talk, write a note, text, call, fly a banner behind a plane, but *never* try to mask one problem with another. Drink socially, if you'd like, but never to forget. *Always* keep your memory free and clear to remember back to how you feel right now. And if all else fails," he stops our walk to the backyard and grasps both my cheeks, "call your daddy. He'll fix it." He kisses my forehead, his tears dripping onto my nose. "I love you, daughter. I never dreamt I'd get to be a part of your wedding day. Nothing, ever, will replace it as my life's culmination; it's the best moment ever in store for me."

"I love you too, Dad. Now let's go," I hedge him, denied again.

"But, if you change your mind, I have the car out front running, ready to go."

Oh, it feels good to throw my head back and gut laugh to the heavens. *That* line—classic. Undoubtedly going to be used on my own daughter when the time comes.

"Move it, Father Time. He's gonna give up, and you're certainly not getting any younger." I wink at him, taking his arm, and the lead. "Don't worry, Dad, I got this."

"Here she comes! Cannon, I see her! You are very, *very* pretty, Sister!" Conner's screaming, pogoing without a stick, the minute we come into view.

Cannon smirks but sweetly hushes him when our wedding song starts. Together, we'd chosen "And I Love

Her" by…it's *my* wedding, do I really need to point out it's The Beatles?

While he's calming Conner, I use the slice of time he's distracted to absorb the man who is about to become my husband. He's in pressed black slacks and a white dress shirt with the top button undone. His hair is tamed, sticking up just enough in the front, and his smile, the glow to his cheeks, the pride and excitement in his high, broad shoulders…he probably shouldn't look better than the bride, or chocolate cake, but damn if he doesn't.

When he moves, talks, sings, strums, touches, winks, smirks, laughs or drives his miraculous body lovingly into mine…everything he does mystifies me. And not only does *he* want *me*, but he wants me *only*, and forever.

"Dad," I whisper, "pinch me."

"No need, darling, it's real. Can you imagine what *he* must be thinking right now? Probably trying to figure out which star was the perfect one he wished on, or how he got so in God's favor. *You're* the prize, beautiful Elizabeth, and he knows it."

Our guests stand and face me, but I'm looking at one person only, and he now is doing the same. "Stole my breath," he mouths and winks at me, stepping slightly forward when we reach him.

My father removes my hand from his arm, kisses the back of it, then offers it to Cannon. "I believe you to be worthy, son, so I give to you my only daughter, my baby. When you think you've shown her enough that you love her, cherished her, treated her like a queen," he dips his head with an almost silent sniffle, then looks back up, "try harder."

"Yes, sir." Cannon nods, then turns us toward she who will unite us for life, my dear Alma.

She recites the traditional verbiage…then comes to *our part.* "You've prepared your own vows?"

We both nod and Cannon quirks his right brow, but I shake my head. "You first, babe."

He slips a paper from his pocket (probably a list) and clears the lump in his throat. "You were born Elizabeth Hannah Carmichael, and I love her, but to me, you are Lizzie Little Bit Witchy Siren Blackwell, and you have been since the second you *begged* me to board your bus. You always shine, from the inside out, but you positively blind me. I vow with this, my last, and every breath in between, to adore you, appreciate you, and hold you up, let you lean, lean on you, carry you or shut my mouth and nod along—anything you need, anytime you need it. I will always put you above all else, especially myself, and if I don't *have* what you need, I'll find it, build it, invent it, just to see you smile. I love you, Lizzie." He puts the note away and steps into me, cupping my cheeks. "You were instantly, are now and will always be, my prettiest instinct."

"That was very, *very* nice, Cannon," Conner says, the gallery all chuckling, my laugh accompanied by a subtle swipe of my tears.

"Elizabeth?" Alma indicates my turn.

Deep breath in for him, out for me, I begin, no piece of paper required. "Cannon..." *Oh nice, one word and my voice cracks on a sob.*

He smiles, taking both my hands in his to reassure me. "One more, baby, in for me," he does it with me, nodding encouragingly, "now out for you."

"Better." I nod and start again. "Cannon, love is *not* patient; I couldn't wait until you looked at me the way I did when I stole peeks at you. Love is *not* always kind; I can be moody, defensive, and snarky, but, thankfully, you have that selective hearing thing nailed." He chuckles where only I can hear him and winks. "Love *does* envy; I'm jealous of every moment of your time I don't get to share. Some nights I stay awake and watch you sleep, so peaceful and beautiful, and hate every creeping second of night until you wake, to light up my day. Love *does* boast." I turn to the crowd and point to him. "This magnificent man is *mine!*" That gets a laugh out of everyone. "But the rest is pretty accurate. I *will* always protect and trust you, and give you only reasons to trust me. I *will* always hope for one more minute with you, one more kiss, one more embrace. And my love for you will *never, ever* fail. I instantly did, do now, and always will belong solely to you in mind, body, heart, and soul. Thank you for choosing me, Cannon, for never giving up, for seeing and unlocking what I never dreamt existed. I will spend my life thanking you. I love you."

Male crying is *not* unattractive or unmanly; the love falling down Cannon's cheeks is breathtaking. "Yours," I mouth, reaching up to help wipe his tears.

"Yours was better, Bethy!" Conner boasts *loudly* and claps.

While everyone else laughs, even Cannon joining with a tiny snicker, I can't help but frown. It wasn't at all, and I don't want my love doubting what his poetic vows meant to me. "It's not true, babe. What you said was magical. It meant the world to me."

"And you mean the world to me, but Lizzie love, there's a reason you write the lyrics." He pulls me into his chest and whispers, "need a nibble." That tiny taste right below my ear turns into a dip of my body and a deep kiss that scorches me from toe to hair follicle.

"All right," Alma improvises, "may I present to you Mr. and Mrs. Cannon and Elizabeth Blackwell!"

"Woo hoo! Quit kissing, now comes cake!" *Any guesses who screeched that?*

We come up for air all smiles and swollen, moist lips. Since our wedding's at our home, I exercise my gloriously option. "I'm running up to change, babe, meet you back here in ten."

"I'll come with." He starts to follow, abruptly halted by my firm hand on his chest.

"Not a chance." My knowing brow calls him out. "I felt your plans on the dip, and we have a yard full of guests. You stay, think about gross things, and I'll be back in ten." I scamper away quickly, dress hoisted to un-trippable level, and dash to our bedroom to wear clothes made of anything other than what they used to make that itchy dress.

On my trip back, I'm stopped by each and every guest with hugs, kisses, well-wishes, envelopes of gifts— which I feel bad taking—and three especially long, heartfelt and teary talks with Bruce my Moose, Jarrett...and Rhett. I'm just promising him a dance later when the voice I've come to call solace speaks over the mic. It's dusk by now, but the lanterns in the trees allow me to make him out perfectly, shirt unbuttoned one more and untucked, the sultry desire in his eyes clearly visible from here.

"My beautiful wife, it's been more like forty minutes. Remember the whole 'love is not patient' part? Yeah, me, you, first dance now. I'll meet you right there," he points to the middle of the dance floor that's been laid out, "and I picked the song. Ready, Siren?"

I eagerly bob my head at him across the dusky yard and make my way to where he'll be waiting. "Dance with me, beautiful," he croons, pulling me into him, one arm low around my back, the other grasping my hand and tucking it between our chests. He rests his forehead on mine, slowly swaying our bodies to "Hold You in My Arms" by Ray Montagne as he nips lightly and brushes his lips against mine. "Can you believe we're here?" he asks. "Married, a home, family? Seems surreal."

"I know exactly what you mean," I agree with a sigh. "I couldn't ask for anything more, wouldn't change a thing about you and me. Sometimes I look at you and get scared, like how could *he* possibly want *me*? Do I really get to keep him forever?"

He swipes his thumb under my eye, catching a stray tear. "Sweet Lizzie, I have no idea who bewitches who." He shakes his head in disbelief. "Love you." He glances around at all the guests, then pulls me tighter with a frustrated groan. "When do they all go home?"

# LIZZIE

**2 years later**

What? You thought you'd hear about two blissful years of Cannon and me honeymooning, having wild monkey sex four times a day, spending time alone, and enjoying getting to know each other even better?

When have Cannon and I *ever* had time alone? Think about it—we met, lived, and courted on a tour bus with four other guys, one a very impressionable, nosey busybody whom I adore. Then, we bought a house, with another house ten feet out the back door, occupied by...see reference to busybody above.

Alma's always over, checking on Conner twice a day, and I'm pretty sure Vaughn and Bryson think they live here.

So much like before, Cannon and I have made a seductive, taboo game of finding time alone courtesy of subliminal body and eye signals and seemingly harmless sentences with underlying meaning in a language only we speak. We are fluent in innuendo.

Ergo, the joke we hear most often is usually some varied form of *"when* did you find time to get pregnant?"

I can tell them the minute it happened, not that I ever will, but it was at approximately 2:15 am last September 16th. No one was in the house but us, a mild thunderstorm woke me up, and I figured, what better birthday present for my husband??

We made our daughters on his birthday, to the rhythm of a warm, gentle storm outside our window, and today, June 7th, they turn one.

I'm working feverishly trying to ensure *Yo Gabba Gabba* covers every available space in the kitchen and back deck while the girls get their nap, so they'll be party perky instead of gabba grumpy. Daddy's run to pick up the cakes— something about they each get to explore and/or demolish their own—and I'm praying I'll have enough time for a quick shower before the doting masses show up.

Or Conner.

*Thinking he's so sly.*

"Hi, Sister!" Okay, even for Conner, usually at about a 15, he's rocking every decibel of 25. "Where are my babies?" This time he leans toward the hall, where he *screams* it.

"Conner!" I aim narrowed eyes at him and point a raw hot dog his way, not set on the cooking platter yet. "Be quiet. The girls will be grumpy if they don't have a nap, and I *know* you're trying to wake them up!" I hiss quietly. "I mean it, mister!"

"Oh, did you hear that?" He cups his ear, wide-eyed. "I heard I think my babies."

Did I mention Conner thinks his nieces are better than all the fish in all the world?

"No, Bubs, I didn't hear—" I knew better than that! Turn my back for one second and he's off! I quickly wash my hands, heading for their room, but I stop, listening over the monitor.

"Good morning, birthday Sophia," he coos at her, and she makes soft, happy gurgle in response.

Did I mention the girls think their uncle is the best person in the whole wide world?

I mean, they love me, and are *very* partial to their Daddy, but Conner? You'd just have to see it to understand.

"Tell your mean Bethy mom you were already awake, okay, Sophia? You are a very, very cute baby, my baby. Your mom and dad got brown eyes, 'cept yours are blue. That's how I know you're my baby. Sophia Conner Carmichael, queen of the wild babies."

Her middle name is Anna, and *obviously* her last name is Blackwell...tomay-toe, tomato.

"Bethy mom said I can change your diaper, long as I do it on the floor, so come on." She babbles at him as I listen. No thump, meaning he laid her down gently, tabs ripping open, raspberries on belly, one-year-old giggle, lid on wipes popping open...sounds good from here. He's watched me a hundred times, wanting nothing more than to perfect taking care of them.

"Daddy's home!" Cannon walks in precariously and I rush over to save one of the wobbling cakes.

I kiss him soundly. "Hey, you."

"Girls still asleep?" He waggles his eyebrows.

"You tell me." I lay a finger over my lips to shush him.

"That was a very good job, Sophia. Now, let's go try not to wake up your sister," Conner conspires over the monitor. "It would be very bad if we tickled her feet, Sophia, so we cannot do that. And we should not blow in her face or shake her bed."

"Be right back." He sets the cake on the counter and takes off down the hall. "Hey, Con, whatcha doin?" He chuckles. "Hello, sweet Sophia, come see your daddy, you big birthday girl."

"Cannon, I want Stella to wake up right this minute."

"Really? Huh, well, wake her up, Bubs, soft and quietly. Don't startle her, okay?"

"Stella Conner Carmichael!" he yells, at about a 9. Oh, and her middle name is Elizabeth, not named after me, but rather Cannon's mom- her full name. And since she's Sophia's twin...*also* a Blackwell.

Potay-toe, potato.

"Con, why don't you help Soph into her pink party dress and I'll get Stella up?" Cannon offers to save his daughter a startling wake up call, and I lean against the counter, listening to it all over the monitor with a smile you couldn't beat off my face.

"No, Sophia wears the blue dress like mine and hers eyes. Stella gets pink because hers are brown like you guys."

"My bad," Cannon laughs, "you're right. So Stella's our baby then?"

"Psshh." Conner's abhorred. "Her chubby cheeks is mine *and* she always looks at the fish. She is mine too."

"What'd you get them for their birthday?"

"I got Sophia a snail and Stella a toad. I found them both on my sidewalk."

*Oh dear God, tell me I'm hearing things.*

"Cool! They can see them every time they come to your house, right?"

*Adore* my husband.

With the first knock on the door, I turn off the monitor, mentally say goodbye to my shower and go greet our guests with a smile. Of course Libby's here first and that *may* be Marshall behind her, or the FAO Schwartz delivery man, completely buried. Walking right up behind them is my dad and family...*are those Power Wheels Barbie jeeps?*

They're. One.

Everyone else arrives within minutes of each other. Bruce mans the grill, Jarrett tackles Vaughn and Bryson in the yard, and Hope sits enraptured as Sommerlyn braids her hair.

I search around for Rhett, I know I saw him come in, finally spotting him out back. Ahh, of course—he's assembling a playhouse. I mean, they're one after all.

And then, I hear them, a babbling chorus of "Ma" and baby claps and I turn to see my girls.

Stella Elizabeth and Sophia Anna Blackwell, my twin angels, one in pink, one in blue, one in Daddy's arms and one in Uncle Conner's, both the absolutely most perfect little people I've ever helped create.

"Ma!" Stella dives for me, the only chance I stand, since Sophia leans toward all the wonderful men in her life like glue.

"Happy Birthday, my beauty." I kiss her cheek as I take her and sniff her head—which never gets old. "Are you one?" I hold up a finger and she mimics me. "Good girl! Yes, you are one!"

"I hear them!" Libby comes flying in the room, Laura standing to the side, politely waiting her turn. "Where's Nana's babies?"

"You gotta share, Nana!" Conner frowns at her.

As I watch them all showering love over my children, I simply smile, basking in all my little family is blessed with...so much *more* family, all of them fawning over the girls constantly. I feel those familiar, strong arms come around my waist from behind and I sigh, letting my head fall back on his shoulder. "Already one," I say a little nasally, "can you believe it?"

"Love, I look around my life every day and never believe any of it. At the center of it all is you, my Siren. All of this, you gave me freely. I love you so damn much, Lizzie."

"I love you too." I peer back and up at him and pucker.

"Oh yeah, Imma need a nibble." He winks and takes it.

# Pretty Remedy

https://amzn.com/B00U2521PU

# Rhett's story

# Available Now!

S.E. Hall resides in Arkansas with her husband of 18 years and 4 beautiful daughters. When not in the stands watching her ladies play softball, she enjoys reading YA and NA romance. She is the author of amazon bestselling series, Evolve Series book 1 Emerge, book 2 Embrace, book 2.5 (novella) Entangled, book 3 Entice. She has also written Pretty Instinct as well as co-authored Stirred Up 1 and Stirred Up 2.

**Fan pages**
https://www.facebook.com/S.E.HallAuthorEmerge
https://twitter.com/SEHallAuthor
https://www.goodreads.com/author/show/7087549.S_E_Hall?from_search=true
http://www.mysehallauthor.com/
http://www.amazon.com/S.E.-Hall/e/B00D0AB9TI


**Buy links**

Emerge: myBook.to/Emerge (FREE)
Embrace: myBook.to/Embrace
Entangled: myBook.to/Entangled
Entice: myBook.to/Entice
Sawyer Beckett's Baby Mama Drama Guide For Dummies: myBook.to/BabyMamaDrama
Endure: myBook.to/Endure

SE Hall

## Finally Found Novels

Pretty Instinct: myBook.to/PrettyInstinct
Pretty Remedy: myBook.to/PrettyRemedy

## Co-Written with Erin Noelle

Conspire: myBook.to/Conspire

## Co-Written with Angela Graham

Matched: myBook.to/Matched
One Naughty Night: myBook.to/1NN
Stirred Up: myBook.to/StirredUp
Packaged: myBook.to/Packaged
Handled: myBook.to/Handled1
Handled 2: myBook.to/Handled2

## Spotify Links -
**Pretty Instinct -**
http://play.spotify.com/user/evolveauthor/playlist/7cOMMeC
Moav4zAxoCnsNpB

## acknowledgements

These are in no particular order...and until you've had to decide who goes where...oh, and made sure not to forget anyone while your stomach churns since you KNOW you're going to do just that...don't judge me. Xo

IF I forgot you- I'm sorry.

First and foremost, I thank God, for giving me the inner strength to keep going, my own mind to use as hard and well as I can and the beautiful people who surround me and bless me every day.

My husband Jeff- could NOT function, let alone write books, without you babe. In a few days, it will be 18 years, and they've been the best of my life. You were MADE for me, the only person I'd go through this crazy maze called life with and come out on the other side with only a few scratches.

My girls- thank you for being the independent, understanding, patient young ladies that you are! I'm so damn proud of every single one of you. Lyndsey- you go girl, proved em all wrong- you WILL persevere, grow stronger, do great things; and I cannot wait to watch you float across that stage like the princess you are! Brookie- just do you baby, find your way a lil more every day and keep that kind heart and warm smile! You're a sweet baby girl! And Shelby Jo- well, you rock kid, kicking ass on every forum you grace!

Mom- I love you. I have you to thank for my "keep going til they kill ya" spirit and love of words (yes, I remember practicing for the spelling bees walking up and down U of A campus.) For my humor, that I think is funny at least…and for the way you adore my girls. Thanks Mom xo

To my family- all of you- we are my favorite kind of crazy!!! I have the best fam in the whole world, always there when I need you, for a laugh or support, to remind me what I'm made of, how far I've come and that I can still go further! The women in my family taught me strength, independence and humor…the men, how to demand myself be treated…how to write romance basically.

Erin Roth- With me since Emerge, you're an amazing editor! I love your lil comments when I hit your funny and insight when I don't. I'm so thrilled with how our relationship has blossomed and I couldn't do it without your professionally stubborn, keen eye. Love you!

Toski Covey- Not only for all my beautiful cover photos, or the phone calls and texts, or amazapimping, or beta reads…but for being my friend; my true friend, who cares about me, as a person, and helps me see what really matters and what doesn't and reminds me some friendships are meant to be…outside of book world.

Carrie "Cookie" Horton Richardson- For picking up Emerge, and starting a trail of fire that changed my life, a room that brought me to people now my friends, staying with me all this time, supporting me endlessly and trusting me with your kind heart.

Cyndi Lane- YOU have changed my life, made it easier. You take care of my worries before I know they're there. You lift me up, think ahead of me and just basically ROCK!!! I am SO lucky to have you, never leave me…I will find you.

Sommer Stein- Girly Swirly, you are da bomb!!!!!! I love you so much, I might name a character after you …oh wait, I did that! ;) In all seriousness, I can't ever repay you for your generosity, eye for detail and love of me and my books. Xo

Nessie Wallace- Woman, you will never know what your support and actual caring, about me as a person, means to me. You have gone above and beyond to become my friend. If I never wrote another book, I know I'd still talk to you every day. I love you. For the typing, the teasers, the muse search, the shot glasses, the texts, the love…..everything you do that makes you you and restores my faith in the good of people…thank you!

Angela Graham - to more just like Stirred Up, it was so much fun taking our more than just a CP friendship that started at Emerge to a co-writing level! Thanks for the ear and great ideas! We always "bounce back," and I'm thankful for that. Xo

Ashley Suzanne- For all the times you've made me feel loved, respected, appreciated and the time you've put into me, my work and my heart- thank you boo! Here's to many years of bitching each other out, to call tearfully making up…to finish that scene (while eating Fruit Loops or some other delicious "snack")

Erin Noelle- I love you. You're genuine, kind, honest, reciprocating and a good person!!!! I pray we are always friends! You ARE my lady crush.

Sam Stettner- I won't ever not love you. To this day, you continue to help me with all sorts of things and you are my friend, now and forever.

Ena Burnette- To the lady who has rocked out all my cover reveals and blog tours, and somehow, does them better and better every time…..I owe you girl, you're fabulous!

Bethany Castaneda- THANK YOU sweet girl for all your help and support xo

Lisa Marie Kreinheder- THANK YOU so much for all your help xo

Shayne McClendon, Harper Sloan, Shantel Tessier and Hilary Storm- for the above and beyond! Xoxox

Michelle Grad- one of my originals, you kinda spin my world girlie! Much love xo

Tera Chastain and Amber Warne- Girls, you GO HAM on the teasers and the pic posts of "congrats" and "welcome!" Yes, I notice, and appreciate it, my lil slutmonkey and sweetpea xo

SE Hall

Renee Entress- You're too good to me woman, luv ya xoxoxo

Whitney Lynn- for the swag and extra help xoxoxo

Sean Smith- Thank you for being my Cannon Blackwell muse and all the support! https://www.facebook.com/SeanSmithFitness

Book Geek Boutique- Thank you for the awesome, timely, affordable swag! Xoxoxo

Mom by Design- your shot glasses and hand-work are amazing!!!!!

Book trailer makers- Kara, Jasmine and Kasey- THANK YOU- I love them!!!!

Brenda Wright- coming in like the clutch beast formatter, THANK YOU!!!!! Here's to a long relationship together xo

To S.E. Elite- I tried to thank as many of you in sneaky ways in PI as I could, and will get the rest of you next book, but THANK YOU ALL so very much for all you do. I truly would put my ST up against any on the planet, you're amazing, you're family!!!!!!!

Evolve Crew Cuties- Thank you so much for all the love and support, it means the world to me!

Beautiful Betas of PI- Thank you for all the love and feedback, you helped so much and I appreciate it beyond words!!!

Bloggers- Thank you, from the bottom of my heart, for taking a chance on this lil ole' Indie and giving her work voice! I hope I say thank you enough, if not, THANK YOU!!!!!!!

Kellie Montgomery and all the ECB girls- all 5 picks for 2013???? Your blog truly has been perhaps my biggest supporter, never even have to ask.....THANK YOU! You changed the game for me and I will never be able to repay you!

To the readers.....each and every one of you- THANK YOU. For reading, loving, recommending, blogging, tweeting, sending me a message of support.....it's all for you!

382

Sky Sky- good lookin' out Pretty…loving that window up there ya got, always using it to watch over Mama. I miss you every single day. Every. Single. One. But while I'm still down here, I promise, I will always try my hardest to FLY SKY HIGH.

Made in the USA
Columbia, SC
08 April 2018